Deadly Deceit

Deadly Deceit

JEAN HARROD

© Jean Harrod, 2016

Published by York Authors Coffee Shop

Maps
Turks & Caicos Islands & The Bahamas Political Map
© Peter hermes Furian | Dreamstime

ISBN 978-0-9929971-4-4 (Paperback)
ISBN 978-0-9929971-5-1 (epub)
ISBN 978-0-9929971-6-8 (mobi)

Book layout and design by Clare Brayshaw

Prepared and printed by:

York Publishing Services Ltd
64 Hallfield Road
Layerthorpe
York YO31 7ZQ

Tel: 01904 431213

Website: www.yps-publishing.co.uk

For Jane

Acknowledgements

Throughout the writing of my second novel in this 'Diplomatic Crime' series, I've had the same wonderful team helping me, as well as many readers urging me on.

Many, many thanks to my sister Jane for her unflagging advice and support; and to my writer friends Christine, Fiona, Paul and Margaret, who again have been with me every step of the way on this journey.

I owe thanks as well to Lisanne, who is a superb editor; and to John, Alicia, Clare, and Paula.

A special thanks too to all the wonderful people I met in The Turks and Caicos Islands.

The events in this novel did not happen. Its plot and characters exist only in my imagination.

About the Author

Born and educated in the UK, Jean was employed as a British diplomat for many years, working in Embassies and High Commissions in Australia, Brussels, the Caribbean, China, East Berlin, Indonesia, Mauritius, and Switzerland. She has travelled extensively around the world and writes about all the countries she has lived in, or visited.

'Deadly Diplomacy', set in Australia, was her debut diplomatic crime novel, and the first of a series featuring diplomat Jess Turner and DI Tom Sangster.

'Deadly Deceit', set in the Turks and Caicos Islands, Caribbean, is the second in the series.

Jean now lives in North Yorkshire. An active contributor to regional theatre, she has written and staged several plays.

www.jeanharrod.com

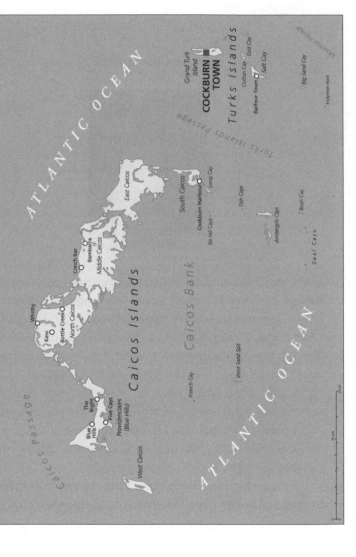

TURKS AND CAICOS ISLANDS
(UNITED KINGDOM)

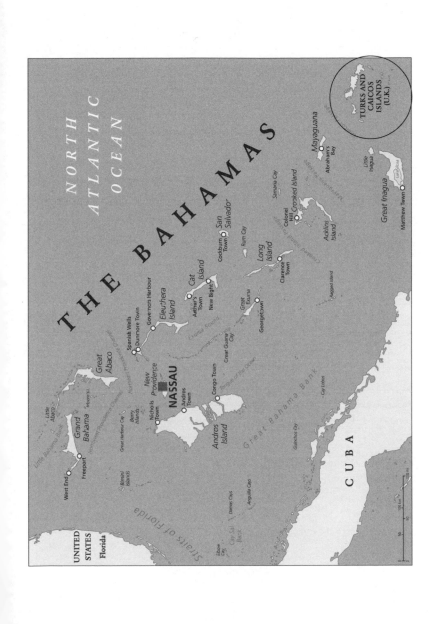

1

Bay of Cap-Haitien
North Coast of Haiti, Caribbean

The sloop slipped out of the bay on a strong swell in the dead of night. The sea was already rough. Too rough.

Nobody spoke, but in the dark she could feel their fear. Soft crying and moaning echoed all around. And retching. Bile rose in her own throat as the smell of vomit filled her nostrils, making her want to heave.

A soft whimper made her gaze down at her baby, squirming in her arms. She pulled the shawl around her little one, and started softly singing...

> *Dodo titit*
> *Si ou pa dodo*
> *Krab la va manje ou...*

She could feel pins and needles creeping into her toes. Uncrossing her legs, she stamped her feet. She wanted to stand up and move about, but she couldn't. They were squashed together in the bowels of the small boat. Eighty women and children. Maybe more.

She took deep breaths of the fresh air squeezing through the cracks of the hatchway, while the wind rattled around the edges of its ill-fitting wooden cover. At least she was sitting right under it. She'd watched the men in the village building the sloop by hand from old planks, while the women stitched together bits of fabric and nylon to make the sails. It was a rough vessel. Just like the one her papa used to fish from, until the sea had taken him, and brought her family nothing but grief.

She closed her eyes, and pictured him: big, round face, with smooth skin made even darker by working in the sun, curly black hair, and dark eyes that lit up whenever he saw her. He'd tell her stories of the sea whenever he came home. She'd loved that. Loved him.

She flinched as the sloop shuddered. It was travelling upwind into the waves, so she expected a rough crossing. She respected the sea, knew its ways. Even here, below deck, she could feel the swell getting higher. We should go back, and wait for better weather. But she knew they couldn't. The police might catch them, and scupper the boat. Then they would lose all their money. It had taken Pierre years of hard work to save up for their passage. He'd gone first. Now he'd sent for her, and the child he'd never seen.

They had to go on.

Everything will be all right when we reach Pierre, she told herself over and over. She pulled an envelope out of her pocket, drew out his photo and kissed it in the dark.

The baby moaned again. Was it hungry or sick? Or perhaps just sensing the fear all around? She offered her breast but the baby refused to latch on. "You're going to meet your papa soon, child. Very soon." She finished the lullaby...

Sleep little one
If you don't sleep
The crab will eat you...

When the baby was asleep, she pulled the shawl tighter around her, and tied the ends in a knot around her waist to bind them even closer together. Never to be parted. Singing the lullaby again, more to comfort herself than the child, her mind returned to happier times, to her mother and father, and to her wedding to Pierre. She lost herself in those happy memories.

Later, tipping over sideways into the lap of the woman next to her, she sat up straight wondering where she was. She'd dozed off. Her stomach turned as she felt the sloop rolling up and down, side to side, on the rising waves.

She could hear men on deck shouting to each other. The wind still howled through the sails and rigging. The rickety vessel's wooden frame creaked and moaned, as if protesting about being out on the ocean on such a stormy night. Was it light yet? They seemed to have been travelling for hours.

When you see light in the sky, you'll be here, with me. That's what Pierre had written. Here, below deck, it was still pitch black. She wriggled her toes and rubbed her feet again.

The shouting became louder, more urgent. Her heart started pounding. She could hear many footsteps running around above her. She listened intently.

Land! That's what they're shouting. *Land!*

She felt a surge of happiness.

Suddenly, she was jolted and catapulted forward as the old vessel smashed into something. It stood still for a moment as if dazed by the blow.

"*The reef!*" Voices were screaming.

She heard a loud crack, and felt the vessel roll and tip over to one side. Piercing cries rang out above as men were plunged into the sea. All around her, women and children started screaming as they tumbled on top of each other. Suddenly, a wall of water rushed through the cracked hull, sweeping her and the baby up through the hatch, and out into the sea.

The cold. The shock...

Water rushed into her mouth and lungs. Spluttering, she felt herself being dragged under by the weight of her long skirt. With one arm in a vice-like grip around the baby, she scrabbled with the other through the water, kicking furiously, not knowing whether she was swimming to the top, or the bottom, of the ocean.

A moment later she surfaced, gasping for air, and sobbing with terror. *My baby!* She turned onto her back to get the child clear of the water.

Light in the sky! She could see light breaking in the sky, as Pierre had promised.

Voices all around her shouted for help, then she heard: "*Requins!*"

Sharks? Hysterical, she screamed as something brushed past her. But it was just a piece of wood floating by. Grabbing it, she pulled her baby out of the shawl and lay it on the plank.

A man swam past, heading for shore.

"*Help,*" she cried. "*Please, my baby!*"

He didn't even look her way.

Holding the baby in front of her, she kicked and pushed her way towards lights in the distance. It had to be shore. It looked so far away, yet the waves seemed calmer now. She must be inside the reef, and that gave her hope. She kept steady, pushing and kicking. Pushing and kicking. She could hardly breathe with the exhaustion, but she kept going. Pushing and kicking.

"Nearly there, child," she kept saying, to urge herself on. The baby didn't move or cry, as if sensing their fight for life.

Her toes brushed something. She froze, but it wasn't a shark.

The soft seabed! She put one foot down cautiously, then the other. Now, she was standing on wobbly legs, shoulder high in water. Sobbing with relief, she picked her baby up from the plank and waded towards the beach.

Scrambling out of the waves, she flopped onto soft sand, and rolled onto her back. Dizzy with exertion and shock, her heart was pumping so hard she thought it would burst.

Someone was beside her now. Hands were pulling at her. Her baby started crying. She clutched it tight. But the hands wouldn't let go.

"No!" She struggled to sit up. A blow to the back of her head sent pain searing through her body. Her head spun. Another blow. Then another.

As she slipped into darkness, she heard her baby screaming as it was wrenched from her arms.

2

Michael Grant paced around the old lighthouse on the northern end of Grand Turk, overlooking the infamous north-west reef. He couldn't see much. The night was pitch black with cloud cover, but he could hear the Atlantic rollers pounding onto the reef in the distance, and feel the spray carried on the wind in his face.

The storm had raged all night. The noise of torrential rain battering the roof of his old house, and the wind rattling the plantation shutters, had driven him crazy. He'd tried to work in his study, sifting through the sequence of events over the last year – dates, times and conversations. It was important to get everything right, to forget nothing, but being cooped up in those conditions only added to his torment. When the storm eased, he'd slipped out of the house and driven up here.

Can't you just look away? Those words were whirling around in his head.

That's exactly what he had done. Looked away. But he couldn't get their screams out of his head. They haunted him, even during waking hours. If he had any guts, he'd wade out to sea and drown himself right now. That way it would be over quickly, and Jayne and the kids wouldn't have to live with the shame too.

He slumped down on the wet lighthouse steps and buried his head in his hands. Water seeped through his trousers, but he didn't care. He pulled a packet of cigarettes and lighter from his pocket. His hands shook as he lit up and inhaled tobacco deep into his lungs.

Why the hell had he applied for this job? What made him think *he* could succeed when so many had failed before him? These islands were *cursed*. And now he'd blown everything he'd worked so hard for over two decades.

He came out in a cold sweat just thinking about the time and effort he'd put in. Working all hours, always the last to leave, always helpful and loyal, pandering to the morons above him. Everything, so diligently planned and executed to propel himself up the career ladder, lay smashed to bits on the rocks.

A distant rumbling. He pricked up his ears. It sounded like an engine. A car? More like the roar of a motorbike. He stood up and ducked behind the lighthouse. Silly really because his Land Rover was in plain view. He peered back down Lighthouse Road. No sign of any headlights. He listened hard, but the only sound he could hear was the sea.

He sat back down on the steps and pulled his torch out of his pocket to check his watch. 4.30. He looked up at the sky. Light would soon be breaking on the eastern horizon. He sighed. Of course he should never have brought Jayne here too. He *knew* she'd soon be bored and start hankering after her old life in London, with the shops and restaurants. That was the trouble, he thought bitterly. His UK salary was never enough for the lifestyle she craved. Poor Jayne, none of this was her fault, he chided himself. She'd made an effort to settle here. Had even been content for a while, especially as their young son was with them. Of course she missed their daughter at boarding school in the UK, and tried not to show it. But it hadn't been long before she started making excuses to go back to the UK for one reason or another. Still, thank God she was over there at present with the children.

The irony was they were set up for life now. She could spend whatever she liked. He'd paid the school fees, the mortgage and all their debts. Except now the guilt and fear of discovery was paralysing. He couldn't work, couldn't sleep, couldn't eat.

He pulled a notebook out of his pocket and studied what he'd written with his torch. He'd tried several times to start this letter, to tell Jayne everything, to explain. But he'd never got past the second paragraph. How to explain something so terrible? He tore out his latest attempt and folded the piece of paper up into a small square.

A shuffling noise startled him.

"Who's there?"

A harsh sound rang out.

He leapt to his feet, but it was only a donkey braying back at him in the dark. The animals wandered freely around the island, a legacy of the days when their ancestors worked the salt mills.

He shook his head and looked down the road again. Still no headlights. He turned back to the sea. Of course his career would be over. He'd probably end up in prison. People in his position had to be made an example of. All the money would be confiscated. Then what would happen to Jayne and the kids?

He was even more nervous now poor old Clement Pearson was dead. He shivered. This had to stop. *He* was going to stop it, even if it meant his own ruin.

He flopped back against the wall of the old lighthouse with the sheer weight of his decision. The structure had stood since the 1850s, surviving storms, hurricanes and tidal waves. Its bright light beamed out to sea, warning ships of the hazard of the reef. Made of cast iron, it was permanent. Something that would never crumble. Something that would never break.

Not like him.

He threw the cigarette butt to the ground and stamped on it. Now, he was going to do what he should have done a while ago. Face the music. He wouldn't be frightened or intimidated. He'd go back to the office right now, and explain everything to London. It was the only way. He'd send a classified telegram for greater security, rather than an email.

Steeling himself, he got into the car and fired up the engine. Pulling out of the lighthouse car park, he started down the road back into town. With no street lights or other cars around, it was deathly quiet in the dark. He put his foot down and sped along. It was a bumpy ride as the tyres sloshed and bounced through water filled potholes. As he drove, his mind was rehearsing exactly what he was going to say.

Approaching the crossroads, he suddenly saw a truck hurtling along from another direction in the darkness. Why did it have no lights on?

He slammed his foot on the brakes. Nothing.

They were going to collide.

He pressed down on the horn in warning, but the truck wasn't stopping. Frantic, he pumped the brakes.

Nothing.

Yanking the handbrake on, he tried to swerve. Too late. He raised his arms to cover his face, but couldn't block out the sound of his own desperate cry, as the truck smashed into his door with tremendous force.

Semi-conscious in the silent aftermath, he tried to move. The steering wheel pinned him to the seat. He could smell petrol.

Then he heard the crackle of flames.

3

Providenciales
Turks and Caicos Islands

Jess followed the first group of well-heeled American tourists as they hurried across the tarmac. Judging by their noisy banter, they'd made the most of the open bar on the plane and were already well into the holiday spirit.

By contrast, the returning islanders sauntered along with all the time in the world, their flip-flops slapping on the ground as they went. Dark-skinned women wore cotton dresses. The men left their short-sleeved shirts loose over their trousers to keep cool.

Jess looked down at her high heels and navy-blue trouser suit. She felt way overdressed, but then she was here to work.

She still couldn't believe how quickly her life had changed in 24 hours. Yesterday, she'd been in Washington on special unpaid leave from the Foreign Office, with her diplomat partner Simon, when London had called out of the blue. Would she go to the Turks and Caicos Islands immediately on temporary duty to cover for the Head of the Governor's Office, David Evans, whose mother was gravely ill in the UK?

She'd hesitated, because it meant leaving Simon alone in Washington to continue his job in the Embassy. But

London had wanted a decision on the spot, so she'd just said 'yes'. How could she refuse to help? She'd been passing the weeks going to coffee mornings and ladies' lunches, even enjoying her new found freedom for a while. And she'd played so much tennis she was developing the calves of a mountain climber. But, as a diplomat too, she missed working and felt the need to get back to it.

So, this morning, she'd jumped on a plane from Washington to Miami, then transferred onto a flight to the islands. Now, here she was on Providenciales, the main tourist and economic island in the British Overseas Territory of the Turks and Caicos. What a turn of events.

Brilliant sunlight reflected off the white-washed walls of the international terminal, dazzling her. She felt her spirits soar for the first time in ages. As she stepped through the door, a steel band struck up in the far corner of the arrivals' hall to welcome the tourists. *Definitely in the Caribbean!*

After clearing passport control, she hauled her suitcase off the single baggage belt, and walked through customs. Now she had to transfer onto a domestic flight to the island of Grand Turk, the capital and seat of Government. She was relieved to discover the domestic terminal was in the same building. Now, she could see the Island Airways check-in for Grand Turk on the other side of the cavernous waiting area.

She went over. There were two desks, each with a set of weighing scales, and a line of 'queuing' suitcases. But no sign of any check-in staff, or passengers. No security officers either to monitor the unattended baggage.

In the far corner, a café heaved with people. They had to be the owners of these suitcases, she thought. They weren't all going over to Grand Turk: flights to other islands were up on the departure board too. She had another look at the café and decided to give it a miss. She wasn't going into that scrum, no matter how desperate she was for coffee. She pulled her suitcase over to a row of plastic seats and sat down to wait for check-in to open.

She switched on her mobile to call Simon and let him know she'd arrived. She waited for a signal... and waited.

No signal.

Other people were on their mobiles in the terminal, so she could only think her US provider didn't cover the Turks and Caicos. *Damn!* She'd have to phone Simon on a landline when she got over to Grand Turk.

Relaxing back into the seat, she watched everyone. Airports were fascinating and gave a real insight into the locals. Flying brought out the worst in people, but this lot didn't seem at all worried. They were too busy eating and drinking.

She smiled thinking back to the conversation with her Personnel Officer in London. She told him she'd barely heard of the Turks and Caicos Islands, let alone worked in a Governor's Office in a British Overseas Territory before. He was upbeat about it, although she detected a note of desperation in his voice. She guessed she was the only person available to drop everything at a moment's notice and jet off to the Caribbean, and he wasn't about to let her off the hook. "You're one of life's troopers, Jess," he said with as much honesty as he could muster. "You'll cope." And that was that.

He'd instructed London's Overseas Territories Department to email her a background brief on the Turks and Caicos overnight. She'd spent the entire journey reading it over and over to get the facts straight in her head.

The history of these islands made interesting reading. They'd first been claimed by the Spanish, then the French, with the British Empire finally gaining control in 1764.

Initially the islands were annexed to Jamaica, and governed from there. When Jamaica became independent, the islands were annexed to the Bahamas. However, when they gained independence, the Turks and Caicos voted to remain British, and finally got their own resident Governor, on Grand Turk. And that's where Jess was now heading.

Suddenly, a young woman in red trousers and jacket, with black hair tied back in a ponytail, clambered over some weighing scales and stood behind one of the desks. She wore a huge Island Airways badge on her lapel.

The stampede from the café that followed was unexpected. The relaxed crowd turned into a crush as people pushed and shoved to check in their bulging suitcases.

Jess watched fascinated.

Suddenly the crowds parted as a man swept out of the café and walked straight up to the desk. Must be someone important, Jess thought, as he swaggered along dressed in a smart business suit. His curly hair was rigid with gel, and his black skin, above the collar of his white shirt, glowed with good living.

The check-in girl gave him a big smile. A baggage attendant appeared from nowhere and lifted his suitcase onto the weighing scales. Jess couldn't see if the man acknowledged either of them, because he had his back to her. He certainly didn't stop talking on his mobile for a moment. As he walked away from check-in, a little girl darted in front of him, causing him to stumble and drop his briefcase.

"Keep that kid under control!" he barked at the child's mother. His penetrating voice reverberated around the terminal. People stood shocked and hushed.

The woman pulled the child close, her eyes lowered submissively as he continued his rant.

Jess stood up.

He caught the movement, and glared at her. Then he picked up his briefcase and went over to security.

The crowd closed in again at check-in and the chaos resumed.

Rude oaf! Jess watched him pass through security. He obviously thought he was some kind of 'Big Shot'. She sat down again to wait until everyone else had checked in. Huge suitcases, pushchairs, boxes, food hampers, and trunks were all being weighed. Nothing, she noticed, was ever turned away.

Suddenly an old lady was lifted up onto the baggage scales by two passengers. Were they weighing her?

Then Jess realised... *Oh God!* She jumped up and rushed over to the window. Outside a row of propeller planes stood gleaming in the sunshine – not a jet in sight. Now she knew why the weight of the bags and passengers mattered so much. Her stomach turned. She hated propeller planes. Every movement, every turbulent bump, every lash of rain seemed magnified inside them.

It was at that precise moment she wondered just what she was letting herself in for. Had she been a bit hasty in accepting this assignment? Almost immediately, she dismissed her uneasiness. She'd agreed to do this job for a couple of months, and that's exactly what she was going to do.

At the check-in desk, she put her ticket on the counter and her suitcase on the baggage scales. The other passengers had gone through the metal detector arch, and were sitting in a tiny room on the other side.

"Weight?" The check-in girl barked without looking up.

Jess looked at her suitcase on the weighing scales.

"Your weight." The girl's eyes never left her computer.

"Fifty-six kilos."

The girl looked up in disbelief, her lips pursed under a single slash of bright red lipstick.

Jess couldn't blame her for being sceptical, given the size of the other passengers.

The girl looked her up and down, and slapped a boarding card on the counter.

In the tiny departure lounge there were only half a dozen seats, not enough for all the passengers. Big Shot sat by the door leading to the tarmac, and was now deep in conversation with another man. Jess had noticed this other man at check-in, not only because of his blond ponytail, but because he was the only other white person around. With sun-bronzed skin and dressed casually in a black polo shirt and jeans, he had a rugged look about him, as if he spent his life outdoors.

He must have been aware of her eyes on him, because he looked over and flashed her a smile.

It was such a warm smile that it deserved one in return.

As soon as the door opened, Big Shot stood up and pushed through it. A crush to get through after him followed. Jess went out last. She was in no rush. At least the plane had two propellers, she thought, as she climbed the small portable steps and entered the cabin. The pilot and co-pilot sat up front, with no door to shield them from the passengers. Jess couldn't stand up straight, because there wasn't enough head room. With only a single seat on either side of the aisle, and a row of three across the back, there couldn't have been more than 24 seats in all. She looked at the number on her boarding card, then at the seat. Who should be sitting in it, but Big Shot? He averted his eyes. He had no intention of moving.

"Sit anywhere," the pilot shouted to her over his shoulder.

The only spare seat left was in the middle of the back row. Bent over double, she walked to the back and sat down between two burly men. With no arm-rests dividing the seats, their fleshy hips pressed against her. The heat radiating from their bodies made her feel uncomfortable, and she perched on the edge of the seat. No wonder everyone had stampeded to get onto the plane, she thought. And now she knew the ropes, she wouldn't get the worst seat again either.

The pilot taxied over to the single runway, swung onto it, and stepped on the gas in a running start. Jess wondered, heart in mouth, if they'd ever get off the ground with all the weight on board. But they were soon rising above stunning, white sandy beaches and aquamarine sea, in brilliant sunshine. She forgot about being squashed in the middle, because it gave her a terrific view out of each side window. She smiled at one of the men sitting next to her.

He just looked out the window.

Why were the Islanders so uncommunicative in this Territory, she wondered? No-one had spoken to her, or even looked her in the eye, since she'd arrived, except Blond Ponytail. She could see him now sitting towards the front, reading a newspaper. All the American tourists seemed to have been left behind in Provo.

She peered out the windows again. Blue sea shimmered all around, and merged on the horizon with crystalline sky. White foam swirled over coral reefs, as waves crashed onto them. She'd never seen anything so beautiful.

According to the brief London had sent her, the islands were surrounded by the third largest coral reef system in the world. So it wasn't surprising, over the centuries, that many ships had ended up in a watery grave close to these shores. That's how the islands had come to be populated by people of African descent. Some had been slaves who survived those shipwrecks. Others had been slaves of American Royalists who had come down to the islands after the American War of Independence to set up cotton and tobacco plantations.

Jess wondered if the islanders' demeanour could be a consequence of their ancestors' grim experience of slavery? Or of the trauma of being ship-wrecked? Could experiences like that be passed genetically through generations? Or maybe living in an isolated society in the middle of the North Atlantic just made them subdued and wary of foreigners? They could hardly like having a British colonial government either, except they had voted to keep it.

Only then did it occur to her that she hadn't noticed anything British about the Territory. Had there been a Union Jack flying at Provo airport? She couldn't remember seeing one. The Oprah Winfrey Show had beamed out of the terminal TV. And people spoke with a slight American accent, rather than a British one.

All very puzzling.

As Jess sat there, uncomfortably considering her first impressions of the Turks and Caicos, Big Shot turned round and gave her a penetrating stare. It was as if he knew exactly what was going through her mind. He didn't smile or acknowledge her, so she didn't respond either. She was already getting the hang of this.

At that moment a more sinister thought popped into her head. Maybe there was another reason why people didn't talk to each other here, let alone to strangers. Maybe they didn't want to draw attention to themselves? Perhaps they were afraid to?

4

There was no steel band to welcome them when they walked into the Grand Turk domestic terminal, and no holiday feel to the place either. Jess's flying companions stood silently waiting for their luggage at the single baggage carousel. Miraculously, hers came out first. She hauled it off and walked into the main hallway. She wasn't expecting a welcoming committee, which was just as well, as there wasn't one. Hadn't David Evans said he'd meet her?

After a while, she saw a black limousine draw up outside, and Big Shot get in. She went over to the door and watched the car disappear into the distance with an uneasy feeling in the pit of her stomach. He *was* someone important, and she'd just made a terrible first impression.

Too bad, she thought, as she looked again in vain for David. Not that she'd met him. There were just no other white faces in the terminal.

A young man sidled up to her. "Taxi, Miss?" he asked, smiling.

It was the first time any islander had smiled at her since she'd landed in the Territory. His trousers and shirt looked clean and freshly ironed, which she liked. And he didn't try and grab her suitcase or herd her towards his taxi. She nodded.

He smiled again. "Wait there!"

He crossed the road to the car park in front of the terminal and got into an old Ford, which was covered in fine sand. She was soon to discover that almost everything in the islands was. She started having second thoughts when the old car wouldn't start. But after the third attempt, it shuddered into life, and he drove over to where she was waiting.

The battered bonnet, and the front number plate hanging off, didn't fill her with confidence either. But his friendly smile heartened her, and she decided to take a chance.

He jumped out, stashed her suitcase in the boot, and held the passenger door open. "Where are you going, Miss?" he asked as she got in.

"Governor's Office, please."

He nodded and ran round to the driver's seat. He drove along the airport approach road for about 200 yards. At the T-junction, he turned left. Moments later, he swung through an open iron gate, and pulled up outside a small building. "Governor's Office, Miss," he said, switching off the engine.

Jess looked at him. She could have walked it in five minutes. That's when she realised he was no taxi driver at all. Just a local, keen to make a quick buck. Oh well, she thought, at least she'd made it in one piece.

Ahead of her, the building looked more like a white-washed bungalow than an office. The brass plaque, screwed into the wall next to the front door, confirmed it was the Governor's Office. She tried the handle, but the door was locked. She walked along and peered through one of the windows. Everything was in darkness inside. She looked at her watch: 4.30. Had everyone already gone home?

Wearily, she sat down on the front door step. She'd been travelling all day and now she'd arrived, not only was there no-one to meet her at the airport, the office was closed. But, as she looked up at the huge orange sun hanging low in the sky, and heard the rhythmic sound of waves lapping onto the shore in the distance, she felt entirely calm.

Seeing another set of iron gates further along, she rose, brushed off her trousers, and walked towards them, pulling her suitcase behind her. Although the sun was close to setting, it was still hot on her face. The humidity wrapped around her, and little drops of sweat trickled down her back. She stopped to take off her jacket and tuck it under her arm.

Beyond the gates, a driveway led up to a beautiful old house, standing framed in the late afternoon sunlight. It looked just like one of those old Bermuda-style houses in story books, with a wide verandah and wooden railings on every side. Dotted around the grounds were squat palm trees and low-lying shrubs.

She grabbed the handle of her suitcase again, and set off along the drive. The going was uncomfortable. Sand squeezed through the open toes of her shoes until the soles of her feet felt like they were getting a sand scrub pedicure.

When she reached the house, a sign above the door said: *Trafalgar House*. Beside it stood an old bronze cannon, with its barrel pointing up the drive as if ready to blast any unwanted visitors. Someone had a sense of humour, she thought, as she rang the bell and waited. No reply. She rang again. Where was everyone?

Leaving her suitcase at the door, she walked along the wooden verandah. It led around the side of the house, to a paved courtyard at the back. Party preparations were underway. A trestle table was set with a white tablecloth, and sparkling china and glass. Several bottles of booze were lined up on the bar in the far corner. Everything looked ready, except there was no-one around.

She couldn't see the sea from the courtyard, but she could hear it. Walking across the back garden towards some scrub-like bushes that seemed to border the property, she peered through a gap, and saw a beautiful, white coral beach, and aquamarine sea.

Mesmerised, she watched the huge sun hover on the horizon before slipping out of sight.

A cry from behind made her jump.

She spun round and saw a plump woman, wearing a domestic uniform and white pinafore staring at her. The woman nervously pushed some stray curly black hairs behind an old-fashioned comb that was keeping her bun in place. "Miss Jessica?" she asked.

"Yes."

"Oh my goodness." Tears welled up in the woman's black eyes and slipped down her cheeks.

Jess was startled.

"Th-the Governor..." The woman fanned herself with her hands as if trying to summon up air to breathe. "He had a car accident this morning."

"An *accident*?"

The woman buried her head in her hands.

Hearing footsteps running along the verandah, Jess turned to see a man with dishevelled sandy-coloured hair appear. She knew immediately who he was, and held out her hand. "Hello, David?"

He shook her hand, warmly. "I'm so sorry I wasn't at the airport, Jess, I was late getting there." He sounded breathless from running. "I thought you hadn't come."

"I've just heard the awful news about the Governor," she said.

David went over to the woman, who was dabbing her eyes with the edge of her apron, and put a comforting hand on her shoulder. "This is Maggie," he said. "The Governor's housekeeper and cook."

Jess smiled at Maggie.

David went on. "The Governor's car ran into a truck early this morning on his way down from the Ridge. He was badly injured and burned. The police took him to the clinic but there wasn't much they could do without the right medical equipment. He's been flown to a hospital in Miami." He gave a sort of sigh as he stopped talking, as if all the air had been sucked out of him.

"Is he going to be all right?" Jess asked, anxiously.

David shrugged. "We don't know yet."

"And your mother?" Jess asked, thinking how weighed down with worry he looked.

"Not good." He looked away, to compose himself. "We were organising a welcoming dinner party for you." He pointed at the table and preparations. "The Governor wanted to introduce you to a few people before I left in the morning. Maggie's been cooking all afternoon... I suppose we should have cancelled it really."

Both he and Maggie looked at her.

Jess could see they were reeling with shock over the Governor's accident, and didn't know what to do about the party.

"Are the guests still coming?" she asked.

David nodded. "Just a few expats living here." He hesitated. "The locals don't socialise with us much."

"Is the food all prepared?"

Maggie nodded.

Jess turned to David. "Socialising is probably the last thing you want to do, but shouldn't we try and carry on as normal? It seems to me that you've done everything you can for the Governor. He's in the US getting the best possible medical treatment. There's nothing more you can do for him now."

David nodded. "I'm sure you're right." He sighed. "I don't suppose London will let me leave in the morning, not now."

Jess heard the sadness in his voice.

"Trust me, David, you need to be there." She paused. "Look, I don't know much about these islands, or our operation here." The truth was she knew absolutely nothing except what she'd read in the background brief. "But I can tick things over while you're away. As long as we're not expecting any crisis."

His eyes brightened. "Really?"

She nodded. "Why don't you ring London? Tell them I've arrived, and I'm happy to hold the fort while you're away."

He looked at her. "Are you sure?"

"Absolutely. I'll talk to them too if you want."

"And Sally's here to help you of course," he said, eagerly.

"Sally?"

"The Governor's PA."

"Of course." Jess knew from the brief the Governor's PA was the only other UK-based member of staff, although there were several local administrators. "That settles it then." She smiled at David. "If London are happy, so am I."

"Thanks, Jess." He dashed into the house to phone.

When she turned back, Maggie was staring at her wide-eyed. "No, Miss Jessica!" She shook her head. "*No!*"

Jess gave her a reassuring smile. "Now don't you worry, Maggie. We'll be fine here on our own, for a while."

5

By the time Jess had showered and changed, the darkness of night had swept in. She threw open her bedroom shutters and windows, and looked up at the velvety black sky and bright stars. The sound of the sea lapping onto the shore, and the crickets' nocturnal song, reminded her just how much she loved the feel of the tropics.

The original plan had been for her to live in David's house in town while he was away. Now, with the Governor's accident, David wanted her to stay at the Residence rather than leave it empty. That was fine with her. It would be convenient to have the office at the end of the drive. Anyway, the Residence was a charming old house. It seemed to sigh with age every time she took a step on the waxed floorboards, or turned on a squeaky tap. Even the wardrobe doors groaned when opened, and the dressing table drawers had expanded so much with the humidity she could hardly move them. There was no air conditioning, but that didn't bother her. The draught from the ceiling fan kept the air moving. A net hanging from the ceiling over her double bed, and fly-screens over the windows, suggested there was a mosquito problem.

A strange feeling came over her. It had only been a short plane ride from Washington, but she felt she'd gone back in time, to a bygone age...

Smashing crockery broke the spell. She looked down to the courtyard, where Maggie was muttering under her breath and reaching for a broom to sweep up what looked like pieces of a broken plate.

Poor Maggie. She must be upset about the Governor, Jess thought, as she slipped out of her bedroom to go and help with the preparations. On the landing, a crystal chandelier hung over the staircase, lighting the way. She looked at the portraits of previous Governors mounted along the wall as she went down the stairs. But there was no picture of the present Governor, Michael Grant. He'd probably only take his place on the wall after he'd finished the job. *If* he ever came back.

Like her, the Governor was a British diplomat, only more senior. He chaired the local Government which, apart from him, was made up entirely of local islanders. Although both she and the Governor were members of the Foreign Office, she'd never met Michael Grant before.

Stopping at the phone in the hallway, she decided to give Simon a quick call to let him know she was there. It might be too late after dinner. She hesitated as she picked up the receiver. She was still troubled by the look in his eyes when she'd told him she was coming down here for a couple of months. Of course she should have discussed it with him first. And she would have, if London hadn't demanded an immediate answer. It simply hadn't occurred to her that he would mind, being so busy with his own job.

She took a deep breath and dialled his Washington office. No reply. She tried their home number. No reply there either. When she got no reply from his mobile, she felt uneasy. She knew he didn't have a work function, because they were supposed to have been going out to dinner, to celebrate the anniversary of their second year together. He'd arranged it, saying they needed a night out for a change, to talk. Of course she'd apologised for spoiling his dinner plans, but he'd told her not to worry about it.

So where was he now?

She redialled their home phone number to leave a voicemail. The first thing he always did when he got home was check that machine.

"Hi Simon, I've tried your office as well, but I guess you're out for the evening... Well, I'm here... Amazing place! I feel like Robinson Crusoe... except I arrived to terrible news. The Governor was seriously injured in a car crash this morning. He's been flown out to a Miami hospital... David Evans, the person I'm replacing, is still hoping to go to the UK in the morning so I may be holding the fort on my own for a while... Oh, and my mobile doesn't work here. That's why you haven't been able to get me if you've been trying. I'll get a new one tomorrow and text you the number... I'm staying at the Governor's Residence by the way... There's a dinner party tonight to introduce me to some expats. I don't know what time it'll finish. It may be too late for me to phone again after that. If so, I'll catch you in the morning... Sleep tight..."

She put the receiver back, feeling a bit more cheerful. Simon would be fine once he'd got used to the idea of her working down here. It had been a surprise, that's all. Anyway, it was only for a couple of months, and that would fly by.

By the time she got out into the courtyard, Maggie had already swept up and gone. But David was there, lining up glasses along the bar.

"What did London say?" she asked.

"They didn't like the idea of me leaving you on your own, but they agreed I could go."

"I should think so too."

He nodded and started cleaning the glasses with a tea towel to remove any smears. "I'm booked on the first flight out in the morning."

She watched him. "Do I need to write barman into my job description too?"

He smiled for the first time. "The Governor's driver usually does all this. He's driver, aide-de-camp, butler, barman, you name it. But he's so upset about the Governor's accident, he can't work."

She frowned. "I didn't think he was in the car."

"He wasn't. That's *why* he's so troubled. Poor man. He feels if he'd been driving, the accident would never have happened." He paused. "God knows what the Governor was doing up on the Ridge before dawn."

"What exactly *is* the Ridge?" she asked.

"The highest point on the island," David explained. "There's an old lighthouse up there and the remains of a former US naval base. Developers have been building more houses up on the high ground in recent years, where it's safer." He glanced over. "These islands sit smack bang in the hurricane belt. They're so flat, they're vulnerable to tidal waves that can follow these storms." He paused. "You should read the disaster management file as a priority in the morning, Jess. Familiarise yourself with the hurricane procedures. We've just come into the season."

"Hurricanes? *Oh great!*"

David smiled again. "Don't worry. It's been years since there's been a direct hit. Now, Ma'am." He wrapped the tea towel over his arm. "What can I get you?"

Jess laughed "Gin and tonic please." She pulled up a rattan bar stool. "And while we've got a few minutes, can you fill me in on who's coming this evening?"

David measured out some gin and poured it into a glass. "The most senior guest is Dominic Canning, Chief Justice of the Supreme Court, and his wife Rebekah. Her name is spelt with the biblical *kah* at the end, as she will remind you if you ever get it wrong." He bent down to get a can of tonic from the fridge under the bar. "The position of Chief Justice has always been held by a Brit. Dominic's a retired British barrister."

"I guess it's important to keep an impartial judiciary."

"Exactly!" He paused. "Rebekah's his *third* wife." He gave Jess a knowing look. "High maintenance. Fond of the grog too."

She nodded. "So, where's the Governor's wife?"

"Oh, Jayne took their young son Sam back to the UK for a week to pick up their daughter from boarding school. They were all supposed to be coming back together to spend the summer holidays here with the Governor." He sighed. "She's left the kids with their grandparents in the UK, and is on her way to the Governor's bedside in Miami."

A familiar sadness settled on Jess. "How awful for them."

"Yeah." David pushed her drink towards her. "Apart from the Governor's PA Sally, the other three guests are all American. There aren't many Brits on this island."

"So I've noticed. This could be another State of America for all the UK presence."

"Shame, isn't it? But we have no economic or strategic interests here." He paused. "Problem is, the islanders want to remain British."

"So I read in my background brief."

"They like having British passports, the safety net of British defence, foreign affairs, that sort of thing. And local politics can be partisan and poisonous. They might not trust us much, but they trust each other even less."

She smiled.

"It's a bit like the Falklands really," he went on. "Until the people here *vote* to become independent, we won't leave."

"Must be a bit of an uphill struggle, trying to get anything done though?"

"Spot on," he said, wearily. "They like the security of being a British Overseas Territory, but they don't want British officials here. They especially don't want us running things, or telling them what to do."

She gave a wry smile. "So, tell me, who are these American guests?"

"Two are brothers – Brad and Charles Regan. They run the local dive company. Brad's lived on Grand Turk for years. Came over as a young man, loved the diving and set up a business. He runs the day to day operation, mostly for tourists." He glanced at Jess. "His brother Charles is a New York banker. I think he's the financial backer. The business can't make that much money because we don't get the volume of tourists over here that Provo does. Charles is a pretty competent diver though. Visits as often as he can."

Jess nodded. "Are they bringing wives?"

"No." David shook his head. "Charles is divorced. His ex-wife lives in New York with the kids. And Brad has never married. Well, not as far as I know anyway." He smiled. "He likes the ladies, and they like him – if you get my meaning."

Jess nodded. "So who's the third American?"

"Carrie Lynch." David's eyes lit up when he mentioned her name. "She runs the local kindergarten. She came down here on holiday, and fell in love with the island too. There was no kindergarten, so she set one up. Runs it with the help of a couple of local women." He counted on his fingers. "Oh, and of course, the Governor's PA Sally is coming too, which makes eight of us." He glanced up. "We'll need to keep an eye on Sally tonight. She's very upset about the Governor's accident."

Jess wasn't quite sure what he meant about keeping an eye on Sally, and he didn't explain.

Instead, he looked at his watch. "I'll pop through to the kitchen and get more ice before everyone arrives." And with that, he disappeared into the house.

Jess spotted a pad and pencil at the end of the bar and went over to get it. She'd picked up a tip from an Ambassador's wife, a wonderful hostess, who'd advised her to keep a list of guests' names in her pocket and check it regularly. That way she'd never find herself in the embarrassing position of forgetting one of her guests' names.

Jess always followed that advice, and now wrote out a list of this evening's dinner guests in the pad.

(UK) Dominic Canning (Chief Justice), and wife Rebekah.

(UK) Sally – Governor's PA – and David, Head of Governor's Office.

(US) Brad Regan (dive company) – his brother Charles Regan (New York banker).

(US) Carrie Lynch – teacher/owns kindergarten.

Jess tore out the piece of paper, folded it up and slipped it into her skirt pocket. She sat back on the bar stool and took a long sip of her gin and tonic. Delicious! Hearing the whine of a mosquito, she flapped it away from her ear. She was worried now about being bitten. Her long, black skirt covered her legs and ankles, but her strappy top exposed her arms. She was about to go into the house to find some insect repellent when she heard heavy footsteps on the verandah. She got up and walked over to greet the first guest.

When the man turned the corner and saw her, his eyes widened. "The lady on the plane!"

Jess recognised him at once – Blond Ponytail. She smiled and held out her hand. "I'm Jessica Turner, and you must be..."

"Brad Regan." He spoke with a soft American accent as he shook her hand.

He was still wearing his hair in a ponytail, which she'd normally have thought naff for a man who looked to be in his 40s. But, wearing a printed shirt loose over dark trousers, he seemed at ease with himself. She liked that about him. "You run the dive company, I believe?"

"You're well informed, Jessica."

His whole face lit up when he smiled. She could see why he was a hit with the ladies.

"Call me, Jess."

"Do you dive, Jess?"

"Afraid not."

"Then you're missing something special." He pointed in the direction of the ocean. "Just a few hundred yards offshore, the seabed suddenly drops to 7,000 feet. We call it the wall." He paused. "You must let me take you out there. It's *fantastic*."

She shivered. "I'm not a fan of the deep and what's out there."

"There's very little in the deep," he said. "The sea-life exists all around the coral reefs and inside, where the food is, although you can see the migrating whales pass through the Columbus Passage during the winter."

"The Columbus Passage?"

"It's a deep water trench that runs between the Caicos Bank and the Turks Bank." He paused. "It's sometimes called The Turks Islands Passage. Here, let me show you." He beckoned her to follow him behind the bar where an old map of the islands hung on the back wall. He traced his finger along the map. "The Turks and Caicos Islands run directly south of the Bahamas, and south-east of Miami."

Jess knew the geography from the map attached to her background brief, but she let him tell her anyway.

"There are lots of islands in the chain, but only a few are inhabited." He pointed to them.

"The Islands of West Caicos, Providenciales, North Caicos, Middle Caicos, East Caicos and South Caicos all sit in a sort of semi-circle on the northern edge of the Caicos Bank." He moved his finger to the east. "And here's Grand Turk, where we are, sitting on top of the Turks Bank, and Salt Cay lies just south of us." He ran his finger over the ocean between the Caicos Bank and the Turks Bank. "Here's the Columbus Passage."

"Ah, I see."

He looked at her. "These two Banks are like flattened mountain summits. The islands sit above sea level, with shallow water all around them. As you get to the edge of the two banks, it's like going over a cliff. That's where our 7,000 feet drop comes in."

Jess gave an involuntary shiver.

He grinned at her reaction. "It's *wonderful* out there, Jess. *Please* let me teach you to dive."

Jess couldn't think of anything worse. But he was so enthusiastic, she heard herself say, "Maybe I'll give it a go sometime."

"How about Saturday?"

She hesitated.

"Hi Brad!" David called out, as he returned with a large bucket of ice. "I see you two have met."

Jess was glad of the interruption. "Brad was on the same plane as me coming over from Provo." She stopped, wondering whether to mention the scene with the child and Big Shot in the terminal.

But she didn't have to because Brad got in first. "You'll have to forgive Roger Pearson," he said. "He's just been appointed Immigration Minister. It's turned his head a little."

"*A little?*" David walked back behind the bar, with a sour look on his face. Clearly he didn't think much of Roger Pearson either.

Jess frowned. "The surname Pearson seems familiar."

Brad laughed. "The Pearson family are a dynasty over here. Half the islanders have British surnames from colonial days." He turned to David, serious now. "How's the Governor? Have you heard anything more about what actually happened?"

David shook his head. "It was a hit and run. A vehicle slammed into the Governor's Land Rover at the crossroads on his way down from the Ridge early this morning. The police think it was the truck that was stolen from the supermarket compound late last night. They're out looking for it now." He shook his head. "Probably kids out joyriding... bloody idiots!"

Brad frowned. "What was the Governor doing up there in the early hours?"

Before David could answer, a loud female voice rang out. "For Chrissakes! We're not eating out here all night with these mozzies, are we?"

Jess turned to see a petite woman with shoulder-length auburn hair standing at the entrance. Her short black dress and plunging cleavage were eye-popping.

The woman walked over to Jess and held out her hand. "Good to meet you, Jess." She had a cut-glass accent. "I'm Sally, the Governor's PA."

"Hello." Jess shook her hand.

"It'll be great to have another woman from home in the office," Sally said. Then she spotted Brad at the bar, and went straight over. She squashed him in her cleavage as she reached up to kiss him on both cheeks.

David rolled his eyes.

"*Shit!*" Sally slapped her arm in a dramatic gesture. "I'm going in to get some mozzie spray before I'm bitten to death." And with that she teetered into the house, high heels clattering on the flagstones.

"Now you've met Sally," David said, flatly.

Jess smiled, as more footsteps by the entrance made them all turn again.

"Hi Carrie." David came out quickly from behind the bar and walked over to a tall, young woman wearing black culottes and a halter neck top. With her blonde hair tied back in a ponytail and tanned skin, she looked the stereotypical all-American girl. David kissed her on both cheeks and gave her a warm smile which, Jess noticed, Carrie returned. He beckoned to Jess. "Let me introduce you two."

But Carrie didn't need his help. She walked over to Jess and shook her hand warmly. "Lovely to meet you, Jess, even if it is in such awful circumstances." She turned back to David. "How's the Governor?"

"Still in an induced coma, while they assess the full extent of his injuries."

"Terrible," Carrie said, quietly. "Has he been able to talk about the accident?"

David shook his head.

"So sad. We took the children to church this afternoon to say prayers for him."

Jess remembered that Carrie ran the local kindergarten.

At that moment, Sally came back out of the house. She didn't give Carrie the warm welcome she'd given Brad. She just nodded at her, and thrust a can of repellent at Jess. "They'll love your new blood."

"Thanks." Jess took the can. "I'd better go and change my top."

"We can go inside if that's what everyone wants to do,"

David said.

"Don't worry on my account." Jess excused herself. "I'll just be five minutes."

★

Upstairs in her bedroom, Jess put on a long-sleeved blouse and sprayed on the mozzie repellent. She walked over to the window and looked down to the courtyard where David was chatting to Carrie. She also noticed Sally link arms with Brad, in a proprietary way.

So engrossed were the four of them in each other, they hadn't noticed another couple arrive. From David's earlier description – an older man with a younger woman – Jess knew they were the Chief Justice, Dominic Canning, and his wife Rebekah.

As soon as he spotted them, David went over, kissed Rebekah on both cheeks, and shook Dominic's hand.

From her vantage point, Jess found herself watching Rebekah, who stood rigidly next to her husband. When he put a hand on her back to usher her in, Rebekah shrugged it off and walked away. They've had a row, Jess thought.

The Chief Justice immediately took David aside for a private chat, but Jess's attention went back to Rebekah, who stood aloof from everyone. She was a beautiful woman, tall and slim, with flowing dark hair. Jess could see what had attracted the Chief Justice to Rebekah, but what was in it for her? Money? Status? Jess knew she was being cynical, but that was the reality of life.

Seeing Rebekah on her own, Brad immediately uncoupled himself from Sally's grip and went over to talk to her.

Jess had to admit Brad was attentive and charming. He seemed to get on with everyone, even Big Shot at the airport, whom Jess now knew was the incoming

Immigration Minister Roger Pearson. What had Brad and the Minister been talking about so intently in that tiny departure lounge, she wondered?

Pearson? There was something familiar about that surname. She'd heard it somewhere else today.

Of course! She went over to her handbag and fished out a newspaper article she'd torn out of the *Miami Post* on the plane over, thinking it would be big news in a small community like this. Unfolding it, she read again:

CARIBBEAN NEWS, 17 AUGUST
AP
TURKS AND CAICOS MINISTER
COMMITS SUICIDE

Newspaper reports in the Turks and Caicos Islands say that local Immigration Minister Clement Pearson was found hanged in his garage early on Tuesday 4 August. Mrs Pearson retired early on Monday evening, leaving her husband working in his study. When she woke up the next morning and saw he hadn't been to bed all night, she searched and found him in the garage. She called the paramedics, but he couldn't be revived.

Government sources said the Minister had been suffering from depression after the death of his 20 year old son from a drugs overdose. Earlier that day, the Minister had been giving evidence to the British Government Inquiry into illegal immigration into the Turks and Caicos, and the sinking of two Haitian sloops off Grand Turk in recent months. Speculation is increasing that the pressure of the Inquiry added to the Minister's fragile state of mind.

Today a pathologist gave the provisional cause of the Minister's death as hanging, with the police treating it as non-suspicious.

So, Big Shot Roger Pearson had just been appointed

Immigration Minister, in place of the deceased Immigration Minister Clement Pearson. Did that mean the two men were related? Things couldn't work like that in a British Overseas Territory, could they? She felt frustrated. She should be going through everything with David in the office before he left in the morning, not having dinner with a bunch of strangers.

She put the cutting back in her bag and returned to the window. She frowned as she watched the guests below. They all knew each other very well, but the atmosphere down there seemed awkward – strained, even. Of course the Governor's accident would be enough to dampen any gathering. Was that the reason for the tension? Only Brad seemed relaxed enough to move easily amongst everyone. But there was one person missing – his brother Charles still hadn't arrived.

At that moment Brad looked up, as if aware she was watching him. He smiled and beckoned her down.

Jess nodded and took a deep breath. She had the feeling this was going to be a long evening.

6

Miami

Detective Inspector Tom Sangster put his bare feet up on the hotel balcony railings, and took a swig of cold lager. Travelling on planes gave him a real thirst. He relaxed back in the chair to breathe in the humid Miami night. August was the hottest month of the year, according to the blurb on the plane. Not that it bothered him. He was used to those temperatures back home in Australia.

He closed his eyes to let the atmosphere wash over him. The sounds and smells of a new place were always exciting, and Miami didn't disappoint. On the pavement below, people chatted happily as they strolled along. The rhythmic beat of drums and flamenco guitar drifted over rooftops from the next street. The music seemed to be pulling them like a magnet. His taxi driver had told him to go out and sample Coconut Grove's nightlife, it was some of the best in Miami. Now the noisy hubbub was tempting him to do just that, despite the late hour.

Standing his lager bottle on the balcony floor, Tom returned to his latest portrait sketch. With his graphite pencil, he adjusted the mouth into an open smile. Definitely not the tight mouth of the reserved person he'd drawn the first time he'd met Jessica Turner.

He'd recognised her immediately at Miami Airport earlier. He rarely forgot a face, especially one he'd sketched. So why hadn't he gone over straightaway and said hello? He'd been asking himself that all the way to the hotel. Jess obviously hadn't seen him, and by the time he'd got his act together, she'd disappeared through a departure gate for some place called Providenciales.

Where the hell *was* that anyway?

He got up and went inside for his iPad. Googling Providenciales, he wasn't surprised to see it was the capital of a British Overseas Territory in the Caribbean called the Turks and Caicos Islands. That made perfect sense. Jess *was* a British diplomat, after all. Was she working there, he wondered, or just visiting?

Back on the balcony, he stared at the face he'd recreated from memory and that fleeting glimpse in the airport. Dark memories flooded back from their first meeting in Brisbane. It hadn't gone well. Jess had been cool, to the point of icy. But, then, he had just bawled her out for traipsing over his crime scene, before finding out she was the British Consul.

Her soul-less eyes back then had unsettled him, mostly because he hadn't been able to work her out, and capture them on paper. Later, he understood that frosty exterior was her way of coping with the death of her husband and young daughter in a car crash in Indonesia. He knew Jess hadn't been in the car with them at the time, and that she somehow blamed herself for their deaths. He didn't know why, because she never spoke about it. He'd only found out about the crash from the British High Commissioner, who'd told him while they were at the hospital waiting for Jess to come out of surgery after that psychopath shot her.

Shit – what a case that was! The murder of British businesswoman Ellen Chambers had been the most challenging investigation of his career.

Jess had been so determined to protect the murder victim's British sister that she'd ended up taking a bullet herself. The woman had guts, no doubt about that. She'd flushed out the killer, even acted as bait. The irony was *he'd* been credited with tracking down the killer and saving *her* life. Sometimes, he wondered if it hadn't been the other way around.

Still, that case had given him a national profile. An offer of a transfer to the Canberra Federal Police soon followed. That had surprised him. He thought he'd be policing the streets of Brisbane forever. In Canberra, he'd been assigned to an intelligence unit responsible for identifying criminals smuggling illegal migrants to Australia by sea. He never expected to be involved in intelligence work, and found it stimulating. But it was a far cry from what he was used to on the front line.

Anyway, he must have been doing something right because, in no time, he'd been selected to join the Prime Minister's new multi-agency task force to combat illegal people smuggling to Australia.

Funny where life takes you, he thought, as he took another swig of lager. Now here he was, on this humid night in Miami, on a fact-finding mission with a colleague, to see how the Americans coped with illegal boat people from Haiti and Latin America. They'd already visited Italy and Greece to see how those Governments were dealing with people-smuggling from the Middle East, and Africa. They'd been in Paris and London too, examining the problem of migrants trying to get across the Channel by boats or through the tunnel.

The bleep of an email arriving on his iPad caught his attention.

Dear Detective Inspector Sangster,

Welcome to Miami.

I write to confirm we have arranged a two-day program for you and your colleague with our Miami Air & Marine Branch. A car will pick you up from your hotel at 1000 in the morning for a day of roundtable talks with experts at HQ.

On day two, air enforcement agents will take you out in our Eurocopter AS35083 AStar, which patrols the Florida waters and a large part of the Caribbean. It provides the backbone of our marine interceptor fleet that protects the south-east US maritime border from smugglers and terrorists.

I hope you have a useful and informative visit, and I look forward to meeting you at tomorrow's roundtable talks.

Bill Shorten

US Customs and Border Protection, Miami

Tom sent a cordial reply back, and put his iPad down on the table. He could relax now their programme was in place. He leant back and closed his eyes again, but he wasn't sleepy. The flight from London had taken the best part of ten hours, and his body clock was still somewhere over the Atlantic.

Tapping his foot to the music, he could smell food on the breeze now. He was hungry again.

A text sounded from his mobile. It was from his colleague, in a room just down the corridor.

You still up, mate? Jetlag's killing me. Fancy a beer at the Tango Café on the corner?

Tom smiled and looked at his watch. Almost midnight. But he knew he wouldn't sleep much tonight anyway.

See you in the lobby in 10 minutes, he texted back.

Before he went to change, he picked up his iPad again and opened his contacts' list. He never deleted anyone unless he knew they were dead.

Yes, there she was – Jessica Turner. They hadn't been in touch since Brisbane, and he only had her old Canberra British High Commission address and phone number listed. But he also had a generic FCO email address for her. Hopefully she could pick up her email for that account wherever she was, even in the Turks and Caicos Islands. He'd give it a go.

7

Back at the Governor's Residence, Sally was doing her best to make sure the evening wouldn't be boring. She'd been diligent in topping up everyone's wine glasses, especially her own, and keeping up a stream of inane chatter.

David kept glancing nervously at her.

"Honestly!" Rebekah Canning gave a dismissive laugh. "If you believe *that* Sally, you'll believe anything."

Sally's eyes narrowed. "I'm telling you, Captain Jack Sparrow was based on a pirate from the Bahamas. He plundered ships around these islands and buried the booty on Provo's Grace Bay Beach."

"Huh! You're showing your gullibility, along with your..." Rebekah cast her eyes over Sally's ample cleavage.

Sally sat bolt upright. "And you're showing you know nothing about the country you live in."

Rebekah's eyes flashed.

Sensing trouble, Jess intervened. "Well, I wouldn't mind finding Johnny Depp on the beach when I get up in the morning."

Everyone laughed and relaxed back in their chairs, except for Sally who continued to glare at Rebekah.

Tension eased, Jess reached over and moved the wine bottle well out of Sally's reach. Now she knew why David wanted them to keep an eye on her. Sally was like a powder keg ready to blow.

Jess shifted in her chair as perspiration trickled down her back. Her feet and ankles were itching like mad from mozzie bites. So were the backs of her arms. They were biting through her clothes.

"Try Charles again," Rebekah said to Brad.

"I've tried loads of times. He's not answering." Brad shook his head. "It's not like my brother to be late, especially if there's good food and wine around."

"Are you *sure* he got back from his dive okay?" Rebekah's voice was tense. "He's not still out there, is he?"

"No." Carrie broke off from talking to David. "I saw Charles driving away from the Dive Centre this afternoon, on my way back from taking the kids to church."

Carrie had one of those soft American accents that flowed effortlessly, not at all guttural or harsh. In the soft glow of candlelight, with her sun-burnished skin and bright blonde hair, she looked radiant. Jess could quite see why David was smitten.

"Will you go and look for him, Brad," Rebekah asked.

"No." Sally put her hand on Brad's arm. "Your brother can look after himself. He's probably just fallen asleep."

Brad nodded. "He's not used to all that physical activity, working in a New York bank."

Sally smiled. "Maybe he's engaged in some physical activity now, with some woman?"

Jess noticed Rebekah flinch. The woman seemed to wear her heart on her sleeve. With her long, dark hair and beautiful face, Jess wondered if there was some Spanish or South American heritage in her. She certainly seemed on tenterhooks tonight, especially about Charles. Friendly concern? Or something more?

Maggie popped her head out of the kitchen door. "Can I serve the main course?" she asked David.

"Of course."

Moments later, Maggie came out proudly carrying a tray of steaming bowls. "Conch stew," she announced.

Rebekah groaned, and Maggie's face fell.

"*Wonderful*, Maggie," Sally said, loudly. "I *love* your conch stew."

Maggie's smile returned as she placed a bowl in front of each guest.

Jess was surprised at Rebekah's rudeness, and glanced at the Chief Justice who stared at his wife with a stony expression, but said nothing. Jess turned to Brad, who sat on her left. "What exactly is conch?" she asked.

"A massive pink snail." He smiled and pointed to the bar. "See those huge, shiny sea-shells decorating the shelves. They're conch shells. The islanders cook the conch's edible muscle in soups and stews. It's a local delicacy."

Rebekah wrinkled her nose. "They drag themselves along the seabed with that muscly foot. Just imagine what it's gone through."

Dominic gave his wife another warning look. He seemed to know she was ready to blow up too.

Jess noticed that, despite sitting on either side of Charles's empty chair, the Cannings had not spoken a word to each other all evening. "Shall we remove Charles's place setting?" she asked.

"No," Rebekah said, quickly. "He'll be here."

Jess shrugged, and dipped her spoon into the stew. After tasting it, she looked over at Maggie, who was hovering by the kitchen door. "Lovely," she said.

Maggie nodded gratefully, and went inside.

Jess turned back to Dominic, who sat on her right. Despite his unremarkable appearance – short, grey hair and a middle aged paunch, she found him knowledgeable on a wide range of issues as she would expect a senior barrister and judge to be. He had a razor sharp brain, giving quick, succinct answers to her questions about the Territory. In just 15 minutes of conversation, she'd learnt more about the Turks and Caicos Islands from him than from the whole of her London brief.

The other noticeable thing about the Chief Justice was his observant grey eyes. They darted around the table, watching everyone, especially his wife who was now matching Sally in the amount of wine she was drinking. It was only when Jess asked Dominic about Clement Pearson's death that he became evasive. But she was determined to probe. "I saw an article in the *Miami Post* on the plane over today about Clement," she said.

Dominic looked down at his food.

"It said he was found hanged in his garage," she went on. "The police were reported as saying there was nothing suspicious about his death, which suggests he committed suicide." She paused. "Is that what happened?"

Dominic nodded.

"The article implied the Minister had been depressed about the death of his son from a drugs overdose," she persisted. "Is that true, do you think?"

Dominic shrugged. "I don't know all the details, Jess."

"I also read that earlier on the day Clement Pearson died, he'd been in front of a British Inquiry into the sinking of two Haitian sloops. Can you tell me about that?"

Dominic gave her a sideways look. He wiped his mouth on his napkin, and shifted his chair closer to hers, to speak more privately. "The first sloop sank about five months ago. The weather wasn't particularly good at the time. The second sloop went down two months later." He paused and gave her another look. "After a lot of pressure, the British Government ordered an Inquiry, and sent UK officials out to do an investigation."

"What were their findings?"

Dominic was practically whispering now. "*Both* were deemed to be accidents, in bad weather." His eyes were piercing. "I kept asking the Governor to set up talks with the Haitian Government, to put some pressure on them to stop these sloops leaving Haiti in the first place." He paused. "The Governor *said* he'd reported everything to London, and that there was nothing to be done. Not even the Haitian Government could stop these sloops."

"Why not?"

"Because most of them set sail from Cap-Haitien, on the north coast. It's a pretty lawless area. The poor souls on board think they're paying passage for a better life in the US. But they end up here. We're only about 90 miles away." He shook his head. "The British Government *should* be doing something about it."

Jess just let him talk. She was learning a lot.

"I'm going back to the UK tomorrow," Dominic said. "I'm giving a speech to a global law conference."

She looked over.

"Yes. Then I'm going into the Foreign Office to discuss all this. They've *got* to do something about this illegal migration." He paused. "The locals are fed up with the increasing numbers coming over, and tensions are bubbling." He sighed. "This bloody voodoo doesn't help!"

Jess stared at him. "Voodoo?"

He nodded. "It's like a religion to the Haitians. Their voodoo God, Bondye, is similar to the God of Islam, Judaism and Christianity. But there are lots of spirits in voodoo – good and bad."

Jess laughed. "All I know about voodoo is what I've seen on films. Zombies and people sticking pins in little dolls."

He gave her a reproachful look. "They take this seriously, Jess. Anyway, poppet dolls, as they're known, are the black magic voodoo of bad spirits, which we've outlawed in these islands."

She looked at him. "Do you think it still goes on, in secret?"

"Possibly, but the central aspect of voodoo is about *healing* people with herbs, faith and even Western medicine these days. Both men and women can be priests. They perform religious ceremonies to call up, or rather pacify, the spirits."

"I see."

"All priests hold ceremonies. They tell the future, read dreams, cast love and death spells. That sort of thing." He paused. "In Haiti they carry out sacrificial practices, but that's outlawed here too."

"It's *supposed* to have been outlawed," Sally piped up.

Jess looked up to see everyone was listening to her conversation with Dominic.

"Go on, Dom," Rebekah urged. "Tell her about the recent goings-on."

He shook his head. "Jess doesn't want to hear about that."

"They've started their sacrifices again." Rebekah's voice caught in the back of her throat. "That's what's happened to my Benji, I'm sure of it. They targeted us because Dom's the Chief Justice. *Payback!*"

Jess looked startled.

"Benji's their pet Labrador," Brad explained. "He disappeared a couple of weeks ago."

"He's not the *only* pet to go missing," Sally said, darkly. "The Governor's had calls from other islanders whose cats and dogs have disappeared. The police found bones lying around the remains of a fire on the beach the other day. The locals got mad and started accusing the migrants of sacrificing their pets. The police had to step in to calm the situation down. But feelings are running high."

Jess looked at David.

"It's true," he said, calmly. "But it's all a fuss about nothing. There's no evidence that sacrificial practices are going on. Everyone has parties on the beach of a night. They light fires, and have barbecues."

"So what did forensic tests on the bones show?" Jess asked.

David shrugged. "A local doctor said they weren't human, if that's what you're wondering."

"Have they been properly analysed in a laboratory?" she persisted.

David shrugged again. "Doubt it."

Carrie, who'd been sitting quietly, said: "It would explain what's happened to all these pets, if they have been sacrificed."

"Oh!" Rebekah gave a strangled gasp.

"Sorry, Rebekah," Carrie said. "I didn't mean to upset you, but these ceremonies go on all over Haiti in July and August. And they *do* use animals." She shivered. "I live near the beach, and I've heard drumming and chanting in the middle of the night."

David put a comforting hand over Carrie's. "It's nothing to be frightened of."

Sally picked up her glass and emptied it in one gulp. "Well, if you ask me, Rebekah, you shouldn't have let Benji out to roam around on his own. You should have taken him out on a lead."

Rebekah reacted as if she'd been punched.

"So you've only got yourself to blame really," Sally added.

There was a stunned silence.

"*You bitch!*" Rebekah shouted at her, and jumped to her feet.

Everyone around the table sat frozen, as they listened to Rebekah's footsteps stomping around the verandah and out of the Residence.

"Rebekah?" Dominic called after his wife. "Come back." He jumped up and went after her.

Jess stared at Sally in disbelief.

"Well, she winds me up," Sally said, through gritted teeth. "Lady-la-di-bloody-da!"

Jess expected David to go after the Cannings, but he sat like a rabbit in headlights. She threw her napkin on the table, and hurried after them. "Dominic," she called.

He stopped and turned.

"I'm so sorry," she said. "Sally's rudeness is inexcusable."

Dominic's face softened. "Don't worry. Rebekah's just, well, she's just upset about Benji, that's all." He glanced over Jess's shoulder to check they were alone, and lowered his voice. "Look, we haven't got time to talk privately before I go to London. Just keep your head down and hold the fort for a few days."

"But, I need to..."

"Don't ask any more questions about Clement's death, or about the Government Inquiry. I'm going to talk to London about it all. So just leave it until I get back." He stopped as footsteps approached from behind.

Brad came up. "I'd better take Sally home. She's had too much to drink."

Jess nodded. "That's putting it mildly."

"Don't be too hard on her, Jess," he went on, "she's really upset about the Governor."

"So's everyone else!" She wasn't going to let Sally off the hook so easily.

When she turned back, Dominic had walked to the end of the verandah by the front entrance. He gave a fleeting glance over his shoulder before disappearing into the night after his wife.

Jess frowned. The look on his face at that moment would play on her mind for some time. If she'd had to explain it to anyone, she'd have said it was a look of fear.

8

They call this place the graveyard of souls.

Bad spirits wait here for unsuspecting sailors, to scupper their boats and drag them down into the deep, so the locals say. Not everyone is superstitious of course, but they all keep their distance and navigate their vessels around the area.

And who can blame them after what's happened over the centuries?

No-one comes here, except me. I love being in the boat, especially on a dead calm night like this, when the inky sky and black sea merge and wrap themselves around me. Navigating by the stars, I'm at one with the sea.

I can breathe out here, with the trade wind in my face, and waves slapping onto the bow as they try to push the boat towards the reef. I'm not afraid, because I belong here. I feel it deep inside.

Sometimes, sitting here, I imagine I hear the roar of the wind and cracking wood as another overladen vessel smashes apart on the reef. I hear terrified screams as its human cargo plunges into the ocean. I see them thrashing about in the water. I see their life ebbing away as water floods their lungs, and they sink down to join the other sunken-eyed skeletons in that watery graveyard below.

Why are they so afraid of drowning? Death is as certain as life itself. And being taken by the sea is the only way to go. Why thrash about? Why scream? Why not go serenely and calmly to the next life? It's a mystery to me.

I keep asking myself if I care? The truthful answer is no, because I know they no longer suffer.

Sometimes I wonder if I will become like the ancient mariner, incurring the wrath of the spirits when he shot the albatross? Will I be doomed to bear the burden of my crimes and wander the seas for eternity? Except that would be no hardship for me.

I've been thinking about that a lot lately, trying to pin-point the turning point, the exact moment. But I can't. I had a simple, happy childhood. I had everything I needed. Since then, I've lived my life exactly how I've wanted to live it. So when did it happen?

When did I become this person I am now? Still, think of what the Bible says: "Let the little children come to me, and do not hinder them, for to such belongs the kingdom of heaven."

9

Jess lay in bed, exhausted from travelling, but with her mind so alive she was finding it hard to get to sleep. She'd been up twice to get a drink of water to counteract all the food and alcohol at dinner. Why did she have that coffee after everyone had gone? Now, apart from the sound of waves caressing the shore, all she could hear was the ceiling fan clunking rhythmically above.

Tossing this way and that in the heat, her arms and legs itched like mad from mozzie bites. She'd been counting sheep, even trying to meditate herself to sleep.

Clunk... clunk.

She had to get some sleep, or she'd be fit for nothing in the morning.

Clunk... clunk.

Her eyes felt heavy...

The pavement glowed white in the moonlight as she ran. Only the sound of her ragged breathing cut into the silence of the night. Throat constricted with terror and dizzy with exhaustion, she was running as fast as she could without getting anywhere. *Run!* She screamed at herself. *Run!*

She looked over her shoulder. She couldn't hear any footsteps, but she knew he was there.

Fear flowed through her. She had to get inside where she'd be safe... if only she could get to the door. Why couldn't she get to the door? Why couldn't she move?

She could hear her teeth chattering, then another sound...

A familiar sound, carried over from her waking life. If only she could understand it. Was someone crying? A child? But the sound escaped back into the recesses of her dreams, lost or irretrievable in her befuddled mind.

A loud noise crashed in her ears. Jess snapped awake, and looked around at unfamiliar dark shapes and shadows.

Where was she?

Of course! Everything came flooding back... the Governor's Residence.

Lying naked, she stared into womblike darkness, listening to the rain lash against the windows. Her hair was sticking to her damp forehead and neck, as little beads of sweat trickled between her breasts.

The latch on her bedroom door clicked.

She gasped and sat up. "Who's there?"

No reply.

Her heart hammered as she jumped out of bed and went over to the door. She peered out to the landing. No-one there. The house was dark and still. Closing the door, she turned the key in the lock and went over to the window. As she opened the shutters, spray from the hammering rain blew in her face. It was so refreshing, she breathed in deeply to banish the suffocating heat, and looked down into the courtyard. She could see nothing in the dark and rain. It must have been the wind earlier blowing through the house's old timbers and rattling the latch on her bedroom door. Why was she so jumpy?

She went back over to the bed, then stopped. There was no way she'd be able to go back to sleep without checking the house.

She put on her robe. Barefoot, she went back to the door, and put her ear against it. No sound. She unlocked the door and crept out onto the landing. Total darkness. She listened again. There was no-one there, but she could feel a cool draught of air floating up the staircase. Where was it coming from? Eyes attuned to the darkness, she went down the stairs and followed the draught along the hallway, and into the kitchen, where the back door stood wide open.

What on earth?

She hurried over and peered outside. Through the rain, she saw a light moving around in the distance. It looked like a flashlight. Then it faded and disappeared.

Her feet suddenly felt wet. She bent down and touched the tiled floor. She was standing in a puddle of water.

Her stomach fluttered. Someone must have come in through this door from the rain, and gone out again. Quickly, she slammed the door shut and threw the top and bottom bolts.

Feeling around the walls, she found the light switch and flicked it on. Her eyes watered in the glare, but she could see nothing out of place. None of the cupboards or drawers was open, or ransacked. She went into the dining room and switched on the lights. Same there. In the main reception room, everything was neat and tidy too.

There was no sign of any forced entry, which meant someone must have got in with a key. Perhaps Maggie had forgotten something and come back for it? But she wouldn't go out and leave the back door wide open, would she? It didn't make sense.

Jess was in two minds as to what to do. Should she call someone? And say what? That someone had been in the house, but there was no forced entry and nothing apparently missing. Who would she call anyway? She decided to wait until morning.

She climbed the stairs back up to her room. Passing the landing window that overlooked the front entrance, she noticed a light on in the Governor's Office at the end of the drive. Who was working at that time of night? Perhaps David was trying to clear his desk before leaving in the morning? Yes, she thought, that was likely. It cheered her up to think a colleague was close by.

She went back into her room and flicked on the light. As soon as the darkness and shadows were banished, she felt even better. But that didn't stop her checking the bathroom, inside the wardrobe and under the bed to make sure no-one was there. This time she locked the door, securely.

Oh God, she suddenly thought. Perhaps David had been in the house? Had he popped his head round her bedroom door and seen her naked? She got up again and slipped on her nightdress. She'd just have to put up with the heat.

She lay back on the bed. The breeze from the ceiling fan chilled her damp skin and made her shiver. She was overwrought with travelling, that's all. But she was even less sleepy now than before.

Lying there, her eyes cast lazily around the room. As they settled on a chair in the corner, she sat bolt upright again.

A rag doll was sitting on the chair, propped up against the cushion.

Where had that come from? It hadn't been there earlier. She would definitely have noticed it. Her mind flashed back to what the Chief Justice said at dinner about poppet dolls and bad spirits. *Voodoo?* Her heart quickened again.

She got up and went over to the doll. It was made entirely of black cloth, and plumped up with some kind of stuffing. It had two buttons sewn on for eyes, and two strips of red material for lips, in the shape of a smile. As Jess picked it up, sand sprinkled out of the doll's black hair. It's red gingham dress felt wet too.

She put it back on the chair. This was no voodoo doll to stick pins in, this was a child's toy. Suddenly that sound in the fog of sleep earlier came back to her. Had she heard a real child crying? Or was her memory just playing tricks?

A familiar wave of sadness came over her. She went over to the wardrobe and pulled a framed photo out of her suitcase. Staring at Jack and Amy, she brushed her lips across the glass before standing it on the bedside cabinet. It felt comforting to have them with her, in this strange place.

That was the trouble, she thought. It *was* a strange place, with a strange atmosphere. That, and the shock of the Governor's accident, was playing with her head. She'd be fine in the morning, she told herself. Nevertheless, she lay tossing and turning for a long time, before slipping back into a restless sleep.

*

When she woke up again, light was streaming through the open shutters. She looked at the clock. 6.10am. Getting up, she went over to the window. Gone was the incessant rain, dark shadows and oppressive heat. In its place was beautiful blue sky and sunshine, and the sound of gentle waves lapping on the beach. Her spirits rose as the fresh morning air blew in her face, dispelling last night's fears.

Hot and sticky from her disturbed night, she decided to go for a quick swim before breakfast. It was early enough. She put on her swimsuit and beach robe, and went downstairs. Another glance in all the rooms confirmed that there'd been no burglary. It must have been Maggie or David in the house last night after all. She unlocked the kitchen door, and went out into bright morning light.

She walked across the courtyard and garden, and stepped onto the beach. Her bare feet sank into fine sand, which was already hot, but not so hot that she couldn't walk on it. She scanned the beach both ways as she headed straight towards the sea. No-one around, except in the distance she could see about five or six ponies grazing on a patch of grass adjoining the beach.

The water looked like a turquoise millpond. White, foamy breakers in the distance indicated the reef's location. Beyond that, dark blue sea stretched into the horizon. She remembered Brad's words. "Just a few hundred yards offshore, the seabed drops to 7,000 feet."

She swam out a little way, then stopped and put her feet gingerly on the bottom. Nothing but soft sand. This really was paradise. More confident now, she swam along the shoreline, rather than go out of her depth. Hearing a distant splash, she looked up to see the ponies had gone into the sea, and were swimming and playing like young children. It was surreal. Magical even.

She kicked out her legs and floated on her back. Her head started to clear, and she thought about what she had to do that day. As soon as she got into the office, she'd phone Miami to find out how the Governor was doing. Then she'd ring the Police Commissioner and ask for a copy of the police report on the car crash to send to London. And all that talk over dinner last night about voodoo and missing pets was weighing on her mind. She'd ask him to do a proper analysis of the bones found at that beach bonfire.

Suddenly something touched the top of her head. Startled, she scrambled to put her feet on the bottom and turned...

A pony!

She panicked as the herd surrounded her. But it turned out they were just curious. One came close enough for her to stroke his nose. He nudged her arm gently again and again. She didn't understand what he wanted at first. Then she realised, and grabbed hold of his mane. She laughed as he pulled her back to shore and deposited her close to the beach, before swimming back to his friends. They must play this game with the local children, she thought.

That was the friendliest experience she'd had since arriving on the island.

Reluctantly, she set off back to the Residence. On the way, she stopped to pick up small shells, or to study pieces of driftwood and black seaweed. As the house came closer, she noticed two porthole windows right at the top. Must be an attic above the bedrooms, she thought. Those windows looked like sentries' eyes, keeping a watch out to sea.

Through the gap in the bushes, she spotted a woman watching her from the Residence garden. Dressed in a navy blue suit, and with her jet black hair tied firmly in a bun, the woman had a confident air about her.

Jess approached her with a smile.

The woman looked her up and down.

Jess knew she must look a sight in her beach robe, with wet hair hanging down, but she held out her hand. "Hello. I'm Jessica Turner."

The woman averted her eyes and shook Jess's fingers, limply. "Alvita Pearson." Her voice was stiff and formal. "I'm responsible for the local staff and administration in the Governor's Office."

There was that surname Pearson again, Jess thought.

Heavy footsteps came pounding along the verandah, and they both turned.

"*There* you are, Jess." David came rushing over. "I'm glad you two have met," he said, breathlessly. "I've written some handover notes for you." He thrust a brown envelope at Jess. "Sorry to leave you in the lurch like this, but I have to go. I'm booked on the first flight over to Provo."

"Thanks." Jess took the envelope. "Is there a police report on the Governor's accident in here?"

David shook his head.

"Then I'd better call on the Police Commissioner first thing and get a copy for London."

Alvita intervened. "He usually calls on the Governor at 3pm every Wednesday to report the latest incidents of crime."

Jess turned to her. "Could you ask him to come this morning instead? We need to talk urgently about the Governor's accident."

Alvita shrugged. "He may not want to come at all in the Governor's absence."

"Yes he will." David turned to Alvita. "The Governor's accident is the most pressing issue. Please ask him to come at 11am."

Alvita gave a curt nod, and walked away.

"Don't mind her," David said to Jess. "She'll be okay, once she gets used to you."

Jess shrugged. She was already used to the islanders.

"Anyway, Sally will help you find your way around. She'll be your eyes and ears in the office too."

"Sally?" Jess frowned at him. How could she depend on her? "Her behaviour was outrageous last night. *So* rude."

He looked worried. "I know, but..."

"She has a drink problem."

He hesitated. "She does drink a lot, but she's not an alcoholic or anything like that. She's just temperamental.

When she gets upset, like she is about the Governor, she drinks and goes over the top." He hopped from one foot to the other, anxious to leave. "I'm sure you *can* rely on her, Jess."

Jess didn't think she would ever rely on Sally for anything, but she didn't voice that opinion. David was feeling bad enough about leaving as it was. "Go on. Off you go." She smiled. "Or you'll miss that flight."

He hesitated. "I'm so sorry to dump everything on you."

"I'll be fine," she said. "You just concentrate on seeing your mum."

He nodded. "Thanks."

"I hope it goes... as well as can be expected back home."

He gave her a friendly hug. "Bye Jess. See you in a couple of months." And with that he hurried away.

Watching him go, she felt suddenly apprehensive. She hadn't been able to ask him anything about the job, or even about the goings-on in the house last night. Still, in the light of day, she was beginning to think she'd overreacted last night. And that was probably down to being in a new place, the travelling, and the shock of the Governor's accident. She'd be fine, she told herself, as she strode into the house. Anyway, she'd agreed to do the job for a couple of months, and that's exactly what she was going to do.

She just wished the uneasiness in the pit of her stomach would go away.

10

It was the way the Police Commissioner placed his peaked hat between them on the back seat that Jess noticed. It was done carefully, as if he were deliberately marking out his authority, a line she should not cross. Not that she could ignore his importance. All the locals nodded or waved at his official Land Rover as it made its stately way at 20mph along the main road leading from the Governor's Residence to Grand Turk's capital, Cockburn Town. Clearly everyone wanted to keep on the right side of Dexter Robinson. He held a powerful position in these islands, and reported directly to the Governor, rather than to any local ministers or officials.

He was a hulk of a man, almost six feet tall, with a large, jowly face, although his personality was anything *but* larger than life. He spoke quietly, with an unassuming manner, for someone in his position. Unlike the other islanders, he looked Jess in the eye when he spoke to her, so that was something. Now, his black skin glistened as he shifted uncomfortably in the humidity, and adjusted the leather belt on his khaki uniform.

Jess had to admit she was uncomfortable too. It wasn't even midday but her eyes were heavy, and she felt stuck to the leather seat. The Land Rover had air conditioning installed, she noticed, but the driver hadn't put it on.

Either it was broken or they didn't like it. She was too polite to say anything, especially as Dexter had offered to take her to the scene of the Governor's accident.

She looked up and caught the driver studying her in his rear view mirror. As a new member of the Governor's Office, *and* a woman, she knew the locals would be curious about her. She smiled, but he averted his eyes back to the road ahead.

She turned to Dexter. "How long have you been Police Commissioner here?" she asked.

He seemed surprised by the question. "Five years."

"Are you from Grand Turk or one of the outlying islands?"

"Grand Turk."

She already knew from her brief he was one of the few police officers actually from the Turks and Caicos Islands. Most were recruited from neighbouring Caribbean countries, a policy put in place by the British Government to prevent nepotism and corruption on these small islands. "I'm still not clear about what happened when the Governor had his car crash." She paused. "Why was he driving down from the Ridge at that time?"

Dexter shrugged. "I don't know."

"It seems a strange thing to do in the middle of the night."

He nodded.

"You said it was a hit and run?"

"Yes. A truck was stolen from the supermarket compound hours before the crash. We believe it was the other vehicle involved."

"And the driver just drove off?"

"Yes."

"Did he report the accident?"

"No."

"Did he phone for an ambulance?"

"No."

Jess sat back in the seat. This was hard work. Dexter was a cautious man, and chose his words carefully. She pressed on. "What makes you think a truck was involved?"

"Because of the extensive damage to the Governor's car." He pulled a large white handkerchief out of his pocket, shook it out, and mopped his brow.

"Wouldn't that driver have been injured too?"

He shrugged.

She could tell he was uncomfortable with her questions, but she persisted: "It must be difficult to hide a truck on a small island like this, especially one that's been in an accident. Surely someone's seen it, or knows where it is?"

He said nothing, and just lowered his side window to get whatever breeze he could from the late morning air.

Jess looked out, and saw a large pond, almost rectangular in shape. A tall windmill towered over it, gracing the skyline. Its metal vanes were almost rusted away.

"That's a salina," he said. "A salt pond. At one time, salt used to be the only way of preserving food. The industry lasted over 200 years in these islands, until the 1960s and refrigerators." He sighed, as if regretting the passing of time. "That's all that's left of it now."

Jess studied the still, brackish water as they drove alongside it. A green-coloured heron stalked along the edge. "How did they gather the salt?" she asked.

"You see those walls?" He pointed to what looked like stone channels.

She nodded.

"They're man-made canals linking a whole network of salinas on the island. The windmills pumped sea water continuously through the reservoirs and sluice gates. Mineral deposits would emerge through evaporation, and the salt settled into crystals."

It hadn't escaped Jess's attention that he was happier to explain the history of the salt industry than talk about the Governor's accident. She got back to the point. "Are drugs a problem here?" she asked.

He looked at her as if surprised by the question: "They're becoming a problem. We've experienced an increase in supply over the last couple of years."

"Where do they come from? The US?"

He shook his head. "Central and South America mostly. Some get diverted here on their way *to* the US. There are smuggling routes through other Caribbean countries too." He fell silent and looked out the window again.

Jess wasn't sure whether to ask him about Clement Pearson's suicide or not. In the end, she decided she would. "I read about the Immigration Minister's suicide, in the *Miami Post* on the plane over." She paused. "How has that affected everyone here?"

He let out a deep sigh. "We're heartbroken. Clement was born and brought up here."

It was said with such feeling Jess knew he meant it. "Do you have any idea *why* he committed suicide? I mean... was he upset or depressed about anything?"

The Police Commissioner looked at her. "People tend not to show their feelings outwardly here, Miss Turner." He paused to consider his words. "You will know from the newspaper that Clement's son died of a drugs overdose recently. Clement was devastated, as was his wife."

She nodded. "I understand on the day he died, the Minister gave evidence to a British Inquiry into the sinking of two Haitian sloops. What can you tell me about that?"

He was silent for a while, then he said: "UK officials came out to do the investigation. Their report concluded that the two sloops met the same fate, while sailing in bad weather."

"Both of them?"

He nodded. "They ended up on the north-west reef, like so many other vessels over the centuries."

"Do you have a copy of that report?" she asked, thinking she ought to read it.

"I do." He nodded. "The Governor has a copy too."

Jess made a mental note to look for it when she got back. "Well," she said, sympathetically. "It's a shocking thing to happen once, let alone twice. It must have upset everyone here, especially Clement.

He nodded, gravely.

An attractive, white-washed building caught her eye as they drove past. It had tall pillars at the entrance and fancy balustrades around its verandahs. She leant closer to the window. The sign said it was the House of Assembly. The car park was empty, so she guessed Parliament wasn't in session.

Soon, they were driving into town. They passed a two-storey office block, which she saw was the Police HQ, then an old prison, a museum, and a few shops before reaching a single roundabout. Turning right, they started to make their way up to the Ridge. Jess glanced at the Police Commissioner again. He was sitting so quietly she decided to leave him to his thoughts.

When they came to what looked like a small settlement, he surprised her by suddenly starting to talk. "They're the problem." He tapped on the window to emphasise his point. "Coming illegally in their sloops night after night. We send them home, and they come straight back. There are eight million of them just across the water in Haiti, and less than 50,000 of us. We're getting overrun." He looked at her as if she were personally responsible. "Something *has* to be done about it."

Jess saw the driver nodding his head in agreement. Out the window, she could see the houses were made of plywood, and corrugated metal roofs covered with sheet plastic. Washing lines hung between the houses, with colourful clothes pegged to them, while children and dogs chased each other around in the sunshine.

When Jess looked back at the Police Commissioner, little beads of sweat trickled down his forehead. Was he steamed up about the Haitians? Or just hot?

"You obviously allow some of them to stay here," she said.

He nodded. "These people have been here a while. Some of them have jobs as domestic cleaners, and gardeners. Some help build houses. But all new arrivals are transported to Provo, and flown straight back to Haiti."

"What kind of processing do you do before deporting them?"

"We take the name they give us, fingerprint them, and send them back to Haiti."

"Do any of them claim asylum?"

He stared at her. "We send them straight back."

She took that to mean no other processing was done. Then she remembered what the Chief Justice had said the night before. "I've heard about the inter-communal tensions," she said.

"Can you blame our people? They are being squeezed out of their homes and jobs."

"I've heard about the missing pets too," she said. "What do you know about voodoo? Is it being practised here?"

He gave her a scornful look. "I know very little about it."

She didn't believe him, and wondered why he was being evasive. The Police Commissioner, of all people, would know if voodoo was practised on the island and any consequences resulting from it. She looked at him. "I understand that bones were found after a bonfire on the beach. I'm told the locals believe their pets are being sacrificed in voodoo ceremonies."

He nodded. "Bones have been found, but I don't believe they have anything to do with voodoo."

"Have they been analysed in the laboratory?"

"Why should they be? They're not human."

Jess knew when she was being fobbed off. "Don't you think it would be a good idea to get those bones analysed, to find out for sure if they're human or animal?"

"Police resources are already stretched," he said.

"I'm sure they are, especially if you have all these community tensions to police. But if you get the bones analysed, you'll hopefully be able to tell the locals with certainty that they don't belong to their missing pets. That would de-escalate the situation."

Suddenly, the car came to a halt at crossroads. "We're here." The Commissioner got out.

Jess was relieved to be able to get out too, and take in some air. She looked around. The Governor had been travelling back from the lighthouse, in the direction of town, when that truck hit. She crossed diagonally over the road and studied the tarmac on the other side. A few fine pieces of shattered glass, and a scorched patch on the grass verge, were the only signs left of a crash. Everything else had been cleaned up efficiently. That surprised her. "Did forensics find anything interesting or unusual?" she asked.

He shook his head.

"Obviously the Governor's car was travelling down from the lighthouse. So which direction did the other vehicle come from? East or west?"

"It hit the Governor's door, so it would have come from the west."

Jess looked along the deserted road, and felt uneasy. Who would steal a truck from a local supermarket in the middle of the night, go joyriding – if that's what they were doing, accidentally plough into the Governor's Land Rover, then disappear without a trace and without calling the emergency services? She turned back to the Police Commissioner. "This doesn't make any sense," she said, truthfully.

Immediately his eyes became wary. "The accident report will tell us everything," he said, in a voice that brooked no more questions.

Why was he being so cagey? She was sure he knew more than he was telling her. "I'm going to relay my initial findings to London when I get back," she said in a businesslike voice. "And I'd like a copy of the accident report please to send them." She paused. "I'd like to see the Governor's car too."

He nodded. "You will have a copy of the accident report as soon as it's ready," he said. "The Governor's Land Rover is in the Government Garage, which is close to the Governor's Office."

She nodded. "I'll take a look at it later."

"Of course."

Jess looked along the road and saw the lighthouse standing on top of the Ridge. What had the Governor been doing up there, she wondered? "Can we go up to the lighthouse while we're here, if it's no trouble?"

He nodded and walked back to his Land Rover.

Jess followed and got in beside him.

The driver proceeded to the top of the Ridge, and drew up outside a low picket fence that surrounded the lighthouse.

Jess got out quickly, and for the first time felt a strong breeze in her face. She took some gulps of air, relieved to be able to finally breathe. She walked through a small gate in the fence, and headed for the lighthouse. It was an impressive structure, tall and solid. According to a plaque embedded in the wall, it was made of cast iron and built by the British. She climbed the few steps to the door. A sign said it was open to the public every day, except there was no-one around and the door was locked when she tried it. She went back down the steps, and across the grass to the edge of the headland.

An amazing sight greeted her. High, foamy breakers crashed onto the reef out to sea. Below she could see only rocks and turbulent waves. Further along the headland, there was a cliff path, and a track leading down to a small beach.

The Police Commissioner joined her, and stood staring out to the reef.

"Is that where those two sloops went down?" she asked.

"Yes."

"Did they all die out there?"

He gave her a straight look. "They've been dying out there for centuries, Miss Turner. Many ships have run aground on the north-west reef."

They fell silent.

His mobile rang. He looked to see who the caller was, then walked away to answer it.

Glad he'd gone, Jess went back to the lighthouse and sat down on the steps in the shade. She didn't know what to make of the Police Commissioner. He was polite and respectful, yet guarded. She felt he was answering all her questions honestly, but somehow not telling her the truth. She sensed strong emotions bubbling under that quiet exterior too. It wasn't going to be easy to get to know Dexter Robinson.

As she leant against the locked door, Jess spotted something on the grass through a gap in the steps. It looked like a folded piece of paper. Curious, she leaned sideways, pushed her arm under the steps and picked it up.

Unfolding the paper, she smoothed it out. The writing was distinctive, with firm, long strokes, in black ink. Water had blotched some of it, but she started reading ...

My Darling,

Words cannot describe how much I love you and the children, and how truly sorry I am. I've been a fool. I've betrayed you and everything I hold most dear.

The next bit was blotched. Then it went on.

I have to explain in a letter because I don't know when I will see you again. I hope that one day you will be able to forgive me...

Jess turned the paper over but there was nothing on the other side and no signature. The letter was unfinished.

She read it again. *I've been a fool. I've betrayed you and everything I hold most dear... I don't know when I will see you again.* Those words stood out. It was some kind of confession. To a lover maybe?

When she heard the Police Commissioner's quick footsteps coming back, and for a reason she would not have been able to explain, she folded the letter back up and slipped it into her pocket.

He came up to her, arms rigid by his sides. But it was his face that told her something was seriously wrong.

"We need to go back, urgently," he said.

"Why? What's happened?"

"There's been another... death."

Her breath caught in her throat. "Who?"

"She was found hanging in the garage this morning...
Mrs Pearson!"

It took Jess a moment to figure out who he was talking
about. "Clement Pearson's *wife*?" she asked, incredulously.

"Yes."

"Dear God! Has *she* committed suicide too?"

"No." As he shook his head, the colour seemed to drain
from his lips. "She was found hanging by her feet, with
her throat cut."

11

Back in the office, Jess sat shell-shocked at David's cluttered desk, trying to concentrate on his handover notes. It was an odd constitutional set-up on these islands. The British Government – represented by the Governor – retained responsibility for foreign affairs, security, defence, policing and financial regulation. All other internal policies had been devolved to local Ministers, who had their own Parliament to discuss them. Bizarrely, the Governor wasn't allowed to set foot in Parliament while it was in session, yet he chaired the Cabinet of Ministers that agreed all these internal policies anyway. Who'd thought up that arrangement, she wondered?

She rubbed her eyes. The atmosphere was so stuffy she could scarcely breathe. The air conditioner wasn't working; and the windows had been painted shut by the decorators. Not only that, they were covered with security grilles and the glass was frosted. For all she could see out, she could have been sitting in the Foreign Office in London, with the central heating on full blast.

She got up and opened the connecting door to let in some cool air from the comfortable open plan office the three local administrators shared. She noticed how quiet they were. Mrs Pearson's brutal murder, coming straight after the Governor's accident, had them totally shocked.

Jess wondered whether to let them go home early, but that was really a decision for Alvita. They thought of her as their boss.

Alvita was a bit of an enigma. She hovered around the office, watching everyone and listening. Whenever there was a rustle of stockings, or a creaky leather shoe, Alvita was close by. She was like a haunting presence, and Jess didn't know yet if she was a good or malevolent spirit.

Jess took a sip of coffee and a bite of the ham sandwich Sally had brought in for her. It was meant as a peace offering, she knew that. Talk about a personality shift. Today, Sally was smart and efficient, and nothing like the woman at the party last night. Jess understood now why the Governor put up with Sally's occasional bad behaviour, but she wouldn't tolerate it.

Sally popped her head round the door. "Can I have a word?"

Jess nodded.

Sally came in, pushed the door to, and sat down. "Mrs Pearson's murder has really upset all the staff."

Jess put the handover notes down. "I know, it's an awful shock."

"Hung by her *feet*, with her *throat* cut. Who would *do* something like that?" Sally paused. "What did the Police Commissioner say?"

"Very little. He'd only just found out himself. I asked him to ring with more information as soon as he could." She hesitated. "Tell me, Sally, has anything like this ever happened here before?"

Sally stared at her. "Why? Do you think there might be a serial killer out there?"

"No," Jess said, quickly. "I wasn't thinking that. I just wondered if there was anything in the history of these islands that might tell us why she was killed in that way." She paused. "Did you know Mrs Pearson?"

"I knew *who* she was. I saw her and her husband around a lot. But I wouldn't say I *knew* either of them." Sally paused. "The Governor did though. He was really upset when Clement committed suicide. Never seen him so upset."

"Really?" That interested Jess. "What sort of a man was Clement? I mean, was he well liked on the island? Well respected?"

Sally nodded. "The Governor always said Clement was one of the good guys."

"What did he mean by that?"

Sally shrugged. "Well, you told me about the way Roger Pearson behaved towards that little girl in the terminal. His uncle Clement would never have done that."

"Is that how Clement and Roger were related, uncle and nephew."

"Yes. The Pearsons are a prominent local family." Sally leant forward. "What does it all mean, Jess? First Clement commits suicide, then his wife is butchered like an animal. What did she do to deserve that?"

Jess shook her head, and they fell silent.

Hearing the rustle of stockings, Jess got up quickly and poked her head out of the door in time to see Alvita disappearing round the corner. She'd obviously been listening outside. Jess frowned and shut the door. "I need to report Mrs Pearson's murder to London," she said, "but I'd better wait for the Police Commissioner to ring first in case he has more details." She paused. "What time is it?"

Sally checked her watch. "3.25." She paused. "Oh, I forgot to tell you, Jess, your Simon phoned while you were out."

Jess looked at her.

"He seemed a bit put out that you hadn't phoned him."

"I did phone, last night. I left a message on the machine." Jess frowned. "Did you explain about the communications, or rather lack of them, down here?"

"Yes," Sally said. "I've got a new mobile for you too. It's open to international roaming so you'll be able to call Simon any time. And I've sorted out your Foreign Office email account, so you can log onto David's computer and pick up your emails."

"Hallelujah!"

"Oh and I've put some classified electronic telegrams from London on the Governor's desk. Better read them in there."

Jess knew the locals weren't allowed to see the classified e-grams and reports, nor did they have access to a small confidential area in the building. That must cause some resentment, she thought. "Have you typed up that statement for the local media about Mrs Pearson's death?"

"Yes. And I've drawn up a condolence letter from you to the family. It's also on the Governor's desk for you to sign."

Very helpful and efficient, Jess thought. No, Sally's not a secretary you would want to lose, but she had to tackle her about her drinking. "Don't send that statement to the media until the Police Commissioner's confirmed everything, will you?"

Sally nodded and went out.

Jess switched on David's desktop computer. Her mind was buzzing while she sat waiting for it to power up and run through its security programmes. *What do you think she did to deserve that?* Mrs Pearson's murder had been horrific. Jess couldn't help but feel the manner of her death was significant. But what did it mean?

A familiar chain of emails popped up on the screen and she started to scroll through them, glad to be back in business. She'd missed this flow of information from British embassies all over the world.

Suddenly one particular email got her attention.

Hey Jess,

I might have put on some weight and have a few more grey hairs, but I don't reckon I've changed that much. So why did you walk past me at Miami Airport yesterday and disappear on a flight to Providenciales? I had to google it to find out it was in the Turks and Caicos Islands. Where?

Seriously though, it was good to see you, briefly. I'm in Miami for a couple of days on a fact-finding mission to see how the Americans patrol their south-east maritime border and handle illegal immigration from your neck of the woods. It's a long story but I'm not in Brisbane any more. I'm working for the Federal Police in Canberra, on a multi-agency task force to combat illegal people smuggling.

I see your islands are close to Haiti. It would be good to get a look first hand at your operation down there and see how you deal with illegals. I've got a couple of days extra I can build into my trip before going back to Australia. I'm not sure whether you're working there or just visiting. But, if it's convenient, I could come down. If not, no worries. We'll catch up another time.

All the best,

Tom Sangster

Jess flopped back in her chair in surprise. *Tom Sangster!* The gruff Aussie policeman with an artistic soul. She hadn't seen him for a couple of years – since Brisbane to be exact. She conjured up his steely grey eyes. He couldn't have changed much in two years, she thought. So how on earth did she manage to walk past him in Miami airport?

She read his email again. His job sounded interesting, and the people-smuggling angle highly topical. It would be useful to hear from him what the US were doing to combat it. And it would be good to see him again too. He might even be able to give her some practical advice on police procedure relating to Mrs Pearson's murder and the Governor's accident. Yes, she thought, she would invite him down.

She smiled and pressed reply.

Dear Tom,

I'm so sorry I walked past you yesterday, but you would be the last person I would have expected to see at Miami Airport of all places. Your job with the Federal Police sounds great. What an opportunity to do some travelling too.

I'm working down here for a couple of months on a temporary placement in the Governor's Office. I should be really happy to see you if you can get down for a couple of days. We have a big problem with illegal Haitians on our islands, as I'm beginning to find out. I'm sure you'll find a visit worthwhile.

She paused. Should she tell him about Mrs Pearson's murder? No, she'd wait until he got here. But she would mention the Governor's accident in case he'd seen it in the Miami press.

The Governor had a serious car accident yesterday morning and has been medivaced to Miami. He's in a bad way and we're all really worried about him. I'm staying at his Residence. There are a number of guest rooms, so you would be welcome to stay here too.

If you can make it, let me know which day and flight you will be arriving on. I'll meet you at the airport.

Best wishes,

Jess

As she sat back in the chair, memories of the Ellen Chambers' murder started flooding back, which wasn't unusual. She relived it all the time in her dreams, or rather nightmares. She's running as fast as she can, but she can't move. She hears his footsteps after her, but she can't get away.

Her throat tightened, and she unconsciously rubbed the spot above her left breast where the bullet entered. The truth was it had scarred her mind more than her body.

Suddenly Sally burst through the door. "Rebekah's just phoned. She's in a state. She wants to see you."

Jess looked up. "What's happened?"

"She's found Benji's collar outside on the patio." Sally sounded breathless.

"So?"

"She drove Dominic to the airport to get his flight for London. When she got back, she found the dog's collar on the patio, next to his bowl. She puts fresh water out for Benji every day, in case he comes back." Sally swallowed. "The collar had some nails punched through it." She lowered her voice. "Coffin nails... that's why she's hysterical."

"Coffin nails?"

"It's a voodoo curse." Sally closed the door to speak privately. "Coffins are dug up, and the nails used to seal the lid are pulled out. It means that whatever the person in the coffin died from is transferred to the person who is presented with the nails."

Jess stared at Sally. "We are talking about a dog, aren't we?"

"That's just it," Sally said. "Rebekah says she's the one the nails are meant for. Someone's going to kill her, in the same way they've killed her dog Benji."

12

The Toyota sparked into life as Jess turned the key in the ignition of the office car. She laid Sally's handwritten directions to the Chief Justice's house on the passenger seat. All she had to do was drive to the main roundabout in town and go straight over, rather than turn right onto Lighthouse Road and up to the Ridge.

Nosing the car through the gates, she pulled out onto the main road. At least they drive on the left here, she thought, not like in America.

Sally had wanted to go with her to see Rebekah until Jess reminded her about the scene at last night's dinner. Sally had had the decency to look shame-faced. "I'll be the last person Rebekah wants to see then."

Jess had simply nodded. She wouldn't stoke the fire by reminding Sally that Rebekah had called her a bitch. The two women clearly had a history of flaring up at each other. It wasn't just Sally's fault; Rebekah had goaded her too. Still, Jess would confront Sally about her drinking and behaviour. It was totally unacceptable.

She pulled the driver's sun visor down, as the sinking sun was right in her eye line. She was glad to be out of the office, where the atmosphere had been hushed and tense all day. Finally, she was independent, and driving herself around.

What a day! She loosened her tight grip on the steering wheel, and tried to relax back in the seat. As she drove towards Cockburn Town, she made a mental note of all the landmarks she passed. First on her right came the airport, then an old hotel with an outdoor beach bar, and the salina. Nothing on her left except the sea, and a few houses, until she got nearer to town. She liked the way the buildings and houses were gaily painted in different colours. They looked straight out of a picture book.

Approaching the small Baptist church on her right, she spotted a familiar figure coming out of the gate. A line of cute toddlers followed. Jess checked her rear view mirror, swung across the road and pulled up alongside the kerb. Lowering the window, she called out: "Hi, Carrie."

Carrie smiled in recognition, then turned to her little charges. "Don't move!" she shouted at them.

They stood to attention while Carrie bent down to talk through the window. "Are you finding your way around okay, Jess?"

"I'm trying to get my bearings." Jess waved at the children, and they giggled shyly. The boys were all dressed in t-shirts and shorts, the girls had their curly black hair braided with ribbons and wore pinafore dresses with t-shirts underneath. To a child they wore tiny white plimsolls and ankle socks.

Carrie's face clouded. "Have you heard about Mrs Pearson?" she whispered, so the children couldn't hear.

"Yes. Awful, isn't it?"

"It's hard to believe that could happen here. It's... frightening."

Jess could see the shock on Carrie's face. "Did you know Mrs Pearson?" she asked.

"Yes, but I know her daughter better. I look after her son while she works." Carrie hesitated. "Was it a burglary gone wrong, do you know? She was always walking around decked out in gold jewellery."

"I don't think the police know yet." Jess was thinking the murder seemed too brutal for a burglary gone wrong, but she didn't want to say that and frighten Carrie. She remembered only too well Carrie's fear at last night's dinner about voodoo chanting and fires on the beach near her home. For that reason, she didn't mention anything about Benji's collar turning up with those nails in it either.

Carrie shivered. "Better make sure all the doors and windows are locked tonight, just in case."

One of the toddlers started getting restless, and pushed another towards the road. "Stay on the pavement!" Carrie barked at them.

They immediately stood still again.

Jess smiled. "I'd better let you go."

"Okay, Jess. See you soon." Carrie turned, and lined the children up again before leading them back to the kindergarten.

Carrie certainly had a firm hand with those children, yet she'd seemed so gentle at dinner. Jess wondered what a teacher like Carrie got out of running a kindergarten. She'd be more like a nanny with such young children, and that couldn't be very challenging. Or was it? Maybe getting them very young had its rewards? Who was it said, *give me a child until they're seven, and I'll give you the man*? She seemed to remember it was some kind of Jesuit saying.

There was no traffic at the roundabout, and she drove straight over. In Washington, it would be the start of the rush hour at this time, and the roads clogged with people. Not here though.

Jess followed Sally's directions, and turned left at the next crossroads. Soon, she spotted a Union Jack flying on a flagpole in the front garden of a house; the first in a little residential complex of about ten houses. It had to be the Chief Justice's house with that flag, she thought. Dominic was doing his bit to raise the British presence.

The metal gates to the property stood wide open. No sign of any security here either, she noticed, as she swung through. Two cars were parked in the driveway. A smart, silver Jeep, which looked new, alongside a bright red Mini. Did Rebekah have company?

The house was a modern, two-storey home, probably built within the last 10 or 15 years, and nothing like the Governor's old Residence. Painted a pastel pink, with white plantation shutters at the windows, it looked like something out of a Florida lifestyle magazine. Palm trees lined the property's perimeter, the grass on the front lawn was mown short and the shrubs neatly clipped. Rebekah's influence, no doubt.

Jess parked the car and walked towards the front door. A black cat, with white paws, sprang out of nowhere onto the porch, barring her way. Arching its back, it hissed at her in a show of bravado, then bolted into the bushes. Another friendly local, she thought.

The front door was wide open. Behind it, a metal screen door was closed to keep flies and mozzies out. She couldn't see a bell and called out.

"Hello? Rebekah? It's Jess." Silence.

"Rebekah? Are you there?" Still silence.

Jess tried the screen door handle, and it clicked open. She pushed it and stepped onto the doormat inside. "Rebekah?" she called again. There was still no reply.

Someone had to be here with the front door wide open, and the cars parked in the drive, she thought, as she walked down the hallway. Where was Rebekah? That voodoo warning was making Jess anxious. Whoever had left Benji's collar on the patio wanted to frighten Rebekah, or they wouldn't have waited for the Chief Justice to leave the island before putting it there.

Walking through the first door she came to, Jess found herself in a bright, airy sitting room. Two sets of chintz sofas and armchairs were carefully arranged at either end, alongside antique tables and lamps. An impressive grandfather clock stood against the far wall. Its loud ticking was the only noise in the house.

Still no Rebekah, though.

Jess went over to the window and looked out onto the back garden.

Relief flooded through her when she saw Rebekah out there, although she wasn't alone. A man stood facing her, holding her by the shoulders to keep her still while he talked to her. Who was he? Jess couldn't see his face. But when he tenderly pushed a stray lock of hair off Rebekah's face, and she laid her forehead on his chest, Jess realised what was going on. She felt uncomfortable watching them, but she didn't move.

Suddenly Rebekah tried to pull away, but the man wrapped both arms around her and kissed her passionately. At first Rebekah returned his kiss. Then she pulled out of the embrace, and pushed him lightly away.

He went to grab her again, but she turned and strode back to the house.

Embarrassed, Jess quickly retraced her steps, and slipped out the front door as if she were just arriving.

Rebekah appeared in the hallway, looking hot and flustered. She flinched when she saw Jess, then said: "I'm so glad to see you." She opened the fly screen door. "Please come in."

Jess followed her down the hallway and into the sitting room.

"Can I get you some tea, or anything?" Rebekah asked, politely.

"No thanks, I'm fine." Jess sat down on the sofa. "I came as soon as I could. Sally told me what happened."

Rebekah's eyes welled up, but she held it together.

"Have you got Benji's collar?" Jess asked.

Rebekah went over to the sideboard. Her hands were shaking when she came back with it.

The collar was a thick, red leather strap, with a silver buckle to adjust the size. Three nails had been punched through the leather, at what looked like an equal distance, their pointed ends hanging clearly out the other side.

The door creaked open, and they both turned.

Now Jess saw the man's face, she immediately knew who he was. She stood up and held out her hand. "You must be Charles."

"And you must be Jess." He shook her hand in a perfunctory way, without smiling. "You've worked out that Brad and I are not only brothers, we're twins," he said.

She could see that. The same bright blue eyes, except Charles had short, brown hair rather than Brad's sun-bleached locks and ponytail. Charles also looked like he was carrying plenty of New York business lunches around his midriff.

"Sorry about missing your dinner last night," he said, casually, as if he wasn't sorry at all.

She didn't blame him for missing it, but the fact that he offered no explanation for his absence irritated her. Although he struck her as the kind of man who didn't much care what anyone thought of him. Unlike his brother, Charles seemed to have no charm about him. His poker face gave the impression he didn't want to show anything of himself or his feelings.

Still, now Jess knew why Rebekah was so worried about Charles not turning up for dinner last night. They were probably having an affair, and she'd expected him to be there. So what did Charles have to do last night that was more important, Jess wondered?

Watching them both, Jess could understand their mutual attraction. Charles oozed the arrogance of a successful banker. He was probably loaded too, which might appeal to someone like Rebekah. Did the Chief Justice know about his wife and Charles, she wondered? Would he have gone off to his London law conference if he had?

"It's voodoo," Rebekah said, turning back to the dog collar.

Jess nodded. "Sally explained about coffin nails."

"It's meant for me." Rebekah's hands were still shaking. "It's a curse. It means I'm going to die the same way as Benji."

"Oh come on, Rebekah," Charles said. "You don't know that Benji's dead."

"Yes, I do," she fired back. "I can feel it."

"Even if that were true," Charles said, gently, "it doesn't mean that someone deliberately killed him. Maybe he was run over by accident? Or perhaps he went for a swim and drowned. You know he loves going in the sea."

Rebekah shook her head. "I've driven all over this island looking for his body along the roadside. He wasn't run over by a car. And he would never go into the sea unless I gave him permission." She paused. "That's the way I trained him. Not to go into the sea unless I told him he could."

Jess felt sorry for Rebekah, who was deeply upset about her dog. "Have you told the police?" she asked.

"Tell them what exactly?" Charles intervened.

"That Benji's missing, and that his collar has turned up with three nails in it. I'm sure they'll understand the voodoo implication."

"I don't think that's necessary?" Charles answered.

Not only did his authoritarian tone grate on Jess, he was clearly averse to going to the police. Why, she wondered? "Hasn't Benji been missing for a while?" she asked.

Rebekah nodded. "Two weeks to this day." A tear slipped down her cheek. "Every morning he used to go out to roam around for a couple of hours. That morning he went out as usual and never came back."

"Well, then I think it's sensible to tell the police," Jess said. "Not least because someone's trying to frighten you with these coffin nails. And that should be reported." She looked at Rebekah. "Can you think of any reason why anyone would want to do that?"

Rebekah glanced at Charles.

He shook his head.

Jess asked: "Would you like me to talk to the police, Rebekah?"

"No, I'll phone them, he's my dog."

Charles sighed.

"Good." Jess fished her new mobile out of her bag and looked at the number Sally had stuck on the back with some tape. "Here's my mobile number." She wrote it down on her note pad, ripped the piece of paper out, and handed it to Rebekah. "Call me if you need to."

Rebekah took it. "Thanks, Jess."

"No trouble." Jess looked at her watch. "Now, I'm sorry, but I have to get back to the office."

"Of course." Rebekah gave her a small smile.

"Are you going to be staying in the house alone?" Jess asked.

"No need to worry on that score," Charles intervened. "I'll make sure she's all right."

Yes, I'm sure you will, Jess thought, especially with the Chief Justice away. She looked over at Rebekah, who nodded in agreement.

As Jess looked at Charles again, she found him impossible to read behind that stony facade. If he was as passionate about Rebekah as he'd appeared to be in the garden earlier, wouldn't he call the police and do everything he could to help and protect her? It didn't make sense, especially after Mrs Pearson's brutal murder.

She gave him a curt nod and walked back to her car.

★

Driving along on the other side of Cockburn Town, Jess checked her watch. 5pm. She ought to phone Simon back in case he was leaving the office early for a function. She pulled into the next lay by, opposite the main beach, and dialled his direct office line.

He answered. "Ah, there you are. Thought you'd forgotten about me."

"Sorry, Simon, communications are terrible down here. I've just got a new mobile that actually works."

"I phoned hours ago. Spoke to your PA, Sally."

The pique in his voice surprised her. "Yes, she told me, but I've been out around town most of the day."

"I should know by now that when you get involved in a job, it takes you over."

She was taken aback. What a strange thing to say. "I haven't been working for over six months," she said, flatly.

He sighed. "Yeah, I know. I was just worried, that's all. You might have phoned and left a message to say you were okay."

"I did leave a message. Last night, on our home phone." She hesitated. "Didn't you pick it up?"

There was something in the silence that followed that made her ask. "*Have y*ou been home?"

"Yes, of course, I have. I got back late last night, and left early this morning. Must've forgotten to check the machine."

90

He sounded unusually tense, which wasn't like Simon. He was always cheerful, annoyingly so sometimes. "Anything wrong?" she asked.

There was a pause. "Everything's fine."

He didn't sound fine, but she let it go. "Well, I've got this new mobile now, so you can ring me anytime you like."

"I heard about the Governor's accident on the news," he said. "That's why I was so worried."

"Yes, I did mention it in my voicemail last night. It's been a real shock for everyone here."

"I phoned our Consulate in Miami earlier to see how he was getting on," he said. "They say he's still critical."

"He's in a coma apparently." She paused. "It was a strange accident though."

"Why? What makes you say that?"

She wasn't sure herself. "Well, the Governor was driving himself, in the early hours of the morning, when a truck smashed into him."

"So what's unusual about that?"

"Well, the police think the truck was stolen from the local supermarket just before the accident. It was a hit and run. But they haven't found the truck, and they've no idea who was driving it."

"Kids out joyriding, I expect."

"Mm. Maybe." She paused. "I don't know why, but it just doesn't feel right somehow."

"Well, I hear from the Washington folk that it's not an easy Territory to govern. They're a maverick bunch down there."

Simon wasn't telling her anything that she hadn't worked out for herself. She wanted to tell him about Mrs Pearson's murder, and about the tales of voodoo, but something stopped her. He sounded stressed. Was that because she'd come down to work here? Or something else?

"Is David Evans still there?" he asked.

"No, he left this morning."

"So you're on your own?" He sighed again. "Honestly, Jess, you do manage to get yourself into some tricky situations. I'm afraid I can't come down to help you."

"Of course not. I wouldn't expect you to."

"But how will you manage on your own?"

"Don't worry. I'm not on my own. The Governor's PA Sally is here and our local staff. We'll be fine." In truth, she felt anything but fine, but she wouldn't say so. "You sure everything's all right?" she asked again.

"Yes," he said, quietly. "I'm just busy, that's all. I've... er, I've got to fly to Los Angeles this evening to cover a couple of meetings for the Ambassador."

Jess knew Simon had a busy job as First Secretary Political in the Washington Embassy. He travelled a lot around the States, attending conferences, and meeting high profile figures. He often represented the Ambassador on these occasions. "Oh, I see. Will you ring me when you get there?"

There was a pause. "I've got a whole series of meetings lined up. I'm going to be pushed for time over the next couple of days."

Surely not too tied up to phone or send a quick text, she thought. But she didn't want to put him under any more pressure, and said nothing.

He added quickly. "Look, can you just tick things over down there until London send reinforcements, as I'm sure they will in the circumstances?"

"What else would I do?" she asked, lightly.

"You do tend to throw yourself into everything, Jess."

"Throw myself into everything?"

"You know what I mean," he said. "Well, I've got to go home and pack before getting on that plane."

"Right, well, I hope it goes well in LA."

"Take care," he said, softly. "See you soon, Jess." And with that he was gone.

Jess sat staring at the phone. That was the strangest conversation she'd ever had with Simon. It was almost as if they didn't know what to say to each other. They'd sounded more like colleagues than lovers. There was something up with him, she could sense it.

She sat back in the seat and looked out to sea. It was so beautiful, she wished Simon could see it too. The trouble with him was that he worked too hard. Never mind what he said about her, he was the workaholic in the family. What he needed was a good break. She'd try and persuade him to come for a holiday the next time they spoke. It would do him good.

She started up the engine again and set off for the Governor's Office. As she drove along, she was so lost in her thoughts she soon found herself in unfamiliar territory, and pulled up outside some gates. The sign said it was the Government Garage. Great, she thought, she'd have a quick look at the Governor's car while she was there.

She drove through the gates and pulled up in a gravel courtyard. With the sun now gone and the light fading, it was all pretty gloomy. Ahead, she could see three timber garages, or sheds, all standing in a row, on the far side of the courtyard. To the left stood a small brick building which looked like some kind of office.

She grabbed her bag, got out of the car and went over to the office. She poked her head in the door. There was a desk cluttered with papers, but no sign of anyone. She walked across the gravel courtyard, over to the nearest garage. Its doors stood half open, and she looked inside. A car was up on the ramp, and tools strewn about underneath. Still no-one.

"Hello?" she called out. "Anyone here?"

No reply. She walked back outside. Where was everyone? They wouldn't go home and leave the garages open and their tools out, surely? She suddenly felt uncomfortable walking around the place and going into all the garages without permission. Still, it was the Government Garage, she told herself, and she did work for the Government.

The doors to the next garage were closed. She went over, lifted the latch, and pulled them open. It was dark inside, with no windows. She didn't need much light to know the vehicle was the Governor's wrecked Land Rover.

As she stood looking at the mangled metal, and smelt the burning residue, her heart started racing. Memories came flooding back. She could see her Amy and Jack being ripped apart by the explosion and flames as they sat trapped in the car. She struggled to push the image out of her head. *Don't go there!* she told herself over and over. *Not now!*

Resisting the urge to run out, she took a deep breath and opened the garage doors wide to let in the last of the daylight. Then she forced herself to inspect the car.

The driver's door, and passenger door behind, had taken the full impact of the collision. No wonder the police thought a truck had hit it. All four wheels had collapsed on their axles, and the paintwork was burnt. None of the windows had any glass in them. She noticed there was no glass on the garage floor either, which made the clean-up job at the crash site even more impressive.

How on earth had the Governor got out of that alive, she wondered? The driver's door was completely buckled in, so he must have climbed over and somehow got out the front passenger door.

She pulled her camera out of her bag to take some photos and email them to London. They needed to see the intensity of the crash. It was so dark in the garage, she put the setting on automatic to enable the flash if necessary. As she moved around the Land Rover, photographing it from every angle, she was surprised to see so much of the inside of the vehicle burnt out, as well as the boot.

She felt guilty about taking photographs with no-one around, and was eager to get away. Quickly, she closed the garage doors, leaving them in the same position she'd found them, and got back into her car. Her hands were shaking as she gripped the wheel and put the gear in drive. That burnt out car had disturbed feelings she thought were well under control. She glanced in the driver mirror and saw her face was wet with tears. She wiped them away, sadly, and drove on.

★

By the time she got back to the office, everyone had gone home, and the building was in darkness. There was no external security lighting on either. Why was everyone so relaxed about security on this island, she thought, crossly? She parked the car, let herself in with David's keys, and flicked on the lights.

On her desk, Sally had left a message from the Police Commissioner. He wanted Jess to attend a hurricane planning meeting in Provo the following morning. It had been postponed twice already, and was now urgent because the hurricane season had started. He would be happy to chair the meeting in the Governor's absence, as Jess was new to the island.

Jess re-read it with irritation. What about Mrs Pearson's murder? Not even a *mention* of that, and she'd been waiting hours for him to phone with more details for her to report to London.

Sally had left a postscript on the note to say she'd booked Jess a seat on the 9am flight to Provo in the morning, in case she wanted to go.

Jess was in two minds about going. It would be a good opportunity to see Provo and meet some people over there, but she didn't want to leave Sally and the local staff here on their own.

She heard the bleep of a text message and opened it.

I've phoned the police about Benji and his collar. They're sending an officer round now. I'll keep in touch. Rebekah.

Jess was pleased Rebekah had done that. At least the police were taking it seriously and sending an officer round. She picked up the telephone directory to call the Police Commissioner. But when she tried to make the call, she found the switchboard was shut down. Using her mobile to phone the central police station, she got a recorded message saying they were closed for the night. There was an emergency number, but she decided she couldn't ring that. She'd have to phone again in the morning. She'd make sure she got his mobile number then too.

She yawned and rubbed her tired eyes. She'd had enough for one day. Swivelling round to her computer, she scrolled to her inbox to check her emails before going back to the Residence.

Dear Jess,

Great – we're on. I'll be on the Trans Air flight 556 from Miami to Provo tomorrow, arriving at 4pm. There's a domestic flight to Grand Turk at 5pm, so I'll catch that and get over to you for about 5.30pm. Hope that's okay? If there's any delay, I'll call. What's your mobile number?

Look forward to catching up tomorrow.

All good wishes, Tom.

Jess smiled, happy to finally get one piece of good news. She pressed reply.

Dear Tom,

That's fine. As it happens, I shall be in Provo tomorrow and will meet you on arrival at Provo airport. We can travel back to Grand Turk together on the 5pm flight. Do please ring my mobile number 09807 103476 if there are any problems.

Look forward to seeing you too.

Best wishes, Jess.

It would be good to have a friendly face around, she thought, and a policeman. She remembered her first meeting with Tom. He'd been so offhand at the time, but he'd turned out to be rather kind under that gruff exterior. And she treasured that lovely sketch he'd done of Amy from an old photo. He'd captured her little face and spirit so well.

As memories of that brutal time in Brisbane came flooding back, she felt a chill shiver up her spine. That had all started with a woman's murder too, and ended up with four people losing their lives.

It couldn't possibly be happening again, could it?

13

The humid night air wrapped around her as Jess stepped out of the office front door. She peered along the drive. There wasn't a single light along the way to the Residence. Now she knew why there were torches strategically placed on tables at the front and back doors of the house. She only wished she'd picked one up on the way out.

Adjusting her eyes to the dark, she started to walk the couple of hundred yards to the house. It was a lovely night, with hardly a breath of air. The sky was covered with stars, although she couldn't identify the constellations from this unfamiliar location.

Her stomach grumbled. It was already 8pm. It had taken her ages to send a report to London about Mrs Pearson's murder, because she was so unfamiliar with the operation of the classified telegram system in the office. She'd got it off eventually. But she was still cross with the Police Commissioner for not phoning her.

As she walked along, apart from the chirruping crickets and waves lapping onto the shore in the distance, the only noise was the sound of her shoes crunching on the drive's sandy gravel. Even the spiky leaves of the dwarf palms were silent in the still air. Taller trees couldn't survive the hurricane-force winds that battered these islands.

Now, she could see the Residence. It was in total darkness, except for the light from the chandelier on the top landing. The house had a forlorn look about it. It should be the centre of island life, she thought, full of people and parties. Had it been like that once? What secrets could it tell?

A dark shape swooped across her path. Oh God, bats! Goosebumps rose along her back and arms.

That's when she heard the crunch of a footstep behind her. It was just one crunch, but definitely a footstep! She looked over her shoulder, but couldn't see anyone. Heart quickening, she ran down the rest of the drive, and around the verandah to the back of the house. Seeing the light on in the kitchen, she ran across the courtyard and burst through the kitchen door.

"Oh!" Maggie, who'd been dozing in the rocking chair, jumped up.

"Sorry Maggie." Jess was breathing hard. "Didn't mean to scare you."

"What's wrong, Miss Jessica?"

Jess felt foolish now. "Oh, I ... er, I thought I heard someone following me down the drive in the dark."

Maggie frowned. "Who was it?" she asked, sharply.

"I don't know. I didn't stop to find out."

Maggie went over to the back door and turned the key in the lock. Then she went to the window and looked out.

"Can you see anyone?" Jess asked.

Maggie shook her head.

"Sorry." Jess sighed. "It was probably the bat that spooked me. I can't stand them." She smiled at Maggie now. "Anyway, what are you still doing here?"

"Waiting for you, Miss Jessica," Maggie said, as if it was obvious. "I've cooked your supper."

Jess felt both grateful and guilty. When Maggie said she would prepare some supper for her, she'd assumed she meant something for her to cook or heat up herself when she got back.

"I'm sorry, Maggie. I didn't realise you'd wait for me. I'm very grateful, but you should have gone home hours ago."

"It's no trouble." Maggie went back to the stove. "It's chicken, baked with tomatoes. One of my own recipes."

"Sounds wonderful." Now they were talking about food, Jess realised how hungry she was. "I'm famished."

Maggie nodded. "I thought you would be." She switched on the electric oven and pushed the casserole inside. "The potatoes just need to boil." She turned on the ring under the pan.

"I can serve myself when it's ready. You go home now." Jess paused, remembering the disturbance in the house last night. "Who else has a key to get into this house, Maggie?"

"A key?" Maggie paused to think. "Only me, and the Governor, and of course his wife." She looked at Jess. "And you now."

That made four copies already. "Do you each have keys to the front and the back doors?"

"Yes." Maggie turned to the back door. "Except the key in the lock now is always kept on the first hook up there." She pointed to a key rack on the wall, laden with keys of one description or another. "And I remember the Governor couldn't find his keys to get in one night," Maggie went on, "so he keeps a spare set in the office."

Keys everywhere, Jess thought. That meant everyone in the office probably had access to them too.

"Why do you ask, Miss Jessica?"

Jess looked at her. "Well, I was woken up in the middle of the night by a noise in the house. And when I came down here, the back door was wide open."

Maggie gave her a sceptical look. "Perhaps the wind blew it open?"

Jess shook her head. "Someone came in here, I'm sure of it. It was raining heavily outside at the time, and there was a puddle of water on the floor by the door."

Maggie looked back at the potatoes on the stove.

Jess went on: "I also found a child's doll on the chair in my bedroom. Is it still there?"

Maggie turned back and frowned. "I didn't see a doll when I made your bed."

Jess was about to go up and look for it, when Maggie asked gently. "Are you going to be all right here on your own, Miss Jessica?"

Jess nodded. "I'm used to being on my own," she said, defensively. She had the impression Maggie thought she was overwrought.

"But are you sure you'll be all right?"

"Yes."

There was a pause.

"That's a lovely photo in your room, Miss Jessica."

Jess knew that Maggie was talking about the photo of Jack and Amy on her bedside cabinet. She didn't want to talk about them, but she could see Maggie was curious. "My husband and daughter," she said.

"Forgive me for asking about them, Miss Jessica, but your eyes are sad."

Jess felt the usual weariness creep all over her when anyone mentioned Jack and Amy. She pulled out a kitchen chair and sat down, heavily. "They were killed in a car accident," she said, simply.

Maggie nodded, as if she already knew. "I lost my husband too, not long after we were married. It's a hard thing to have to live with."

Jess didn't ask any questions, because she couldn't bear to hear the answers. "I'm sorry, Maggie."

They were both silent with their memories, until the potatoes boiled over and water hissed onto the electric hob.

Maggie leapt up, and turned down the heat. Wiping up the spilt water with a dish cloth, she rinsed it, and hung it over the edge of the sink. "I'd better get off home now," she said.

"Of course. Thank you for cooking my supper and waiting for me. I really appreciate it."

Maggie smiled and picked up her bag. "Now lock the door after me."

Jess nodded, but didn't move.

"Now, please, Miss Jessica. I want to know the house is locked."

Jess got up and went over to the door.

"Don't open it to anyone during the night," Maggie said as she stepped out.

"Really, Maggie, I..."

"*Please!*"

"All right."

"Goodnight, Miss Jessica."

"Goodnight, Maggie." Jess closed the door and turned the key in the lock. She went back to the kitchen table and sat down again. Alone now with her thoughts, all she could hear was the sound of the sea and bubbling potatoes.

She could picture Amy playing on the beach out there and paddling in the sea. She'd be seven this year. What would she look like now, if she'd lived? But Jess would never know. In her mind, Amy would be for ever three.

One thing's for sure, she thought, as she stood up and went over to take the potatoes off the heat. She wasn't going mad, despite what Maggie thought. Someone had definitely been in the house last night.

★

Later, after changing and eating, Jess's thoughts turned back to work. She went into the Governor's study, where Sally had set up Jess's laptop on his desk, and typed in the wireless code. She wanted to download her photos of the Governor's car and email them to London. At least they'd have something to go on, in the absence of the police report.

She switched on the ceiling fan to get the stuffy air moving. Would the Governor mind her working in his study while he was away? She hoped not, in the circumstances.

His desk stood adjacent to the window for maximum light. Behind that, the wall was covered from floor to ceiling with books on fixed shelving. A two-seater sofa and chair filled the other side of the room, and in the corner stood a globe of the world. It was a cosy room, she thought, and set up for work.

She sat down, powered up her laptop, and quickly downloaded her photos of the Governor's car from her camera. Then she saved them to her memory drive, as back up, as she always did. However, when she tried to get onto the internet, she ran into problems. Nothing but buffering, and *page cannot be displayed*. Eventually she gave up: she'd have to email the photos from the office tomorrow.

She looked at her watch. 10.20. Her eyes were heavy, but she still had to prepare for the Provo hurricane planning meeting before going to bed. She picked up the disaster management file and went over to make herself comfortable on the sofa.

The file made worrying reading. Hurricanes, she discovered, were rated in five categories. Even the lowest, Category 1, could produce dangerous winds capable of knocking out power lines, and damaging buildings and houses. And she didn't need an expert to tell her any storm surge following a hurricane could cause a tsunami-type wave that could wipe out the entire coastline, and that would include the office and Residence.

The file said that the Disaster Management Centre was located up on the Ridge. She was surprised she hadn't seen it when she went up there earlier with the Police Commissioner.

The next section in the file, marked 'hurricane preparedness', was a list of things to do. Check the roofs, put up storm shutters to protect windows, check drains to prevent flooding, stock up on lamps, candles, provisions. Check the generators have been serviced. Generators? She hadn't even *seen* a generator. So much to do...

She yawned and laid her head back on the sofa, listening to the rhythmic clunk of the overhead ceiling fan.

Clunk... clunk.

She was so tired. She really ought to go to bed. In the stillness, she could hear the sea washing onto the shore. Everywhere she went in the house, she could hear the sea.

She stretched her aching back, and looked at her watch. Past midnight!

She became aware of a pounding noise, and it wasn't her heart. She listened. It sounded like drumming.

Was someone having a party on the beach? She listened again. Now she could hear voices. Low and rhythmic.

Her stomach turned, as she remembered Carrie's words. *These sacrificial ceremonies take place all over Haiti around July and August.* Hadn't Carrie said she'd heard drumming and chanting on the beach in the middle of the night?

Jess got up and went out to the kitchen, where the noise was a little louder. She unlocked the back door and opened it slightly. It was definitely coming from along the beach. Then she had an idea. If this was some kind of voodoo ceremony, she'd take some photos to present to the police as evidence. They'd have to investigate, and stop this nonsense once and for all. She went back to the study to get her camera, and then let herself out the back door.

On the beach now, the drumming and chanting was louder. She could see flames shooting into the sky. It was still pitch dark, with no moon. Little spots of rain blew in her face. She walked slowly towards the flames. The deep sand underfoot made progress slow, but at least her approach was silent.

Suddenly, a streak of lightning lit up the sky like a security light. She stopped and jumped behind some scrub-like bushes bordering the beach, hoping she hadn't been seen. She was nervous now. As the rain fell harder, she wondered whether to go back. But she pressed on, creeping closer to the fire under cover of the bushes.

Smoke began drifting her way, as the rain dampened the flames. She stopped dead when she saw a group of people standing in a circle around the fire. Arms raised to the heavens, they were chanting something over and over that she couldn't understand. It certainly wasn't English.

A figure in a long robe stood apart from the group, head and face obscured by a hood, leading the chanting. Jess stood in astonishment. It looked like a scene from a movie.

She pulled her camera out of her pocket, and stopped. The flash was different to lightning, and might draw attention to her.

Now, she could smell burning, like charred flesh!

She ducked down in fear as a loud clap of thunder reverberated around the sky. The heavens opened. Rain hammered down, soaking her, but she couldn't drag herself away.

Through the noise of the rain, she heard a twig snap. She froze, as someone walked past a couple of yards away, towards the gathering. She recognised that figure... that walk.

The crowd parted as Alvita went up to the robed figure. She said something that Jess was too far away to hear. One by one the members of the group embraced Alvita, then disappeared into the night.

Jess waited until everyone had gone, then went over to the remains of the fire. In the smoking embers, she could see something small laid out on a wire mesh. A dog? Or a cat maybe? It was too charred to identify. It was too small to be a human... although perhaps a baby?

Nonsense, she was letting her imagination run riot. She pulled her camera out of her pocket. Looking furtively around, she took a picture, shoved her camera back in her pocket, and hurried back to the Residence as fast as she could wade through the deep sand.

14

Jessica Turner is going to be a problem. She looks young and harmless, but I've seen her eyes. They are cool and sympathetic on the surface, but she is watching everyone. Was she sent here by London to spy on us? A woman of course is less conspicuous than a man, and she blends in well. Already people are accepting her, and she's only been here a few days. That's annoying.

When will the British Government understand they don't own these islands? They belong to those who live here, and have done through the centuries. The islanders know British people haven't even heard of the Turks and Caicos Islands, let alone know where they are. And that's just fine.

That's why it's so easy for me. People here don't need fancy restaurants, flashy cars and clothes. No, they want to live the same relaxed and peaceful life they have over the centuries. They don't want any change. They just want enough money to live on. As long as they can look after their families, everything's fine.

But they also know if they step out of line, they will regret it.

"And what is Death? Is still the cause unfound?
That dark, mysterious name of horrid sound? –
A long and lingering sleep, the weary crave.
And Peace? Where can its happiness abound? –
Nowhere at all, save heaven, and the grave."*

---

* Poem 'What is Life' by John Clare

Does Jessica Turner know her English poets? She probably thinks only illiterate fools live here. Just how educated is she? Does she know how Mussolini died? If she did, she would know why that old woman was hung up by her feet and left for dead.

I heard what happened to Jessica's husband and child. Very careless. So I think she would understand if she knew the truth. But she would ruin everything too, and I can't let that happen.

I've seen her a lot today — in town, at the lighthouse, at the Government Garage, and now on the beach this evening. Perhaps I can find a chink in her armour? It'll be fun trying. A cat and mouse game, something to amuse me for a while, until she too ends up in that watery graveyard of souls with all the others.

Because that's where I've decided she will go.

15

Tom Sangster felt a familiar rush of adrenaline as the helicopter rose from Key West's Naval Air Station. The whirring rotary-wing Eurocopter, and the smell of fuel, made him feel right at home. Policing the vast Australian coastline was very similar. He put on headphones to cut out the noise, and to hear what the pilot was saying.

"Take your last look at the most southerly point of the Continental States of America." The pilot sounded deliberately theatrical as he manoeuvred the helicopter in a wide circle out to sea.

Tom couldn't believe he was up there. He looked down at the gleaming white cruise ships lined up along the quayside, as they waited for their passengers who were shopping in Duval Street. He wished he could have visited Ernest Hemingway's house before leaving, but there was no time.

Having seen his colleague back off to Australia the night before, he'd planned to do some sight-seeing in Miami this morning, before catching his afternoon flight to the Turks and Caicos. So when the US guys suggested he join them on an early morning helicopter trip down to their naval base at Key West, he didn't have to be asked twice.

"That's Cuba over there," the pilot cut into his thoughts, "just 96 miles due south."

Visibility was good on this beautiful morning, and Tom could just make out the island of Cuba. With a light south-westerly breeze, and clear blue skies, flying conditions were perfect.

Completing the circle, the pilot set a northerly course, back up the Florida Straits. "The Bahamas are about an hour's flying time out in the North Atlantic," he pointed eastwards. "And the Turks and Caicos due south of them." He glanced over. "What time's your flight this afternoon?"

"2.15."

"Plenty of time, then." All the while he was speaking, the pilot's eyes scanned the vessels below.

Tom knew they were looking for one ship in particular, the *Haitian Prince*. It was suspected of having illegal migrants on board.

He remained quiet as they flew close to a series of sand-fringed islands stretching back to the US mainland. The Florida Keys looked stunning from the air. Linked by road bridges, the traffic flowed freely across them in both directions. Offshore, yachts bobbed about in the sparkling emerald sea close to swanky beachside properties.

When the helicopter suddenly banked to the right, Tom followed the pilot's gaze to a cargo ship in the distance. Something about that vessel interested him.

As they hovered above it, Tom scanned the stacks of metal containers on deck. Nothing particularly suspicious, he thought, except there was no-one about. Crew members would normally come up on deck if they heard a helicopter.

The pilot descended a little, and circled around the vessel. "Is it the *Haitian Prince*?" he asked.

Tom screwed up his eyes to try and see. "I can't make out the lettering on the hull. It's too rusty." But he could see through the window of the bridge. "It's *way* too quiet in there though."

"Yeah." The pilot gave him a grim smile. "They're hopin' we'll go away." Immediately he radioed the co-ordinates back to base, with an instruction for the US Coastguard to locate, and board, the vessel. Flying one last sweep around the ship, he gave a satisfied nod and pulled back on the throttle. The helicopter rose into the air again.

Tom was unfazed. The core job was the same back home, except boats had to cross the Timor Sea from Indonesia to get to Australia. Illegal immigrants risked their lives, packed together in flimsy vessels, crossing those waters. And identifying the criminal traffickers facilitating that trade was Tom's main job. They collected masses of intelligence on these criminal networks, but it was a global problem that depended on the co-operation of foreign governments. "Where did you get the intelligence that there were illegal migrants on board the *Haitian Prince* from?" he asked.

"Out of Haiti originally," the pilot replied. "A British naval ship spotted the vessel last night and radioed in its location."

That surprised Tom. "The British Navy is active down here?"

"Yep. They have a ship on patrol in the Caribbean every hurricane season in case any of its Overseas Territories are hit. They're helpful to us too."

Tom was surprised the British and US Governments shared intelligence in the area. He made a mental note to ask Jess about that when he saw her, and settled back into his seat. It had certainly been an interesting and useful visit to Florida and Miami. The US guys were already talking about coming over to Australia to see how they did things back home. Tom would start the ball rolling with an official invitation as soon as he got back.

Now, he was looking forward to seeing how the British Government coped at the sharp end with the flow of illegals from Haiti to the Turks and Caicos. And he had to admit he was looking forward to seeing Jess again too. Had he done the right thing contacting her? It had been on impulse. But the more he thought about it, the more he knew he'd have been disappointed to return to Australia without seeing her. And that thought troubled him.

16

Jess shifted in the seat. "Start the car up, Sally, it's stifling in here."

Sally turned the key in the ignition, and the engine and air conditioning purred into action.

Jess felt grumpy this morning. Not only was she tired, but that experience on the beach last night had rattled her. It had clearly been some kind of ceremony, with all that drumming and chanting going on. If it was voodoo, and those people were Haitians, what was Alvita doing out there with them?

She turned back to Sally, wondering whether to tell her about it. But she didn't want to frighten her, and changed the subject. "By the time I got back to the office from Rebekah's yesterday evening, there was no-one in Overseas Territories Department to answer my telephone call."

"London would be closed at that time," Sally said. "They're four hours ahead of us."

"So I had to report Mrs Pearson's murder by classified e-gram. I also mentioned the voodoo, and what happened to Rebekah and her dog since she's the Chief Justice's wife. I asked them to call me back this morning, but all I got was an email acknowledging my report and asking for regular updates."

Sally pulled a face. "It's always the same in August. One member of staff holds the fort while everyone else goes on leave."

Jess nodded. "And I'm still waiting for the police to produce the accident report for the Governor's car crash. I went round to the Government Garage and took some photos of the car before I came back yesterday too. What a mess! I'm surprised he got out of that alive, you know."

Sally nodded, sadly.

"I haven't got time now," Jess went on. "But I need to email those photos to London when I get back. I couldn't get onto the internet in the Residence on my laptop last night."

Sally looked surprised.

"If London ring while I'm over in Provo, can you take a message and ring me straight away?"

"Are you happy for me to do that?" Sally asked. "Only I don't usually get involved in talking to London."

Jess looked at her. "Why not?"

"The Governor and David insist they do all that."

They were either paranoid about advancing their own careers with London, Jess thought, or worried Sally was a loose cannon. "Sally," she said, firmly, "the Governor's lying seriously injured in a Miami hospital, and Mrs Pearson's been brutally murdered. This is a serious situation. I'm counting on you."

"Of course." Sally sat up straight. "Look, I behaved badly at dinner the other evening, and I know that has shaken your confidence in me."

Jess said nothing.

"But Rebekah really winds me up," Sally said. "Believe me, there's something not quite right about her."

Jess stared at her. "What do you mean?"

"Oh I don't know … she just, well, she just seems to like causing trouble," Sally said. "But I assure you, I can do my own job, Jess, and more."

Jess wondered if Sally knew about Rebekah and Charles, and was hinting at it. But she wouldn't get into that now. Her mind was on that voodoo ceremony and why the locals were so grim and silent here.

"There's a strange atmosphere on these islands," she said. "Quite unlike anything I've experienced anywhere before."

Sally nodded, as if she knew exactly what Jess was talking about. "They don't want British officials here. That's the truth of it."

"I know, but I think it's more than that." Jess paused. "How does the Governor get on with the locals? I mean, he chairs Cabinet and supervises local Ministers. What sort of a relationship does he have with them?"

Sally shrugged. "He never opens up to me. But I don't think he finds it easy here. None of us do. I think it's been getting to him."

Jess looked over. "What makes you say that?"

"He's been so irritable lately, jumping off the deep end at any little thing. And that's not like him." Sally paused. "Then there was that blazing row he had with Clement Pearson."

"Row?"

"It was the day Clement committed suicide," Sally went on, "that's why I remember it so well. Clement turned up at the office unexpectedly that afternoon, demanding to see the Governor."

"Really?"

"Yes. It was about five. I remember all the other staff had gone. The Governor told me to go home too. I said I'd be happy to stay as I had a lot of work to do, but he insisted I leave and that he would lock up." Sally pulled a face. "That was a first. He never locks up the Office."

"So you left?"

"Yes, but halfway home, I realised I'd left my purse in my desk drawer and went back for it. The front door was locked when I got there, which was odd. I had my key though and let myself in." She paused. "As soon as I opened the door, I heard them arguing. That really surprised me because I'd never heard the Governor even raise his voice before. Clement was a quiet sort of man too. But they were really going at it."

Jess was intrigued now. "What was it all about?"

Sally shrugged. "I didn't hang around to find out, I wasn't supposed to be there." She bit her lip. "It was later that night Clement hanged himself, and his wife found him in the garage. Now *she's* been murdered." She stared at Jess. "I keep wondering if that argument had something to do with Clement committing suicide."

Jess's head was whirling. What had the two men been arguing about? And had that row prompted Clement to take his own life.

"What are you thinking?" Sally asked.

"Well," Jess glanced over. "Since that argument, Clement has committed suicide, his wife's been murdered and the Governor's had a serious car crash."

Sally nodded, and fell silent.

Jess looked at her watch. "Come on," she said. "Let's get going or I'll miss my flight."

"All right." Sally buckled up her seat belt, and reversed out of the space.

Another thought occurred to Jess. "Was David in the office when the Governor and Clement had that row?" she asked.

Sally hesitated as she put the gear in drive, then shook her head. "No, he was at meetings in Provo that day."

"What about Alvita?"

Sally had to think. "She *was* in the office, but I can't be sure if she was still there then." Sally's face hardened. "To be honest, the less I see of her, the better. She hates us here on *her* islands, as she calls them. I'm sure she thinks she should be in charge of the Governor's Office."

Jess nodded, although in a way she understood Alvita. She'd been born in these islands. They were her home, her whole life. She would resent people coming from London into positions of authority, when they knew little about the islands and the people.

Sally put her foot down on the accelerator and the car pulled off. "It's not easy working with people who don't want you here."

"Does Alvita treat you okay in the office?" Jess asked.

Sally pursed her lips tight. "She gets it back in bucket loads if she starts anything with me."

Jess smiled. Sally could look after herself, but Alvita was a worry. What had she been up to on the beach last night? And why was she so cosy with the Haitians? Everyone else seemed to blame them for everything.

Sally said: "I thought I might go and see Rebekah today. I feel awful for what I said about her not looking after Benji properly."

Jess didn't want Sally going anywhere while she was away. The Office and phones had to be properly manned. Not only that, the Governor's accident was weighing on her mind, or rather the manner of his accident. Was it somehow connected to his argument with Clement Pearson? Why had Clement committed suicide anyway? Jess didn't know how these things fitted together, but instinct was telling her that they did. So, until she knew more, she wanted to be sure Sally was safe. "I'd like you to stay in the office all day while I'm in Provo please."

Sally caught the edge in her voice. "Why?"

Jess didn't want to scare her. "I want you to be careful, that's all."

But Sally looked startled. "What are you saying? That something's going to happen to me too?"

"No, I'm definitely not saying that, but I would like you to be careful. So please stay in the office, man the phones, and keep me informed of any developments. You can ring me any time on my mobile. Any time," she repeated. "I want to know everything that's going on. Understood?"

"Understood," Sally said, softly, as she pulled the car up outside the airport terminal. "What time shall I pick you up?"

"We're booked on the 5pm flight from Provo, so let's say 5.30."

"We? Oh, yes, of course you'll have that Aussie policeman with you, won't you?" Sally looked interested. "What's he like?"

Jess smiled. "I haven't seen him for a couple of years. We worked on a consular case together in Brisbane. He's not only a policeman, you know, he's an artist."

"Ooh, how interesting." Sally paused. "Bit unusual for a cop, isn't it?"

Jess nodded. "I suppose it is really. He does portraits, that kind of thing."

Sally glanced over. "Do you think he'd do one of me?"

Jess couldn't help but smile. The vision of Sally holding Brad to her bosom at dinner sprang into her mind.

"Will you ask him, Jess?"

Jess had been really wondering what Tom would make of *her* now. She cringed, thinking about the tragic face and blank eyes he'd drawn in his first sketch of her. It hadn't been long after she'd lost Jack and Amy, and before she'd got together with Simon.

And thinking of Simon now, she didn't know whether she felt hurt or cross. She'd sent him a text last night to say *goodnight* and another this morning to say *hi*. He hadn't replied to either. Not yet anyway. What was up with him?

She turned to Sally. "Can you ring our Consulate in Miami while I'm in Provo? I called them this morning to find out how the Governor was doing. They said they'd ring back, but they haven't."

"Okay. Will do," Sally said. "And I'll come back at 5.30 to pick you up."

"That'd be great." Jess picked up her bag and briefcase and got out of the car. "Remember," she said through the open window, "stay in the office."

"Absolutely. I won't leave the building until I come back and pick you up."

17

Back in Provo again, Jess climbed out of the plane and straightened up. Even at 9.30, the heat was stifling. She could feel the soles of her shoes sticking to the tarmac as she walked over to the terminal. At least she was wearing flats today. The island's sandy ground was impossible in high heels.

With no checks on domestic flights, she entered the building and followed the signs to the taxi rank. The terminal was deserted this morning, compared to her arrival. As she passed by the café, she glanced through the window, and stopped.

That uniform was unmistakable . . .

The Police Commissioner sat at a table in the far corner. His companion had his back to her, but that curly, gelled hair was instantly recognisable – *Big Shot!*

The pair were engrossed in conversation. She knew the Police Commissioner was in Provo for the hurricane planning meeting. It only then occurred to her that Roger Pearson would be attending too, as the new Immigration Minister. For some reason, hurricane planning came within that ministerial portfolio.

A welcome blast of air conditioning blew in her face when she went into the café to speak to them. Neither man looked up. She hesitated. The Police Commissioner pulled his ever-present white handkerchief out of his pocket and wiped his brow. He looked sickly this morning, but it was his low, urgent voice that caught her attention. It sounded like he was pleading with Roger Pearson, although Jess couldn't hear what about.

Roger still had his back to her but, by the way he kept jabbing a finger at the Police Commissioner, it looked like he was giving him a dressing down. He must be upset about his aunt's murder, she thought. She knew only too well from her job that people reacted differently to shock and grief. Some collapsed in despair, while others lashed out at anyone within range. The café staff politely kept their eyes down, and busied themselves drying up cups and saucers. They didn't want to be seen to be listening. What a way to treat the Police Commissioner in public!

Not wanting to get caught up in all that, she quickly withdrew from the café and walked out of the terminal to stand in line at the taxi rank. Almost immediately her mobile started ringing. "Hello," she answered.

"Hi Jess."

She recognised the voice. "Hello, Brad."

"Sorry to disturb you." He sounded tense. "I know you're over in Provo, but I didn't know who else to call."

"What's wrong?"

"It's Rebekah. I'm at her place now, with my brother Charles. She's . . . well, she's a bit . . . hysterical about this voodoo warning. She says she heard footsteps outside the house in the middle of the night, but she was too afraid to go out and investigate."

Jess didn't blame her. "Has she told the police?"

He sighed. "They called round yesterday to take a statement about Benji's collar and those coffin nails." He paused. "They didn't take the collar. Wouldn't even touch it, according to Rebekah. Too scared."

"Oh for God's sake," Jess said, irritably. She was surprised Rebekah had been on her own last night. She'd have thought poker-faced Charles would have taken the opportunity of her husband's absence to stay over. "Is Rebekah on her own?" she asked.

"My brother's with her now." Brad sighed. "The thing is Jess, Rebekah refuses to talk to the police again. She says they're a waste of time." He paused. "She wants to see you."

Jess sighed. She didn't blame Rebekah for being upset about her dog, but it was a matter for the police. She would definitely have a word with the Police Commissioner when she saw him. His officers *must* take this seriously. "I'll pop round and see Rebekah this evening when I get back," she said. "In the meantime, you might want to call the doctor and ask him to give her something to help her rest."

"Good idea." He paused. "You know, Jess, everyone's upset with what's happening. First Clement, then all the talk of voodoo and pets being sacrificed, then the Governor's accident, and now Mrs Pearson. People are afraid."

"I understand that, Brad."

"Well, I was thinking it might be a good idea for us all to get together again this evening. It always helps to be in company, rather than at home alone dwelling on things, don't you think?" He paused. "Why don't you come over for dinner at my place? Charles can bring Rebekah, and save you a drive over to hers."

A repeat performance of their first dinner did not appeal to Jess. "I'm sorry," she said, quickly, "but I've got a friend arriving to stay at the Residence."

"Oh, bring him along too, and Sally," he said. "The more the merrier."

How did Brad know her friend was a man? Unless Sally had been talking. "We won't get back to Grand Turk until about 5.30. He might be tired from travelling."

"That's a point." Brad paused. "Tell you what. Why don't I bring some food over to you, and we can all meet up at the Residence? If that suits you, of course."

She groaned inwardly knowing Brad wasn't going to be put off. Still, at least it would be an opportunity for Tom to meet a few people, since it looked like she was going to be too busy to take him out and about. "All right," she said, "but it'll be easier if Maggie prepares something simple at the Residence."

"Perfect." The relief in Brad's voice was palpable.

Why was he so eager to meet up, she wondered? "Would you ring Sally and ask her to speak to Maggie about it, please? Tell her we only want something simple, and not to go to any trouble. The poor woman has had enough to cope with."

"Great. I'll do that." He paused. "Is it okay if Carrie joins us? She's feeling the strain too."

"Of course." Jess had moved to the front of the queue now, and could see a taxi turning in the direction of the rank. "Look, I must go, Brad. See you all at, say, seven?"

"Okay. Thanks Jess. See you then."

She pocketed her mobile. Another dinner was the last thing she wanted but, in the Governor's absence, she felt she had a duty to do something to help everyone. She got into the back of the taxi.

"Where to, Miss?"

Jess looked up to see a smiling row of teeth. "The Disaster Management Centre, please."

The young man gave her a blank look.

She tried again. "The control centre where they manage natural disasters . . . hurricanes and things."

He shrugged.

Jess pulled the disaster management file out of her briefcase, and read out the address.

He gave her a doubtful look.

She was just wondering what to do when Roger Pearson strode out of the terminal, and jumped into the back of a black limousine. He had to be going to the same place.

"See that Mercedes," she said, pointing through the windscreen. "Follow it."

The taxi driver grinned, and pressed down on the accelerator in pursuit.

The first thing Jess noticed about Provo was the smooth tarmac road, and neatly clipped bushes of brightly coloured bougainvillea along the central reservation. Then came newly built houses and luxury hotels. It felt a world away from the old charm and history of Grand Turk. On the pavement here, black and white people mingled more comfortably. The common denominator probably being wealth, she thought.

Jess started gripping the seat nervously as the taxi driver picked up speed along the dual carriageway. He weaved his way through the traffic, determined not to lose the Mercedes. When the taxi's engine started making a rattling noise, she began to regret her *follow that car* order. Suddenly, the sight of a stunning bay, with white sand and more turquoise sea, came into view. Reaching into her handbag for her camera, she felt around but couldn't find it. Reluctantly, she took her eyes off the road to look inside. Definitely not there. *Damn!* She remembered she'd left it in the Governor's study last night. She frowned. She still had to download that photo of the charred remains in the fire on the beach last night too and email it to the Police Commissioner.

The taxi driver suddenly slammed on the brakes.

She jerked forward.

When the Mercedes turned left into a narrow lane, the taxi driver followed.

"Just a minute," she said. "Are you sure this is the right way?"

"I'm following that car, Miss." He flashed her a glance in the driver's mirror. "Just like you said." He drove on, determined to keep up.

The taxi was engulfed in sand from the Mercedes' tyres on the unsealed track as they bumped over stones and potholes. Jess was more worried about how she was going to explain to Roger why they were following him, than being shaken about in the back.

Finally, the taxi shuddered to a halt. Once the cloud of sand had subsided, she stared at a single-storey, concrete building nestling into the side of a hill. Several cars were parked outside, in a haphazard way.

Was *this* the island's Disaster Management Centre?

★

Roger Pearson could turn on the charm, she thought, as she watched him chair the meeting. He clearly enjoyed being the centre of attention, and in control. Jess could feel the tension in the room though, and wondered if that was due to Mrs Pearson's murder, or to Roger's mercurial personality? He was all sweetness and light now. But he could turn in a flash as she'd seen with that little girl, and the Police Commissioner, at the airport.

Roger's officials clearly didn't want to get on the wrong side of him. They hung on his every word, and only spoke when invited to. They ranged from the Chief of the Fire Brigade, to the Chief Medical Officer, to representatives of the other inhabited islands in the Turks and Caicos chain. Jess studied them as they introduced themselves.

They were all black, and local islanders, except for the Fire Brigade Chief, who said he was from Trinidad.

Despite an old air conditioner blasting away noisily in the corner of the room, the place was stifling hot. A lick of paint wouldn't go amiss, she thought, although she guessed she was the only person who noticed. The table they were sitting around was made up of several smaller, square tables all pushed together to form a rectangle. A projector screen hung over a whiteboard at one end of the room, with a detailed map of the islands next to it. Apart from some battery operated radios, she could see only one computer which surely wouldn't be enough in any emergency. The electricity supply would be the first thing to go, so they must have a generator somewhere too.

The meeting wasn't like any meeting she'd ever chaired. Senior officials were not free to express themselves here. And when she introduced herself and explained that she was holding the reins while the Governor recovered from his accident, no-one asked how he was, or expressed any sympathy. Why? Didn't they care? She got the distinct feeling there was something unspoken between these people, and they weren't going to open up while she was around.

Jess just listened as the meeting went on, soaking up all the information on hurricane disaster planning like a sponge. She studied a small map the Minister circulated, indicating the location of all the hurricane shelters on every island, and the safe harbours for shipping. She wrote down the radio and TV frequencies for emergency messages in her diary, and slipped the latest list of emergency telephone numbers inside the back cover. She'd have programmed them into her mobile there and then, except she didn't want to appear rude.

Several questions popped into her mind as the meeting progressed, but she kept them to herself. Not that she was intimidated by Roger Pearson, like everyone else seemed to be. The discussion was just so slow; she didn't want to drag things out further. No-one else seemed bothered about the time, but she was eager to get away and see the Police Commissioner. Where was he, anyway?

After an hour and a half, she excused herself to go outside and phone him on her mobile. But there was no reply from the numbers Sally had given her for his direct office line and mobile. She left voice messages on both saying she wanted to speak to him urgently.

Back in the meeting, Roger Pearson pushed a note along the table to her. *Are you free for lunch after the meeting?* it read.

Oh God! That was the last thing she wanted. *Thank you,* she scribbled back, *but I have to go and see the Police Commissioner.*

The piece of paper slid back in her direction. *He's flown back to Grand Turk to supervise the murder investigation* came the reply.

Flown back to Grand Turk without talking to her? Jess was annoyed he'd gone, and that she was now cornered on the lunch invitation. She knew it would be churlish to refuse since Roger was probably only being polite to a new arrival. *Thank you* she wrote back. *That would be lovely.*

Roger nodded when he read it, and continued with the meeting. As it dragged on, she realised that at least he was well up to speed on disaster management. He did most of the talking though, only occasionally listening to what others had to say. He liked to fire off questions too, which rattled those on the receiving end. His officials were definitely scared of him. Or perhaps more of being caught out by him, and humiliated in front of the others? That created a lot of tension in the room.

The more she watched Roger Pearson in action, the more she disliked him. He seemed to relish his new-found status as Immigration Minister, showing little regard for any officials around the table. The man had a big ego, that's for sure, and seemed keen to stamp his authority over everyone. Just what would his agenda be in his new role, she wondered? And how far would he go to get what he wanted?

18

Jess felt she should pinch herself to make sure she really was sitting in the shade of a palm tree in an oceanfront restaurant overlooking Grace Bay. A stunning 12-mile curving beach, with powder white sand, stretched along the shoreline. While out to sea, white foam bubbled on turquoise water as waves broke up on the reef. What a wonderfully secluded Caribbean paradise!

"I was educated mostly in America." Roger Pearson helped himself to another spoonful of coconut fish curry from the bowl in the centre of the table. "I majored in history at Yale."

"Ah." Jess put her knife and fork down. The curry was delicious, but she wasn't hungry and Roger seemed more than capable of eating it all on his own. "I wondered how you were so knowledgeable about ancient customs."

"Voodoo's nothing for us to worry about," he went on. "It's been practised in Haiti for centuries, like a religion." He gave her a pointed look. "It was brought over from West Africa by our forefathers, on slave ships."

Roger Pearson was a lifetime away from his forebears on slave ships, she thought. Decked out in a designer suit, polished shoes, and glowing with privilege, he only had to lift a hand and every waiter in the restaurant came running. "Do the Haitians here practise voodoo?" she asked.

He shrugged. "It may go on quietly in some corners of the islands, but it's harmless."

"Harmless? Even when people think their pets are being sacrificed?"

"Just be thankful they're not human sacrifices," he said, lightly.

She realised he was joking, but she was thinking of the charred offering on the beach the night before. And people were scared. "Can you be sure they're not?"

"Come now, Miss Turner." He gave her a reproachful look. "It wasn't that long ago humans were being sacrificed in *your* country."

She raised her eyebrows.

"Weren't the Druids barbarians who liked to sacrifice humans?" He went on. "At least the Roman invaders thought they were."

Jess sat back in her seat. "That was over 2,000 years ago," she said, drily. "And as far as I know, there's no evidence in the history books to substantiate such claims. They more likely used animals in their rituals."

"As in voodoo ceremonies." Roger had made his point. "Best not to listen to gossip."

The man was being smug now. "Perhaps we *should* listen," she went on. "Ignoring this kind of thing leads to mistrust, fear even. Wouldn't it be better to investigate these ceremonies, and missing pets, to find out the truth? At least it might restore community relations."

"What a waste of police time that would be."

"Is that what the Governor thinks too?" she asked.

Roger shrugged. "He takes a pragmatic view."

"Is that why he didn't instruct the police to investigate?"

"He always listens to advice," he said, pointedly.

"I see." Jess wondered what kind of influence Roger had over the Governor. She didn't know the Governor, but she doubted the Chief Justice could be easily swayed. He took voodoo, or rather the effect it was having on the community, seriously. "Does the Chief Justice see things the same way as you?" she asked.

Roger frowned. "Has that poor man been going on about voodoo again?" He shook his head. "He's been under a lot of pressure lately."

"Pressure?"

"He has a very heavy workload," he said. "And let's face it, he's not getting any younger. Retirement must be beckoning."

Jess felt her hackles rise. Roger seemed contemptuous of the Chief Justice. He clearly didn't think much of any senior official here – black or white. "Personally, I found Dominic articulate and highly intelligent," she said. "He didn't strike me as being over the hill or under any particular strain."

Roger said nothing more.

Looking at the man, Jess wondered again what his agenda might be now he was a Minister. From what she'd seen, and judging by the fear he provoked in his own staff, he was already a powerful figure in the islands. But how much more power did he want? Complete independence from the British Government?

They fell silent as Roger drained his third glass of white wine. She sat back in her chair wondering whether to mention his aunt's murder. Of course he'd be upset, but then he was tucking heartily into his lunch. She decided to plunge in. "I'm sorry about your aunt. It must have been a terrible shock, particularly after your uncle's . . . death."

Immediately the shutters came down over Roger's eyes. He put his knife and fork down. "It's been terrible for the whole family," he said.

"How's the investigation going?"

"It has only just started, Miss Turner."

He clearly didn't want to talk about the murder, but she felt compelled to ask: "Do you know if the police have a suspect, or a motive, yet?"

He shook his head. "Not as far as I know. As I said, it's early days."

Jess knew she was being fobbed off. But why? "Do you think the *way* Mrs Pearson was killed could be significant?" she went on, gently. "I mean, has such a thing ever happened here before?"

"You ask a lot of questions, Miss Turner."

Jess knew she was being indelicate. "I'm sorry to have to ask you about your aunt," she said, "but you know the British Government are ultimately responsible for police and security issues here. In the absence of the Governor, I have to report back to London. That's why I need to be kept informed of developments."

Roger looked at her. "I'm afraid I don't know any more than you do at the moment."

She nodded. "It's terrible for you and your family that these deaths have come so close to each other." She paused. "Do the police think your aunt's murder is connected to your uncle's death?"

He shook his head, and made a show of looking at his watch. "I really have to get back to work now." He wiped his mouth on his napkin and put it down on the table.

Jess knew this was his way of closing down the conversation. She was sure he did know more about the police investigation; he just didn't want to discuss it with her. "Can I ask you one more thing before you go," she said. "Do you think the police need any help with your aunt's murder investigation?"

He looked up. "Why? Do you think they're not up to the job?"

She heard the edge in his voice. "No. I'm not saying that. I just thought they might need some specialist help with forensics, or extra manpower, that sort of thing."

"If the Governor were here, Miss Turner, he'd tell you that our police are more than up to the job."

"Ah, but he's not here, Minister." She gave him his formal title now. "He's fighting for his life in a Miami hospital." She paused. "Rather a coincidence in the circumstances, don't you think?"

★

The sun glinted on the silver pot as the waiter placed it on the table. Coffee – at last! Jess poured herself a cup, and topped it up to the brim with milk. Little beads of sweat trickled down the back of her neck as she drank the piping hot liquid. But she didn't care, she needed the caffeine.

She was glad Roger Pearson had gone. She hadn't handled their conversation very well, but she found him a difficult man. And she wasn't going to let him bully her like he had his officials.

She pulled her mobile out of her pocket and tapped her inbox. . . *Still* nothing from the Police Commissioner. He obviously wasn't concerned about keeping her informed either. She'd go and see him the minute she got back to Grand Turk.

Her eyes went back to the shoreline. The beach was deserted now, in the hottest part of the day, except for a few tourists still lounging on their sun beds in the shade. Out to sea, a speed boat dragged a paraglider across the sky like a kite. The scene looked like a photo from a glossy holiday magazine.

Suddenly, she became aware of the silence. She looked around. Everyone had gone. Even the waiters had disappeared, which was annoying. Roger had paid for lunch before leaving, but she needed to settle up for the coffee. She checked her watch: 2.45. It was still too early to go to the airport to collect Tom, but she needed to let the restaurant staff clear up.

A light touch on her shoulder made her jump.

She turned to see a woman standing behind her. She looked elegant in a sleeveless, navy blue and white dress, with her curly black hair clasped tightly in a ponytail.

"Can I speak to you, Miss Turner?" she asked.

"Of course." Jess gestured to the chair opposite her, wondering what she wanted.

The woman glanced around and sat down. "How well do you know Roger Pearson?" she asked, quickly. "Only I saw you having lunch with him."

What a strange question to fire off, Jess thought, especially without introducing herself. But the woman clearly knew who Jess was, so she answered truthfully: "As you probably know, I only arrived here a couple of days ago."

The woman bit her lip, looking nervous.

Jess's eyes were drawn to the chunky gold earrings and pendant the woman wore. She looked well off, sophisticated even. "So what would you like to talk to me about?" Jess asked.

The woman looked over her shoulder, and turned back. "I shouldn't be talking to you, but someone has to."

Jess saw fear in the woman's dark eyes now, and sat forward.

"Things are not what they seem on these islands, Miss Turner." The woman shook her head. "It's got worse and worse. People are afraid to speak out."

Jess contained her surprise. "Afraid?"

The woman pointed in the direction of the beach. "Look at those rich tourists! They have no idea what's going on here, or even where they are. All they see is beautiful sea and sand. They don't *care* about these islands. They don't *want* to know the reality." The words were tumbling out now. "I can't stand the lies any more, you see . . . the awful deceit. It's not going to stop. It's never going to stop."

The woman was clearly upset, but she wasn't making any sense. "I'm not sure I understand what you're trying to tell me," Jess said.

The woman leant forward. "You can't trust Roger Pearson. You can't trust any of them!"

Jess stared at her. "Why not?"

The woman just looked away.

Jess tried again. "So what are these lies, and this awful deceit, you talk about?"

The woman shook her head. "You can't deal with this on your own, Miss Turner. You need to get the British police over here. There's no-one else to help us."

A car door slammed in the distance.

The woman flinched. "I can't be seen talking to you." She went to get up.

"Please!" Jess put a hand on her arm to stop her leaving.

The woman shrugged it off and stood up. "Believe me when I say people are too scared to tell the truth." She bent down and whispered. "The Governor was going to confess. That's why they had to stop him."

Jess was stunned for a moment. "What are you trying to say? That the Governor's car crash *wasn't* an accident?"

The woman nodded. "Be careful, Miss Turner."

Jess jumped up.

But the woman turned and ran straight out of the restaurant.

Jess stared after her, then plopped back down on the chair, with the woman's words whirling around in her head. *The Governor was going to confess. That's why they had to stop him.*

How would that woman know the Governor's car crash wasn't an accident, she wondered? Who was she anyway? And why would she stick her neck out to say something when everyone else was supposedly too afraid? But, as Jess remembered the sound of drumming and chanting on the beach the night before, and the smell of charred flesh, shivers ran up her spine. What the hell was going on in these islands?

19

Tom stretched his right leg out in the aisle and flexed his knee. His long legs were always a problem in coach class. Still, it was a short flight to Providenciales – only an hour and twenty minutes from Miami. Now, by his watch, they should be landing in half an hour.

He finished the dregs of red wine in his glass and laid his head back on the seat rest. That Californian wine was very drinkable, but he would have liked a glass of Tasmanian Pinot Noir with that chicken.

Closing his eyes, he wondered what on earth he was doing on a plane to the Turks and Caicos Islands. What had he been thinking when he contacted Jess and invited himself down? He was probably the last person she wanted to see, raking up all those bad memories of Brisbane. Of course she'd told him to come. She was too polite to say no. He shook his head just thinking about it.

He'd told the guys back in Canberra he was going to visit a friend in the Caribbean for a few days. He thought of Jess as a friend. But was she? After all, they'd been working when they were thrown together on that murder case. Did she think of him as a friend? He didn't often feel nervous, but he was now.

Still, his time in Miami had been useful. He'd learnt a lot about their 'illegals' operation. He'd recommend his colleagues adopt one or two US procedures when he got back home. And it hadn't all been one-sided. The US guys were keen to hear about how they did things back in Australia too.

It was only now he had the time and space to think that he realised something was bugging him. It was the way those guys reacted when he told them he was going to visit a friend in the Governor's Office in the Turks and Caicos. They either looked away, or down at their feet. There was definitely something unspoken between them. What was all that about? Did they clam up because he said he was going to visit a friend in the Turks and Caicos? Or because she was in the Governor's Office? Perhaps both? Only the helicopter pilot, on their way back from Key West this morning, had said anything.

"That's gonna be interestin'. They're a pretty lawless bunch down there."

He'd asked the pilot what he meant by that.

"I guess you're gonna find that out soon enough." The pilot had given him a wry smile. "We've got a good contact in the local police on Grand Turk, if you need one while you're down there."

"Oh, I'm not planning on doing any work." Tom had smiled. "I'm taking a few days' leave."

"Sure, buddy." The pilot glanced over. "But if you need any help, be sure to get in touch with Chuck Lynch."

Tom remembered the name Chuck Lynch clearly. He never forgot a face or a name. But he was annoyed with himself now for not asking more questions. Why hadn't he pressed them to explain why they didn't want to talk about the Turks and Caicos? He'd never usually have let something like that go, not when he was working as a detective anyway. Was he losing his touch, he wondered? Sitting there, he remembered how he used to feel at the start of a new murder case. That buzz. The excitement of putting the pieces of a crime puzzle together. It was like a fever that burnt in his brain. He couldn't rest or think about anything else until he'd resolved it. It made him feel alive.

He suddenly realised how much he missed all that.

20

The Governor was going to confess… that's why they had to stop him.

Jess paced around the airport terminal waiting for Tom's plane to land? Could she believe that woman? She might have had another reason for saying what she did. But then Jess had felt things were all wrong from the moment she set foot in this Territory. She'd been treading carefully, feeling her way along with the Police Commissioner and Roger Pearson. Now she had no option but to request a British police team come over to investigate the Governor's accident, and assess the local police response to Mrs Pearson's murder.

She pulled out her mobile. She'd call Sally and ask her to track down the Police Commissioner and get him to call round later. She dialled Sally's direct office line. No reply. She rang Sally's mobile. No reply from that either. She phoned the Governor's Office switchboard, but it just rang and rang. She thrust the phone back in her pocket. What were they all doing over there?

Suddenly the lights of Tom's Trans Air jet came looming on the horizon. She watched the plane line up with the single runway as it approached. Down came the landing gear. The huge wings wobbled in the air currents. Finally, the plane thudded down on the tarmac, rushed past her, and juddered to a stop at the far end of the runway.

Flashing an official airside pass, Jess walked past the single baggage carousel, and up to the immigration desk to wait for Tom there. Standing by the window, she watched the plane taxi over and stop close to the terminal. Steps were manoeuvred up to the plane and the door opened. Her eyes scanned the passengers as they descended. She hadn't seen Tom for a couple of years. Would he look the same?

When she saw him appear in the plane's doorway, an overwhelming sense of relief washed over her. He hurried down the steps and across the tarmac with a sense of purpose that set him apart from all the other passengers and holidaymakers. Single-minded, that was Tom.

Suddenly, he looked over to where she was waiting, as if he knew she was there, and stopped. He smiled and gave her a salute in the same way he had when they last said goodbye.

She laughed and waved.

Clearing immigration, he went straight over to her.

There was no awkwardness between them as they greeted each other with a friendly hug. The intervening years just fell away. He was still as fit and lean as ever, just a little greyer around the temples. "I'm so glad you're here, Tom," she said, anxiously.

He frowned as he studied her face. "What's wrong?"

★

They were sitting in the corner of the domestic departure lounge waiting for their flight to Grand Turk, and as far away from the other passengers as they could for privacy. They hadn't stopped talking for the whole 30 minutes he'd been on the ground. Or rather Jess hadn't. She was trying to explain to him the set-up in these islands. "The Governor is a senior British diplomat from London," she said. "He chairs Cabinet, which consists entirely of local Ministers. They have their own individual domestic portfolios, you know, such as fishing, housing and immigration."

"What's your job then, Jess?"

"I'm the Head of the Governor's Office. You see, under the Constitution, the UK retains responsibility for foreign affairs, defence, policing and security, and financial regulation. I work to the Governor on those issues."

He ran his hands through his short, spiky hair. "So, if I've got this right, just about everyone works to the Governor."

"Yes."

"He's all powerful, then?"

"Well, yes, I suppose he is, except it would be physically impossible for one man to keep an eye on *everything*."

"So what are you saying?"

"That's just it." Jess flopped back in the chair. "I don't know what I'm saying. I only arrived two days ago, to cover the job for a colleague. His mother's gravely ill in the UK. Before that, I was on special unpaid leave, accompanying Simon on his posting to Washington."

"How is Simon?" he asked.

She hesitated. "Oh, fine."

"I can't imagine you not working," he said. "Must've had a lot of time on your hands."

She looked away. Tom had the unnerving habit of looking into her eyes, as if reading her thoughts.

"So," he said. "You got here on Tuesday to find the Governor had had a car accident that morning." He paused. "Except now you think it wasn't an accident."

"Yes." She'd already told him about the woman in the Provo restaurant, who'd said the Governor was going to confess, and that's why they had to stop him.

"Then there was a dinner party that night at the Governor's Residence," he went on. "And later that night, a local lady called Mrs Pearson, was murdered."

"Yes. She was found hanging by her feet at home in the garage, with her throat cut."

"Jesus!"

She nodded. "Shocking isn't it? Her husband, the Minister Clement Pearson, hanged himself in that same garage, a few weeks ago. The inquest confirmed suicide."

Tom paused to think. "Pretty brutal way to kill someone. Hanging them up by their feet and cutting their throat." He hesitated. "Why kill her like that?"

Jess shrugged. "I don't know. I've asked if that's ever happened here before. No-one's come up with anything yet."

"Hmm. There has to be a reason for such brutality. Unless of course that *was* the reason?"

She frowned at him.

"Perhaps the killer wanted to send a brutal message?" he explained. "Scare someone maybe?"

"He's done that all right," she said. "Scared the whole island."

Tom nodded. "You say the Minister was the murdered woman's husband, and that he committed suicide?"

"Yes, press reports said he was depressed after his son died of a drugs overdose."

He nodded. "Could that be what's going on here? Drugs?"

Jess shrugged. "I wondered that too, but these are small islands. Only a few people could afford hard drugs, so it couldn't be that lucrative a trade. Not enough to murder for, surely?"

"Unless the drugs are going through these islands on their way to the US market. That would earn megabucks for the traffickers." His eyes flashed. "And for those facilitating the trade here."

"Mm."

"I'm just speculating," he said, quickly.

"I'm going to ring London when I get back to Grand Turk, and ask them to send a UK police team over to investigate the Governor's car accident. They can assess local police resources and their response to Mrs Pearson's murder while they're here." She looked at him and gave an apologetic smile. "And you thought you were coming for a holiday?"

He smiled. "I'll do whatever I can to help. But I'm afraid I can only stay for three days. I have to be back at work next week, you see. The Illegal Immigration Task Force I'm working for have to include the findings from my overseas trip in their report for the PM. I'm a member of the panel presenting it to him next Friday.

Only three days. She felt deflated, especially after being so relieved to see him walk off that plane. Of course he had no locus in these islands to do any detective work, and wouldn't be able to do any actual investigating. But he'd be company, a friend she could trust. And right now, that's what she needed. "You don't have a problem flying, do you?" she asked, as their flight was called. "We have to go over to Grand Turk on propeller planes."

Those steely, grey eyes she remembered so well narrowed. "I'm an Australian Federal Agent. We fly everywhere on helicopters, single engine propeller planes and whatever else."

"You'll be right at home here, then, won't you?" she quipped.

On the flight over to Grand Turk, Jess stared out the window at the sugary sand banks popping up out of the sea. She tried to relax, but couldn't help worrying. She hadn't managed to get Sally on the phone, and she'd specifically told her to stay in the office.

On a single seat across the aisle from her, Tom sat remarkably still.

She glanced over and saw him drawing in his sketch pad, a habit she found both intriguing and irritating. She peered sideways to try and get a look at his drawing, but she couldn't quite see it. She hoped it wasn't of her.

It was impossible to talk much on the plane. Everyone was so quiet they would have heard everything. She settled back into the seat, but her head was buzzing. It wasn't just Sally she was worried about. Simon hadn't replied to any of her texts. She started sifting through the events of the last few weeks in her mind. Had there been any signs that something was wrong with him? Now that she thought about it, he had seemed rather preoccupied. And he'd been working later than usual. Was something wrong at work, perhaps? She hoped he was all right in Los Angeles. He'd call if he wasn't, wouldn't he? If she didn't hear from him soon, she could always ring his secretary in Washington to check he was okay.

It was a relief when the plane landed to be able to get off. The sun was still hot as they walked across the tarmac to Grand Turk's domestic terminal. She left Tom at the baggage carousel to wait for his suitcase while she went out to find Sally. She looked around, but there was no sign of her in the terminal.

Pushing through the door, she was relieved to see her pacing around on the pavement outside.

"Sally?" she called and waved.

Sally came rushing over.

It was only when she took off her sunglasses that Jess saw her red-rimmed eyes.

"It's the Governor." Sally's breath caught in her throat. "He p-passed away in hospital about an hour ago."

21

Maggie came straight out of the Residence the moment the car drew up outside, as if she'd been waiting by the window for them to come back.

Jess climbed out of the car and went over. The tears in Maggie's eyes said it all, and she put her arm around her. "I'm so sorry, Maggie."

Maggie pulled a handkerchief out of her uniform pocket and wiped her tears. They stood together in silence, until Jess looked over to the car and beckoned to Tom. "We have a guest, Maggie," she said, quietly. "Will you be able to look after him?"

Immediately Maggie straightened up and nodded.

Jess smiled at Tom as he walked over. She knew he felt awkward arriving at a time like this. "Tom," she said, brightly, "this is Maggie, our housekeeper. Maggie already knows who are you."

Maggie shook Tom's hand. "Come in," she said, warmly. "Please." She ushered him through the front door.

Tom stood in the hallway and looked at them in turn. "I'm really sorry about the Governor."

Jess nodded and put a reassuring hand on his arm. "And I'm sorry you've arrived in the middle of all this."

"I don't want to be in the way," he said, quickly.

She shook her head. "You won't be. I can assure you.

I'm very glad you're here. We all are." She turned to Maggie. "Did Sally ring about supper tonight? Only we can cancel it."

Maggie shook her head. "I've got everything in hand, Miss Jessica. It helps me, keeping busy."

Jess looked into Maggie's soulful eyes. "I don't know what we'd do without you?" She turned to Tom. "Can I leave you in Maggie's capable hands to settle in while I go back to the office and make some calls?"

He nodded. "Yep. You go and do what you have to do."

She looked up at the still cloudless sky. The sun had gone, leaving a soft, mellow light. "It's lovely on the beach at this time of day if you want a swim after all that travelling. But don't go out too far... there's no-one to help if you get into trouble."

He frowned at her, as if to say *are you serious?*

"Yes, I know you Australians live at the beach," she said. "But..."

He smiled. "No worries. I'll be careful."

"Right, Mister Tom. Follow me." Maggie looked relieved to have the distraction of another guest in the house. "I'll show you to your room."

Jess left them together, and returned to the car, where Sally sat silently, hands still gripping the wheel. "You okay, Sally?" she asked as she got in.

Sally nodded. "London rang to tell us about the Governor while you were in the air. I didn't know what to do."

Jess could still see shock on Sally's face. "I'm sorry I wasn't here when you got that news," she said, kindly.

That display of sympathy prompted the floodgates to open. Tears spilled down Sally's cheeks. "Poor Jayne, she'll be devastated... and the kids."

Jess felt a lump in her throat too. She hadn't known the Governor, but she knew exactly what his wife and children were going through right now. "At least Jayne was at his bedside when he died."

Sally nodded and wiped her eyes. "London asked if you could ring as soon as you got back."

Jess nodded. "I'll do that. Come on, let's go back to the office."

Sally turned the car round and headed back along the drive. "I got hold of the Police Commissioner. I told him about the Governor." She looked over for reassurance that she'd done the right thing.

Jess nodded.

"He asked me to ring him the moment you got back, and he'd come round."

Jess sighed inwardly with frustration. She'd tried to phone and text him several times during the day. Why hadn't he got in touch? That question was really bothering her. "Please phone him back and ask him to come here straightaway."

★

Dexter Robinson let out a tired sigh as he lowered his bulk into a chair, and placed his peaked hat on the Governor's conference table in front of him. He had the ever present beads of sweat on his forehead.

Jess had decided to see the Police Commissioner in the Governor's office. She wanted him to be under no illusion that he had to deal with her now. And, hopefully, being in a room he was used to would make him feel more at ease.

She noticed the tremor in his hand as he pulled his handkerchief from his uniform pocket and mopped his brow. His face looked drained.

"I'm sorry about the Governor." His voice was grave. "It's the worst possible news."

Jess nodded. "We knew he was badly injured in that accident, but we hoped... well, we hoped he'd pull through."

There was a pause while they both collected their thoughts.

"Has there been any decision about funeral arrangements?" he asked. "Will it be held here, or in the UK?"

"I haven't heard yet, but I expect it'll be at the Governor's home in the UK. We'll hold a memorial service for him here of course." She was thinking aloud now. "And we'll open a book of condolence in reception for people to come in and sign."

He nodded. "I'm sure the other islands will want to open one too, for people who can't get here."

"Of course."

As they talked about the Governor's death and all the arrangements, the Police Commissioner seemed to sink lower and lower into his chair. He looked exhausted, and had now lapsed into his customary silence. Jess was still irritated he hadn't kept in touch during the day, but she decided to try and work with him. He was a man of status in these islands, and well respected by the local people. She had to try and gain his trust. First, she wanted to know what he'd been doing all day. "We missed you at the hurricane planning meeting," she said.

He nodded. "I went over to Provo on an early plane, but I flew straight back. We had a problem with Mrs Pearson's daughter. She wasn't being very co-operative, and my officers wanted me to talk to her."

"Problem?" Jess asked.

He nodded. "She was the one who found her mother's body yesterday." He looked up. "Around midday, when we were up at the lighthouse."

Jess frowned. "Why didn't she find it earlier?"

"Oh, she doesn't live with her mother," he said. "She's married with a child of her own. She'd been ringing her mother all morning, and got no reply. So she picked her child up from the kindergarten around 11.30 for lunch, and drove up to her mother's house."

Jess could just imagine what a dreadful scene the poor woman had walked into. "Must have been terrible for her."

"Yes." He stopped. "Now, she refuses point blank to go back into the house. But if burglary was the reason for the murder, she's the only one who can tell us if there's anything missing. But she insists that she will never set foot in the house again."

"Do you think it might have been a burglary gone wrong?" Jess asked.

He looked down. "We're exploring all lines of enquiry at the moment. But there were no signs of a forced entry. The front door was closed as usual when the daughter turned up. She let herself in with her key." He sighed. "We're interviewing the domestic staff at the moment. They're Haitians."

Jess looked up. "Talking of Haitians," she said. "Your officers don't seem to be taking Mrs Canning's fears about her dog seriously. On my advice, she phoned yesterday to report that her dog's collar had been returned and left on her back patio. There were three so-called coffin nails punched into it."

He nodded, wearily. "Yes. I heard about it."

"So why didn't your officers take the collar away for examination? And why aren't they taking her safety seriously? It might seem like a simple voodoo joke to them, but don't forget she's the wife of the Chief Justice on this island. He's been responsible for jailing local criminals here, so this could be some kind of payback."

"Oh my officers don't think it's a joke." Dexter shook his head. "No, they were... nervous of handling the collar."

"Why? Because of the... curse those nails are supposed to bring with them?"

He nodded. "The local people don't really believe in voodoo, but that doesn't stop them being scared to get involved."

"It's their job," she said. "Would you please ask them to go back and get the collar and investigate the disappearance of Mrs Canning's dog properly?" She paused. "With everything that's gone on, we should be taking this curse, or rather the threat it conveys, more seriously. As the Chief Justice is away, don't you think it would be prudent to put a police guard on her house for a while?"

He sighed. "You're right, of course."

"And could you please keep me informed of developments on these investigations as they progress," she said, pointedly. "I have to report regularly to London." She paused as her mind turned to the Governor's car crash. How could she broach her suspicions that it wasn't an accident, without mentioning that woman in Provo and her warning. "Have you found the vehicle that hit the Governor's car yet?" she asked.

He shook his head. "No, my officers are still searching."

"Do you still think the stolen supermarket truck was involved?"

He nodded. "I do, because we can't find it. Someone has it well hidden."

She wondered just how difficult it could be to find a large supermarket truck on such a small island. "I find the whole incident bizarre," she said. "Why was the Governor driving down from the lighthouse in the early hours of the morning anyway? It seems his car and the truck were the only two vehicles on the road. Funny that they should hit each other, and that no-one saw anything." She paused. "Or have any witnesses come forward now?"

He shook his head. "No witnesses."

Why was she not surprised? "If the Governor's car was travelling as fast as you seem to think, Dexter, the impact would have been serious. Wouldn't the driver of the truck be injured too?"

"We've checked with the clinic and doctors on the island," he replied. "No-one has presented with injuries of that nature."

Something in the way he shifted on his seat before answering her last question suggested he wasn't telling the whole truth. "Are you sure it was an accident?" she asked, in a level voice.

His eyes widened briefly, then he replied: "I have a copy of the accident report for you." He grunted with the effort of bending down to his briefcase on the floor and pulled out a document. "The preliminary findings, anyway."

She got up and took the document. "What does it conclude?"

"That it was an accident," he said.

"An accident? How can it conclude it was an accident when you haven't found the other vehicle and driver yet?"

He went on: "The Governor's car which, as you know, he was driving himself, was travelling at a speed of almost 70mph. That is very fast on that downhill, single-lane stretch of road. At the only junction along that road, a truck coming from another direction ploughed into the driver's door. It was a serious impact. The Governor's car caught fire and, well, we know the rest."

Jess was pacing around the office now, thinking back to the wreck in the Government Garage. The sequence of events sounded plausible, and the damage reported seemed to correspond with what she'd seen. The car was burnt black, so it had been a serious fire. But how had the Governor got out alive?" She looked at Dexter. "I saw the Governor's car in the Government Garage last night. How did he get out of that blaze alive? Not out the driver's door, that's for sure, the metal was too buckled."

Dexter shifted again in his seat. "We think he climbed across the seat, and out the passenger door."

Jess turned that over in her mind. It was the impact that caused the serious injuries to the Governor, not burns from the fire that followed. If he'd been so badly injured at impact, how could he have climbed across the seat and got out the passenger door? She looked at Dexter.

But he just looked away.

Her mind turned to the argument that Sally had heard between Clement Pearson and the Governor just before Clement committed suicide. Again, she wouldn't tell the Police Commissioner about the argument, but she would ask him about the two men. "How well did the Governor and Clement Pearson know each other?"

"Very well," he replied. "They were colleagues."

"Did they get on well?"

"They were both gentlemen," he said, as if that answered her question.

So what were they arguing about, she wondered? And why? "There's a sequence of events here, Dexter, that are puzzling. First, Clement Pearson commits suicide. Why? Then the Governor has a serious car crash, and later dies. Then *Mrs* Pearson is brutally murdered. Again, why?" She paused. "These events are shocking. The question is, how are they connected?"

Dexter mopped his forehead again. It was too chilly in the cold air conditioning for him to be sweating this time. He was buying time to think.

"Do you know how they are connected?" she asked again. "Do you have *any* leads or motives?"

The colour had drained from Dexter's lips. "You're getting ahead of the investigation, Jess."

She sat back in the chair, and rubbed her eyes. She was getting nowhere.

"We need to be patient," he insisted, "and wait for the evidence to emerge."

But Jess had no more patience. She would definitely request UK police assistance, but she wanted Dexter to agree to this. "Have you got enough officers and resources to continue to investigate Mrs Pearson's murder as well as to find the vehicle and driver who killed the Governor?" Her words were rather blunt, but she wanted to shock Dexter into doing something. "The Governor's crash was a hit and run. So until you have found the truck and driver and established it really was an accident, don't you think we should keep an open mind?"

For a brief moment, she saw panic in his eyes.

Then he replied: "I am quite sure we can manage both the investigation into the Governor's accident, and Mrs Pearson's murder, with the resources and manpower we already have here."

"Can you, Dexter?" She knew it would be easier to bring UK police officers onto the island with his co-operation. He was the Police Chief, and commanded the respect of the locals. "Wouldn't it be helpful to have more boots to cover the ground? And more forensics, and other, experts."

The Police Commissioner said nothing.

She went on: "Once the British media get to know about the question marks still hanging over the Governor's car accident, *and* the horror of Mrs Pearson's murder, they'll be all over these islands. They'll poke into every nook and cranny until they get to the truth."

He stared at her.

"The pressure will be intense You do realise you'll be in the firing line if there's no quick resolution." She paused. "Wouldn't it be better to work with outside assistance to share the pressure and responsibility?"

She noticed the tremor in his hands again. He was clearly weighing her words up carefully in his mind, like the measured man he was.

After a while he said: "I am not requesting outside police assistance, Jess, but I can see that I won't be able to stop you. Nor can I stop London sending police officers to the island."

She nodded. She interpreted his words to mean that he didn't want to be *seen* by his own people to be requesting outside help. "Good," she said. "I'll request police assistance in the Governor's absence. To everyone outside this room, it will be a case of London sending assistance whether we want it or not."

The door creaked open and they both looked round.

Sally poked her head in. "The Director's on the phone for you, Jess."

The Police Commissioner took his cue and hauled himself wearily out of the chair.

"We need to be in constant contact, Dexter," she said. "I can't wait a whole working day for you to call me back. Likewise, I wouldn't expect you to wait that long for me either."

He nodded and picked up his hat. "Shall I call on you here every day at 5pm to discuss developments? If there's anything important you should know before then, I will telephone."

"Yes, thank you."

At the door he turned. "I am really sorry about the Governor, Jess. He was a good man at heart. I hope you will relay my sincere condolences to Jayne."

It was said with such sincerity, Jess believed him. The trouble was the Police Commissioner was a difficult man to read behind that quiet, unassuming manner. She also couldn't forget that scene in the café this morning. Roger Pearson looked like he was in complete control of Dexter Robinson. She'd already decided that she couldn't trust Roger, which meant she couldn't trust the Police Commissioner either.

She went back to the desk and picked up the phone.

22

Jess sat behind the Governor's desk waiting for Sally and Alvita. Outside, the light had faded, and the room was cast in shadows. The gloom matched her own mood. Only a couple of days ago the Governor had been sitting at this desk working. Now he was dead.

Not for the first time she wondered what kind of man he'd been. His office was an exact replica of his study in the Residence – same furniture, same book shelves, and same world globe. What did that say about him? Organised? Predictable? A safe pair of hands rather than a risk taker? She picked up the framed photo of Jayne and his two children sitting on the end of his desk. She could see it had been taken outside on the beach because the Residence was in the background. And she guessed the Governor had been behind the camera, because his family's eyes were so full of love.

Now, they would never see him again.

Tears welled up in her eyes. It had been four years since Jack and Amy had died in that terrible accident, and it still felt like yesterday.

At that moment, Sally and Alvita walked in. They looked at her and hesitated.

Jess put the photo back in its place and stood up. "Come in." She walked over to the conference table and gestured to them to sit down. "I was just looking at that photo of the Governor's wife and children." She sighed. "They'll never get over this tragedy."

Alvita nodded sadly, and sat down.

Jess went on: "I lost my husband and young daughter in a car crash while I was working in Jakarta, you see. So I know what they're going through."

Sally stared at her. "I had no idea, Jess."

"Why would you? It's not on my CV." She gave a sad smile. "Sometimes, things catch me unawares, like that family photo, and everything bubbles up."

"I'm sorry to hear that, Jess," Alvita said. "It's tough losing your family like that."

Sally didn't seem to know what else to say.

"Right," Jess said. "I'm okay now, so let's press on with some work." She paused. "Our Director in London just phoned from Cyprus. He's on holiday with his family there. That's why it's taken so long for him to call."

Alvita pursed her lips so tightly they almost disappeared.

"August is our holiday month in the UK," Jess explained. "Schools are on holiday, and officers try to take leave with their families. Departments operate a skeleton staff while everyone's away." She paused. "Anyway, the Director's breaking his holiday and flying back to the UK today to take charge of the situation."

"I should think so too," Sally said.

"Human Resources are trying to identify someone to take over the position of Governor," Jess said.

"That'll take ages!" Sally huffed.

"Yes. To find someone, and go through the accreditation process will take weeks. Meanwhile, the Director's trying to find a couple of officers to come down to help temporarily. Hopefully, they'll have some experience of working in an Overseas Territory."

Alvita raised her eyebrows. "No-one has ever known a thing about these islands before coming here."

Jess couldn't argue with that. "Yes, but when they do get here, we'll all need to work as a team." She was trying to send a message.

Alvita knew it was directed at her, and looked away.

Jess changed the subject. "Do we have a condolence book for the Governor?"

Sally nodded. "We always keep a spare one in case the Queen or Prime Minister pop their clogs."

"Well, let's put it on a small table in reception for the general public to come in and sign, alongside a framed photo of the Governor." Jess paused. "Can you take charge of all that, Alvita?"

Alvita looked interested now.

"Can you also place an advert in the local papers inviting people, and I mean everyone, not just dignitaries, to come and sign the condolence book?"

Alvita was warming to the task. "I'll ask the radio and TV broadcasters to advertise it too. And I'll put some flowers on the table."

"Good idea," Jess said. "The Police Commissioner thinks the other islands will want to open their own condolence books too." She paused. "As you know them best, Alvita, can I ask you to organise that directly with them?"

She nodded. "I'll find some more condolence books, and of course some fountain pens for signing. We must do this properly."

"Absolutely." Jess was pleased to see Alvita being co-operative. "And if you think of anything else we should be doing, please let me know."

Alvita went to get up.

"Before you go," Jess said, quickly. "I want you both to know I've asked for a British police team to come over and help."

Alvita looked up, sharply.

Jess wasn't going to tell them yet of her suspicions about the Governor's accident. "The Police Commissioner feels he has enough resources here to do the job, but I think they may need extra help investigating Mrs Pearson's murder." She looked at Alvita. "How are the locals bearing up?"

Alvita spoke slowly. "They're shocked and frightened, but they have faith in *our* police to catch the killer." She paused. "Don't you, Jess?"

Jess hesitated. "I just think resources will be overstretched, and that it would help to have forensics and other experts to help out. You know, once the British media get wind of it, they'll be over here like a shot. They'll dig around this island until they find out the truth." She paused. "It was my decision to point this out to London, and request police assistance."

"Do you have the authority to do that?" Alvita asked.

"Yes." Jess paused. "Now I don't want either of you talking to anyone outside the office about this. No speculation, and no gossip please."

Alvita gave Jess a look she couldn't quite read. "These islands may be under British rule, Jess, but they don't operate like the UK." She seemed to be choosing her words carefully. "There's a certain... *order* to them. If you rock the boat too hard, you may capsize it. Then everyone will drown."

The words were spoken in a level voice, without a hint of malice, but Jess got the distinct impression it was a warning. Or was it a threat?

There was a pause.

Alvita took the opportunity to get up. "Sorry, but I have to get home."

Jess just let her go.

Sally jumped up. "We've got to go too, Jess. It's nearly 6.30. Everyone will be at the Residence in half an hour for dinner."

Oh God, yes, Jess thought. Another dinner. She looked at Sally's weary face and dark eyes. "I'd understand if you wanted to drop out this evening. You look tired."

"Oh no." Sally shook her head. "I don't want to be at home on my own, I'll only brood about everything."

Was Sally afraid to be in the house alone after Mrs Pearson's murder, Jess wondered? "You can come and stay at the Residence for a few nights if you'd like to. Until things settle down a bit."

Sally's face brightened. "But you've got your policeman there."

"He's not *my* policeman. Anyway, there's plenty of room for you too, if you'd prefer not to be on your own."

Sally's face was saying she'd like nothing more than to stay at the Residence, but still she hesitated.

Was Sally worried about intruding? "I won't take no for answer," Jess said, firmly. "I'd like you to stay with me until all this is over."

"Well, if you're sure," Sally said. "I've got a change of clothes in my office. I keep them here to save me going home if I'm invited out unexpectedly in the evening."

"Right, well you go and get them while I lock these papers away. We can walk over together."

While Sally went to get her clothes, Jess sat down at the Governor's desk again, trying to make sense of everything. If only he were here to explain himself. If that woman in Provo could be believed, he'd been about to confess to something. What? He'd had a brilliant career, a top job, and a lovely family. Why would he do anything to jeopardise that? Of course if this was about drug running through the islands, as Tom thought it might be, huge sums of money would be involved.

That's when it occurred to her that if drugs were finding their way from the Turks and Caicos into the US, the authorities over there would have got wind of it. In which case, the US National Security Agency were probably monitoring all their phone and internet communications. If the NSA knew about it, the CIA would too. Could any of the Americans down here, or locals even, be working for the CIA, she wondered?

If only she could have a chat with Simon, he'd start digging straightaway. She looked at her watch. Los Angeles was three hours behind the Turks and Caicos, it was just after lunch there. She picked up the phone and dialled his mobile. When it immediately switched to voicemail, she hung up without bothering to leave another message. She'd left enough already. She would just ring his office in Washington, and make sure everything was okay.

For some reason, she had butterflies in her stomach when she picked up the phone again and dialled his office. Being on the same time zone, she hoped Simon's secretary would still be there at 6.30. They both usually worked until seven. But the phone just rang and rang. She was about to hang up when a female voice came on the line: "British Embassy switchboard."

"Oh hi, I was trying to ring Simon Hill's office," Jess said.

There was a pause. "Sorry Ma'am, he's on leave right now."

On leave? For a moment Jess didn't know what to say. "He's... he's working in Los Angeles, isn't he?"

"It says on my chart that he's on leave until 3 September, Ma'am."

Two weeks' leave? That couldn't be true, surely? "Do you know if he's on local leave in Washington?" she asked. "Or has he gone away?"

"I'm afraid I don't know, Ma'am."

Jess's mind was racing in all directions. "Well, can I speak to his secretary, if she's still there?"

"Just a moment, Ma'am."

As she waited, Jess's heart was pounding.

The switchboard operator came back on. "Sorry Ma'am, she's on leave too."

Jess tried to steady her voice. "Do you have a contact number for him? I need to talk to him urgently. I'm his..." Jess stopped. How could she say she was his partner? What a fool she'd look when she didn't even know he was on leave.

"I'm sorry Ma'am, I can't help you," the telephonist said. "But if you phone back in the morning and speak to the Management Officer, he may be able to give you more information."

23

Tom Sangster took another sip of cold, white wine. It felt weird to be in the Governor's dining room with a bunch of people he'd never met before, on an island he'd never heard of before going to Miami. Surrounded by antique furniture, gilt-framed paintings, and a table covered with sparkling china that could have come straight out of Buckingham Palace, it was like being on a film set.

Except this was no fantasy island, this was real.

Jess smiled from the other end of the table, as if reading his thoughts. She'd probably had the same reaction when she arrived. Now, she seemed to fit right in.

He pressed the cold glass to his cheek to get some relief from the stifling heat. Had no-one thought of installing air conditioning? He put the glass down, and rubbed the back of his neck with the same hand to cool down. He didn't think anyone had noticed until Jess smiled at him again.

"Stuffy in here, isn't it?" she said. "Believe me. It's better than being eaten by mozzies out in the courtyard."

"Too right." Sally scratched her arms.

"Mozzies don't like my blood," Tom replied.

"Lucky you!" Sally groaned. "Anyway you're probably immune, from spending your life having barbies at the beach."

Jess laughed. "Australians don't spend their *entire* lives at the beach, Sally."

"We would if we could," Tom joked.

"Well *I* do," Brad piped up.

Everyone laughed.

"Do you dive, Tom?" Brad went on. "I'd be happy to take you out."

Tom smiled. "I love to dive, but I don't have any gear with me."

"No worries, mate," Brad joked. "I'll fit you out. How long are you here for?"

"Only a few days," Tom replied.

Brad nodded. "Leave it with me."

They fell silent as Maggie came in with a large oval platter of a local chicken and rice dish.

"Put it in the middle of the table, Maggie," Jess said. "We'll help ourselves."

Tom watched Jess in these unfamiliar surroundings. He felt he knew her well, but in truth he knew little about her life. He didn't even know where she'd been born, or if she had any family, or what books she read, or what music she liked. He tried not to stare because she knew he studied faces, and she didn't like him sketching her. No wonder, he thought, after that one he did of her in Australia, with blank eyes. She'd been like some ice queen back then. Of course he hadn't known about her husband and child.

At Miami Airport the other day, he was surprised at how happy she looked. Now, her face was tired and drawn. Not only that, there was sadness in her eyes again.

Brad interrupted his thoughts. "So what do you do for a living, Tom?"

"I work for the police." Judging by the lack of reaction around the table, he guessed everyone already knew. "The Federal Police, in Canberra."

"Is that where you and Jess met?" Brad asked.

"No." He wondered how much Jess would want her guests to know about her. "We met on a murder case involving a British citizen in Brisbane."

"So, you are colleagues?"

Was Brad trying to suss out his relationship with Jess, Tom wondered?

Jess intervened. "We *were* colleagues. I was the British Consul in Australia at the time. Now, Tom and I are friends."

Tom smiled at that.

"What does a Consul do?" Rebekah asked.

"A Consul is responsible for the protection of British citizens," Jess replied. "If a Brit gets into trouble in a country, the Consul's job is to try and help them. They'll liaise with the local police on any investigation, and with the next of kin or relatives of whoever is in trouble."

"Why don't we have a Consul here?" Rebekah sounded petulant. "God knows we need one."

"Because we *are* the Government," Jess replied.

"Huh! Dom says no-one in London gives a *toss* about these islands."

Jess couldn't disagree with her.

When the conversation fell silent again, Tom had a mouthful of fried chicken. It was a simple dish, with rice and vegetables, but it hit the spot.

On the wall behind Jess hung a painting of a former Governor, with wrinkles and grey hair. People wouldn't be used to having a woman in charge here, he thought, especially a younger woman. Just how old was Jess? She hadn't changed in the two years since he'd seen her. Back then he'd thought she was in her mid to late thirties. She was still slim, and her hair blonder than he remembered.

He noticed her attractive brown eyes were alertly watching everyone, including him.

She might not be the Governor, but she was definitely in charge. He could tell that by the way Sally stopped having a pop at Rebekah immediately Jess gave her a pointed look. Rebekah too had insisted on having a private word with Jess when she arrived, and seemed calmer after their chat. What was that all about, he wondered?

It didn't escape his attention that Jess moved the wine bottle out of Sally and Rebekah's reach at every opportunity. It was clear those two ladies liked the grog.

Even the American twins, Brad and Charles, deferred to Jess when she spoke. They were an interesting pair, and Tom itched to pick up his pad and pencil to capture them on paper. Apart from their hair, their features were identical, yet their personalities so different.

Brad looked at ease in his surroundings. Charming and funny, he kept the conversation flowing, without mentioning any of the recent troubles. Tom could see Jess was grateful for that. Brad acted like a man who breezed through life. Running his own dive company, he obviously spent his days doing what he loved. Most of the beach guys back home with ponytails and sun-tans were bludgers on the social. Brad was not in that category.

Tom became aware of a trickle of sweat running down his back, and hoped it wouldn't seep through his shirt. Brad on the other hand, dressed in that colourful Hawaiian shirt over his trousers, didn't even look hot.

Brad's twin Charles was different altogether. He had the same bright blue eyes and laconic smile, but his hair was short and dark. He was a New York banker, according to Jess. She thought Charles financed the brothers' dive business. He certainly looked like a highly paid executive, with his flabby paunch and expensive clothes. He had a dead pan expression. Poker-face, that's what Jess had called him. He was sharp too. A little too sharp for Tom's liking. Many of his quips were more cutting than clever. Had the two brothers been educated at the same school or university, he wondered? Of course, it wasn't unusual for one son in a family to be brighter than the other. Did that apply to twins too?

The most interesting thing about Charles was his preoccupation with Rebekah. He barely said anything to anyone else. Whenever he wasn't eating, his arm lay possessively along the back of her chair. He fussed over her and leant closer whenever he could. Rebekah on the other hand, alternated between leaning into him and moving away, as if she couldn't decide which way to turn. Tom wasn't surprised to see her there without her Chief Justice husband, because Jess said they were all friends. But Rebekah's obvious relationship with Charles intrigued him.

Those two have been between the sheets, he thought. No doubt about that. Rebekah was gorgeous, and spoke with a posh English accent. Anyone could see she was high maintenance, though. He couldn't be doing with a woman like that. Jess said Rebekah's husband was away at a conference in London. And it looked like Charles had stepped effortlessly into his shoes in his absence. The pair of them were comfortable, as if they'd known each other for some time. Everyone else around the table seemed to accept their obvious closeness too.

Tom tried to engage Charles in conversation. "So what do you do, Charles?" he asked, for something to say, even though he knew.

Charles looked over. "I'm one of those boring bankers that everyone has loved to hate since the recession."

"Only since the recession?" Tom raised his eyebrows in mock surprise. "Bankers have been loathed in Australia for decades."

"It's true." Jess laughed. "Aussie banks even put out funny adverts on the basis that they are the root of all evil."

The smile Charles gave didn't reach his eyes.

He didn't like that, Tom thought. This man takes himself seriously. "Do you ever do business in Sydney?" he asked.

Charles shook his head. "I've visited a couple of times, but I'm more interested in the big players, like London, Frankfurt and Tokyo."

It was a put down; but Tom didn't bite. Something just didn't seem right about these two Regan brothers, not in a place like this. He couldn't quite work out what it was as he sat watching and listening. Of course he had no jurisdiction to do any police work, and he wouldn't cause trouble for Jess, but he thought he might ask the guys back home to run a few discreet checks on her American guests. It would be interesting to see what they came up with.

He took another sip of wine. The old timbers around the house creaked as they contracted after the heat of the day. Good job the air was so humid, or any small flame could send this old place up like a box of matches, he thought. In the dry heat back home, eucalyptus trees could spontaneously combust. It was nature's way of renewing itself.

His ears pricked up as he heard voices along the hallway: he thought Maggie was working alone in the kitchen. He looked up. No-one else around the table seemed to have heard anything. Then it went quiet out there again.

Concentrating back on Jess's guests, he found it weird that the conversation seemed contrived not to touch on anything upsetting. Hadn't Jess said they were getting together because everyone *was* upset. So why weren't they talking about the murder, or the Governor's death? He couldn't help but notice they were all watching each other closely too.

Aside from his eyes on Rebekah, Charles kept glancing at his brother Brad. Why? The Governor's PA Sally was all over Brad, touching his arm or shoulder, laughing a little too much at his jokes, whereas Brad hardly said a word to her. The only person *he* seemed to have eyes for was Jess. He'd assumed the role of host, filling up glasses with wine, offering more food, and generally looking after everyone. Very presumptuous of him.

The only person who appeared normal in this group was the American girl, Carrie, who sat on his right. Most of the time, she sat listening quietly to the conversation. He found it hard to study her without turning and making it obvious, but he'd felt her eyes on him from time to time. She was pretty, tall, and blonde. He wondered about her. "So what brought you down to Grand Turk, Carrie?" he asked.

She smiled at him with perfect white teeth. "I run the local kindergarten. My story's much like Brad's. I came down to Grand Turk on a diving vacation, and fell in love with the place. I quit my teaching job in the States and opened a kindergarten here." She paused. "There wasn't one, you see."

"When was that?" he asked.

"Seven years ago."

"*Seven* years?"

She gave him a playful look. "Why should that surprise you?"

"Don't you miss the nightlife, the shopping, the hustle and bustle of the States?"

She gave a small laugh. "I go to Miami regularly. I've opened another kindergarten over there. They do lots of fund raising around the States to help us here with money, books and crayons, that kind of thing. From time to time, I take the little ones and their parents to Miami for a special party or event. Sometimes the American children and their families come here. There are lots of exchanges," she said proudly. "It's going well."

He smiled. "Are your family over there too?"

She shook her head. "I haven't spent all my life in America, Tom. I was brought up in Africa, mostly. My family are still there."

"In Africa?"

She nodded. "My father gave up his teaching job when I was young to become a missionary. He took my mother and me with him. So you see, I'm more used to a simple way of life than the greedy excesses of America."

It was said lightly, but her words didn't ring true somehow. She seemed self-assured, and at ease around that table, as if she were more used to wining and dining in fashionable restaurants than sitting in mud huts in Africa. Perhaps she was just comfortable in her own skin? Perhaps she was the kind of person who was comfortable in any social situation? "Which African country did you live in?" he asked.

"In Ghana, mostly, and Nigeria."

"Ah, so you'll know a bit about voodoo, then? Am I right in thinking it came over to the Caribbean with the slaves from West Africa?"

A frown flitted across Carrie's face. "Yes."

"So what do you make of what's going on here? Jess told me about the missing pets, the sacrifices, and strange ceremonies on the beach in the night."

Carrie looked at him. "Nearly every voodoo service has an animal sacrifice. By killing the animal, life is released. The theory is the spirits receive the life sacrificed to them and are rejuvenated."

"So it's okay to take people's pets?"

She shook her head. "That's just gossip. Voodoo is more about healing people's illnesses with herbs – a kind of faith healing."

"And what about black magic?"

"Voodoo is a peaceful, happy religion," she said, patiently. "I grant you there is black magic voodoo, but it's banned here."

"Tell me about it," he said.

"Well..." she glanced around the table.

He followed her gaze and saw that everyone else was listening too.

"Perhaps we should have dessert now," Jess said, loudly.

"Please," Tom persisted. "I'd like to know more from Carrie about voodoo."

Carrie shrugged. "Black magic is the voodoo of angry and mean spirits. It's all about death curses, zombies and... wild sex orgies."

"Ah!" Tom smiled. "So *that's* what's going on of a night on the beach."

Carrie looked serious. "The human mind is strange, Tom. If people believe in black magic voodoo, then it's real to them. And that makes it dangerous."

Rebekah flung her napkin on the table. "Those *bastards* took my Benji!"

"Benji's her dog," Carrie whispered to Tom.

Rebekah choked "N-now they're coming for me too."

Tom felt his jaw drop, literally.

Jess explained: "Yesterday, Benji's dog collar turned up outside Rebekah's on the patio. It had three coffin nails punched into it."

"Exactly!" Rebekah exclaimed. "Coffin nails are a voodoo curse. It means I'm going to die the same death as my Benji. And he was *sacrificed*, I'm sure of it."

Tom thought the woman had completely lost it.

"Come on, Rebekah." Charles put his arm around her. "You know nothing like that is going to happen to you."

"It *will*. I know it will." As Rebekah pushed him away, she knocked her glass of red wine over. It ran right across the table's shiny surface and straight into Sally's lap.

"Oi," squealed Sally, as she pushed her chair back, and glared at Rebekah.

Rebekah stared back, then stood up: "I've got something to tell you all."

"*Rebekah!*" Charles put a firm hand on her arm.

Rebekah shrugged it off. "I'm *going* to say it."

There was a hushed pause.

"*Please Rebekah…*"

"Charles and I are in love," she said, dramatically.

An embarrassed silence followed.

Charles stood pale and rigid.

Tom looked over at Jess in horror, realising his talk of voodoo had been like throwing a hand grenade at her guests.

"Jess told me to be truthful about the affair," Rebekah insisted.

"I meant *with the police*," Jess replied.

"Your poor husband," Sally said, bluntly. "No wonder he's gone off to London. Who wouldn't want to get away from you two?"

Rebekah tossed her head. "Dom doesn't know about us."

"Of course he bloody well knows," Sally said, as she wiped her wine-soaked dress with her napkin. "We all know. It was obvious. *Staring* into each other's eyes all the time. *Touching* each other. You humiliated that poor man."

"Listen to that… that *strumpet* over there," Rebekah flung back at Sally, "with her boobs hanging out. She can't *stop* touching Brad!"

"*Enough!*" Jess stood up.

Rebekah slumped back down on her chair.

Even Charles was at a loss for words.

At that moment there was a cry from the kitchen, followed by a crash.

Everyone looked at each other.

Tom jumped up, ran down the hallway and into the kitchen, to see a smashed bowl of trifle splattered across the floor, and Maggie kneeling beside it with her head in her hands.

He put a hand on her shoulder. "Are you all right, Maggie?"

She looked with fearful eyes at the back door.

"Who was it?" he asked.

Maggie shook her head, and covered her face with her hands.

Tom ran outside, in time to see a figure disappearing into the bushes along the beach.

★

Tom laid his head back on the rattan chair, and flapped a mosquito away from his ear. The stillness of the tropical night belied the turmoil inside his head. What must Jess think of him? She'd been so careful to keep the conversation light. Then he'd pushed Carrie to talk about voodoo, and caused a real blow up.

Then there was that crash in the kitchen.

The kitchen door squeaked open. Jess came out and flopped down in the chair next to him. "They've all gone, thank goodness. And Sally's gone to bed, still moaning about her dress."

"I'm sorry, Jess." He was anxious to apologise. "I shouldn't have gone on about voodoo."

She touched his arm, gently. "Don't worry. Something was going to set Rebekah off tonight. It was just a matter of time."

"What a drama queen!"

Jess nodded, as she slipped off her shoes. "Except I know deep down she's really worried about her dog, and that voodoo curse. And about her affair with Charles."

"Do you think her husband knows?"

Jess nodded. "Rebekah wants to believe he doesn't. But he's too smart not to have worked it out." She paused. "Rebekah told me their marriage was toxic. Strange word to use, I thought – *toxic*." She shrugged. "Anyway she came clean about her affair with Charles when we had that private chat before supper. What she didn't know is that I'd already seen them kissing when they thought were alone."

Tom nodded. "She's very stressed. I could see it in her eyes. It's like she's about to snap, if you know what I mean?"

They fell silent with their own thoughts, until he asked: "Has Maggie said any more about what happened in the kitchen?"

Jess shook her head. "She's sticking to her story that she was working with her back to the door, and didn't see or hear whoever came in."

He gave her a sceptical look.

"I know it doesn't make sense, Tom. But I saw fear in her eyes."

Tom could see nothing but weariness in Jess's, but he had to tell her the truth. "I heard voices in the kitchen way before any scream or smashed crockery."

Her face fell. "Are you saying Maggie's *lying*?"

"I was closest to the door." He paused. "And I definitely heard raised voices before Maggie cried out."

Jess stared at him. "You mean she was *arguing* with someone?"

He nodded. "I'm not sure if it was a man or woman. They were quite a way off."

Jess sank back into the chair and stared into the distance. "Is there *no-one* I can trust?"

The sad way she said that really unsettled him.

Laying her head back on the seat, she looked up at the night sky and flapped away a mosquito.

Tom glanced at a cloud of hypnotised insects swarming around the single strip light over the patio bar. They really had a mosquito problem on this island.

"Well, there's nothing more we can do tonight, Tom," she said. "Fancy a nightcap?"

He smiled. "Thought you'd never ask."

She went to get up. "There's an open bottle of wine in the fridge."

He put a hand on her shoulder. "You stay there." He got up and went back into the kitchen. He was surprised to see Maggie had washed up and cleared the kitchen before leaving, despite her fright. The only remains of dinner was a stickiness underfoot where the trifle had landed. He lifted the bottle of wine out of the fridge and was just closing the door when he heard a voice in the house. He listened. It had to be Sally. Everyone else had gone.

He went over to the door and peered down the hall.

Sally's recognisable voice floated down from upstairs.

"We must tell Jess," Sally whispered. "We can't keep her in the dark."

Tom instinctively pressed himself against the wall so as not to be seen.

"You *promised* you'd come over," Sally whined. "What does it matter if I'm staying at the Residence?"

Sally was on her mobile, on the landing above. Must be a better signal there than in her bedroom, he thought. But it was the urgency in her voice that made him want to listen.

"Oh all *right!*" She sounded peeved now. "It'll have to be later, after Jess and her cop have gone to bed." She paused. "I'll meet you at the moorings. What time?"

Sally must have hung up after that because it went quiet. Tom waited until he heard her footsteps cross the landing and the latch of her bedroom door close. Interesting, he thought, as he went back into the kitchen. He picked up two glasses from the kitchen table and held them up to the light to check they were clean.

Outside, Jess had moved onto the small rattan sofa, and was now lying stretched out on her back. Her blonde hair fanned out over the cushion at one end and her tanned legs dangled over the other. Eyes closed, she lay still, as if asleep. She looked lovely, lying there, with her skirt ridden up over her thighs. He felt a tightness in his throat.

She opened her eyes. "I'm so glad you're here, Tom."

"Because I've got the wine?" he joked to cover his confusion.

She laughed, sat up and tucked her legs under her. "You know I've often wondered how you're getting on."

He looked at her.

"I've found it hard to forget that awful time in Brisbane." She paused and smiled at him. "So, tell me, how has life been treating you?"

"Well..." He put the glasses down on the table, and poured the wine. He was going to tell her about Sally's conversation, except she looked in such need of sleep, he thought he'd find out what Sally was up to himself first. "I've told you most of it," he went on. "I got promoted after our Brisbane caper and was sent to work for the Feds in Canberra." He shook his head in disbelief. "Who would have thought it? Me, a Federal Agent!"

"Why not? You're good at your job." She hesitated. "I still have nightmares about that maniac... I'm running through the streets of Brisbane with him after me... I wake up when I feel the bullet pierce my skin." She shivered. "Did they ever find his body in the river?"

"Nah." Tom handed her a glass of wine. "I told you he'd be feed for the sharks."

A shadow came over her face. "I wish his body *had* been found. At least we'd be certain."

"We *are* certain," Tom said, firmly. "He can't have survived."

She took a sip of wine.

Now they were at ease with each other, he took the opportunity to say something more personal. "You know, when I saw you at Miami Airport the other day, it was the first time I'd ever seen you looking... relaxed."

"Thanks," she said, drily.

"Sorry, that didn't come out right." He paused to find the words. "They were difficult times on that murder case. We were both exhausted..."

"And scared."

"And scared," he repeated. "So when I saw you, I felt pleased you were happy, especially after everything you've been through. But tonight, Jess, I have to say you look... sad again."

She stared at him. "You're not doing another sketch of me, are you?"

"No, definitely not."

She looked away. "Everything's fine. It's just this place."

The way she averted her eyes made him think everything was *not* fine.

She slapped her ankle. "These bloomin' mozzies!"

He sat back in his chair, knowing the moment had passed.

"*Damn!* I've just remembered I still haven't emailed those photos to London."

"Photos?" He looked at her.

"Yes, I went to the Government Garage last night to see the Governor's car. What a wreck! I took some photos and downloaded them onto my laptop to email to London. Would you like to see them?"

He nodded.

"Come on then." She slipped her feet back in her shoes. "My laptop's in his study." She picked up her glass. "Bring your wine. At least we won't get bitten in there."

Following her inside, he glanced up at the landing, but there was no sign of Sally this time. He went into the study and closed the door. He'd already had a look in this room on his way down to dinner. His police training had taught him to recce his surroundings thoroughly.

Jess sat down at her laptop on the Governor's desk. As she powered up and scrolled through to find the photos, he strolled over to the bookcase and scanned the titles. All the British classics you would expect in a Governor's office, plus books on the Caribbean, volumes of poetry, and reference books. A large map took his interest...

"Oh, they've gone!"

He turned round.

"The photos," Jess said. "They're not here."

"Must be there, somewhere," he said.

"They're not," she said, quietly. "They've been deleted." She pushed her chair back, went over to the sofa and started searching frantically in her bag. "I downloaded copies onto my memory stick too. Now where is it?" She found it and inserted it into the computer. "Here we are," she said, as the photos popped up. "Take a look." She got up.

He slipped into the seat and started to look through the photos. "Wow, that's a helluva smash!"

"Mm."

"Have you got the police accident report?"

"Yes."

"Mind if I read it?"

She pulled the report from some papers in the desk tray and handed it to him.

"Tell you what, I'll have a read through," he said. "Then I'll go and take a look at the car in the morning."

She frowned. "It's at the Government Garage. I don't think they're just going to let you walk in and take a look at it."

"I'll think of something to tell them." He glanced over. "I won't push it, if I'm not welcome."

"Oh, I'm not sure, Tom." She didn't sound convinced.

"Don't worry. It'll be fine."

She sank down onto the sofa. "I'd like to know who deleted those photos from my laptop."

"Maggie would know if someone's been in here, wouldn't she?"

"Yes, but would she tell me?" Jess sounded weary. "If you're going to do some detective work, even in an unofficial capacity, you'd better know exactly what you're up against, Tom."

He sat down on the sofa next to her. His thigh was touching hers, but she didn't move away.

She pushed her hair back off her exhausted face. "I keep thinking about what that woman said in Provo today. She couldn't stand the lies any more. The awful *deceit* is how she described it. Then she said the Governor was going to confess, and that's why they'd had to stop him." She paused. "Whoever *they* are."

He nodded. "You already told me about her."

She sighed. "I wish I knew what she'd meant. You know, the more I think about everything, the more I think this all started with the suicide of Clement Pearson."

He looked at her.

"Clement called on the Governor hours before he took his own life. He just turned up around 5pm that afternoon. The rest of the staff had gone, except Sally. The Governor insisted she leave too. But, halfway home, she realised she'd forgotten her keys and came back to get them. That's when she heard the two men arguing."

"What about?"

Jess shrugged. "Sally said she was too nervous to stay and listen. She just picked up her keys and left. But it was later that evening, or rather in the early hours of the following morning, that Clement committed suicide."

"So we've no idea what the row was about?"

She shook her head. "And now both Clement and the Governor are dead."

He put his arm across the back of the sofa. "Convenient that, isn't it?"

She nodded. "These deaths fit together somehow, I just don't know how."

He was quiet for a while. "Was anyone else in the office when they had that row?"

"Sally said the staff had gone home." Jess paused. "But there's a lady called Alvita, who often stays late. She heads the local staff. It's always possible she was still around."

"Have you talked to her?"

Jess shook her head. "She's not exactly helpful."

"What about the police?" he asked. "Have you talked to them?"

"Hardly. If the islanders don't trust them enough to be able to speak out, how can I?"

"Well, we'll just have to do a bit of digging ourselves." He looked around. "And we could start with this study."

Jess looked shocked.

"This is the first place I'd search if it were my investigation, starting with the Governor's desk." He got up from the sofa. "You do it, if you feel more comfortable."

Jess really didn't want to go poking around the Governor's private study. It felt like too much of an intrusion.

"Go on," he urged.

She sighed and got up. "What am I looking for?" She went over to the desk.

"Anything unusual. Or anything that looks like it doesn't belong here." He went over to the bookcase and started searching the cupboards below.

They worked together, silent and methodical.

Tom found nothing of interest in the cupboards and started on the shelves. Pulling the books out in turn, he tipped them upside down to see if anything fell out.

"Look at this, Tom."

He turned to see Jess holding up a tiny brass key.

"It doesn't fit any of the desk locks," she said.

"Try these cupboards." He pointed to the ones under the book shelves he was searching. "There's a keyhole in the door."

She went over, and pushed the key in the lock. "Nope. Doesn't fit."

Suddenly, a piece of paper fluttered to the carpet as Tom shook out one of the books.

Jess bent down and picked it up. "I've seen this writing before," she said, quickly. She went over to her handbag and rummaged inside until she pulled out another piece of paper and unfolded it. "I found this under the lighthouse steps." She held the two papers side by side. "They're the same!"

Tom peered over her shoulder. "Looks like a letter." He started reading it out loud.

"My Darling,

Words cannot describe how much I love you and the children, and how truly sorry I am. I've been a fool. I've betrayed you and everything I hold most dear. I have to explain in a letter because I don't know when I will see you again. I hope one day you will be able to forgive me..."

"It's an unfinished letter," Jess said, as she turned both papers over.

He frowned. "Looks like someone's had several goes at writing it. There are lots of crossings out." He stared at her. "By the look on your face, this means something to you."

"It's the *Governor's* writing," she said, excitedly. "I don't know why I didn't recognise it before, it's all over the files. It's a letter to his wife, Jayne, asking for her forgiveness." She paused. "So that woman in the restaurant was right. He *was* going to confess to something."

Tom frowned. "But why would he leave something like this at the lighthouse?"

Jess shrugged. "Perhaps he dropped it, and couldn't find it in the dark?"

"So what's up there, at this lighthouse?"

"It's just a lighthouse. A working lighthouse, to warn ships about the north-west reef." She went over to her bag again, pulled out the Miami newspaper article and handed it to him. "Read this."

He read the headline out loud. "Turks and Caicos Minister commits suicide."

"It's about Clement Pearson," she added.

He read on, then looked up: "I know about this. It says he was found hanged in his garage by his wife... according to this he was suffering from depression after the death of his son due to a drugs overdose."

"Forget that bit. Read on!"

Tom looked back at the newspaper cutting and continued reading out loud. "Earlier that day he'd been giving evidence to the British Government Inquiry into illegal immigration and the sinking of two Haitian sloops off Grand Turk recently. Speculation is increasing that the pressure of the Inquiry added to the Minister's fragile state of mind." Tom stopped and looked at her.

"There's a copy of that Inquiry report in the Governor's Office," she said. "The sloops went down *off* the north-west reef, despite the lighthouse being there to warn them to stay clear."

His eyes widened.

"Let's think about the sequence of events." She paused. "Clement Pearson gives evidence to the Government Inquiry about the sinking of the Haitian sloops. Later that afternoon, he turns up at the Governor's Office and there's an argument. That night Clement commits suicide."

Tom nodded. "Then, days later, the Governor goes up to the lighthouse in the middle of the night. Why? And why would he take a half-written letter with him?"

"I don't know." She ran her fingers through her hair. "Maybe he was upset about the sloops, and somehow felt compelled to go up to the lighthouse." She paused. "I know I would have been if I'd been Governor at the time. All those people losing their lives. Maybe he couldn't sleep and it was playing on his mind."

"Yes, but why take this letter up there?" he asked.

"Maybe he didn't take it up there? Maybe he was trying to write it up there." She paused. "That article says speculation was increasing that the pressure of the Inquiry added to Clement Pearson's state of mind, suggesting it drove him over the edge to commit suicide."

He looked at her. "So?"

"So, maybe the Governor felt responsible for that? Perhaps the pressure of the Inquiry was getting to him too. And that's why he was up there."

He nodded. "Maybe."

"The thing is, Tom. If that crash was no accident, then someone else must have known the Governor was up there." She paused. "And that person must have planned to kill him on his way back down."

24

Tom lay naked on the bed in the dark under the mosquito net. He wouldn't normally bother with a net, but the mozzies on this island were a real pest. Above him, the creaking ceiling fan was getting on his nerves, but it was also helping him stay awake.

Finally, he heard a click. It was the softest of sounds, but exactly what he'd been waiting for. He lifted up the side of the mosquito net and got out of bed. Stepping into his shorts, he slipped his t-shirt over his head and listened.

The top stair creaked.

He waited, lifted his door latch, and peered out. All clear. Creeping across the landing, he heard the familiar squeak as the back door opened and closed again.

He ran quietly down the stairs and into the kitchen. Opening the back door, he peered out. All clear again.

The air felt cooler as he stepped outside. He took a deep breath, and looked at his watch – 12.30. It was almost a full moon that lit up the sky, making it easy to see his way. He slipped across the garden, and onto the beach.

In the distance, he caught sight of Sally walking towards the boat moorings.

Following her, he ducked in and out of the bushes that bordered the beach for cover.

When Sally stopped at the jetty wall, and looked at her watch, Tom approached cautiously, and crouched down behind a bush, a few metres away, to watch. By the way she was pacing around and staring along the beach, he guessed she was waiting for someone.

It was only a couple of minutes before a figure jogged towards her from the other direction. Tom screwed up his eyes to see who it was. Definitely a man by the size and gait, he thought. There were no surprises when he saw the man's face...

Brad ran up to Sally and wrapped his arms around her. They stood kissing for a long time, until she pulled her head back: "What took you so long?" She sounded peeved again.

"Had to shake my brother and Rebekah off first," Brad said.

"*I* should come first," Sally huffed. "Anyway, Charles can look after Rebekah without you." She paused. "What were you *really* doing?"

Brad nuzzled into her neck. "You always come first my love."

That seemed to mollify Sally, but she still pulled out of the embrace. "Listen Brad, I'm not comfortable about keeping secrets from Jess. We must tell her everything."

"No!" Brad straightened up. "Definitely not."

"She's my boss now, Brad," Sally persisted. "She deserves to know."

"No." Brad's voice was firm. He put his hand up Sally's skirt and started caressing her. "Not yet, my love, she'll ruin everything we've worked for."

Sally moaned, and thrust her hips towards him.

He was rubbing himself against her in slow, deliberate motions.

Sally grabbed the edges of his t-shirt, and pulled it over his head in one quick movement. "*Why* should I keep it a secret?" she asked, provocatively, as she tossed it aside.

"Because I'm telling you to," came the reply.

"You're *telling* me?"

Brad grabbed her arm. "You'll do what I say."

"You can't *make* me keep silent."

Brad yanked Sally's t-shirt over her head and flung it on the sand.

Tom's eyes widened as Sally's bare breasts glowed white in the moonlight. When she tried to pull away from Brad, he lurched forward and pinned her against the jetty wall. Tom tensed, ready to intervene.

But Sally just giggled as Brad held her still with one hand and dragged her beach skirt to the ground. She kicked it away.

Tom couldn't tear his eyes away from Sally's naked curves as she stood shivering in anticipation.

"*Make* me keep silent!" Sally goaded.

Brad slowly pushed her legs apart, until Sally was spread-eagled against the jetty wall.

"Go on," Sally urged.

Slowly, Brad started kissing her face, moving his tongue slowly down her neck... over her nipples... across her stomach.

Sally was visibly trembling. "*Make me!*"

With his hands holding her pert buttocks, Brad dropped to his knees and buried his head between her legs.

Sally threw back her head, delirious, hair flowing.

Tom had never seen such frenzy on a woman's face during sex. Sally was one hot lady! So engrossed was he, his reaction to the faint snap of twig behind him was slow. But when he did turn...

Jess stood staring at him.

If it hadn't been so dark, she'd have seen him flush crimson. He looked over to the jetty, where Sally was moaning with pleasure, and back at Jess's stony white face in the moonlight.

He took her arm and quickly guided her to some bushes further away so they wouldn't be overheard. "Did you hear all that before... before the main show started?"

"I did."

"Brad's playing Sally like a piano. Using sex to control her."

"Hmm." Jess looked over to where Brad was now on top of Sally on the sand. "Impressive, isn't he?" She turned back to Tom. "But I'm not sure who's controlling who in that relationship."

Tom looked from her to Brad and Sally again. Was Jess being *serious*? "Brad's trying to stop Sally telling you something."

"So I heard."

"Well, I heard Sally on her mobile earlier, when I went back into the kitchen to get that wine. She was making arrangements to meet someone. I didn't know who at the time."

"So, when were you going to tell me about it?"

He heard the controlled anger in her voice. "You looked so exhausted," he explained. "I thought I'd find out what Sally was up to first, and let you sleep. I guess we woke you up."

"I wasn't asleep," she said, simply.

"I had no right, Jess. I got carried away."

She flicked a glance over to Brad and Sally, now locked together and rhythmically pounding the edge of the surf. "You're not the only one it seems."

He stood back. "Quite a floor show, isn't it?"

"*And* their last," she said, with conviction. She turned back to him. "Please don't mention this to anyone, Tom. *I'll* deal with Sally in the morning."

"Of course."

She nodded. "I think it's time we went back to the house," she said, stiffly.

25

These islands are like a web, with my networks spun right across them. I know everything that happens, and everyone who comes here. I'm like a spider. When I feel a vibration on an outer strand of my web, I pounce on my prey.

Now, I feel a vibration. Jessica Turner. There's something different about her. And I know what it is. Unlike the others, she doesn't seem afraid of death. Why? I believe it's because her child is dead.

"If anyone causes one of these little ones to stumble – those who believe in me – it would be better for them to have a large millstone hung around their neck and to be drowned in the depths of the sea."*

But my delay in dealing with her has made her dangerous. Already she has brought that Federal Agent here; and she wants to bring in the British police too. I can't allow that to happen. It will ruin everything.

The first time I saw her I decided she would end up in that watery graveyard, but I've had a change of heart. I let Bondye deal with that stupid Pearson woman. Now, I think I might let him deal with Jessica Turner too. Only this time, it will be much more terrifying to see her naked and pleading for her life on the sacrificial altar. She might have some respect for voodoo then.

Her interfering friend will not get away unpunished either.

---

* Matthew 18.6 Bible New International Version

26

Tom threw the plantation shutters open wide and stared out to sea. Relieved finally to see the purple glow of morning breaking, he took a deep breath of salty air and looked at his watch – 5.05. Outside, the scene was as still as inside the house. Jess and Sally must be sound asleep after all that action in the middle of the night.

He went over to the bed and picked up his sketchpad. He looked at Sally's face. He still hadn't got her expression of sexual ecstasy right. He could normally draw anyone, and any expression, in a few minutes. He'd had a lot of practice. Faces had intrigued him from the first moment he'd picked up a pencil. As an only child, he'd started drawing his mother, and then moved on to children in his class. Even back then, he'd found it difficult to forge relationships. So he drew the faces of the children he liked most, and hung them on his bedroom wall. *They* were his friends, in his eyes at least.

He cringed now remembering Jess's face when she found him watching Sally and Brad. Beneath that stony stare of hers, he knew she was upset. Who could blame her? He was her guest, and he'd repaid her by sneaking out in the night to find out what one of her own colleagues was up to. They'd walked back to the house in silence, and returned to their rooms with a simple goodnight. He felt bad about that.

He hadn't bothered to go back to bed, he was too keyed up. He'd heard Sally come back about an hour after him, and wondered if Jess would have it out with her. But after Sally's door clicked closed, the house went quiet again.

He spent the rest of the night creating a log of chronological events on his iPad from the information and papers Jess had given him. When finished, he gathered all the papers up and slipped them safely back into the plastic folder to return to her in the morning.

Then he scrolled through the log.

Monday 3 August – TCI Immigration Minister (Clement Pearson) gives evidence to a British Government Inquiry into illegal immigration and the sinking of two Haitian sloops off Grand Turk.

- Same day, around 5pm, he turns up at the Governor's Office. Governor's PA (Sally) hears them having a row. Doesn't know what it's about. Or does she? Did someone else in the office overhear that row? *Find out if local lady, Alvita, was still at work?*

Tuesday 4 August – Clement Pearson is found hanging in his garage at home by his wife. Inquest says suicide. But was it? *Need to get a look at the scene of the hanging, and post mortem report.*

[TWO WEEK GAP]

Tuesday 17 August – British Governor is seriously injured in a car crash in the early hours of the morning driving himself down from the lighthouse on the Ridge. What was he doing up there in the middle of the night? Who knew he was up there? Murder attempt on the way back?

- Governor's car travelling down from lighthouse. Truck smashes into the car at crossroads (driver side). Governor's car catches fire. Photos show extensive damage and fire. How did Governor get out alive? Did he save himself? Or did someone pull him out? Still no sign of the truck or driver. No witnesses. Murder attempt? Police say accident. Why? Hard to believe. *Where is that truck? Where is the driver? Need to get a look at the Governor's car.*

- Jess arrives to take over from the Head of the Governor's Office (David Evans). At dinner that evening, she meets the Chief Justice (Dominic Canning) who talks to her about Haitian voodoo and impact on islanders. Several pets disappeared. Locals believe they have been sacrificed. A *row over dinner between his wife, Rebekah, and Sally. Those two don't get on. Why*?

Wednesday 18th – Jess finds letter (half finished) under lighthouse steps. Governor's handwriting. Letter to his wife asking for forgiveness for something. What? Why leave letter there? Dropped in dark? Disturbed by someone? Who?

- Dead Immigration Minister's wife, Mrs Pearson, is found hanging by her bound feet in her garage. Throat cut. Why murder her? What did she know? Why so brutal? Why in the same spot as her husband? *Need to get a look at crime scene.*

Thursday 19th – Governor dies of injuries in Miami hospital, without regaining consciousness.

- I arrive in the TCI.

Tom stared at the log for a moment, then typed in another entry.

- Rebekah Canning declares she's in love with Charles Regan, NY banker and co-owner local dive company. Says her husband doesn't know. But everyone else seems to.

Tom ran his fingers through his hair. He wanted to help Jess, although he couldn't be seen to be doing any police work on the island. Still, he could do some digging *off* the island. He scrolled to his email account and typed in a colleague's address in Canberra. He would have to phrase the message carefully in case it was intercepted.

Hi mate,

Arrived safely in the Turks and Caicos Islands. Lovely place, with great scuba diving around the coral reefs. You're missing a treat. I'm going out diving with an American guy, Brad Regan, and his twin brother Charles, who own the local dive company. Fantastic diving off the wall – the sea bed drops suddenly to 7,000 feet a few hundred yards offshore. Can't wait to get out there. Google those guys and take a look at their dive company. Terrific photos on the internet.

It's not all perfect in paradise though. The Governor was injured in a car crash and has since died. Jess and her colleagues are devastated. There's also been a murder, a local woman. Google the press reports and take a look for yourself. Good job I'm on holiday!

He thought about Rebekah. She might be the wife of the British Chief Justice, but there was something weird about her, and she looked under real strain. Could he ask for a check on her too? Yep! He might as well check out

Carrie too, while he was at it.

Jess is really busy coping on her own with things, although she has some backup from the local expat community. Rebekah Canning, wife of the British Chief Justice, is being particularly high profile, along with American Carrie Lynch, who runs the local kindergarten.

Anyway, this is just to let you know I've got my feet up for a couple of days. But I'll definitely be back for the PM's briefing next week. Wouldn't miss it for the world.

Cheers, Tom

He re-read the email and pressed send. He was satisfied his mate would know he was asking him to run checks on Brad, Charles, Rebekah and Carrie.

Next, he scrolled to Jess's photos of the Governor's Land Rover and studied them. It was the burnt, rusty hue of the paintwork from the fire that really caught his attention. It looked pretty even all over the car, which seemed odd in the circumstances. And why, if the truck had smacked head-on into its side door, had the Land Rover not tipped onto its side or been shunted along the road? The more he looked at the photos, and the way the paintwork was burnt, the more suspicious it looked.

He needed to take a look at the vehicle. Why not go now, he thought, before anyone started work at the Government Garage. That way he wouldn't have to answer any questions. And security seemed very lax on this island, so hopefully the Garage wouldn't be locked.

Still dressed in his cargo shorts and t-shirt from earlier, he slipped his feet into his trainers. He found his torch and Swiss Army knife in his suitcase and slipped them into his shorts' pocket. He tucked his iPad under his arm. He wouldn't leave it after what happened to Jess's laptop.

He knew from his map of Grand Turk that the Garage was located on the main road, about half a mile south of the Residence. Rather than walk down the road in plain view, he would try and access it from the beach that ran parallel.

Lifting the latch, he opened the door and went onto the landing. Quietly, he stepped over the creaky top stair, made his way down to the kitchen, and slipped out the back door. No-one heard him leave this time, he was sure of that.

Although light was beginning to break out to sea, it was still dark onshore. The narrow beam of his torch picked out the way as he turned left and headed south, keeping close to the bushes at the back of the beach. His feet sank deep into the sand with every step, which made it heavy going. He resisted the temptation to walk along the flattened sand by the water's edge, where he'd be more visible.

He was surprised how isolated the Governor's house was, with no neighbouring properties, and only scrub and beach for at least half a mile in each direction. When he came across a six-foot high wire fence, with low rise buildings set back, he guessed it was the Government Garage. Checking both ways along the beach, he tucked his iPad down the waistband of his cargo shorts, hauled himself up onto the top of the fence, and jumped down the other side, into tall grass. Staying low, he made his way towards the buildings. He could hear nothing but the sound of waves lapping onto the shore. No dawn chorus of birds, just the sea. Nothing but the sea.

Perspiration trickled down his back as he moved towards the buildings in the semi-darkness. That was due more to nerves than heat. He didn't want to get caught trespassing, but his instincts were compelling him to take a look at that Land Rover.

As Jess described, three timber garages stood in a row in front of him. He switched off his torch in case the beam was visible from the road, and crept forward. His footsteps on soft gravel resonated in the silence. He stopped and listened. No-one. He could see each garage had two large doors, held together by bolts at the top and bottom, and a hasp and staple latch for a padlock in the middle. Only the far garage looked secured with a padlock. He walked around the garages looking for windows, but there were none.

Quietly, he threw back the bolts of the first garage, pulled the doors open and peered inside. A black limousine was up on the ramps. But it was not the Governor's Land Rover. He shut the door, secured the bolts again, and moved to the middle garage. Inside that one, a white minivan was jacked up on one side, with the front wheel removed. Not that one either. He closed the door, and moved to the garage secured with a padlock. The Governor's car had to be in here.

He rattled the padlock. Locked. Pulling his knife out of his pocket, he retracted the hook pick, and inserted it into the lock. It clicked open. Add breaking and entering to trespassing, he thought, as he slipped off the padlock. He opened one of the doors and flashed his torch inside.

But he was disappointed. It was empty. He went inside and shone the beam around. This garage was very tidy. Tools were neatly laid out on benches and shelves around the walls; and the floor was meticulously clean. Too clean, he thought, as he walked around with the torch inspecting it. Not only had the Land Rover gone, someone had swept the garage clean of any evidence it had ever been there.

Closing the garage door, he heard a car pull up outside the compound gates, on the main road. He clicked the padlock back in place, and slipped round the side of the garage to avoid being picked out by the car's headlights. As soon as the driver switched off the engine and lights, he started running back to the fence.

Suddenly, a deep growl rang out in the silence. *Shit!* Over his shoulder, he saw a dark shape in pursuit, and heard the rapid patter of paws. He sprinted to the fence, and clambered onto the top. A black dog sprang at the fence, snapping at his legs and barking furiously.

Practically falling down the other side, he picked himself up and hurried back along the beach as fast as he could jog through the deep sand, until he reached the Residence. His heart was still pounding, and he was gasping. But now he was convinced Jess was right. The Governor's car crash was no accident. The police wouldn't have moved the Land Rover otherwise, and cleaned up the garage of any evidence it was ever there.

He had to find that vehicle. But how? He couldn't exactly ask the police to show it to him. He would have to find someone else to help. Then he remembered the helicopter pilot's words on their way back from Key West. *If you need any help, be sure to get in touch with Chuck Lynch.* Of course, Chuck was the US police contact on the island. They obviously trust him, Tom thought, but could he?

He jumped as he heard a noise. Someone was coming. He lay flat on the sand in the gloom and saw a woman slip around the side of the house, carrying a child. Then he heard voices.

"I told you not to come back," a woman hissed.

He knew that voice... it was *Maggie!*

"Take the child." The other woman urged.

"I can't." Maggie sounded weary. "There are too many people in the house."

"Do it!" The other woman snapped as if she were in charge. "What other choice do you have?"

Intrigued, Tom crawled behind a bush and peered round to see Maggie talking to a woman in a dark suit, with her hair tied in a bun. She was holding a little girl of about two or three, in a cotton dress. The child wasn't making a sound.

The woman pushed the child into Maggie's arms. "*Take her!*"

Suddenly, Maggie slapped the other woman hard across the face.

The woman gasped, and her hand flew to her cheek.

Tom held his breath, wondering what would happen next. But Maggie just grabbed the child.

The woman stared at her, then turned and stalked off.

Only then did the child start to whimper.

Maggie spoke softly to the little girl, as she bounced and cradled her in her arms. She shook her head as she watched the other woman walk away. Only when she was out of sight did Maggie turn and walk into the house.

27

Opening the heavy steel door, Jess stepped out of the communications room into the humid air in the corridor. She shivered. She'd been so absorbed in her work, she hadn't noticed the air conditioning control was on such a low setting.

She checked her watch – 08.25.

It had taken over an hour to send a classified e-gram to London. She was relieved to have sent the photos of the Governor's car and relayed her suspicions about the accident. She'd also told them about that unfinished confession letter to the Governor's wife. She knew London would get into a flap when they read it. She was disappointed not to be able to give them any more details on Mrs Pearson's murder. But she repeated her worry about the missing pets and reports of voodoo sacrifices. She wanted them to understand exactly what was going on, and the urgency of the situation. They needed to send UK police assistance.

Closing the door, she scrambled the combination lock. All she could do now was wait.

She rubbed her cold arms and headed down the corridor towards the kitchen. She was desperate for a cup of tea, having left the Residence before seven with no breakfast. Just as she was passing the Governor's office, she heard a strange noise coming from inside. No-one should be in there, apart from Sally, and she wasn't in yet.

She pushed open the door and peered inside. Overgrown shrubs outside the window swayed in the breeze, casting eerie shadows around the walls. She didn't like this office. Not only was it gloomy, the heavy furniture made it feel oppressive. A twig scratched against the window pane in the wind, like chalk on a blackboard. That was the noise she'd heard.

As she stood looking around, she was more convinced than ever that the Governor and Clement Pearson's row had kicked off this terrible chain of events. Was there something in here to shed light on what it was about? If Tom were here, he'd search the whole place from top to bottom. She closed the door, she'd do it herself later.

As she entered the kitchen, a cockroach scuttled across the floor, and disappeared under the unit. Cockroaches didn't bother her. They were inevitable companions in hot climates. She yawned as she filled up the kettle. With only a few hours' sleep after Sally and Brad's antics on the beach, she was already tired.

She was cross with Sally. The girl was out of control. Drinking too much, constantly arguing with Rebekah, and having sex on a public beach. That would be enough to get her sent home from any overseas mission. But Jess hadn't mentioned Sally in her e-gram to London, because she was a good PA. And Jess needed her help. She would give her a warning though. One more upset, and Sally would be on the first plane home. Jess would rather work alone than have a loose cannon on the team.

First though, she had to find out about that secret Sally and Brad shared.

She shoved a teabag into a mug, and poured in some boiling water. She liked tea made from leaves in a pot, but she was so parched, she'd drink anything.

Her ears pricked up as the front door slammed. The staff were arriving. She'd scheduled a hurricane planning meeting for the whole team at 08.30 to keep everyone focused on the job.

She took a carton from the fridge and poured some milk into her tea. Mug in hand, she walked out of the kitchen and straight into Sally.

"Morning, Jess." Sally sounded cheerful. "You missed a great breakfast. I'll have to stay at the Residence more often, and have Maggie wait on me."

"Did you see Tom?" Jess asked, coldly.

"Nope. Guess he was spark out." Sally looked at her sideways. "Must have had an exhausting night."

Jess was about to give Sally a piece of her mind when the door opened again, and Alvita walked in.

"Morning," Alvita mumbled.

"Morning," Jess replied, in a business-like tone. "Can you please get all the staff into the Conference Room now. I want to start the hurricane planning meeting promptly in five minutes." Without another word, she went straight into her office to get the papers for the meeting.

She would deal with Sally after that.

★

Hurricane planning checklist laid on the table, and pen in hand, Jess looked around. On her instructions, all the local staff had been invited to the meeting, including the gardeners who looked after the grounds. But she might just as well not have bothered because Alvita answered every question directed at them. And they were happy to let her.

"Have all the dead tree branches near the office and Residence been cut back?" Jess asked the head gardener, an old Haitian man. "We don't want them flying around and causing damage."

He looked down.

"Yes," Alvita replied. "All the gutters have been cleared and secured too."

Jess studied the old man while his eyes were averted. She couldn't see any difference between his features and the locals. His hair was just as curly, and his skin as black. He was more wrinkled from working out in the sun all day, but who wouldn't be?

"So where do we keep the hurricane shutters for the windows?" she asked.

Alvita piped up: "The boards for the office windows are in the store room round the back. The Residence ones are in the garage."

Jess ticked that off her checklist. "What about battery operated radios? How many have we got?"

"Four," Alvita said. "Two in the Residence, and two here."

"Have we got a supply of spare batteries?"

"Yes," Sally answered this time. "They arrived last week."

Jess nodded. "Do the radios have the local emergency frequency stuck to them somewhere?"

Alvita frowned at her.

"I'm not a complete novice, Alvita," Jess said. "I was working on the island of Mauritius, in the Indian Ocean, when a cyclone hit. The electricity and phones were cut immediately, and the only form of communication was battery operated radio, on an emergency frequency."

Alvita looked down.

"What about drinking water containers?" Jess knew the water supply would be cut off too, or at least contaminated. "Where are they kept?"

"*I* wouldn't drink out of the old ones we have in the store room," Sally said.

"They're fine," Alvita replied.

It was only then that Jess noticed a red mark on Alvita's cheek, or was it a scratch? "Let's buy a few new ones, assuming the shops haven't sold out by now."

Alvita shook her head. "There's really no need."

"Just *do* it, please!"

Alvita nodded.

"Good... now, do we have candles, and battery operated lanterns?" Jess asked. "And a good supply of batteries?"

Sally nodded. "I got some spare batteries for the lanterns too."

"Good. What about stocks of tinned and dried foods?" Jess looked around the table. "Have you all stocked up at home?"

The local staff averted their eyes, which Jess took to mean they hadn't. Of course, they lived with the constant threat of hurricanes, and took the risk in their stride. Still, she'd raised the issue, it was up to them what they did in their own homes. She made a note to talk to Maggie about Residence stocks though.

She looked up. "Where's the Disaster Management Centre on Grand Turk?"

"On the Ridge, near the lighthouse," Alvita replied.

Jess frowned, she hadn't seen it when she was up there with the Police Commissioner. "Let's go up after lunch, Alvita. You can show me where it is. We'll make sure everything's in working order while we're up there."

Alvita looked surprised. "All right."

"Good, well that's everything on my list for now. Has anyone got anything else to say?"

The staff all looked away again.

"Good," she said. "If there's nothing else, we'll draw the meeting to a close."

Everyone leapt to their feet without another word, and filed out.

Sally was about to get up too.

"Not you, Sally," Jess said. "I want to talk to you in the Governor's office. It's more private in there."

"Okay," Sally said. "I'll get us some coffee first."

"Forget the coffee." Jess walked down the corridor, with Sally trailing behind her.

"Shut the door." Jess sat down behind the Governor's desk.

Sally did as she was told, and sat down in a chair on the other side of the desk. The secretive smile that had hung on her lips throughout the hurricane planning meeting faded as she looked at Jess.

"Is there something wrong?" she asked.

Jess put her elbows on the desk and looked at her. "You tell me."

Sally's brow furrowed. "I don't understand."

"Oh I think you do."

A faint look of alarm flitted across Sally's face.

"You're good at keeping secrets, aren't you?" Jess went on.

"I-I don't know what you mean."

"Well, let's see if you can remember what happened last night. Or in the *middle* of the night, to be precise." Jess paused. "Do you sleepwalk, Sally?"

"Oh." Sally squirmed in her chair. "You mean me going for a walk. Sorry if I woke you, I have trouble sleeping."

Jess could feel her irritation bubbling up. She looked at her watch. "You have precisely two minutes to tell me exactly what's going on." She kept her voice low and firm. "Otherwise, you'll be on the first plane home to London."

Sally flinched.

"I won't have a UK based member of staff behaving *lewdly* in public."

Sally paled. "You saw us?"

"Yes."

Sally had the decency to look shamefaced. "I'm sorry, Jess. It won't happen again."

"You're right it won't." Jess snapped. "And the only secrets you should be keeping are those belonging to the British Government."

Sally slumped down in the chair when she realised Jess had not only seen, but heard everything too.

Jess raised her eyebrows. "So?"

"I wanted to tell you, Jess, but Brad made me keep quiet."

Jess knew that much was true. "It looked like you enjoyed every minute of that coercion."

Sally blushed and looked away.

"If Brad has that kind of control over you, Sally, your position here is compromised. You need to go back to the UK."

Sally's face fell. "No, Jess. Please." The seriousness of her situation struck home. "I want to stay here."

"Then you'd better tell me what this secret is the two of you share. Then we'll decide what's best to do in the circumstances."

Sally bit her quivering lip.

Jess stood up to break the tension, and walked over to the window. She had to be straight with Sally.

"You behaved outrageously at both dinner parties. You clearly drink too much. You were rude to our guests, and you had sex on a public beach." She turned back. "Tell me why I should let you stay."

Sally looked up. "I'm sorry, Jess."

"Tell me why I should let you stay."

Sally sighed. "I can't defend myself because it's all true." She paused. "I was *so* lonely here with nothing to do in my spare time, and no-one of my age for company, I-I started drinking to make it bearable," she explained. "I used to get sloshed just to lose track of time."

"I see."

"That all changed when Brad and I got together," Sally went on. "Now, I love my life here. And I love him. He means the world to me."

Jess knew that Sally was mad about Brad, but did he feel the same way about her? He didn't pay her much attention. Did he just want sex, or did he love her too? "So, do you two have long-term plans?" she asked.

Sally nodded. "I think so. I can't bear the thought of losing him."

Jess took that to mean Brad hadn't made any real commitment yet.

"*Please* don't send me home," Sally pleaded. "I won't drink, and I won't behave badly. I promise."

Jess walked back to the desk and sat down. Sally's face was earnest enough, but would she keep that promise? *Could* she keep that promise if she had a drink problem?

"You'll need to tell me what this secret is." Jess paused. "I want the truth, Sally."

Sally recoiled. "Brad won't let me tell anybody."

Jess shrugged. "If your loyalties are to Brad, then your position here is compromised. You need to go home," she repeated.

"No!" Sally shook her head. "Please Jess... Look, if I tell you, you won't tell Brad I told you, will you?"

"I'm not making any promises." Jess was blunt now. "A woman's been murdered." She held back her suspicions about the Governor's car accident.

Sally's jaw dropped. "You don't think Brad had anything to do with *murder*, do you?"

Jess leant forward. "You tell me."

Sally looked aghast. "Brad's no killer." Her voice cracked with emotion. "N–nor am I."

"Then you can tell me what this secret is."

Sally slumped back in her chair, with a resigned sigh. "Brad's found a Spanish galleon offshore."

"*A sunken galleon?*" Jess repeated. "That's the big secret? Brad's found an old shipwreck?"

"Not *just* a shipwreck, Jess." Sally's eyes lit up. "It's a galleon from the old Spanish treasure fleet." She leant forward. "With a *massive* shipment of silver coins and gold bullion on board."

Jess put her head in her hands.

"Treasure hunters have been looking for it for decades," Sally went on. "That's why Brad has to keep the discovery a secret, until he can recover the contents. If even a whisper of this gets out, people will be swarming all over."

"For God's sake, Sally," Jess tried to keep her voice calm. "We're dealing with murder, and all you and Brad can think of is *treasure* hunting?"

"Please, Jess. Let me explain." Sally was sitting on the edge of her seat. "The Spanish treasure fleet was a convoy of ships back in the days of the Spanish Empire. Brad says Spain sent out agricultural machinery, books, and... stuff in these galleons to their colonies in the Americas, and they took back cargoes of gold bullion and silver coins from the mines."

Jess looked at her. "So what's this galleon called?"

Sally's eyes clouded. "Brad's keeping that a secret, even from me, although he did let slip it went down around 1715."

Jess gave an exasperated sigh.

"It's *true!*" Sally paused. "The fleet used to rendezvous in Havana. They travelled in convoy from there to avoid being attacked by pirates."

"Pirates!" Jess groaned.

"I know what you're thinking, Jess, but Brad says this convoy is in the history books. There were 12 ships altogether. When they left Havana to sail back to Europe, they got caught up in a hurricane. Eleven ships survived and made it back to Spain, but one went missing."

"And that's the one Brad's found?" Jess tried not to sound sarcastic. "So how did it get from Havana down to our waters?"

"That's just it." Sally was excited now. "The convoy got separated in the hurricane. The last ship was damaged, and overrun by pirates. They were sailing it down the Cuban coastline, to their pirate port in Haiti, when it went down."

"Exactly where is it supposed to have gone down?"

Sally hesitated. "Brad hasn't told me the exact location yet. It's some miles off our shores, but he's been searching for it since he first came to Grand Turk. He's so excited, it's been his lifelong dream to find it."

Jess could see from Sally's eyes that she was totally swept up in the excitement of the find, but then she'd believe anything Brad told her. "Even if Brad gets the gold and silver to the surface," Jess said, "he wouldn't be able to keep it, would he?"

Sally hesitated. "He'll get something, I'm sure, but Brad's not motivated by the money, Jess. It's the *importance* of the find. He'll be famous in maritime and diving circles. His dive business will flourish. Every diver will want to come to Grand Turk." She smiled. "Brad will go down in history."

Jess couldn't argue with that. "Did the Governor know about the wreck?" she asked.

"Absolutely not."

Jess wondered if that were true. "Well, someone else must know." She paused. "What about his brother Charles? They go out diving together."

Sally shook her head, vehemently. "No-one knows, except me."

"Oh come on." Jess stared at her. "Brad can't possibly go out there diving alone?"

That's when the first look of doubt flitted across Sally's face. "He says he does."

Jess didn't believe a word of it. "Tell him I want to talk to him."

Sally blanched. "Then he'd know I told you."

"You can tell him truthfully that I was going to send you home, if you hadn't told me. And he wouldn't like that, would he?"

Sally looked deflated. "I-I don't know how he's going to take it."

"Look, I need to speak to him, Sally. We have to be able to discount any connection between what Brad's up to out there, and the awful things happening onshore."

Sally stiffened. "I can tell you categorically that Brad has nothing to do with murder. Nothing at all."

"Nevertheless," Jess persisted, "please tell him I'd like to see him this afternoon."

Sally hesitated. "He said he was going to take Tom out diving after lunch."

Jess knew Tom was really keen to go out with Brad. "In that case, please ask Brad to come to the office immediately after they get back."

Sally gave another resigned sigh. "If you insist."

"I do."

"Jess, I..."

"You and I will have another chat after that."

Sally got up and walked out, shoulders hunched like a condemned woman.

28

Tom sat at a table in the sheltered courtyard, tucking into the poached eggs and bacon Maggie had cooked. The soft yolks oozed as he dipped his toast in, just the way he liked them. A sudden gust of wind whipped across the table, rocking the flower vase. He reached out and steadied it. The breeze had certainly picked up since his visit earlier to the Garage.

He noticed Maggie's hands shaking as she poured the coffee, although her face looked calm. Was she still upset about earlier? She'd certainly given that woman a whack. Maybe it was some kind of family row, he thought, as he bit into his toast? Family tensions were not something he had to worry about. He'd never been married or had kids. The demands of his job had destroyed the two serious relationships he'd ever had.

"Mister Brad rang for you," Maggie said. "I knocked on your door, but you were in the shower."

Tom looked up. "Did he leave a message?"

"He asked if you wanted to go out diving this afternoon."

Tom smiled. He'd been itching to go out since hearing it was one of the best scuba diving spots in the world.

"Mister Brad's number is on the notepad next to the phone in the hall," Maggie said. "He said to leave a message if he's not there." She handed Tom the cup of coffee. "Can I get you anything else?" she asked.

He heard the weariness in her voice. "I could have cooked my own breakfast, Maggie. I'm used to doing it."

She glanced over. "You live alone?"

"Yes."

"No wife and children?"

He shook his head. "No wife and children."

She looked thoughtful. "How long have you and Miss Jessica known each other?"

He knew where this conversation was going. "We worked together for a while, in Australia."

She nodded. "Miss Jessica told me her husband and child had died."

"Yes. In a car crash in Indonesia."

Maggie shook her head, sadly. "She's a good lady."

"She is."

Maggie made a show of moving plates around the table, rather than leave. "Maybe she'll meet another man." She glanced at him. "And have another family."

He smiled. "She has met another man. She lives with him in Washington."

Maggie looked surprised. "Are you sure, Mister Tom, only when I look at a person's face, I see a lot. And Miss Jessica doesn't look like a lady in love. She's too sad."

Tom saw a lot in people's faces too, which is why he sketched them. Maggie was right though. Jess did look sad. But this conversation was getting too personal, and he decided to change the subject. Jess wouldn't like them discussing her. Anyway, he had a few questions of his own for Maggie.

"So," he said, brightly. "How long have you worked for the Governor?"

Maggie looked away. "I've worked for several Governors, Mister Tom. I've looked after this Residence for many years." She flapped her hand, dismissively. "Too many to remember."

Tom was used to interviewing people and knew when someone was being evasive. He persisted. "Did previous Governors bring their families with them?"

"No." Maggie shook her head. "They were much *older* than this Governor."

"Ah, I see. So that's why this Governor brought his wife *and* child with him?"

Maggie's shoulders drooped. "That's what makes it so sad."

He nodded. "I bet you've seen many changes over the years?"

Maggie nodded. "Too many, Mister Tom."

He thought back to that scene with the woman and child earlier. "It must be nice to have a child in the house though."

The spoon clattered onto a china plate as it slipped from Maggie's hands. She picked it up, quickly. "I get clumsy as I get old."

Tom wouldn't have said Maggie was particularly old, in her fifties or early sixties perhaps? But it was definitely talk of a child that had made her nervous. Why?

"I thought Jess said the Governor's son was living here too?" he added.

"Oh yes." Maggie's face cleared. "The Governor's boy has been going to the local school."

He nodded. "What about the Governor's wife?"

Maggie pursed her lips in disapproval. "*She* liked to be in Provo, with its fancy hotels, and rich people." She paused. "You stay in Grand Turk, Mister Tom. This is the real Turks and Caicos."

Ah, Tom thought. So Maggie doesn't like Provo, or the Governor's wife, it seems. Still, if Provo was so much better off than Grand Turk, that would cause resentment. He looked at his watch, and wiped his mouth with a napkin.

"Great breakfast, Maggie. Thank you."

She smiled for the first time. "You're welcome, Mister Tom."

He stood up. "What time did Jess go to the office?"

"Very early, and without any breakfast." Maggie frowned. "She said she'd be back for lunch with you at 12 noon sharp."

"Then I'd better make sure I'm back," he joked. In truth he was relieved Jess was coming back for lunch. They had a lot to talk about. "But right now, I have an appointment in town, and I need a taxi."

Maggie nodded. "I'll ring for one while you get ready."

"Thank you, Maggie. I'll just telephone Brad before I go."

*

Tom was pretty sure the man dressed in jeans and polo shirt walking towards him was Chuck Lynch. Agile and fit for such a tall man, he looked confident and at ease. He was also bang on time – 10am. That said a lot about the man. Chuck had wanted to meet on a stretch of beach near town, rather than in a coffee shop or bar. Tom guessed he wanted the encounter to look unplanned.

Chuck had been cagey when Tom first introduced himself on the phone as an Australian Federal Agent. He'd warmed up a little when Tom told him about his job in the illegal migration task force back home, and explained that the US guys in Miami had given him Chuck's name as a contact. Tom deliberately didn't mention recent events

217

on the island, and simply asked Chuck if he had time to meet up and give him some background about how the local police dealt with illegals arriving on their shores. He'd normally go through official channels, he explained, but as he was on the island in an unofficial capacity visiting a friend, he thought he'd contact Chuck instead.

Now, Tom sat on some rocks on the beach near the jetty, about 300 yards from Front Street, a single row of shops and office buildings along the seafront in Cockburn Town. The beach was deserted except for a group of young boys in their swimmers jumping off the jetty into the sea. They played in the water and swam like fish.

"Tom?" Chuck asked, as he approached.

Tom nodded. He didn't offer to shake hands because that would indicate the meeting was deliberate. He just beckoned Chuck to sit down. "I don't have my badge," he quipped, "but you can check my passport if you want."

Chuck sat down, took off his metal-framed sunglasses, and slipped them into the top pocket of his shirt.

"Sorry for being so cautious on the phone," he said in an American drawl. "Things haven't been so easy round here lately."

Tom studied Chuck. His black hair was wavy rather than curly, and his skin coffee-coloured. He looked to be in his mid-thirties, and different from the locals. "Hope you don't mind me asking, Chuck. Are you from these islands?"

Chuck hesitated. "My mom *is*, my dad's American." He glanced at Tom. "I was born in North Carolina and spent the first years of my life in the US."

Tom nodded. "So what brought you back here?" he asked.

"My Mom and Dad split up, and I came back to Grand Turk with her. But I couldn't settle, so she sent me back to live with my dad."

It was said with such honesty that Tom believed every word. "Life gets complicated, doesn't it?"

"Sure does. After my schoolin', I joined the US police. Then I came down here to work in the Turks and Caicos police." Chuck sighed. "I've been goin' back and forth ever since."

Tom nodded. Chuck was okay, he thought. Now, he wanted to get straight down to business. "I need some help, Chuck," he said, honestly.

Chuck didn't look surprised by that request. "What kinda help?" he asked.

Tom wasn't sure how frank to be. On the other hand, he didn't have time to pussyfoot around. "Do you have many dealings with the US Federal Police, Chuck?"

Chuck continued to look at Tom, as if assessing him. "What's that gotta do with the Australian Government?"

"Nothing." Tom noted Chuck hadn't denied it. "I'm not asking in an official capacity, you understand. I'm here visiting a friend."

Chuck nodded. "In the Governor's Office?"

Tom wasn't surprised Chuck knew who Jess was.

"So, how can I help you, Tom?"

Tom plunged straight in. "As you know, the Governor was injured in a car accident, and has since died."

"Tragic," Chuck nodded.

"I want to have a look at his wrecked Land Rover." Tom paused. "Can you help me gain access?"

Chuck frowned. "Can't Miss Turner take you to have a look?"

"Well that's just it," Tom went on. "It was in Government Garage, but it's not there now." He paused. "Would you be able to find out where it is?"

Chuck shifted on the rock. "Why d'ya wanna see the car?"

The question was asked lightly, but Tom knew his answer would have to be right. He decided to be frank. "The damage looks suspicious."

Chuck frowned again. "You've seen it already, then?"

"Only in photos."

"I see."

"I know about Mrs Pearson's murder," Tom said. "Very nasty."

Chuck nodded. He seemed to be watching Tom as closely as he was watching him.

Tom waited, but Chuck didn't volunteer anything else. He was clearly a man of few words – a trait Tom liked.

"I'd also like to get a look at the crime scene, where Mrs Pearson was murdered," he went on. "I understand it was in her garage at home, in the same place her husband committed suicide?" He paused. "Can you help me with that too, Chuck?"

A sudden gust of wind sprang up from nowhere, blowing fine grains of sand in their faces.

Tom brushed them off his face.

Chuck looked out to sea and frowned. "There's a tropical storm out there," he said, simply.

Tom looked out to sea. He could see nothing but cloudless blue sky.

"It's movin' north-west from Haiti, towards Cuba at the moment," Chuck added.

They both sat staring out to sea in silence. Tom guessed if he said anything more, or tried to push him, Chuck would just walk away. He had to wait patiently for him to make up his mind whether to help or not.

Finally, Chuck turned back and nodded. "Let's see if we can get a look at that car first, Tom. We can take it from there."

Tom smiled. "I don't have a cell phone that works on this island right now. I'm going to try and get one from Turks Telecomm on my way back. I'm staying at the Governor's Residence, so you can contact me there."

Chuck nodded, as if he already knew.

Throughout the conversation, Tom had been wondering why Chuck hadn't asked him more questions. Now he understood. Chuck already knew the answers, and must have checked him out before coming to meet him. "I'm only here for a couple of days, Chuck, so..."

"So I'll be in touch this afternoon," Chuck nodded.

"I'm going out scuba diving after lunch for a couple of hours, so..."

"So I'll see you after that, Tom." And with that, Chuck got up and walked away.

Tom frowned as he watched him go. The whole time they'd been talking, Chuck's eyes had been scrunched up against the strong sunlight, which meant Tom hadn't been able to look him in the eye. Could he trust the man, he wondered?

He got up and brushed himself down. He had no other option right now.

29

When Jess got back to the Residence, Tom was out in the courtyard, where Maggie had set up a table for lunch in the shade of a palm tree. He looked relaxed sitting in a rattan chair, with his feet up on a stool. Head bent over his sketch pad, he was busy with pencil in hand, oblivious to her, or anything else.

She went over to the bar fridge and pulled out a bottle of water. "Fancy a beer, Tom?" she called over.

He looked up, surprised to see her. "Oh, hi." He jumped up and put his pad down on the stool.

"There's some wine, if you'd prefer?" she said.

"I'll have water too, please. I need a clear head for this afternoon."

"You're going out diving with Brad, then?" She poured some water into two glasses.

"Yes." He pulled an ice tray from the fridge and started pushing cubes into their drinks. "Can't wait to get out there."

"Rather you than me. I can swim, but I don't like being in the sea. Not out of my depth anyway."

"Don't you like diving?" his voice sounded incredulous.

"Never tried it. Never wanted to." She handed him a glass.

"We'll have to see what we can do about that! You're really missing out."

She shook her head, firmly. "Don't even think it. You won't get me out there. Definitely not."

He held up his hands in a playful gesture of defeat.

"Let's sit at the table, Tom. I'm afraid I don't have long, and Maggie's ready to serve lunch."

"Okay." He held out a chair while she sat down, and then sat down himself.

"About last night, Jess." He cleared his throat.

"Forget it." She could see his discomfort. "You should have told me about Sally before you went following her into the night. And I shouldn't have got annoyed. So let's just leave it at that."

He looked relieved, and took a long swig of water. "So," he asked after a while. "How'd it go with Sally this morning? Bit of a handful, isn't she?"

Jess could see the ghost of a smile on his lips, and knew what he was thinking. She could still see Brad's hands around Sally's bottom too.

"Don't be too hard on her," Tom said. "It must be lonely for a young woman like her on this island."

"That doesn't excuse anything." Jess looked at him, then at his sketchpad on the stool. "Oh I get it. You were drawing Sally when I came in, weren't you? That's why you closed your pad so quickly when you saw me." She could tell by his expression that she was right. "Can I have a look?" she asked.

He hesitated, and looked away.

She knew he didn't like anyone to see his sketches. "Must be raunchy, if you won't let me see."

"All right," he said after a while. He got up and went over to get his pad. He stared at a page for a while, then came back and angled it towards Jess. "Don't say I didn't warn you."

Jess stared at Sally, stark naked from the waist up. Her breasts were huge and perfectly round. He'd drawn her red hair down to her waist, rather than her shoulders. But it was the look of wild delirium on her face that made Sally seem other worldly. "It's amazing!" She paused. "Is that how you see, Sally?"

He shrugged. "I can't get that look of sexual ecstasy on her face right."

"She could be a mermaid, or some mythical sea goddess in this?"

"Or someone high on speed."

Jess couldn't help but smile. "Better not let her see this."

His face fell. "Why? Do you think she'd be upset?"

"Hardly! She'd probably take all her clothes off and insist you draw the rest of her."

He laughed out loud. "Pity she's spoken for."

She nodded. "She says she loves Brad."

"Do you believe her?"

"I don't know *what* to believe." Jess pushed her hair back off her face. "It's this place, it's... surreal."

He smiled. "I know what you mean. I don't think I've ever been anywhere quite like it."

"So you won't be surprised when I tell you what Sally and Brad's big secret is." She paused for effect. "Sunken treasure."

"Sunken treasure?"

She nodded. "*That's* their secret. Brad's found a Spanish galleon off shore."

"Really?" Tom had a spark of interest in his eye now.

"Oh, not you too."

"Well, plenty of wrecks have been found in the Caribbean Sea, and off the coast of Florida." He paused. "Spanish galleon, did you say?"

"Yes." She raised her eyebrows. "And Brad has to keep it a complete secret or other treasure hunters might recover the booty first."

Tom nodded. "That makes sense, Jess. There are plenty of treasure hunters who'd give anything to get there first." He paused. "What's supposed to be down there?"

"Gold bullion and silver coins, according to Sally. At least that's what Brad's told her. Apparently convoys of Spanish galleons used to sail from Europe to the Americas, stopping at Havana on the way there and back. And that's where the pirates got them."

He looked almost as excited as Sally. "What a find, if it were true!"

"*If* it were true," she repeated.

He smiled. "You don't believe it, then?"

"Oh I don't know." She didn't know what to believe. Nothing about this place would surprise her.

He had a gleam in his eye when he said: "So what would you say if Sally came in now, and said she'd seen Captain Jack Sparrow in the Turks Bank in Front Street depositing a swag of silver coins?"

As Jess started laughing, all the built-up tension from the last few days seemed to flow from her.

Tom smiled.

"It's not f-funny." A tear slipped down her cheek.

"No, it's not," he said, grinning.

"S-stop it, Tom!"

He looked at her. "Make me... Go on, *make* me!"

She collapsed with laughter now, remembering Sally on the beach with Brad last night.

Tom was laughing too.

That's when Maggie came out with the lunch. She looked at them both giggling, plonked the dishes down on the table, and went back inside.

"F-for God's sake, Tom!" Jess took a sip of water to stop herself coughing, and wiped her eyes with her paper napkin. "Goodness knows what Maggie must think." She didn't dare look at him for fear of starting up again. "She'll think I'm as hysterical as Rebekah."

He laughed again.

She coughed and composed herself. "Now that's enough talk of pirates and treasure." She lifted the lid of one dish to find fried chicken wings and rice. In the other was a crisp, green salad. "Come on, let's eat."

They both helped themselves to some food, and sat quietly eating for a while. Jess was hungry since she'd had no breakfast. The chicken wings had a sticky, barbecue sauce on them and were particularly tasty.

"Mm." Tom put a chicken bone down on his plate, and wiped his fingers on his paper napkin. "Can I be serious now, Jess?"

"Of course."

"I went to the Government Garage this morning, at the crack of dawn."

She stared at him.

"I thought it would be better to go while no-one was there. To avoid any awkward questions." He paused. "The Land Rover wasn't there," he said, quietly. "The garage had been swept clean too."

She banged down her knife and fork. "What the hell are they playing at?"

Tom looked at her. "This looks bad, Jess. Almost certainly that car crash was deliberate. I don't know if someone intended to kill the Governor, or just frighten him. But it was fatal, and that makes it murder."

The way he said it sent a shiver up her spine.

His eyes pierced hers. "You realise what this means, don't you?"

She nodded. "Why'd you think I've requested UK police assistance? I know I can't trust the local police. I just don't know why, or what's going on?"

"Well, they can't have moved the car very far," he said. "So, I've found someone inside the local police to help me find it."

Her eyes narrowed.

"His name's Chuck Lynch. The Miami police gave me his name as their contact here. Don't worry," he went on, quickly. "Chuck's going to locate the car so I can have a look at it." He paused. "And, well, I think it would be good for me to get a look at the site of Mrs Pearson's murder to... while we're at it."

Jess offered Tom the bowl of salad. "Why? What can you possibly hope to find that the police haven't already?"

"It's not always what you find, Jess." He spooned some salad leaves onto his plate. "It's what you *see*."

She shook her head. "You have no locus to do any investigating. There would be nothing to stop them putting you in jail."

"Trust me. I'll be fine."

"No, it's too dangerous." She frowned as she helped herself to salad.

They fell silent again while they finished eating.

Then Jess asked: "Anyway why would this Chuck want to help you? And how do you know you can trust him?"

"I've been asking myself that," Tom replied. "I'd say he's passing information to the US Federal Police regularly."

"Like an informant?"

"Something like that." Tom paused. "It's the way he reacted, or rather *didn't* react. He knew exactly who I was, who you were, and why I was asking. It came as no surprise to him that the Governor's Land Rover had disappeared." He glanced at Jess. "Wouldn't surprise me if the US Federal Police were keeping an eye on this Territory." He glanced over. "And I think Chuck's their man."

Jess nodded. "Funny you should say that. I'd been wondering if the CIA were active down here. The Territory's too close to their shores for them not to take an interest."

Tom raised his eyebrows.

"They'll be monitoring phone calls, texts, and emails from the NSA in Washington. Probably have someone on the ground down here too."

"Who could it be?" he asked.

She shrugged. "Absolutely anyone. But I tell you something, Tom, if the CIA know, or even suspect, something's wrong down here, I'm sure our UK Security Services will too. She checked her watch. "God, is that the time?" She looked at him. "I'm afraid I've got to get back."

"Of course. Look, take my new mobile number in case you need to call me." He reached into his trouser pocket and pulled out a phone.

Her eyes widened. "How'd you manage to get that?"

"I have my ways."

She pulled her mobile out of her pocket and programmed in the number. "I'm going to visit the island's Disaster Management Centre up on the Ridge this afternoon. And I've asked Brad to come in to see me when you get back from your dive. I want to talk to him about this Spanish galleon." She looked at him. "Please don't mention it to him while you're out there, or to anyone else."

"Of course not."

Jess stood up. "Then I'm expecting the Police Commissioner to call into the office around five. I'll be back after that."

"Right." Tom got up too. "Well, I'm off diving with Brad now." He decided not to tell her he was going to see Chuck straight afterwards. She had enough to worry about.

She frowned. "Please be careful out there, Tom. The wall drops 7,000 feet."

"*Fantastic!* I can't wait."

"We only have a clinic on Grand Turk," she added. "The hospital is on Provo. And there's no decompression chamber anywhere in the Territory if you get the bends."

"Relax, Jess." He smiled, and touched her arm. "I'm an experienced diver. So is Brad. We'll be fine."

★

Jess sat in the passenger seat of the office car, with Alvita at the wheel. She stared through the windscreen at the horse-drawn carriage ahead. It was decoratively painted red and white, and carrying four passengers. She could tell they were tourists by their wide, floppy hats and sunburnt skins. Now, trundling along at ten miles an hour, the horse and carriage were blocking the single lane road. Jess looked at her watch. "We don't have much time," she said.

Alvita stepped on the accelerator, and the car lurched forward. As they whizzed by, the driver shook his horse whip at them. The horse didn't even flinch, and continued its stately trot along the main road into Cockburn Town.

Jess could see Alvita's hands relax on the steering wheel once they'd passed. "Sorry, didn't mean to pressure you," Jess said.

Alvita hit the main roundabout at speed too, and the tyres squealed as she drove around it.

A heat haze shimmered on the tarmac road in front of them as they climbed the hill to the Ridge, which made Jess feel even hotter. She shifted uncomfortably in the seat.

The air conditioning was on, but seemed to be blowing out warm air. She glanced sideways. Face set like stone, Alvita's eyes were glued to the road.

"I hear there's a tropical storm off Haiti," Jess said. Tom had told her about it at lunchtime.

"It's not heading in our direction at the moment," Alvita said, before falling silent again.

Jess noticed the red mark on Alvita's cheek looked more like a deep scratch close up. She turned and stared out her side window, worried. No reply yet from London to her e-gram, and her request for police assistance. She wouldn't panic. They would need time to digest the information and consult others. She'd phone when she got back to the office, if they hadn't been in touch.

There was another call she should have made this morning, to the Management Officer in Washington. Why had Simon lied about going to LA for work? Why not just say he was going on leave? But every time she'd picked up the receiver to call, she'd put it down again. In some way, she didn't *want* to know what he was up to, because that would confirm his lie. But it was gnawing away at her. She decided she would ring when she got back to the office.

There was no sign of life as they passed the Haitian settlement. The only movement was washing flapping in the breeze. Dogs lay flat out asleep in the shade of the tarpaulins. Their owners were inside, avoiding the fierce heat of the day. Up ahead, she could see the lighthouse dominating the skyline. Where was the Disaster Management Centre, she wondered?

Suddenly, Alvita braked and turned down a narrow track. The car bumped along over rough ground until a small concrete structure came into view.

"Here we are." Alvita pulled up outside the building and switched off the engine. "The Centre was built up here on the highest point of the island to withstand any tidal wave. It is common for storm surges to follow hurricanes." She reached over, grabbed her bag from behind Jess's seat, and got out.

The hot sun was intense as Jess stepped out too. There was no shade up here anywhere. Trees couldn't withstand hurricanes. She stared at the building. It was a simple, single-storey structure, with a few small windows and only one door. It could have been a village hall, or a large scout hut, transplanted from the depths of the British countryside.

She turned and looked all around. The stark reality of standing on top of a mountain summit, poking up out of the ocean, with nothing but hundreds of miles of water in every direction hit home. With the highest point at only 170 feet, a storm surge could easily swamp half the island.

"It's open, Jess," Alvita called, and went inside.

Jess followed. The cloying, stale air was the first thing to hit her, then darkness. Coming in from bright sunlight, she couldn't see a thing. "If the wind or sea don't get us," she said, flatly, "we'll suffocate from heat in here."

Alvita didn't react. "There's a kitchen at the other end, with water containers to fill. Candles and matches are in the cupboards. We don't store gas bottles for cooking up here, it's too hot. We bring them up if we need to."

As Jess's eyes began to adjust, she saw the interior of the Disaster Management Centre was a replica of the one on Provo. Several tables had been pushed together in the shape of a rectangle, with wooden chairs placed all around. A projector screen hung over a whiteboard at one end of the room, with a detailed map of the islands next to it. She could see a couple of large, battery operated radios. Again

231

there was only one computer, but this time a couple of old manual typewriters stood on a side table. "They don't still make ribbons for *those*, do they?" she asked.

"We have plenty in the Government store room," Alvita replied.

"They'll be no good. The ink will have dried out if they've been in there for years."

Alvita ignored her. "We have a generator in here too."

Well that's something, Jess thought. "But how's *everyone* supposed to get in here?"

Alvita gave her a surprised look. "Oh... the locals won't come up here, if that's what you mean. They'll stay and defend their homes."

"Against storm force winds and the sea?" Jess was incredulous.

"Believe me, they won't come up here. They'd rather die than leave their homes."

"But they're sitting ducks at sea level on this flat island."

Alvita looked at her in a resigned way. "It's been that way for two centuries."

Jess sighed and sat down at the meeting table, knowing there was nothing she would be able to say or do to change things. "So who *will* come up here?"

"Just us, and members of the Disaster Management Committee," Alvita replied.

Jess remembered the Committee members she'd met on Provo. "Who's on the Committee here?"

"The heads of some Government Departments, the fire chief, the Medical Officer from the Clinic, and one or two others."

"Well, let's get them all up here for a meeting in the next day or so," she said.

"Do you really think that's necessary?" Alvita asked in a way that made it clear she didn't.

"Yes. We need to make sure everyone knows what they have to do in any emergency," Jess insisted. "And let's stock this place up with provisions and everything we need as well... just in case."

Alvita plopped down on a chair at the table opposite her. "Why should you care? You'll be gone soon."

It was said in an even tone, but with a familiar edge that Jess was pretty tired of. "I'm just doing my job, Alvita – or David's to be precise. I have no personal agenda here, I assure you."

"All I'm saying, Jess, is if the British Government don't care about this Territory, why should you?"

Jess could feel her irritation rising. "Of course the Government *cares*."

"No, they don't," Alvita argued. "They don't give us any money or support. Look around." She swept her arms out wide. "Nothing much grows in our soil, our trees and crops get flattened by hurricane force winds. All we have are tourists, and Provo gets most of them."

"I understand that, so..."

"So we've become an offshore tax haven, like other Overseas Territories in the Caribbean. It's the only way we can survive." She stared at Jess, eyes black as coals. "Your Government turn a blind eye to *that* so long as they don't have to fund us. Yet they take every opportunity to criticise us, and the other offshore tax havens."

Jess didn't say anything, because it was true. In many ways, she understood Alvita's bitterness, but her constant hostility was something else. Jess wondered about her personal life.

"Are you married, Alvita?" Jess didn't feel it would be intrusive to ask that question since she'd already told her about Jack and Amy.

Alvita looked taken aback by the direct question. "No. And I don't have any children either."

"Do your parents live on Grand Turk?" Jess asked.

Alvita looked at her as if to say *why are you asking me all these questions?* – but she answered. "They're both dead."

"I'm very sorry to hear that," Jess said, sincerely. "You must have other family on Grand Turk. There are a lot of people with the surname Pearson here."

Alvita put her head on one side. "You seem very curious about me."

Jess shrugged. "I'm always interested in the people I work with. You don't have to answer, if you don't want to."

Alvita sighed. "I'm an only child. My father was a pastor here, at the Baptist church. He was a good man."

Jess could feel perspiration trickling down the back of her neck in the suffocating heat. She desperately wanted to go outside, but she didn't move because Alvita was finally talking to her.

"My father was Clement Pearson's brother," Alvita went on. "My uncle's suicide and my aunt's murder have been a big shock for me. They were the only close family I had left."

Ah, Jess felt great sympathy for her now. Alvita's brusque manner was not just about her job, it was about grief too. She would never see her family again. Never hear their voices. Never feel their touch. Her prickliness was her way of coping, and Jess knew all about that.

"My mother was born on Grand Turk too," Alvita continued. "She died of cancer two years ago, just months after my father. The truth is she didn't want to go on without him." She looked away. "I wasn't enough for her, you see."

Jess didn't know what to say except that she was sorry. "I wish we'd had the chance to talk before."

Alvita nodded.

"So Roger Pearson, the new Minister for Immigration, is your cousin?" Jess asked.

"Yes, but we don't get on," Alvita went on unprompted. "My dad had two brothers. Clement was his youngest brother, and Marvin his oldest. My dad and my uncle Clement always got on well. But my dad and Uncle Marvin fell out before dad died, and never spoke to each other again." She sighed. "Uncle Marvin died of a heart attack just a year after my dad. I think it was the sadness, you see."

Jess nodded. "So Roger is your Uncle Marvin's son."

"Yes."

Now Jess understood why Roger Pearson hadn't seemed that upset about his aunt's murder when they met in Provo yesterday. She looked at Alvita's proud face. "Is there anything I can do to help?" she asked.

Alvita looked at her, then sat forward as if coming out of a daze. She got up, and pushed the chair back under the table. "You people say you want to help, but you come out here and you just, you just turn a blind eye." She headed for the door.

Alvita was back to her normal self, Jess thought. Time to go back to the office.

But Alvita stopped at the door and turned. "If you had any sense," she said, "you'd go back home now." And with that, she walked out.

It was only later, when Jess was back in the office, that Alvita's words kept milling around in her head. *You people come out here and just turn a blind eye.* What did she mean by that? Her voice had been calm and level, but Jess had heard something else. Frustration? Despair? The more Jess thought about it, the more she believed Alvita knew what was happening in these islands. Was she involved? Or just complicit in keeping quiet about it.

Jess remembered the midnight ceremony on the beach, the hooded figure, the chanting, and the flames. Alvita had embraced those people. Why? What was she up to?

If you had any sense, you'd go back home now. Alvita's last words seemed more chilling now, like a warning. Perhaps even a threat?

One thing Jess knew for sure. She couldn't trust Alvita either.

30

"Welcome to the Columbus National Marine Park," Brad shouted, cheerfully, to Tom, as the dive boat skimmed across turquoise water and sped towards the reef. "The Aquarium's my favourite dive spot."

Tom, Brad, Charles and Carrie, all dressed in wet suits cut off at the knees for the warm Caribbean water, sat chatting in the boat for the short ride, while one of Brad's local employees steered.

"You promised me lots of fish," Tom shouted back, over the noise from the outboard engine and the wind.

Brad laughed. "You just wait. The reef ridges rise and fall sharply at that point, creating wonderful sand canyons in between. Fish love 'em. And you'll see boulder star coral and sponges like you've never seen them before."

Tom smiled. Sally must have told Brad by now that Jess knew about his Spanish wreck. If Brad was upset the secret was out, he wasn't showing it. In fact, his infectious enthusiasm was catching. Anyone would think it was *his* first trip out to 'the wall'.

Tom focused on the breakers hitting the reef to the north of Grand Turk, where the Aquarium was located. He was every bit as eager to get into the water as Brad. It had been a while. Now, staring into the distance, he felt Carrie's eyes on him. He hadn't expected her to join them. Charles was Brad's partner in the dive business and on holiday, but Carrie had a job to do. He turned sideways to her: "So, who's looking after the kids today?"

"I give myself Friday afternoons off." She flicked her blonde hair off her sun-tanned face. "The kids come in on Saturday mornings too. They see more of me than their mothers."

"Lucky kids." Carrie was one of the most attractive school teachers he'd ever come across. And he couldn't help but notice how good her model-like figure looked, snuggled into a wetsuit.

Her laugh was deep and flirtatious.

Brad gave him a wink. "You're in there."

Carrie pulled a face at Brad. "Ignore him, Tom. Just because he can't keep his eyes off the girls."

Tom smiled back, thinking how easy they were in each other's company. They were obviously both serious about diving. Back at the Dive Centre, Carrie had been every bit as professional as Brad in the way she kitted herself out, and checked all the equipment. Brad had also taken care to satisfy himself that Tom was a competent diver. He'd insisted on running through all the equipment and emergency procedures in the pool before leaving. He also checked all the oxygen tanks, breathing regulators, masks, and fins before his helpers put them into the boat. Brad was thorough, and Tom liked that.

"*Oi!* Watch my *foot!*" Charles shouted, grumpily, as Brad changed seats.

Charles looked almost comical in his wetsuit, with his protruding gut, and red face. Tom couldn't help but compare Brad's fitness and easy personality with his twin brother's. Even now, while Brad was chatting away, poker face sat quietly. Charles probably wasn't even listening to the conversation. "You okay?" Tom asked him.

No reply.

"Charles...?"

"What? Oh, yes." He nodded.

"How's Rebekah today?" Tom guessed she was occupying his thoughts.

"Still the same. This business with Benji and that voodoo curse has really got to her." He shook his head. "Never seen her like this before."

The way he said that made Tom think Charles had known Rebekah for quite some time. Is that why he came down here regularly, he wondered, to see her? Or was it really to see Brad and to keep an eye on his investment in the Dive Centre?

Tom left Charles to his misery. He was happy to be out on the water, and he wasn't going to let anyone spoil his mood. He smiled again as he leant over the side of the boat and looked down at the brilliant colour and purity of the water below.

"Visibility averages about 100 feet down there," Brad shouted over.

Tom nodded. He loved the ocean, and feeling the wind in his face. He'd been born and brought up at the coast just south of Sydney. Being in or on the water was second nature to him. So it was an irony that he found himself living and working in land-locked Canberra. Initially, he'd been flattered to be head-hunted for such a high profile job. It was interesting, and the travel great. But now he was out and about, he wondered if he really did want a desk job. He looked up to see Carrie studying him.

"Penny for them?" she said.

"Just pondering the meaning of life."

She laughed. "You're *supposed* to be enjoying yourself, Tom."

"I am, but it's hard to leave everything behind."

"Yes, I suppose you get to see everything in your job." She paused. "Nature red in tooth and claw?"

"Tennyson?" he asked

The surprise on her face made him smile. "Even policemen get an education in the colonies," he said, with some satisfaction.

She laughed. "When I lived in Africa, my father repeated that quote like a mantra. Of course over there, the reality was very true. The weak die, and the fit survive. Gives you a different perspective on life."

"Come on you two," Brad shouted, as the boat slowed. "We're here."

When the boat stopped, Brad lined up the oxygen tanks for everyone.

"Don't forget," he said, sternly. "We're only going down to maximum depth of 60 feet today. No more. And I want the four of us to stick together. I'll be Tom's buddy because it's his first dive here." He turned to Carrie and Charles. "You two look out for each other, if we get separated."

They both nodded.

"Right, let's get ready." He handed Tom an oxygen tank, then one to Charles.

A strong wave rocked the boat, and Charles fell backwards onto the deck, ending up with a tank on top of him.

Brad laughed. "You need to lose a bit of weight, bro'. Get your sea legs back."

It was Tom who picked up the tank and stood it on one side while he pulled Charles to his feet. He helped him strap on his cylinder, then put on his own.

Fins and masks in place, they inserted their breathing regulators into their mouths, and sat on the side of the boat. One by one, they leant back and toppled into the sea.

Tom was surprised at how warm the water was outside the reef. He'd expected it to be colder.

Brad touched the forefinger and thumb of his right hand into the shape of an 'o' – for okay. Then he disappeared under the waves.

Tom followed. Descending feet first, he held his nose and blew through it to release the pressure from his ears and sinuses. He felt a rush of adrenaline as the feeling of weightlessness took over. It was the freedom from gravity only diving seemed to give him. Releasing air from his life jacket to counter his buoyancy, he kicked down. Now, he was even more amazed at the clarity of the water. Objects always seemed bigger and closer in water than they actually were. Soon, he was tuning out the bubbling sound of his exhaling breath, and the comforting whoosh of air as he breathed in, to enjoy the eerie silence of the deep.

With Brad in the lead, it didn't take them long to get down to the first canyon. A large, solitary fish swam past. Before they left, Brad had shown him a catalogue of fish they could expect to see at this dive spot. With its tawny colour and stripy markings, Tom reckoned this one was a Nassau grouper. Mouth gaping, the fish was curious and swam up to him for a closer look. Tom wanted to stay, but Brad signalled to keep going.

They swam a few metres on, until Brad pointed to a brightly coloured fish, close to the coral.

Silvery red, and with orange–gold stripes, Tom was fascinated. When he got closer, and saw the fish's large eyes, and rear dorsal fin sticking up, he knew it was the unmistakable long-spine squirrelfish. None of the fish he'd seen so far could be found in Australian waters.

Following Brad up the steep side of the reef, he looked behind to check Charles and Carrie were there. They both gave him the okay hand signal. He signalled back, and followed Brad over the top of the reef and into another canyon. Suddenly, he noticed the current strengthening. It surprised him because Brad said there wasn't much of a current in the summer months. He could feel himself being dragged along, and had to kick and breathe harder to keep up with Brad.

Descending into the canyon, they kept close to the reef wall to get a good look at boulder star coral. Suddenly, Brad pointed downwards excitedly.

A green sea turtle sat quietly on the bottom. Enthralled, Tom swam down for a closer look. The turtle's shell was an olive brown colour, and its skin green. The creature looked huge − about four feet long. Mesmerised, he watched it for a while. The turtle didn't look frightened in the face of this intrusion, but Tom knew a green sea turtle couldn't pull its head into its shell like other turtles, so it was hard to tell if it felt threatened or not. Reluctantly, he decided to move on.

But when he looked up, he couldn't see Brad. He looked back. Where were Charles and Carrie?

He was alone.

Kicking hard, he tried to catch up. But, in just a few yards, he had to stop. He couldn't catch his breath. What was wrong? He checked his pressure gauge. *No air!* The shock rippled through him. Knowing vibrations travel fast in water, he tried to make some noise by banging on his oxygen tank to attract attention.

No-one came.

Now, he had no time to think, or do anything other than make an emergency ascent to the surface. He was around 50 feet down. How long to get to the top, he wondered? Would the air in his lungs run out? His training kicked in. Swift, but steady, he breathed out as he swam up to the surface, slowly inflating his life jacket as he went.

His heart was pounding in his chest, but he knew he had to keep calm or he'd be dead.

On he went... towards the light. Keep going...

Kick...

He felt dizzy... Keep going...

His lungs felt they would burst.

Kick... kick...

Finally, he broke through the surface. Gasping for breath, he tore off his mask and trod water. Trying to control his in and out breathing, he felt like he'd run a marathon. But he kept a controlled rhythm until he finally regained his breath.

Only then did he look around for the dive boat. *Shit!* Nothing but ocean. He started shouting to attract attention, but there was no-one, and nothing, but water. The strong current had dragged him way off course.

He looked up at the sun to get his bearings. Then his blood ran cold when he turned back and saw a black shape looming below. He braced himself as it came to the surface.

Carrie!

She pulled off her mask. "My God!" She sounded as breathless as him. "Are you okay?"

"I had to make an emergency ascent."

"I heard a noise in the canyon. When I turned and couldn't see you, I swam back. I knew there was something wrong when you started your ascent. But I couldn't catch up in time to help."

"I ran out of air."

She frowned. "We haven't been down *that* long. You checked your tank, didn't you?"

"Yes. Must have a problem... And there's no sign of the boat."

As she looked around, Tom noticed how calm Carrie was.

"We've drifted off course in the current." She held onto his arm. "Brad'll come looking for us with the boat. Ditch your lead belt. It'll be easier to stay afloat."

Tom did as he was told. He was surprised at Carrie's strength as they held onto each other. She was holding him up, rather than the other way around. And she seemed completely at ease, as if she were treading water in a swimming pool rather than in the ocean. "What if he doesn't come?" he said.

"He'll be here," she said, firmly. "He knows the currents."

They floated together on the surface for a while, but the swell was increasing with the wind. "We should try and swim back to shore," he said, although he couldn't actually see land.

"No, we must wait. Brad won't leave me out here."

They bobbed about in the waves for what seemed like an eternity, although it was probably only 15 minutes. Then he heard the sound of a motor. Relief flooded through him when he saw the boat heading in their direction.

They both started shouting, and waving their masks in the air, to attract attention.

"What the *hell* happened?" Brad shouted as the boat pulled up alongside them.

"Tom ran out of air," Carrie said. She grabbed the side of the boat and pulled herself up. "I saw him make an emergency ascent from a way off, and followed him up."

Brad and Charles helped her into the boat first, then Tom.

Tom was angry with Brad. "You were *supposed* to be my diving buddy."

Brad looked devastated. "Sorry, mate. Never known the current so strong down there in the summer."

"What are you playing at, Brad?" Charles shouted, his voice hard. "Didn't you check all the tanks?"

Tom turned to see how pale Charles was. Anyone would think *he'd* nearly drowned. Why was he so upset?

"Of course I checked them!" Brad said, defensively. "I don't understand it."

"Well, everyone's safe and sound," Carrie said, evenly. "So let's get back before the wind gets any worse."

"Sorry, Carrie," Brad said, quietly. "Are you okay?"

"I'm fine." She smiled, brightly. "And so is Tom."

Carrie was the voice of reason, Tom thought. He'd been so glad to see her when she surfaced beside him. "Thanks for coming to my rescue," he said. "I owe you."

She touched his arm. "You'd have done the same for me."

The group was silent on the way back, but Tom's head was reeling. Had someone deliberately tampered with his tank? He tried to remember the sequence of events back at the Dive Centre. Brad had checked all the tanks. So had Carrie. He'd even checked his own tank before leaving. He was sure there was nothing wrong with it then.

So who else could have had access to it? A couple of local lads at the Centre had loaded the tanks and equipment onto the boat. It was always possible one of them had tampered with it. On the boat, of course, they'd all had access, except for Brad's local employee who was steering the boat the whole time.

Had it been an attempt on his life, Tom wondered? Why would anyone want to harm him? Maybe it was intended as a warning, to stop him digging into the Governor's accident and Mrs Pearson's murder? Whatever the intention, it only made him more determined to dig harder. Most of all, he wanted to help Jess and keep her safe. He was worried though. It was already Friday, and he was supposed to be flying out to Miami on Sunday afternoon.

Why were the British authorities so slow to react? If this were an Australian Territory, the Australian police would be all over it by now. He just hoped to God that when he got back, Jess would tell him the UK police were on their way.

31

Halfway up the road to the lighthouse, Chuck eased off the accelerator and pointed through his pick-up truck's windscreen. "That's Clement's place."

Tom screwed up his eyes against the sun's glare. The first thing he noticed about the house were the two dormer windows jutting out of the tiled roof, like look-outs. They seemed to be a feature of these island houses. Next was the upstairs verandah that circled the house. Its balustrades were painted blue, as were the plantation shutters at each window. The blue stood out against the white-wash on the rest of the house, and resembled the colour of the deep ocean. He shifted uncomfortably. He didn't want to be reminded of his encounter with the deep. He'd still be down there with that turtle, if he hadn't been an experienced diver.

He forced himself to concentrate.

This was only the second time Tom had met Chuck, who was a man of few words. Tom didn't feel the need to chat either, so they got along fine. He checked his watch; the sun was still strong for 4.30. He opened his passenger window wide to let air blow straight through his and Chuck's windows. It was the only air conditioning on offer.

Tom noticed that Chuck kept checking his driver's mirror. Was someone following, he wondered? He pulled down his passenger sun visor in the hope of finding a vanity mirror to see the road behind, but there wasn't one. He said nothing.

He was surprised to see there were no security guards or electronic gates at the front of the house. Apart from a black railing running around its perimeter, the driveway was accessible to everyone. "Why no security for a Government Minister?" he asked.

"Guess Clement thought he didn't need any." Chuck checked his mirror again, and drove through a stone archway, into the drive. He pulled up outside a large double garage that was integral to the house, like a basement. He leant over, opened the glove box and pulled out a bunch of keys. "Let's be quick, Tom. My truck's recognisable."

Tom looked at him. "Didn't you get permission to access the crime scene?"

Chuck shrugged. "Yes and no." He paused. "*Yes*, in that I said I'd left my sunglasses up here when I attended the crime scene on Wednesday. And *no* in that I didn't say I was bringin' you up here to take a look."

Tom followed Chuck out of the truck, and up some stone steps to the front porch. This time they came across a black metal gate that filled another archway, and barred their way. It was secured with a padlock.

Chuck found the right key from the bunch, and opened it. The gate swung open, and they stepped through onto a patio made of decking. A sudden gust of wind caught the gate, and it clanged shut behind them.

Chuck looked up at the sky. "The wind's changing direction," he said, calmly.

Tom looked down at the dead leaves and petals, from the pots of pink bougainvillea, swirling around his feet.

No-one had tended the plants for a couple of days. In fact, the house stood neglected and silent, as if waiting for them to unlock its secrets. He felt a strange sense of unease.

Even Chuck tensed up at the front door. Did he expect some invisible force to attack him as he entered? He pushed the door open, and stood back to let Tom go in first.

The house had been shut up, with no air conditioning for a couple of days. The claustrophobic heat was overpowering. So was the unmistakable smell of death.

Once he'd adjusted to it, Tom walked through the hallway and into the main living area. It was a large, open plan, lounge diner. From every direction, the windows looked out over an amazing panoramic view of the island and ocean. "Awesome," he said.

Chuck nodded and led the way down some steps. Unlocking another door at the bottom, they went through into a dark basement and garage. The smell down here was stronger.

"Lingers, doesn't it?" Chuck switched on the lights.

The basement and garage formed one huge room that was filled with two cars, gardening equipment, a couple of old tyres, and a small boat already loaded on a trailer with wheels. A fishing net covered the far wall, with a row of fishing rods lined up underneath. A long wooden beam ran the length of the ceiling. It had fish hooks screwed in at certain spots, no doubt for hanging big game fish. "Can we open the garage doors?" Tom asked.

Chuck shook his head. "Might attract attention."

Tom understood. "Can you tell me what actually happened to Mrs Pearson down here?"

"We're still waiting for the autopsy report," Chuck replied. "But it looks like she was killed around midnight on Tuesday. She was found by her daughter the next day, around midday. She'd been phonin' her mother all mornin', but couldn't get a reply. She picked up her young kid from kindergarten at lunchtime, and came straight up here."

Tom nodded. "So what do forensics think happened? Was it a break-in?"

Chuck shook his head. "There were no signs of forced entry. These garage doors were shut, along with the front door, when her daughter got here. She let herself in with her key."

"So Mrs Pearson must have let her killer in," Tom said. "That means she either knew that person, or didn't see them as a threat." He paused. "Were any domestic staff working here on Tuesday, or on Wednesday when she was found?"

Chuck shook his head. "The cleaner was off sick. The gardener was off too, his wife's just had a baby."

"So someone knew Mrs Pearson was alone?"

Chuck nodded. "Looks like it."

Tom walked to the far end where the fishing net hung over the wall. He could see a large area close by where the floor had been scrubbed clean. He looked up at the wooden beam above the spot. "Is this where she was strung up?"

Chuck nodded. "Exactly the same spot as poor old Clement." He swallowed. "He hung himself, you know."

The *same* spot. That interested Tom. It must be significant in some way. "Was it the slash to her throat that killed Mrs Pearson?" he asked.

Chuck nodded.

"So there'd have been a lot of blood."

"It wasn't a pretty sight." Chuck's face paled at the memory. "I was sergeant on duty at the station when the first officers on the scene phoned in. I came straight out." His face looked pained, remembering the scene.

"She was wearing white pyjamas. Her bare feet were tied with rope, and she was strung upside down from the beam up there."

They both looked up.

"Could one person do that?" Tom asked.

Chuck looked thoughtful. "She was small, but plump. Must have weighed over 60 kilos. So whoever strung her up must have been strong."

"Or had some help?" Tom added. "Did they leave anything behind? Footprints in the blood, or tyre marks outside the house?"

"Well..." Chuck hesitated. "There was one thing." He looked up. "A voodoo poppet doll was pinned to the beam up there... next to Mrs Pearson. It had a knife through its throat."

"A voodoo doll?"

Chuck nodded. "These dolls are a way of castin' spells on people. A sort of black magic."

"Was that voodoo doll meant as a curse on Mrs Pearson, and the house?"

"Exactly."

Tom gave him a sceptical look. "I noticed the mirror in the hallway was turned to the wall. Is that voodoo too?"

"Yep. Mirrors represent doorways to the world of the dead. I guess this means Mrs Pearson was refused entry, and is doomed to wander the earth like a ghost or zombie throughout time."

"You don't believe all that mumbo jumbo, do you?" Tom asked.

Chuck looked serious. "Doesn't matter what I believe or not. Those who practise it do." He paused. "I've been out to the Haitian settlement to interview the cleaner and gardener. They're both Haitians, and both terrified. Couldn't get a word out of either of them." He shrugged.

"We get a wall of silence whenever we want to talk about voodoo."

"Is it still practised much on this island?"

"Yeah, in secret. None of us locals get to see it."

Tom couldn't understand why the police didn't deal with it on a small island like this. "Why don't you stop it?" he asked. "Ban it altogether?"

Chuck looked at him. "Can you ever ban anything, Tom? It'll go even deeper underground."

Tom took the point. As he looked at the beam again in the claustrophobic silence, he felt the hairs on the back of his neck stand up. He didn't know Mrs Pearson, hadn't even seen her. But he'd seen enough murder victims to be able to conjure up the fear on her face, the disbelief as the knife cut into her throat, the pain. He could even hear her cries for help, her screams...

Suddenly, the garage doors rattled in a violent gust of wind.

They both jumped.

Chuck shivered despite the heat. "Let's get out of here."

But Tom wasn't going to be spooked. "This boat," he said, going over to it. "Can you tell if it's been out to sea lately?"

Chuck went over and inspected the sides and the trailer. "Hasn't been out for some time, I'd say."

Tom pulled the tarpaulin off that covered the open part of the boat. He climbed in and sat down. "Who benefits from Clement and his wife's deaths?"

"The daughter is their only child now. She inherits everything. But she won't talk to us, or come up here. Too scared. She thinks she'll be cursed if she does, and end up like her mother."

Tom pulled a face. "Not Haitian, is she?"

"Nah. But the whole island's scared shitless."

Tom looked around the garage and basement again. The whole place spoke of the sea, of life *on* the sea, of life *from* the sea. The sea was crucial to all this. He was sure of it. He glanced over at Chuck. "I heard Clement Pearson gave evidence to a British Government Inquiry into the sinking of Haitian sloops on the day he... died," he said. "What can you tell me about that?"

Chuck stepped back. "We need to get out of here now. Let's talk in the truck on the way to the Government Garage."

Tom frowned. "Why are we going there?"

"Seems the Governor's Land Rover was there all along."

Tom stared at him. "Impossible!"

Chuck nodded. "Come on, let's go." He turned on his heels and walked over to the door. He couldn't wait to get out of the place.

Tom was just getting out of the boat, when he noticed something glittering under the seat in front. He bent forward and picked it up. A little, brass key. It looked identical to the one Jess had found in the Governor's desk. "Chuck," he called, excitedly.

But Chuck had already gone.

Tom slipped the key into his trouser pocket, and had a last look around the room before he left. They'll probably end up bulldozing the place, he thought. No-one on a small island like this would ever want to live here again.

★

Chuck drove at a steady pace back down Lighthouse Road towards town.

Tom could feel his tension. He felt guilty for putting him in the awkward position of helping him. But his detective's instincts were on overdrive. He needed to get as much information as he could from him while he had the chance.

"Can we talk about that British Government Inquiry into the two Haitian sloops now, Chuck?" He paused. "I understand Clement was the Immigration Minister when they sank. Was he held responsible for what happened in some way? Did that drive him to take his own life?"

Chuck gripped the steering wheel tight. "The Haitians are the problem. They just keep comin'. Waves of 'em. There's eight million of 'em over there." He pointed out to sea. "We can't take 'em all."

Tom understood. He knew all about illegal immigration. That was the reason he was travelling the globe, to find out how other countries dealt with it. "It's a big problem everywhere, Chuck."

"Yeah."

"How do you process the illegals when they get here?"

"We take 'em over to the detention centre in Provo, then we fly them straight back to Haiti. They're all economic migrants, looking for a better life. Can't blame 'em. They're dirt poor over there." He paused for breath. "But look at us. We're just small islands. There are no jobs for 'em, apart from buildin' hotels and houses. We can't support thousands of Haitians. No," he said, firmly. "Straight back, and that's that."

That was the frankest exchange Tom had had with anyone on the subject of illegal immigration on all his travels. "So what happened to these two sloops?" he asked.

"Terrible... terrible." Chuck's whole frame seemed to tremble. "Grown men weeping as they pulled bodies from the sea. All dead." He wiped his brow on his arm. "The sharks got some of 'em. Legs missin', arms. Some even their heads." He shuddered. "Never seen anythin' like it."

Tom could see this had affected Chuck deeply.

"The thing is they don't want to come here." Chuck's voice had risen now. "They want to go to the States. That's where they think they're goin'. That's where they pay the people smugglers to take 'em." He pressed down hard on the accelerator. "They're bein' cheated out of the little money they have. They were always goin' to end up losin' their lives on the reef."

Tom turned that over in his mind. *They were always going to end up losing their lives on the reef.* That was a strange thing to say.

Suddenly Chuck slammed his fist on the horn, as a donkey strayed out into the road. He was getting all steamed up and liable to crash the truck if Tom didn't stop asking questions. He sat quietly for a while, until Chuck had calmed down. Then he asked: "Isn't there a working lighthouse up on the headland?"

"Ycah."

"So the sloops would have seen the light warning them about the reef. Why not steer clear?"

Chuck shrugged.

They sat silent as they drove alongside the main beach out of town. Despite the wind, the sky was still blue, and the water inside the reef like a turquoise lagoon. The sun was just sinking below the horizon as the waves crashed onto the reef. Tom thought it looked stunning. He wondered if Jess was watching the sunset too. He turned to Chuck and asked again. "Did Clement get blamed for these sloop sinkings? Is that why he committed suicide?"

Chuck shook his head, sadly. "No-one would blame Clement. He was one of the good guys. But it must have weighed on him. He kind of withdrew into himself. Didn't turn up at the office. Just liked to go out fishin' on that boat of his."

"Do you think Clement's wife knew he was having a really hard time?"

"Sure she did. They'd been sweethearts from kids. Always together. Oh yeah, she'd have known everything. She'd supported Clement her entire life."

Now Tom was getting to the heart of things. He wondered whether or not to ask his next question, then decided he had to. "Do you think Clement committed suicide, Chuck? Or was he murdered too?"

Chuck glanced over, then back at the road. He wasn't surprised by the question. "All I know is the autopsy said poor old Clement hung himself. So did the inquest."

"So why would anyone want to murder Clement's wife, and in such a brutal way?" Tom asked. "Why hang her by her feet from the beam in exactly the same spot Clement took his own life? What's the significance of that? Why cut her throat? And why the voodoo curse?"

"That's what we're tryin' to figure out, Tom," Chuck said, quietly. He checked his driver mirror again and frowned.

"Have we got company?" Tom asked.

"We've had company since I picked you up," came the reply.

Tom resisted the urge to look behind. "Look, Chuck, I don't want to get you into trouble. Just drop me off somewhere and forget this afternoon."

Chuck looked over. "Did you say you had those photos of the Governor's car on your phone?"

"Yep."

"Good. I'll park up and take a look at them before we go into the Government Garage."

32

Tucking the telephone receiver between her ear and shoulder, Jess waited for the Embassy switchboard in Washington to put her through to the Management Officer. She felt sick to the stomach, but she had to find out the truth about where Simon was. And why he was lying to her.

Her eyes drifted again to the brass key lying on the desk. It shone brightly, as if recently polished. Less than two inches long, with a simple 'bit' to operate the lock and a hollow shank, it looked more like a key that would open an antique desk drawer, or some kind of trinket box. Was the design of the heart-shaped bow significant, she wondered?

An interesting key, but what on earth did it open?

She gazed around the office for the umpteenth time. She'd found the key in the desk drawer in the Governor's Residence study, but it wouldn't fit any of the locks over there. And none in here either.

"You still there, Ma'am?" the operator came back on.

"Yes."

"Can you hold for another minute?"

"Yes."

Jess rubbed her aching temples. She'd searched this office from top to bottom, going through every drawer, every book on the shelves, and every piece of paper in the Governor's cupboard. It would help if she knew what she was looking for. Just something out of the ordinary, Tom said. Something that would give them a clue about what was going on. Well, she'd been at it for over an hour, and found nothing – at least nothing that had caught her interest.

"Okay, Ma'am," the operator said. "Putting you through now."

"Thank you." Jess heard some crackling.

A male voice came on the line. "Hello, Jess."

"Hello," she said. "We haven't met yet. I'm Simon Hill's partner."

"Yes. Yes, of course. I know who you are."

"Sorry to trouble you." Jess took a deep breath. "I-I'm trying to contact Simon, but he seems to... have gone on leave."

"Yes, he's in the UK for a couple of weeks." There was another pause. "I thought you'd gone with him?"

Simon's in the UK?

"No," she replied, calmly. "I'm in the Turks and Caicos Islands on temporary duty at the moment."

"Lucky you," he laughed. "I could do with some relaxation on the beach. Great diving down there too, I hear."

"Yes," Jess said to jolly him along. "Why did you think I'd gone to the UK with Simon?"

"Funnily enough, I've just been doing the monthly accounts check. It says Simon bought two return air tickets to the UK, so I just assumed..." There was an awkward pause. "I just assumed the second ticket was for you."

"I see." She tried to keep her voice bright. "Did he say he'd be in London?"

"Don't *you* know?"

She could hear him trying to suppress the surprise in his voice, but how could she tell him Simon wouldn't answer her calls or texts?

"I'll try his London flat," she said, quickly.

"Good idea. I expect you'll find him there." His voice was kind and sympathetic, and that made her feel worse.

"If Simon does get in touch with you," she said, "will you tell him I need to speak to him urgently?"

"I'll do that."

"Thanks... Goodbye."

"Bye Jess."

She put the phone down in the cradle, and sat frozen, staring into the distance. Too numb even to get angry or cry.

It was the rattling door handle that brought her back to the present.

"Jess!" Sally called out.

She ignored it.

"Jess! There's a classified e-gram for you from London."

Jess rubbed her face and eyes, and got up wearily to unlock the door. She hadn't wanted anyone to see her searching the Governor's office. Now, she was really glad she'd locked it.

Sally gave her a wan smile. "Everything all right?" she asked, handing over a file. "Only you look..."

"Everything's fine." Jess took the file back to the Governor's desk and sat down.

Sally followed her. "It's from the Director of Overseas Territories."

Jess opened the file cover and began reading.

CONFIDENTIAL AND PERSONAL FOR
JESS TURNER

I was shocked to get your e-gram, and called an emergency meeting in the Foreign Office this morning.

Tomorrow (Saturday), I leave for the TCI, accompanied by a team of three police officers from Scotland Yard. They will assess TCI police manpower and resources on the ground, as well as their response to the Governor's car crash and Mrs Pearson's murder. Further UK police officers will follow if necessary.

A forensic road accident and collision expert in the UK has studied the photos of the Governor's car you e-mailed, and agrees things look suspicious. The Governor of the Cayman Islands has agreed to send over an independent forensic expert to investigate the car wreckage and accident. Being closer to the TCI, their expert should be with you tomorrow (Saturday) evening.

The rest of us will arrive in Miami on Saturday evening, overnight there, and fly down to the TCI on Sunday morning.

I may be jumping the gun because I don't know the full sequence of events or whether the Governor is involved in any wrongdoing, but I have asked the UK police to investigate his bank accounts and other finances. They will also interview his wife, Jayne, on her return from Miami this evening.

I am sorry that you find yourself in this situation Jess, particularly as you are only in Post temporarily to cover for a colleague. David's mother passed away yesterday evening, and he was so grateful to have been at her bedside. I will be seeing him later this evening to find out all he knows about recent events in Grand Turk.

Meanwhile your safety, and the safety of all the staff in the Governor's Office, is paramount. Please take great care, and do nothing to endanger yourselves in any way.

Director of Overseas Territories

Jess sighed and looked up. "Hallelujah. The cavalry's coming!"

Sally nodded, she'd obviously read the e-gram despite its privacy marking.

Jess clicked into business mode again. "Will you organise hotel reservations and hire cars for them all please, Sally?"

Suddenly a thud on the window made them jump. They looked over to see a broken frond from a palm tree pinned against the window pane before sliding to the ground.

Jess frowned. "We need to get some advice from the Met Office about that tropical storm. The wind's definitely getting up?"

Sally looked worried. "I hope Brad and Tom are all right out there diving."

"So do I."

"I really do love Brad, you know, Jess. But, well... when he said he went out to the site of the Spanish ship wreck alone, I knew he wasn't telling me the truth." She shook her head. "He wouldn't dive alone, he's too careful for that. Someone would have to stay on the boat, wouldn't they?"

Jess nodded.

"So who's been helping him? That's what *I* want to know."

Jess shrugged. "I'm afraid you'll have to ask him that."

"I would, but he's not speaking to me." Sally looked hurt. "Said I couldn't keep my big mouth shut."

"Oh don't worry, Sally. He's just upset his secret's out. Probably thinks there's a posse of treasure hunters hotfooting it out to his shipwreck as we speak. He'll come round."

Sally didn't look convinced.

Jess smiled at her. "You did the right thing telling me."

A familiar rustling of stockings made them both look towards the door.

Alvita stood watching them. Had she heard everything? "The Police Commissioner's here for you, Jess," she said.

Jess checked her watch – 3.45; she wasn't expecting Dexter until five. She thought about Simon again, with a heavy heart. But circumstances weren't going to allow her time to mope. "Okay," she said, "please show him in."

★

When Dexter Robinson walked in at a brisk pace, rather than his usual slow gait, Jess knew he was agitated.

"Good afternoon, Jess."

"Afternoon, Dexter." She got up and moved over to the sofa and chairs. "Do sit down."

He eased his bulk into the sturdiest chair.

"You're early," she said. "I hope this means you've got some good news."

"I'm afraid not." He drummed his fingers on the arms of the chair. "Have you heard the news? The storm has intensified into a Category 2 hurricane."

Oh God, she thought, that's all we need

He nodded. "It's over the west coast of Haiti right now."

"What does that mean for us?" she asked, calmly.

"Cat 2 hurricanes mean wind speeds of between 96–110mph," he said. "If it continues on its northerly trajectory, the eye of the storm will pass off the west coast of Provo."

Jess knew from her previous cyclone experience that they would still take a battering.

He nodded, as if reading her thoughts. "It will be strong enough to damage buildings, knock out the power lines, and the phone system," he went on. "There's likely to be considerable flooding depending on the speed with which it passes over."

"What about a storm surge in its wake?"

"Impossible to say," he went on. "These hurricanes form out in the Caribbean Sea, and usually weaken as they blow themselves out over the mountains of Haiti, so it's impossible to predict." He glanced at her. "We are at its mercy."

Jess got up, went over to the antique globe in the corner, and tried to spin it to find Haiti. "Oh!" A loud sound of clinking glass made her stop. It was coming from inside the globe. She grasped the mahogany bracket and pulled. The top half opened to reveal a drinks cabinet inside. Why hadn't she seen this before, she wondered? The bottom section was covered with a wooden insert fitted with custom-made holes. And they in turn were full of dusty bottles and equally dusty glasses. She turned. "Are you a whisky man, Dexter?"

He shook his head. "I don't drink."

"Very sensible." She closed the top of the globe, and found Haiti on the map. She traced the path of the hurricane to the west coast of Provo with a sense of foreboding. From the moment she'd arrived in Grand Turk, it felt like she'd been caught up in an accelerating maelstrom and it was set to get a whole lot worse. "When will the hurricane get here?" she asked, wearily.

"In 36 to 48 hours."

"So sometime on Sunday?"

"Yes," he replied.

"Just when the UK police were due to arrive."

He flinched at her words. "So they *are* coming?"

"Yes," she said. "The Director of Overseas Territories is coming himself, with a team of three UK police officers. They arrive in Miami tomorrow evening, and fly here on Sunday morning."

He stared at her. "So be it," he said, gravely.

The Police Commissioner had a portentous way of speaking English, as if he were quoting directly from the classics. But she guessed he was giving her some kind of warning. Now, all she could do was get on with things until the London team got here. "So," she said, focusing on what was necessary. "We need to put our hurricane emergency plans into action now and get ready."

"I've called a meeting of the Grand Turk Disaster Management Committee for six this evening at the Centre on the Ridge," he said.

She nodded. "I've just been up there with Alvita. She's been showing me the ropes."

He nodded, as if he already knew. "The Minister Roger Pearson is in Grand Turk. He will chair the meeting."

"I thought the Minister only came over from Provo when Parliament was sitting."

The Police Commissioner shrugged. "He came back yesterday evening."

"I see." She paused. "Have you instructed the DMCs on the other islands to meet this evening?"

"Yes. And a bulletin is going out on local radio and TV at six to warn people to make hurricane preparations." He paused. "I'd like to advise airlines to notify passengers and tourists to leave the island before the storm gets here." He looked at her. "The Governor usually gives this order."

She nodded. "I'll approve it in his absence."

"Good."

"Right, I'll see you at the Disaster Management Centre at six," she said, giving him his cue to leave.

But the Police Commissioner was not a man to be rushed. "I wanted you to know we've been taking the disappearance of Mrs Canning's dog seriously, and the coffin nails warning." He paused. "As you suggested, we put a 24 hour guard on her house, for her safety and peace of mind. But..."

Jess waited.

"But she attacked one of our officers last night," he said, quietly.

Jess stared at him. What on earth would make Rebekah attack one of his officers? Had she completely lost it?

"She attacked him with a cricket bat," Dexter went on. "He's in the clinic with concussion."

Jess couldn't believe what she was hearing. "Why on earth would Mrs Canning do that? Was it a mistake? Did she think your officer was an intruder? Or someone who wanted to harm her?"

He shrugged. "We don't know. She wouldn't calm down. So we arrested her and brought her into the police station."

"Oh my God!"

He nodded. "She's refusing to be interviewed, or give a statement. So we're going to charge her with assaulting a police officer."

Jess wasn't surprised.

"She's still causing a scene," he went on, "so I was hoping you might come down to the police station, and... sit with her."

She needs a lawyer, not a nanny, Jess thought.

"Does she have lawyer?" she asked.

He shook his head.

"Well you need to get her one."

He looked dejected.

"What about Mrs Pearson's murder?" she asked. "Has there been any progress?"

"We've brought in her Haitian gardener and cleaner for questioning too."

"Her domestic staff?" Jess paused to think. "What would their motive be? Has something been stolen from the house? Jewellery? Money? Other valuables?"

He shifted in his seat. "Their daughter's still refusing to go in to see what's missing."

"So why have you brought her Haitian domestic staff in for questioning?"

"We found a voodoo doll at the scene." He hesitated. "It was staked to the same beam as Mrs Pearson, with a knife through its throat."

Jess processed that bombshell for a minute before asking icily: "Why didn't I know about this before?"

"We weren't sure of its relevance."

Her eyes narrowed. "Not sure of its relevance?"

He looked away. "I ought to be getting back, there's a lot to do." But, again, he didn't move.

Jess was getting increasingly annoyed. "Is there something else you want to tell me, Dexter?"

He carefully folded his handkerchief and put it in his pocket. "People who don't know this island, and our customs, can soon find themselves in difficulty."

What was he talking about now? Or *who* was he talking about? Her?

"Visitors – or guests to be more precise – shouldn't meddle in what doesn't concern them," he continued.

Guests? Was he talking about Tom? She wished Dexter would stop going round the houses. "What exactly are you trying to say?" she asked, bluntly.

He gave her a stern look. "There was a diving accident at the reef this afternoon. Your Australian guest had to make an emergency ascent when his tank ran out of air."

She gasped. "Is he all right?"

"I think so."

"Is he in the clinic?"

He shrugged.

She jumped up. "Where is he, then?"

"I don't know where he is right now, but he's certainly getting around the island, poking into every corner." His dark eyes fixed on hers. "I suggest you restrain him, before he finds himself in *real* peril." Dexter got up and politely took his leave.

After he'd gone, Jess sat at the desk, her head reeling. *Visitors shouldn't meddle in what doesn't concern them.* It was a warning, clear as day. The Police Commissioner was telling her he knew Tom was digging around into the Governor's accident and Mrs Pearson's murder. Oh God, it was all her fault. She should never have let Tom get mixed up in all this. A diving accident? She shivered. She had to find Tom immediately, and check he was all right. Then she had to get him off this island as soon as possible. She couldn't live with herself if anything happened to him.

33

Jess half ran, half walked along the drive to the Residence. It was well over an hour since the Police Commissioner had left, and Tom still wasn't answering his mobile. *I suggest you restrain him before he finds himself in real peril.* She was certain now Dexter knew far more about what was going on than he was willing to tell her. The man was an enigma. When she talked to him, she felt he was being honest, yet he was clearly lying. Or perhaps not so much lying, as keeping her in the dark.

Then a thought crossed her mind. All along, she'd been asking herself whether she could trust *him*. Maybe he was trying to work out if he could trust *her*, especially if the Governor had been up to no good.

A gust of wind whipped along the drive, covering her in a cloud of sand. She coughed and covered her mouth with her hand. She had sand in her throat, in her nose, in her hair, in her shoes. Everywhere. She put her head down and rushed on.

She should never have let Tom go out diving and nosing around. He was a detective. His instincts were to get stuck in. Thank goodness Sally had managed to book him on a domestic flight to Provo tomorrow afternoon. And from there, onto the last scheduled international flight to Miami. He had to get back to Australia to give that presentation to the PM next week anyway. And if he didn't leave before the hurricane struck, he could get stranded for days, or even weeks.

But where was he now? She started running as fast as she could. The house was silent at the front. "*Tom!*" she shouted. She ran round the verandah to the back. "*Tom!*" But the courtyard was empty and silent. She ran into the kitchen. Empty too. Where was Maggie? She went into the hallway. "*Tom!*" she shouted up the stairs. "Are you here?" No reply. She ran up the stairs and knocked on his door. Silence.

She was alone in the house. All she could hear was the wind rattling the shutters like a prowler trying to get in. Then she heard an engine. She ran downstairs and opened the front door.

Tom jumped out of an old pick-up truck, and waved to the driver as he pulled away. He turned and saw her. "What's up?" he asked.

"You haven't been answering your mobile?" She sounded breathless.

"Oh, I couldn't have it on where we were."

"Where *were* you?"

"Out with Chuck. We've been back to the Government Garage, and up to Clement Pearson's house. He's been showing me the scene of the murder."

Jess was relieved to see him unhurt, yet angry he'd been out investigating. "You didn't say you were going out with Chuck after diving."

He nodded. "But look what I found up at Clement's house." He reached into his pocket and pulled out the little brass key to show her.

She took it from him. "It looks like the one I found in the Governor's desk drawer."

"Exactly!"

She went back into the kitchen, where she'd flung her handbag on the table. Opening it, she pulled out her brass key and compared it to the one Tom had given her. "They look the same."

Tom took both keys and held them up to the light. "Yep, I'm pretty sure they are."

What lock do they fit though, she wondered? "Well, I hope you have better luck finding the lock they fit than I've had."

His face fell. "Nothing?"

She shook her head.

He sighed. "I could do with a beer. How about you?"

She was getting annoyed again. He wasn't even going to mention the diving accident. "I see you're all right, then?"

He opened his hands in a gesture that said *don't I look all right?*

"I know about your diving accident. The Police Commissioner told me."

"Ah, I see. News certainly travels fast." He frowned. "Come on, let's go out into the courtyard, and I'll tell you what I've been up to."

She looked at her watch. "I have to go to a meeting up at the Disaster Management Centre on the Ridge at 6 o'clock. Did you hear there's a hurricane on the way?"

"Shit!" He stopped.

"It's due to hit sometime on Sunday," she said, calmly. She was about to tell him he was booked on flights out of the Territory tomorrow when he interrupted.

"Let's get that drink, and have a chat. Then, I'll drive you up to the Ridge. That'll give me a chance to take a look at the lighthouse. I'll drop you off first, and pick you up after your meeting."

She looked at him suspiciously. "Why do you want to see the lighthouse?"

"Because all roads seem to lead to it, physically and metaphorically speaking." He gave her a smile. "Anyway, it's an important tourist attraction. I've got to see *that* before I leave."

She shook her head, and followed him out into the courtyard.

"Have you seen Maggie? When I got back here the place was empty, with all the doors open."

He turned in surprise. "I haven't seen Maggie since lunchtime."

★

Jess took a long swig of cold beer and tried to relax back on the sofa. It was surprisingly sheltered in the courtyard. The sun was still out, but the sky had turned hazy. The only sign that a hurricane was on its way was the sound of wind whipping through the bushes. It put her on edge. "Sally's booked you a seat on the four o'clock domestic flight to Provo tomorrow afternoon," she said, "and on the 6 o'clock international flight to Miami."

He looked at her in surprise.

"It'll be the last international flight out of the Territory before the hurricane gets here. I'm told it'll be too dangerous for jets to operate after that."

He put his glass of beer on the table beside his chair. "I think I'll stay until..."

"No," she said, firmly. "You've got to get back to Canberra for your presentation to the PM on Friday. The airport could be closed for ages after the hurricane. You're cutting it fine enough as it is."

He shook his head. "I can't leave you and Sally here alone."

"We won't be alone. Our Director of Overseas Territories is arriving from London tomorrow, with three UK police officers."

"Ah!" He looked relieved. "And about time too!"

She nodded. "They were due to overnight in Miami and get here on Sunday morning, but I've told them there's a hurricane on the way. They're planning to get in ahead of that. So they'll aim to get that last international flight in on Saturday evening." She paused. "The same one you'll be able to leave on."

He looked at her. "What if they don't get here before the airport closes?"

She sat forward, took off her shoes and tapped them on the ground to shake out the sand. "Look Tom, I feel bad enough as it is. You came down here for a break for a couple of days, to see me. I've been chasing from pillar to post with hardly a moment to talk to you, let alone take you out and about. There's a murder enquiry going on, plus the Governor's suspicious car accident. Then..."

"Jess..."

"Then you have an awful diving accident. You could have been *killed*. I-I can't have that on my conscience too."

He frowned. "What do you mean? On your conscience *too*?"

She put her shoes back on as she spoke. "I have to live every day with the part I played in the death of my husband and child," she said, quietly.

"I thought they were killed in a car crash."

"They were, but they wouldn't have been in that car if it hadn't been for me." She could hear the emotion in her voice as she spoke. It was still so hard to talk about, but she would have to explain to make Tom understand why he had to leave before the hurricane. "When I was given a job in the Embassy in Jakarta, Jack and Amy came with me." She looked up. "That's where they were killed, in Indonesia."

He nodded.

"Jack was a marine biologist," she went on, "but there was no work like that for him in Jakarta. So he looked after Amy and the house while I worked."

"I see."

"Well that morning... the morning of the crash, we'd had a row. It was all my fault." She took a deep breath. "I had a go at him because the house looked like a tip. I-I was running late and stressed about a presentation I had to make... I couldn't find my computer memory stick, and I still had to drop Amy at the nursery."

He sat quietly listening.

"Jack got angry, picked up Amy and said he'd take her to nursery to give me more time to get ready. He stormed out of the house, sped down the drive in a temper, and pulled out onto the main road right in the path of an oil tanker." She stopped, as that familiar bleakness settled on her.

"It's all right," he said, softly. "You don't have to tell me any more."

"I keep waking up every day, hoping the pain will grow less. But it never does. All I can hear is the screech of tyres, the explosion as the tanker ploughs into Jack's car, then the fire." She buried her head in her hands. "When I close my eyes all I see is Amy waving through the back window of the car as Jack drove off. Her last words to me were *g'bye mummy!* I hear those words every single day of my life. *Every s*ingle day."

"I see," he said, quietly.

"You must go before the hurricane, Tom."

"But I..."

"*Please*. I *can't* have anything happen to you too." There was a pause. "And take Sally with you?"

He looked at her. "What about you?"

"I'm going to stay here."

"This isn't your problem either, Jess. You've been here for less than a week. You're just helping a colleague. You must come with us."

She shook her head. "I'm going to wait for the London team to get here. I have to help them."

"Oh come on." He was getting cross now. "You've got nothing to stay for."

"I've got nothing to leave for either," she flashed back.

He stared at her. "What about Simon?"

"What about Simon?"

He looked surprised. "Is he coming down? What does he think about you staying?"

"No, he's not coming down." She paused. "And I honestly don't know what he thinks about me staying."

"Surely..."

She put up her hand, wearily. "I have to go, or I'll be late for the meeting."

Tom's eyes narrowed. "Right." He emptied his glass. "Let's go."

"I think I should go on my own."

"Give me the keys," he said. "I'll go and get the office car and bring it round. I'm driving you there."

★

Driving past the Office on their way to the Disaster Management Centre Jess saw the gardeners struggling in the wind to fit the wooden hurricane shutters over the windows. Alvita was directing them, pointing and wagging an authoritative finger. She turned at the sound of the car, and frowned as they went past.

Sally too was playing her part, ringing round resident Brits and other foreign nationals on the island, as well as hotels and guesthouses with tourists, to warn them about the hurricane and give them the chance to leave. After that, she said she would go to the supermarket before they got mobbed, to stock up with the provisions for the Residence.

As Tom drove her, Jess sat compiling a mental list of issues to raise at the meeting. The American airline operator would need to get extra planes in tomorrow to evacuate the tourists, who were mostly on Provo anyway; the local radio station would need to broadcast regular bulletins right across the islands; the generator at the Centre needed to be checked it worked; shipping in the area would need to be informed...

She glanced over at Tom, who drove in silence. She was relieved he'd accepted that he should leave tomorrow afternoon. A little wave of sadness rippled through her. She'd miss having him around. He was the only person on the island she knew she could trust. She'd never tell him that though, in case he felt pressured to stay.

On the main road into town, it was a normal Grand Turk rush hour. No-one was driving fast, or in a panic. These hurricanes were part of everyday life in this Territory. Most storms veered off course anyway, before they got near the islands. But the few direct hits they'd had loomed large in island folklore.

The salty water slopped up over the sides of the salina, and the rusty weather vanes creaked in the wind. There were no green herons or other birds to be seen now. They knew what was coming, and had already left.

Tom slowed as they approached the Dive Centre, and pulled up outside. He pushed the gear into park and looked at the building. "Just seeing if anyone's about," he said.

Jess peered at the small hut-type structure. The diving gear and clothes that normally lay out on the grass had gone, and the door was shut tight. "Looks all locked up to me."

Tom shook his head and pointed to the jetty. "Those two dive boats will need to be moved, or they'll get smashed up in the hurricane."

"Will they bring them onshore and store them in a boat shed somewhere?"

"Someone told me there's a natural harbour at the north-west creek," he said. "Boats shelter up there during hurricanes. Brad might take them up there."

Out to sea, the sun had already gone down and in its place was a mottled, purply black sky. "Here comes the storm," she said, quietly.

They sat for a moment, then he pushed the gear into drive and continued along the road.

"You still haven't told me about the diving accident," she said.

"It wasn't an accident."

"*What?*"

He shrugged. "We all went down to the bottom. I got pretty occupied watching a sea turtle. And when I looked up, I was alone. Everyone else had gone."

"Everyone else?"

"Yeah, Charles and Carrie came out with us too." He sighed. "Then I couldn't breathe. I read the gauge and saw the tank was empty. I tried to make some noise to attract attention, but no-one responded." He shrugged again. "Had no alternative but to make an emergency ascent."

She shuddered. She hated the thought of diving herself, although she understood its attraction for others. "You might still be down there now."

He nodded. "Very easily. That's the first time I've ever had to do an emergency ascent."

She stared at him. "I thought you were an *experienced* diver."

"I am. But it's not every day someone tampers with your oxygen tank and tries to kill you."

"*Kill* you? Are you sure? Could it have been an accident?"

"I checked that tank thoroughly before we left, and while we were in the boat. There's no doubt in my mind, someone tampered with it."

Jess was shocked. Only Brad, Carrie and Charles were on the boat, apart from Tom. Was he saying one of them did it?

He glanced over. "Anyone on the boat could have done it. We were chatting, moving around. The noise from the wind and engine was loud."

"But it doesn't make sense. Why would anyone want to kill you?"

He shrugged. "Maybe I've been asking too many questions?"

She shuddered again. "I don't know who told the Police Commissioner, but he knew what had happened. And do you know what he said?" She paused. "He warned me to restrain you or you'd find yourself in real peril."

Tom's steely eyes narrowed. "Did he now?"

Jess could feel her head throbbing, and rubbed her forehead. "I'm sorry about what happened, Tom." It sounded a trite thing to say.

"Why are you apologising? It's not your fault."

"No, but if it wasn't for me, you wouldn't be here."

"Yeah, and if I wasn't here, I might have stepped off the side-walk and under a bus in Miami." He glanced over at her.

The blunt detective she'd known back in Australia came shining through. She stayed silent as they passed the Haitian settlement. A few women stood in a group outside, each with a small child in their arms. The ever-present skinny dogs sniffed around, foraging for food. Jess's eyes flicked over the flimsy shacks and corrugated iron roofs that would never withstand a hurricane. Where do these people go for shelter? Another issue on her list for the meeting.

Suddenly a face caught her attention. She peered through the window. "Is that Maggie?"

"Where?"

She pointed to one side of the settlement. "Over there. Amongst that group of women."

Tom slowed the car and pulled up alongside the kerb. "I can't see her," he said.

"No." Jess sounded confused. "I can't either now. But I'm sure it was her. She had a child in her arms."

He shrugged. "Want to go and have a look?"

Jess checked her watch. "It's nearly six, I need to get to the meeting."

He nodded and drove on. Halfway up the hill, he slowed and pulled up again. "See that house up ahead on the left? That's Clement's."

Jess could see a house standing alone. "Lovely spot."

"Yes. It's got a great panoramic view over the island and sea from the lounge and deck. But..."

"But what?"

He hesitated. "It's a bit weird in there."

She glanced over. "It's bound to feel eerie, with a suicide and murder in the basement. The Police Commissioner told me about the voodoo doll pinned to the beam, by the way, with a knife through its throat."

He nodded. "Did he mention the hall mirror was turned to face the wall?"

She shook her head.

"Chuck says mirrors represent doorways to the world of the dead in voodoo. Someone wanted to stop Mrs Pearson resting in peace. Apparently now she becomes a zombie or a ghost to wander around the house and the island for eternity."

Jess stared at him, but he looked serious. Was all this getting to him too. "The Police Commissioner's fixated on voodoo too. He's brought her Haitian domestic staff in for questioning."

He glanced at her. "Very convenient. Chuck says the brutal way she was killed has terrified everyone." He paused. "You know, Jess, I can't help feeling that's what it was meant to do."

"Mm." She nodded. "Did Chuck say anything about the way she was strung up by her feet, and her throat cut? Is that something to do with voodoo? I mean I know they sacrifice animals, but..."

Tom gave a dismissive laugh. "Sacrificial ceremonies. What nonsense!"

"It's not though" she said. "Don't forget I've seen one. And the Chief Justice takes voodoo seriously too. Rebekah's convinced the Haitians took her dog." She paused. "I believe voodoo *is* practised here, Tom."

"Jesus! No wonder the Police Commissioner's brought Mrs Pearson's domestic staff in for questioning, then."

"You know what's really bugging me," she went on, "the *way* she was murdered. And why?" She paused. "Do you suppose she knew something about her husband, or about his death? Maybe she was going to speak out, and someone decided to shut her up for good?"

They fell silent.

"I think that key you found at Clement's is the link between him and the Governor," she continued. "I mean, why would they both have a copy of the same key?" She paused. "Where'd you find it anyway?"

"In the garage, wedged under the seat in his boat."

"Bit odd, isn't it? Why didn't the police find it? They must have searched the whole house."

He nodded. "Except the open back of the boat was covered with a tarpaulin. I guess the police didn't check it thoroughly. I have to say Chuck was spooked in there. He couldn't get out fast enough. No doubt the rest of them were too."

She nodded. "They did that to Mussolini, you know. Strung him up like a pig. He was executed, then hung upside down in a service station for everyone to see. It was done to confirm his demise to the people."

Tom glanced over. "Is that what's going on here, do you think? Someone wants to confirm the death of Clement and his wife to the locals?"

She shrugged. "Maybe. But whatever the reason, the manner of her death was so horrific, everyone's terrified of being next." She pointed through the window. "Turn right here, Tom."

He turned the car into the narrow track and bumped along to the building. There were several cars parked haphazardly outside. "Is *that* the Disaster Management Centre?" he asked.

"Yes."

"Well, good luck with that," he said, flatly. "I'll pop up to the lighthouse while you're in there." He glanced over. "I'm just going to take a look. Nothing more."

She sighed. "I might be a while, Tom. Nothing happens very quickly in these meetings."

"That's fine. Just call me, I'll be back in five minutes."

She was about to get out of the car when she remembered. "What happened at the Government Garage when you and Chuck got there? Only London have arranged for an accident forensic expert to come over from the Cayman Islands to examine the Governor's car," she said. "He's due to arrive tomorrow."

"You might as well stand him down, Jess. There's nothing to see."

"Is the car still missing?"

"Oh no, the Land Rover's there, and it's the Governor's all right. But that's the only thing that *is* certain." He pulled a face. "The vehicle's now a burnt out shell. Looks like someone took it, set it alight to remove any trace of the accident and forensic evidence, and then kindly returned it."

34

The white-washed lighthouse looked like a ghostly statue against the darkening clouds. Tom opened a gate in the white picket fence that bordered the plot, and went over to it. A fierce wind blew sea-spray in his face. Must be about 50 to 60 feet tall, he thought, as he looked up at the structure. He reckoned the view from the glass observation tower at the top would be stunning, and walked up the few steps to try the door handle. It was locked. He wondered who kept the keys?

Close by stood another small building, which he guessed was the old kerosene store. The lighthouse was electrified now, but still working to guard the northern end of the island.

He sat down on the steps and looked out to sea. It was a fantastic sight as huge waves broke up on the north-west reef. Rays of light beamed down from behind purple clouds like spotlights on the dark, swirling sea. It looked magical, but he was uneasy.

How could he go and leave Jess on her own? He understood why she didn't want to leave, although he would never tell her that. She felt responsible. He'd witnessed her sense of duty in Australia. And he knew well enough that he would never be able to persuade her to do something she didn't think was right.

A loud roar interrupted his thoughts. He stood up and looked back towards the road. It had sounded like a motorbike, but there was nothing coming. Something glinted further along the headland. He squinted, but he couldn't see what it was.

He turned back to the sea, and walked over to the edge of the bluff. Now the wind seemed to be pushing him back. Was it a warning? He smiled at the very idea.

About 50 yards further along, he could see a path along the top of the cliff, and even further along, a dirt track zig zagging down to a small beach. Directly below him, water swirled treacherously around jagged rocks. The rock formation was unusual, and he wondered if there were any caves down there. It was impossible to see from the top, where he stood. He would only be able to check that out from the beach.

He looked up at the sky. Dusk was fast approaching, but he reckoned he still had about 15 minutes or so of daylight. He stood up, pulled a torch from his trouser pocket, and started walking along the cliff path. Reaching the dirt track, he started down. At first the going was good. The trodden down earth was easier to negotiate than he'd thought. As the path got narrower and steeper, the wind strengthened, making it more difficult to keep his footing. He could feel the reverberation of the waves pounding the reef underfoot. He tried to concentrate on the path, but he could hardly take his eyes off the sea. The roar of the wind and the waves was strangely menacing.

Suddenly, loose stones and earth came sliding down from above. When he looked up, he thought he saw a shadow.

Turning back, he slipped. A searing pain shot through his knee as he tumbled over. Arms flailing, he rolled over and over, his hands trying to grasp onto something.

Rolling onto his back, he dug his heels into the earth, and came to a stop on the track. Gingerly he pulled himself into a sitting position, and rubbed his knee. Sore, but not broken. He turned onto his stomach and started climbing back up the track on all fours. Suddenly a crack rang out. He craned his neck to look up.

A figure loomed above.

Something whined past his ear.

He pressed himself flat on his stomach. More bullets pinged into the earth around his feet. He pushed his face so hard into the earth, he could hardly breathe.

Suddenly, the whole scene lit up. The lighthouse. A strong light beamed out to sea.

He held his breath.

★

Jess paced around outside the Disaster Management Centre, wondering why Tom wasn't answering his phone or texts. Where the hell was he? It was pitch black now, everyone else had gone at least 15 minutes ago. She jumped as something touched her leg. It was only a small branch being blown along the ground by the strengthening wind.

She heard an engine in the distance, and peered along the track, but she couldn't see any lights.

Her phone rang, making her jump again. "Hello," she answered.

"Where are you?" Tom shouted.

"Where am *I*?" she asked, sarcastically. "Where are *you*?"

"Listen, Jess." His voice was low, but urgent. "Go inside the building and lock yourself in!"

"Whatever for?"

"Go inside. Now! Please!"

Jess didn't know what was going on, but she heard the panic in his voice. "Okay," she said.

"And stay in there until you hear my voice. Don't open it for anyone else. Someone just fired at me at the lighthouse. They've gone. But I think they may be coming for you." He hung up.

Jess stood shocked. Then she heard the crunch of a footstep on gravel.

She ran inside the building, slammed the door and turned the key in the lock. Ear to the door, she listened hard, but all she could hear was the wind whistling around the building.

The door handle rattled up and down.

"Tom?" she called out.

No reply.

She grabbed a chair and jammed the back under the door handle.

She heard something slam into the heavy, wooden door. *A bullet?* She ran away from the door, and hid under a desk. She could hear nothing but the wind.

Suddenly a car horn rang out in the distance. It kept going as it got closer and closer. A car screeched up to the building. Brakes squealed. Engine still running, a door opened: "*Jess!*"

Tom! She pulled the chair away, unlocked the door and ran outside.

"Thank God you're all right!" He grabbed her arm. "Quick. Let's get out of here."

They ran to the car.

"Someone fired at the door," Jess shouted over the wind.

"Did you see who it was?"

"No." She jumped into the passenger seat.

Tom got in behind the wheel. "Did you hear a voice?"

"No."

He spun the car around and drove fast along the track. The undertray bumped and scraped as they bounced over the rough terrain. At the end of the track, he turned left, and sped down Lighthouse Road towards town.

When Jess finally took her eyes off the road, she looked over and saw he was covered in dirt and sand. Only when it was safe enough to ease his foot off the accelerator did she ask what had happened.

He glanced in his driver's mirror. "I went to the lighthouse. I saw a small, sandy beach below the bluff. There was a trail leading down, so I thought I'd go and take a look."

"You went down in the dark?" Her voice was incredulous.

"It was still dusk," he said, defensively. "There are some rocks directly below the headland. I thought there might be caves down there, and the only way to check that out was from the beach."

"For God's sake!"

"I slipped and fell when I thought I saw someone above. They fired at me. But they couldn't get a clear shot because the bank was steep."

"Did you get a look at them?"

He shook his head. "Shortly after I got to the lighthouse, I thought I heard a motorbike rev up. Whoever it was must have ridden the bike to the headland, and watched me through binoculars. Something was glinting over there. Probably saw me drop you off, and followed me to the lighthouse."

"And then they came back after me," she said, quietly.

"I guessed they would."

Jess stared at him, then turned to look out the back window. "Are we being followed?"

He looked in the mirror again. "Don't know. Can't see anyone."

She turned back. "I don't get it, Tom. *Why* would anyone want to kill you? Or me?"

"Because we're getting too close."

They fell silent, stunned by what had happened. When they reached the roundabout in town, Tom took the road towards the Governor's Office, but then he stopped abruptly at a beachside bar and parked the car in the middle of several others in the car park. Switching off the lights and engine, he sat still for a while to check no-one had followed.

Jess looked at him.

"Let's get a drink before we go back to the Residence. We need to talk... get our heads sorted." He brushed the sand and dirt from his hair and clothes.

They got out and walked over to the bar, which was little more than a wooden shack with a corrugated iron roof. Inside, the place was humming. They managed to find a free table and sat down. It was very basic. No table cloths or napkins, but the place had some life about it, and that's just what they needed.

"TGIF," Tom nodded over to the bar. "There's the sign. Cheap drinks for a couple of hours."

"No wonder the place is full."

"What can I get you?" he asked

"Whatever you're having."

Tom went over to the bar, and came back with two glasses of local rum and two menus. "Might as well eat while we're here."

Jess took a long swig of rum, and grimaced.

Tom knocked his back in one go.

He looked shaken, but she said nothing more. She didn't feel in the least bit hungry, but she was happy to be in the bar with other people around, and Tom. "I can't believe we're thinking about eating."

Tom nodded and opened his menu. "Looks like it's conch stew again, or barbequed chicken wings. No, tell a lie, there's fish and chips too."

"Then it's fish and chips for me," she said, without looking at the menu.

"Me too." Tom got up to order the food.

When he came back, he had two more glasses of rum with him.

Jess emptied her first glass. As she put it back down on the table, she noticed her hands shaking.

Tom put his hand over hers, and they sat in silence until the barman brought over the food.

Jess recognised him. It was the young man who'd been her taxi driver on arrival.

"Evening, Miss." He gave her a beaming smile. "How are you liking Grand Turk?"

"It's wonderful." Her response was automatic.

Tom gave a wry smile.

The young man looked pleased. He put the food down proudly in front of them and touched the side of the old shack. "Hope my restaurant's still standing on Monday night."

"Is there any more news about the hurricane?" Jess asked.

He shrugged. "It'll come and it'll go." And with that he walked off.

Jess couldn't believe how relaxed he was about it. Everyone was. Men were drinking and laughing at the bar. Other people were tucking into their dinner. It was like any other Friday night.

"They might as well enjoy the evening," Tom said, as if reading her thoughts. "What else can they do?"

Jess nodded. Once she'd started eating, she felt a bit better. The rum helped too.

Tom said nothing, but looked grim as he ate his food.

Jess put down her knife and fork. "I don't know what Maggie was doing at the Haitian settlement this afternoon, but it doesn't add up. None of it does."

He nodded. "Maybe she was just visiting? Doing some community work, or something like that?"

Jess shook her head. "Then why didn't she just say so? And why go out in a rush and not lock the Residence doors?" She paused. "She seemed to know those Haitian women well. They were standing in a group, talking, and looked relaxed with each other."

"Well, you'll just have to ask her about it when you get back?"

"Oh I will." She nodded. "You know my mind keeps coming back to when this all started. It was Clement Pearson's suicide *after* giving evidence to the British Inquiry into those two Haitian sloops that kicked it all off." She paused. "So this has to be about the Haitian migrants. The islanders don't want them here, that's for sure."

"They don't want their voodoo either."

They both looked up as loud reggae music suddenly blasted out from two speakers over the bar. The owner gave them another wide grin as some of the locals got up. They cleared a space in the middle of the tables and chairs and started dancing.

Jess and Tom watched them. It seemed surreal after what they'd just been through, and with a hurricane approaching, that everyone should be so happy. After a while, Tom moved his chair round next to Jess, to be able to talk. "Earlier you said you had no idea what Simon thought about you staying here through the hurricane." He paused. "What did you mean by that?"

Jess looked at him. "Simon's not happy about me being here."

"Why not?"

She shrugged. "I wish I knew, but he won't talk about it. Then he told me he was going to LA for work. But I find out he's taken a couple of weeks' leave instead, and gone back to the UK."

"Without telling you?"

She nodded. She couldn't bring herself to say that Simon had bought two return air tickets, and had taken someone else to the UK with him.

"That doesn't sound like Simon." He paused. "Perhaps you need to talk to him."

Jess felt uncomfortable telling Tom this, yet relieved to be finally talking about it. "He won't answer my calls or texts. I don't even know where he is." She sighed. "I guess you never really know another person, do you?"

"True," he nodded.

She looked at him. "Are you with anyone now Tom?"

"Nah. My last partner, Liz, left me around the time of that murder we worked on in Brisbane."

"I'm sorry," she said.

"Don't be. I'm no good at relationships." He paused. "My job always seems to come first. Takes over my whole life, every waking hour, especially when I get a murder case. I can't stop until I've solved it and the killer's behind bars."

"A dog with a bone?"

"Something like that."

"Fine pair then, aren't we?"

He nodded. "Talking of work." He pulled out his mobile. "Finish your fish and chips while I go outside and phone Chuck. I need to talk to him about what happened up at the lighthouse."

She pushed her plate away. "I've finished."

He looked at her. "I'm only going outside to phone."

But she wasn't going to let him out of her sight. "Let's get the bill. I want to get back to the Residence. Sally will be worried."

He got up and went over to the bar. After he'd paid, he came over. "Stay here," he said. "I won't be long."

No chance. She jumped up and followed him out.

35

Jess woke up the next morning to the noise of wind rattling her bedroom shutters, and rain lashing down. Her heart sank. She was hoping the hurricane would veer off in another direction overnight, and miss them altogether. Even more worrying was the sound of waves crashing onto the reef in the distance. At least it was Saturday, she thought, all the staff could look after their own homes and families without worrying about work.

She wondered if Tom and Sally were up, but she could hear nothing above the elements outside. Her mind ran through all the things she had to do before the hurricane hit. The local staff had already put up all the shutters around the windows of the Governor's Office, and secured what they could inside. She'd worked into the night with Sally to dismantle the communications system and store all the electrical equipment on shelves as high as they could in case of flooding. The trouble was the building was single storey. Why hadn't anyone thought to build two storeys on this low lying site? Tom had helped in any way he could, carrying and lifting.

She shuddered, thinking about the showdown the night before. Sally had refused point blank to leave on the afternoon flight to Provo. There was no way she'd abandon her post, she'd said, and leave Jess on her own.

Jess knew Sally's reluctance to leave was due more to Brad than to her, and gave up in the end.

It was different with Tom though. He was not a colleague. He was a friend. After what had happened to him out diving and up at the lighthouse, she had to get him off the island and out of danger. Someone saw him as a real threat. Of course he'd argued to stay too. "Either all three of us leave together, or none of us go," he'd said, bluntly. She'd stood her ground, rehearsing all the arguments. This was not his problem, his job and reputation were on the line back in Canberra. And she'd be safe because the London team would get here ahead of the hurricane. In the end Tom grudgingly accepted he was leaving. Not that she wanted him to go. Far from it. She enjoyed having him around. Felt safer with him in the house. But her instincts were telling her it was the right thing to do.

Getting out of bed and walking over to the window, she found herself standing in a puddle of rainwater from having left the window open a fraction to let some air in overnight. The wind was blowing straight off the sea, at the house. She closed the window tight. At least the electricity was still working, she thought, as she looked up at the whirring ceiling fan.

Coming down the stairs, she heard loud reggae music, and smelt bacon frying. She went into the kitchen, but it wasn't Maggie at the stove.

"Morning." Sally gave her a small smile as she jiggled the pan.

Sally looked pale without her make-up. Her hair was hanging limp, and her eyes were red-rimmed, either from lack of sleep or from crying. "Did you get any sleep?" Jess asked.

"A little," Sally replied. "How about you?"

"A few hours on and off."

Jess went over and turned down the radio.

"I've been listening to the hurricane bulletins on the local station," Sally said.

"Any news?"

Sally shook her head. "Still a Cat 2 heading our way."

"Well," Jess sighed. "At least it hasn't intensified into a Cat 3 overnight. That's something, I suppose." She studied Sally. "Heard from Brad, yet?"

"No. He's not answering my calls. I've sent several texts. Nothing. He didn't even text me goodnight." Sally's voice was shaky. "And he always does that."

Jess knew how that felt too. "He'll come round," she said, without much conviction. "He's probably busy securing the Dive Centre and his boats. There's a lot to do."

"I phoned Charles," Sally said. "He hasn't seen him either."

"Where is Charles?"

"At the police station. They've still got Rebekah in the cells."

Jess frowned. "They've kept her in there all night?"

"Apparently."

"I bet she's in a state," Jess said. "I'd better go down and try and sort things out."

"Charles told me Rebekah wouldn't leave the island without Benji. So they're staying for the hurricane." Sally frowned. "She's a funny woman, Jess. Believe me."

"She won't be going anywhere for some time if the police press charges. Assaulting a police officer is serious." She paused. "Can you try and get hold of the Chief Justice in London, Sally. We need to tell him what's going on, in case Rebekah hasn't been able to do it herself."

Sally nodded. "I'm more worried about Brad. No-one's seen him since yesterday evening."

"Tell you what," Jess said, "if you haven't heard from him by this afternoon, we'll take a run down to the Dive Centre after we've dropped Tom off at the airport. I bet we'll find him there busy battening down the hatches and storing the boats. It'll give us a chance to have a chat and clear the air. Okay?"

Sally brightened a little. "I'm glad I was here last night with you and Tom, and not in my own house alone. It's frightening listening to that sea. I kept imagining a tsunami swamping us. I had to get up in the end and do something."

Jess nodded. "It sounds awful out there, but don't forget this house has stood for centuries. I find that reassuring anyway."

At that moment, the back door opened and Tom walked in, drenched to the skin. He closed it quickly, and took off his sandals. "That's a helluva storm brewing, and it's still 24 hours away."

Sally shivered and threw him a towel. "Your eggs and bacon are ready. Sit down at the kitchen table. I'll serve up."

He pulled off his t-shirt and put the towel around his shoulders as if he'd been for a swim. "Thanks Sally." He sat down to a huge plateful of breakfast.

Jess stared at him. "What have you been doing?"

He looked up. "Getting the hurricane shutters out of the garage. I've put some up on the ground floor at the front and sides of the house."

"Oh thanks, Tom. But why didn't you wait for us?"

"Couldn't sleep with that racket out there. Thought I'd do something useful."

Jess nodded. It seems they'd all been awake half the night. "I'll give you a hand after breakfast."

"Me too," Sally joined in. "Teamwork!" She glanced at Jess as if to say 'am I forgiven?'

Jess nodded, and turned to Tom: "No Maggie, then?"

"No."

"I'm really worried about her," Jess went on. "Maggie wouldn't just not turn up for work."

Tom nodded. "Maybe we should call the police, and report her missing?"

"I'll go down to her house first, and see if she's there," Sally said. "She lives on the outskirts of town.

"No." Jess knew as soon as Sally left the house she'd head straight to Brad's. "I'll call the Police Commissioner. It may be a false alarm, but I need to do something."

At that moment, there was a knock on the front door.

"I'll go," Jess said. "You have your breakfast." She walked along the hallway and opened the door.

Alvita stood outside in a long, white sou'wester, with her hood up like a monk. On her feet were flip-flops. No-one ever seemed to be worried about getting their feet wet on this island.

"Is Maggie here?" Alvita asked.

"No." Jess shook her head. "Come in out of the rain."

Alvita hesitated, then stepped over the threshold and followed Jess into the kitchen. She stopped when she saw Tom and Sally eating breakfast. "I don't want to intrude."

"You're not intruding," Jess said. "Sit down and have a cup of coffee."

Alvita pushed back her hood and sat down, but she didn't take off her raincoat which dripped all over the kitchen floor.

"I went up early to the Disaster Management Centre," Alvita said. "Everyone's working to get things up and running."

Jess smiled. "That's great. Thank you."

Alvita nodded. "On my way back, I stopped at Maggie's, but there was no answer. Her neighbour told me she hadn't been home all night. I thought she might be here."

Alvita's voice was calm, but her eyes looked troubled. "I was just about to call the Police Commissioner," Jess said. "None of us have seen her since lunchtime yesterday."

Alvita stared at her. "Lunchtime yesterday?"

Jess nodded. "Except, well, I thought I saw her at the Haitian settlement yesterday afternoon."

"What on earth would Maggie be doing there?" Sally interrupted.

"Are you sure it was her?" Alvita asked, sharply.

Jess nodded. "She had a child in her arms." She looked over at Tom, for him to back her up. But he was just looking at Alvita.

Alvita jumped up. "I'll go to the settlement and see if she's there."

"Should I call the police?" Jess asked.

"No, I'll phone them if I can't find her there." Alvita hurried out of the kitchen and back along the hall.

"Hold on." Jess called out as she followed. "I'll come with you."

"No. Stay here, Jess, where you'll be safe." Alvita slipped out of the door.

She looked a lonely figure as she hurried along the drive in her cape and hood. When Jess went back into the kitchen, Tom asked: "Who is that woman?"

"That's Alvita. The head of our local staff in the Governor's Office. Why?"

"I saw her yesterday morning having a row with Maggie." He pointed to the back door. "Out there in the garden."

"A row?" Jess frowned. "What about?"

"Alvita turned up with a little girl, and wanted Maggie to look after her. Maggie was reluctant. They had a row, and Maggie slapped her face."

Sally nodded. "I'd like to do that sometimes."

Jess didn't laugh. "What happened then?"

Tom shrugged. "Maggie took the child anyway, and Alvita walked off."

"What happened to the child?" Jess asked.

"Maggie brought her in here." He paused. "I didn't see her again. She wasn't here when we got back for lunch. At least, I didn't see or hear her. Did you?"

Jess shook her head and plopped down on a chair. "Was it the same child we saw Maggie holding at the Haitian settlement?"

He shrugged. "Difficult to say."

Jess picked up the cup of black coffee and took a sip. "Why didn't you tell me that yesterday?" she asked him.

"I didn't think it was important," he replied.

"Why would Maggie take a child to the Haitian settlement?" Sally stopped and looked at them both. "You don't think... oh my God... you don't think she was *giving* the child to them to..." She could hardly bring herself to finish the sentence. "T-to sacrifice?"

"Sally!" Jess plonked her cup down on the saucer. "How could you *think* that?"

"Well," Sally went on, darkly, "with all these ceremonies and fires on the beach... and those bones turning up. What if they're not animal bones? What if they're human? What if they're *children's* bones?"

Jess's blood ran cold at the thought. "That's enough, Sally." She stood up and went over to the stove to cook herself some breakfast. On her way, she glanced over at Tom, who sat deep in thought.

"Right," she said, in her business-like voice. "We'll just finish breakfast, then we'll put the rest of the hurricane shutters over the windows, and prepare the house for a flood. That'll keep us all busy for a few hours." She looked over at Tom. "Then we'll break for lunch, and help Tom get packed and ready to leave."

He raised his eyebrows, and tucked into his eggs and bacon.

★

Their mood was sombre as the three of them got ready to set off for the airport. Jess had spent the last hour in the laundry room trying to get Tom's clothes dry enough to pack. She found herself lingering in there rather than having to look at his glum face. He'd made it very clear he didn't want to go. Eventually, she came out with the neatly folded clothes and handed them to him. "We'd better get over to the airport early," she said, brightly. "It'll be pandemonium. Everyone'll want to get out this afternoon."

"Why don't I drive round now and check him in?" Sally said. "Make sure no-one nabs his seat." She looked at Tom. "Give me your ticket and passport, Tom. I'll take your suitcase too. It'll give you and Jess time to... have a chat."

"Are you allowed to check me in?" he asked.

Sally nodded. "They know I'm from the Governor's Office."

Tom ran upstairs and soon came down with documents and his packed suitcase. "I'll put this in the car for you."

"No bother." Sally put on her raincoat and hat, easily lifted his suitcase with one hand, and took his documents. "No point taking a brolly, it'll be inside out before I close the front door." She waved cheerily at them both. "I'll be back in about 15 minutes." She went off down the hall and banged the front door closed.

Tom looked over at Jess. "I'm going to say this one more time. I don't want to go and leave you both here."

Jess's eyes softened. "I know, Tom. I don't want you to go either. It's just that I feel you must go, for your own sake."

"Do you *really* think you know what's best for everyone?" he said in his gruff way.

She looked away.

He sat down at the table. "I remember those last hours in Australia. You just kept going headlong into danger, with that maniac on your tail. You wouldn't do anything I said. I thought at the time 'when is this woman going to be scared enough to just stay put?'"

Jess sat down opposite him. "I was trying to save someone else. You know that."

"But what about *you*, Jess? When are you going to save yourself for a change?"

She looked at him. "Do you remember I told you at the time that I thought I was somehow *touched* by death?"

He nodded.

"I've lost almost everyone I've ever loved." She paused. "I'm not afraid of dying too, Tom."

"No," he said. "It's living you're afraid of."

She said nothing.

"Look, Jess." He leant forward and touched her hand. "Come with me."

She stared at him.

"At least to Miami, where I know you'd be safe. There, you'd have some time and space to decide what you want to do."

She shook her head slowly. "You know what Tom, I'd like that, but I have to wait for the London team to get here. I *have* to help them resolve all this. I can't just walk away."

He ran his fingers through his hair. "So there's nothing I can say?"

"No, but I'm really glad you tried." She got up to ease the tension and started washing up the breakfast dishes.

He picked up a tea towel and dried them up. Neither of them spoke again as they did the chores, until they heard Sally coming back through the front door.

"Right." He hung the tea towel on the hook. "I'd better be off."

She nodded and they walked down the hall together.

Sally was standing by the front door. "All checked-in," she said to Tom. She pulled a raincoat off the hall rack. "Wear this, Jess. It's Jayne's, but she won't mind."

Jess put on the raincoat, gratefully.

Outside, the rain was being carried along on gusts of wind. It blasted Jess in the face as she walked to the car. She got into the driver's seat, with Sally in the passenger seat and Tom in the back. The car shook in the fierce wind, and Jess had to hold the wheel tight to keep it on the road. No-one spoke.

Jess looked in the mirror at Tom, but he wouldn't catch her eye.

Outside the airport, it was as chaotic as she feared. The car park was completely gridlocked. Desperate drivers had dumped their cars anywhere along the road and pavement to drop off passengers. "I can't get any closer to the terminal," she said.

"Drop us here," Sally said. "We'll run the rest of the way."

Jess turned and smiled at Tom. "You both go through security to the departure lounge. I'll meet you there when I've found somewhere to park."

Tom nodded and got out. He ran with Sally in the driving rain over to the terminal.

Jess found herself stuck now between two stationary cars, and had to wait for one of the drivers to return and let her out. That took ages. Then she drove round and round the car park hunting for a space. Impossible. Out of desperation, she drove back to the main road, and parked the car up on a grass verge.

Sloshing through puddles, she ran back to the terminal and into the main lobby. Suitcases and people filled the floor space. The check-in was frantic. The departure board showed only two more domestic flights leaving for Provo before the airport closed. Tom's flight was one of them. There was a queue of close to 100 passengers for only a few more seats. People were shouting at the two check-in girls, who carried on calmly in their usual way, checking in those who were booked and refusing those who weren't. Jess stopped, wondering if she could help. But what could she do?

That's when she caught a glimpse of a familiar blond ponytail. She stared across the lobby. Was that Brad talking to Big Shot Roger Pearson by the door? She was knocked sideways by a woman with a large suitcase. When she turned back, Brad and Roger had disappeared.

Hurrying through security with her airside pass, she went into the departure lounge to see Sally rushing over.

"You've missed him," Sally shouted. "Quick." She dragged Jess over to the glass window and pointed to one of the two planes on the ground.

"Over there, it's about to go."

Tom stood in the doorway of the plane, looking over at the terminal.

Jess waved through the glass, and mouthed goodbye.

He gave her a broad smile, and his usual salute. Then he turned and went inside.

Immediately the co-pilot pulled up the steps from inside and closed the door. The propellers started up and the pilot taxied to the end of the runway.

The little plane was buffeted around by the wind as it lifted off the ground, and into the air. She stood still, watching its tail lights flashing in the stormy sky, until it was completely out of sight.

"Goodbye, Tom," she whispered.

36

Jess drove towards town in silence, with Sally equally quiet in the passenger seat. The noise of the windscreen wipers scraping back and forth on full speed was getting on her nerves. She turned them down a notch, but couldn't see through the blinding rain and had to turn them up again.

So, Tom had gone. He'd been the only person she could trust on the island. She was alone now, except for Sally. How much could she trust her though when Brad was clearly her number one priority? Still, the London team would arrive soon, and that cheered her up.

As they reached the section of road which ran alongside the beach, she glanced over at the angry sea. Huge waves smashed onto the reef offshore. Gone was the turquoise lagoon inside. Now, only grey swirling water rushed onto shore, almost covering the entire beach. Soon, it would reach the sea wall and the road would be flooded. "Hope we can get back along here in an hour or so," she said to Sally.

Sally sat with her hands clasped nervously in front of her. "Something's wrong, Jess. I can feel it."

"Look we're almost at the Dive Centre. We'll stop here first and see if Brad's about."

"If he's not, can we drive to his house?"

"I've got to go to the police station first and get Rebekah out of there before the hurricane hits."

"After that, then?"

"We need to go to the Disaster Management Centre, Sally. That's where we should be right now."

"*Please,* Jess."

"All right," she said. "If we're quick." Pulling up alongside the pavement, she could see the Dive Centre all locked up and windows boarded with hurricane shutters.

But Sally sprang out of the car anyway, and raced over.

Jess switched off the engine and looked around. The wind was rocking the car, and lashing it with rain. She wound down the driver's window and looked over at the Baptist church on the other side of the road. All locked up, with the windows boarded too. There were one or two cars still on the road. And a few people, covered from head to foot in sou'westers, were working to finish their chores and hurricane preparations. A loose frond from a palm tree hit the windscreen, making her jump.

She looked back to the Dive Centre and saw Sally disappear inside. She got out and ran over. "How'd you get in here?" she asked, as she stepped inside.

Sally held up a key. "Brad hides this spare one under of the grooves of the corrugated iron roof."

A roof which was unlikely to survive a hurricane, Jess thought, although she didn't say that. "Well, he's clearly not here." She looked round the dark, airless room. "Let's go."

"Hang on." Sally went over to his desk drawer, plugged a desk lamp in the socket and switched it on.

Jess was surprised when Sally started rifling through the desk drawers. "What are you doing?"

"Looking for his spare set of house keys. He keeps them in here somewhere."

"Don't you have your own set?" Jess asked.

"No." Sally's face looked stony as she continued searching.

Jess said nothing more, and wandered over to some cupboards. She opened one and found boxes of gaily coloured cotton beachwear stacked on the highest shelves. No doubt to try and keep them out of flood water. Little chance of that, Jess thought. The building was just off the beach, and the sea was already creeping its way up to it.

She opened another cupboard to see rows and rows of oxygen tanks. She stared at them, wondering which one had been Tom's. But it was too dark to inspect them closely. Not that she knew what to look for anyway.

It was only on opening the third cupboard that she smelt something musty. "Ugh, what's in here?"

Sally looked over. "No idea."

"Is there a torch anywhere?"

Sally grabbed the desk lamp and pulled it as close to Jess as the cable would allow.

"It's a tarpaulin."

"Pull it out," Sally said, holding the lamp higher.

Jess dragged the tarpaulin out of the cupboard.

"Open it out, Jess. See if there's anything inside."

Jess dragged the tarpaulin closer to the lamp and opened it out. It was empty except for some damp patches right along the middle section. She bent down and touched them, then recoiled.

"What's the matter?"

"It feels sticky, like blood!"

"*Blood?*"

Jess rubbed her mucky fingers on the cleanest part of the tarpaulin. "They've probably been hauling game fish around in here."

Sally's voice was shaking when she said: "I've found his keys. Let's go and see if he's at home."

"We have to stop at the police station on the way."

But Sally wasn't listening. She unplugged the lamp, pushed Jess out the door, and locked it.

They both ran back to the car and jumped inside.

Jess had the car keys so she drove further along the road and stopped outside Police HQ. She glanced over at Sally's white face. "I'm going in to see the Police Commissioner first, Sally, and get the latest information on the hurricane. I'll find out if they've let Rebekah go."

Sally nodded.

"Wait here. I won't be long."

"Please hurry, Jess."

Jess jumped out of the car and ran into the building.

★

Dexter Robinson sat behind his desk looking strained. "The mobile signal is already down," he said, glumly. "Who knows when it will be back up again?"

Jess took her mobile out of her pocket. No signal. "Are the landlines still working?"

"For the time being."

Jess sat down on a chair opposite him. "Is Mrs Canning still here?"

He nodded.

"That means she's been in custody for over 24 hours. You either have to charge her or let her go."

He nodded. "I was about to release her."

"Why have you kept her so long?" Jess asked.

He looked Jess in the eye. "She hit one of my officers over the head with a cricket bat. He's up in the clinic with concussion, and she refuses to answer any questions or give a statement. She says she has a right to remain silent."

"Does she have a lawyer?"

"She refuses to have one."

Jess frowned. "Has Charles Regan been here to see her?"

"We haven't let *him* see her." Dexter pulled a disapproving face. "Their... liaison is a scandal," he said. "She's the wife of the Chief Justice."

Jess sat back in the chair. Was the Chief Justice the only person on this island who didn't know about his wife's affair? And why wouldn't Rebekah answer a few questions, and get herself released? It didn't make sense. "I realise this is serious," Jess said. "How is your officer? Any lasting damage?"

Dexter shook his head. "Only concussion. There's nothing broken."

"Well that's a relief," she said. "Will you release Mrs Canning before the hurricane gets here?"

He hesitated. "She's not well, Jess."

Jess looked at him, quizzically.

"You'll see and hear that for yourself when you see her." He paused. "I'm prepared to release her before the hurricane hits. I don't like to hold anyone in the cells at times like these. But we will pick her up again when it's over. We will insist she answers our questions and gives us a statement. Then we'll decide about charges."

Jess nodded. "Can I see her now?"

He got up, led Jess out of his office, and called to a young officer at the desk.

The young man grabbed some keys and led them down into the cells.

Now, Jess could see Rebekah in her cell, sitting still on the bed, and staring up at the sky, through the window. She still looked beautiful, but so different, with her hair back in a ponytail, face scrubbed clean of make-up, and dressed in jeans and t-shirt. She looked like a young Latino woman, with dusky skin. Rebekah crossed herself, and lowered her head as if in prayer.

"Are you all right, Rebekah?" Jess asked, steeling herself for a stream of abuse about why she hadn't come before.

But Rebekah surprised her. She turned and gave Jess a level stare, as if looking at her for the first time. They were intelligent eyes. Calm eyes. "Have you come to get me out of here?" she asked, quietly.

Jess stared back. Rebekah's posh English accent had fallen away, and in its place was an American accent.

Rebekah must have seen the astonishment on Jess's face, and gave a wry smile.

Had Rebekah completely flipped, Jess wondered? "Are you feeling all right, Rebekah?" she asked.

"I'm fine." She looked at Jess. "I'm not mad, if that's what you're thinking. I'm perfectly sane. This is who I am."

Jess didn't understand what was going on, but she was irritated now. "Well, it's quite a transformation," she said. "So who are you?"

"I'm Rebekah Canning."

Yes, Jess thought, but his woman was completely different from the Rebekah Canning she'd known before. "So why the English accent?" Jess asked. "The charade?"

"You'll have to ask Charles?" Rebekah replied, as she bowed her head and closed her eyes.

Is she praying, Jess wondered? She turned to the Police Commissioner. "Have you seen Charles Regan today?"

He nodded. "He was in the waiting room all morning. He left at lunchtime when I refused to let him see her."

"Can I go now?" Rebekah asked.

The Police Commissioner unlocked the cell door and opened it wide. "We don't keep anyone in the police cells during hurricanes, unless we have to," he added, sternly. "But you will be picked up again after it. Then we will expect you to answer our questions and give a statement."

Rebekah walked calmly out of the cell and followed the Police Commissioner up the steps, with Jess behind. In the main waiting area, Rebekah sat down on a chair. "I'll wait for Charles here. He'll be back for me."

"I can give you a lift home," Jess said.

"No, thanks. I'll wait here for Charles." Rebekah closed her eyes and put her head back on the seat, without another word.

The Police Commissioner beckoned Jess back into his office. "What do you think?"

"I really don't know." Jess was stunned. "We were going to ring the Chief Justice in London to tell him that Mrs Canning attacked one of your officers. Now we'll have to tell him about... this latest development." She stared at him. "I don't know who that woman is."

He nodded. "We're running an international check on her," he said.

"Can you let me know when you get the results, please."

He nodded, wearily.

"In the circumstances, I think it would be a good idea if you ring Charles Regan and ask him to pick her up." She paused. "He's probably the only person who can deal with her right now."

He nodded again.

She looked at her watch. "I'd better get back to the Residence. The London team are arriving on the 6.30 from Provo."

He frowned. "The last flight in?"

"Yes." She paused. "Look Dexter, I know things are really difficult, but our priority now is to keep people safe and ride out the hurricane. There's nothing more you can do about Mrs Pearson's murder or the Governor's car accident until things get back to normal."

He nodded. "Are you going to remain at the DMC for the hurricane?"

"That's the plan," she said. "As soon as our Director and the police get here."

"I'll see you up there," he said.

"Right."

"Be careful, Jess," he said. "Very careful."

"You too, Dexter." She sprinted over to the car to avoid getting soaked, and jumped in the driver seat.

No Sally!

She looked all around, but there was no sign of her. Then she saw a piece of paper lying on the passenger seat. She picked it up. It was a note.

Gone with Charles to look for Brad. Really worried about him. I'll call or text as soon as we've found him. Will see you back at the Residence soon. Sally.

Jess scrunched the piece of paper up into a ball and flung it down on the seat. What was Sally thinking? Running around looking for Brad in this weather. She sat staring at the rain, wondering what to do. She couldn't go and look for Sally because she didn't know where Brad lived. With no mobile signal, she couldn't call her either. She turned the car round and headed back towards the Residence.

But, as she drove back, she couldn't get Rebekah's eyes or voice out of her head. Why had she put on such an act? Did Dominic really know the woman he was married to? He must do, she thought. No-one could hide something like that from their husband, surely? And what about Charles? He clearly knew because he was having an affair with Rebekah.

But just who was Rebekah Canning? That question played over and over in her head.

37

Jess let herself in the front door. The house was dark with the hurricane shutters over the windows. It felt even more stuffy and claustrophobic inside than usual. She switched on the lights and ceiling fans. At least the electricity was still working. Quickly, she went round closing all the curtains to stop the house feeling like a prison. Despite the barricades, the wind still whistled through the timbers of the old house. She was dreading the full hurricane force wind when it came.

Refusing to give way to nerves, she carried on with the hurricane preparations. First, she went into the kitchen and filled the sink and large cooking pans with fresh water from the tap. Then she went upstairs and filled every bath and sink with water too.

On her way back down, a violent gust of wind shook the house. The lights flickered. She looked up at the chandelier on the landing, and held her breath. It stayed on. Electricity would be the first utility to go, followed by the landlines. It was just a matter of time.

At the phone in the hallway, she stopped and looked at her watch. 5.30. It would be about 9.30 in the UK. Would Simon still be up? She had to try and talk to him, before the lines went down. It wasn't in her nature to think the worst, but it could be the last time she ever spoke to him.

She dialled his mobile, feeling ridiculously nervous as it rang. But her hopes were dashed when it transferred to voicemail. She took a deep breath...

Hi Simon. Me again. Look, I know you're in the UK on leave. I... I don't know why you told me you were going to LA for work. I feel very sad about that, but you must have your reasons. Anyway, I hope you get this message, because, well, because as usual life has a habit of being unpredictable... You may have heard there's a hurricane heading for the Turks and Caicos. It's due to hit us tomorrow... Sunday... I'm sure we'll all be fine, but we're likely to be out of communication for some time and I wanted you to know... in case anything happens... that I've loved every minute of the last couple of years with you, Simon. So... whatever it is you're doing now, I hope you're happy. I just want you to be happy. Always.

She stood staring at the receiver as his voicemail hung up. Had she said the right thing? Had her voice conveyed her real feelings? Now, she was annoyed with herself for not having worked out what she was going to say before leaving a message. She sighed as she put the receiver back. It was too late to worry about that now. She couldn't wallow in self-pity.

She went back into the kitchen. Sally had gathered up all the hurricane lamps and torches and left them on the table before going out. Jess now busied herself checking the batteries were working, and the lamps were filled with oil. Slipping a slim torch in her trouser pocket, she went round the downstairs rooms, putting a lamp and box of matches in each one, ready for when the lights finally went out.

Hearing what sounded like an engine revving up outside, she ran to the front door and looked out into the darkness. Was that Sally coming back? No sign of any car or lights. Where on earth was that girl?

She checked her watch again; half an hour before she had to go to the airport to pick up the London team. Sally had made beds for them upstairs, as hotels were closing. No-one would fly into a hurricane, except of course emergency relief teams. The Director had made it clear he was coming with the UK police no matter what. He would not leave Jess and Sally to face things alone.

Jess climbed the stairs to check everything was ready for them. There were six bedrooms on the first floor. Sally had one bedroom. She had another. That left one spare guest bedroom, the Governor's master bedroom, and two smaller children's rooms full of their clothes and games. Most of the bedrooms had en-suite facilities, as well as a house bathroom, and a house toilet off the landing. So many doors. She went into each bedroom one by one and was pleased to see Sally had got everything ready.

Back on the landing, she heard a creaking sound and stopped. Outside, the sea roared like an angry demon, but this noise was inside the house. She listened hard, then looked up. It seemed to be coming from the attic. Not having been up there before, she didn't know where the stairs were. Her eyes scanned the doors. She'd been through all of them, except for one in the far corner.

Suddenly another violent gust of wind shook the house. The chandelier flickered, and this time went out.

Startled, she stood still to accustom her eyes to the darkness. Senses attuned, it sounded as if that creaking noise was directly above her. She had to go and investigate. Pulling the torch out of her pocket, she flicked it on, and went over to the one door she hadn't been through. Turning the knob, she opened it and shone the beam up a curved staircase that led to the attic. Curiosity drew her in. One by one she climbed the stairs, keeping a hand on the wall to steady herself.

At the top, she took a couple of steps forward and shone the beam around.

"Oh!"

The bulging eyes... the pallid face... the blood...

Jess gasped and dropped to her knees. "No," she whispered, "no." She stared at the body swinging back and forth as the wind rattled through the old timbers... back and forth... back and forth. The blood from the woman's slashed throat dripped onto the floor, as she hung by her bound feet from the beam.

"*Maggie!*"

Jess sprang up and frantically tried to find a pulse. But Maggie's wrists were bound too tightly behind her back. Jess pressed her ear to her chest. No heartbeat. No breath of life from her lips, only a lingering warmth in her cheeks. A sob burst from Jess's throat, a disbelieving sigh of grief.

Suddenly, the attic door clicked shut. Heart racing with fear, she turned and shone the beam down the stairs. No-one. She crept down, turned the door knob and peered out through a crack. She couldn't see anything in the dark.

She tip-toed out the door and across the landing to the staircase. Were they footsteps she could hear in the kitchen? Had someone come into the house and created a draught of wind? Or was Maggie's killer still inside? Trembling, she switched off the torch. She had to get out of the house, it was her only chance.

The top stair creaked as she trod on it. She froze.

It all went quiet downstairs.

She waited a moment, then kept going, listening as she went. No sound. At the bottom of the stairs, she made a dash for the front door.

Someone grabbed her from behind.

She screamed, and struggled blindly to get free...

"*Whoa!*" A familiar voice rang out.

She stopped. "*Tom?*" She turned and almost collapsed with relief.

He caught her. "What's wrong?"

"Maggie!" She could hardly speak. "Upstairs... d–dead."

"*What?*" He switched on his torch, and stared at her. "You're covered in blood? Are you hurt?"

"No." She looked from his shocked face to her hands. "It's Maggie's."

"Wait there!" He went running up the stairs.

"You'll need a knife," Jess called out, "to c–cut her down."

He stopped and ran back down to the kitchen.

She heard him open a drawer and rummage around inside before coming back with a knife.

"Wait there!" he whispered again.

"I need to show you the way." She led him up to the attic door and opened it. "Up there," she said.

Tom climbed the stairs first.

Still shaking, Jess followed.

Even Tom reeled backwards at the sight. "*Jesus!*"

"Cut her down, Tom."

"No. Don't touch anything. Forensics need to see this." He was in professional mode now. "Don't walk about, there may be footprints in the blood on the floor."

"We can't leave Maggie... like that."

He hesitated.

"*Please*, Tom! The police won't come until the hurricane's gone, and perhaps not then for days, a week even. They'll concentrate on helping the living."

Still he hesitated.

"Anything could happen tonight with this hurricane. We could all be swept away. I can't bear the thought of Maggie... like that."

He looked at her, then dragged a chair over to where Maggie was hanging and stood on it. "She's going to be heavy." He started sawing the rope with the knife.

Jess supported Maggie's head and shoulders, while Tom held onto the rope that bound her feet. Cutting through it, the rope snapped. Together they took Maggie's weight and laid her gently on her side on the floor. "Oh God, Maggie." Jess's hand shook as she stroked her hair.

Tom crouched down, sliced through the rope that tied Maggie's wrists together and felt for a pulse.

"It's too late, Tom."

He felt for a heartbeat and for breath from Maggie's mouth. He sat back on his heels. "She's gone," he said, softly.

Jess nodded.

He flashed his torch up at the beam that supported the high attic ceiling. A voodoo poppet doll was pinned to it with a knife through its throat. "Pretty sick," he said.

Jess stared at the doll's grotesque face, but Tom was already flashing the torch beam all around.

"What is this room?" he asked.

Jess looked properly around for the first time and saw a baby's cot and a little bed. On the bed lay a rag doll, just like the one she'd found on her bedroom chair that first night in the house. The doll's red lips smiled at her. She got to her feet to go over.

"No!" Tom held her back as his torch beam moved over a row of bottles standing on a small table next to him.

"What are they?" Jess asked.

He peered closer. "Sedatives... the label says they're for children."

"Oh my God!" Jess put her head in her hands. "Sally can't be right, can she? Surely they can't be sedating and sacrificing *children?*"

★

Back in the kitchen, Jess sat shivering in Maggie's rocking chair. A hurricane lamp threw out a glow that filled the room with shadows.

"Here!" Tom handed her a glass of brandy, then gulped his down in one go.

Jess went to get up. "I must call the Police Commissioner."

"The landline's not working."

"But Maggie..."

"I've put a sheet over her, until we can get her to the morgue."

Jess swigged her brandy which made her eyes water, and glanced over at Tom. "How come you're here?"

"Well, when I got to Provo, I found out the Trans Air flight had turned back to Miami, taking your Director and the UK police back with it."

Jess nodded. "I suppose the weather was too bad to land a jet on that small runway."

"You're not surprised, then?"

"Not in the circumstances."

"You just wanted me gone?"

She shook her head. "I wanted you to be safe, Tom."

"Well, I take my hat off to your local pilots. Those guys are fearless. They were so anxious to get back to their families here, they flew the plane back empty, except for me."

"Now who's got a death wish?"

"Never seen a sky like it. All shades of purple, red and black. Those guys knew what they were doing though, dodging around the darkest clouds to avoid lightning. But the turbulence up there. *Unbelievable!*" He poured himself another brandy and drank it down.

"I'm sorry for putting you through all that."

"Well, I couldn't leave you and Sally alone, could I?" He looked around. "Where is she anyway?"

"Gone to find Brad." Jess explained that Brad was cross with Sally for blabbing about the shipwreck. She also told him about the blood-stained tarpaulin they'd found in the Dive Centre, and about Rebekah's transformation. "I can't believe it, Tom. She was like a *completely* different person at the police station today. Quiet, thoughtful. Eyes wary. She's nobody's fool, I can tell you. But what got me the most was her *voice*." Jess shook her head. "I can still hear it now. She spoke with an *American* accent. Gone was all that pretence. Even *I* thought she was English, before today."

He nodded. "That's another reason I came back. My mate in Canberra ran some checks on your American dinner party guests *and* Rebekah."

Jess frowned at him, but said nothing.

"Rebekah's real name is Gloria Diaz. She was born in Colombia, on 6 June 1982."

"*Colombia?* I *thought* she looked Latino."

"And you were right. Her family moved to the US in 1990. A year later, her father was convicted of drug smuggling and given a long prison sentence. The following year her mother died, when Gloria was only ten."

Jess raised her eyebrows. "What happened to her, then?"

"She was taken into care for a while, then adopted by an American family in Chicago."

Jess could hardly believe it. That background was a far cry from the refined English lady Rebekah had pretended to be.

"Apparently, she ran away from that family a few years later. Hung out on the streets, did a number of waitressing jobs, before becoming an actress."

"*An actress?*" Jess stared at him. "And a bloody good one she is too!"

He nodded. "She spent her early career on the stage mostly, and in minor films. But it turns out she and Charles were an item way back in their twenties."

Somehow that didn't surprise Jess. "Charles is very possessive of her. He can't leave her alone. Always demanding her attention. Leaning over her. Draping his arm along the back of her chair." She looked at him. "You *must* have noticed that?"

He nodded.

"When I saw the pair of them kissing in the garden, it was Charles who grabbed Rebekah and wouldn't let her go. Not the other way round."

"Maybe it's been going on all these years?"

Jess nodded. "I wonder if the Chief Justice knows?"

Tom shrugged. "The funny thing is the guys back home couldn't get anything on the Regan brothers. Restricted access, apparently."

She stared at him.

He nodded. "Carrie Lynch is the only one of your guests whose story checks out. She is who she says she is."

"Well, that's good to hear."

Tom went to pour her another brandy, but she shook her head. "I'd prefer a cup of tea." She got up and pulled a small pan out of the cupboard. "So what do you think the Regan brothers have done for the US authorities to restrict access to their information?"

"I don't know. Maybe they have them under surveillance, and don't want their investigation compromised by the likes of us?"

"Perhaps Rebekah only married the Chief Justice to get half his money in any divorce?" She filled the pan with fresh water. "Maybe it's a scam? Maybe she and Charles have done this before?"

Tom gave her a sceptical look. "Charles doesn't seem short of a bob or two, does he?"

"Well Rebekah gave me the creeps yesterday." She shivered. "I wish Sally would come back."

"Stop worrying. She'll be with Brad."

"But is she safe?" Jess lit a gas burner and put the pan on it. "Do you reckon the wind's dying down?"

He shook his head. "It's going to last all night, at least. So if you're thinking about going out to look for Sally, forget it. Flying debris is what kills people in these storms."

Jess looked at his set face. "Oh all right. We'll go during the eye of the storm." She went over and got the milk out of the fridge. "I lived through a cyclone in Mauritius when I worked there. It went eerily calm for a couple of hours as the centre of the storm passed over us. Gave us the chance to go out and assess the damage before it started up again."

"How big is the eye? How long will it last?"

"I don't know the science, Tom. I just know it happened. The sky turned blue and the hurricane wind stopped. After a couple of hours or so, the storm came back with a vengeance."

Tom looked sceptical. "Let's just see what happens."

"I feel bad about not being up at the Disaster Management Centre. I should be helping out."

"There's nothing you or anyone else can do right now, except stay inside."

"Yes, but I need to know what's going on."

"And what could you do, if you did know? The emergency services can't operate. There's no electricity, and all the phones and broadband are down."

That was Tom, she thought, plain-speaking and practical. She walked over and flicked on the battery operated radio.

Reggae music blared out again. "At least we can listen to the local news bulletins."

"For as long as they stay on the air."

★

Jess jolted awake as something touched her face. She opened her eyes and realised she'd fallen asleep on the sofa in the Governor's Residence. Had she slept through the entire hurricane, she wondered, hopefully? No such luck. The wind whipped around the house as strong as ever, shaking its foundations from time to time. Across the coffee table, in the glow of a hurricane lamp, Tom was fast asleep in the chair, with his feet up on a footstool. His breathing was soft and rhythmic as if he didn't have a care in the world. Poor man, she thought. All this because of her. She was glad he'd come back though. Very glad.

She felt a familiar itch and rubbed her eye. A mosquito must have bitten her eyelid while she was asleep. Was it morning yet? It was impossible to tell with the hurricane shutters over the windows and the curtains drawn. She sat up and looked at her watch. 2.10. Still the middle of the night.

Her stomach turned as she thought of Maggie upstairs. She couldn't go to her room and sleep, not with Maggie in the attic like that. Tom hadn't thought he would get any sleep either with the hurricane raging. So they'd made themselves comfortable in the Governor's study and sat chatting, going over and over everything for hours until Tom eventually dropped off. Look at him now, she thought, sleeping soundly despite the roar of the sea and wind.

Perhaps another brandy would help her get back to sleep. Except the bottle was still on the kitchen table and she didn't want to open the door and wake Tom up. Her eyes rested on the globe in the corner of the room. An identical globe in the Governor's office was used as a drinks cabinet. Were there bottles in this one too?

Careful not to disturb Tom, she lifted the hurricane lamp off the coffee table and went over to the globe. Opening the lid, she saw an identical wooden insert inside, but all the holes for bottles and glasses were empty. *Damn!* Then something glinted through one of the holes in the lamplight. She gently pulled the insert to see if it lifted out. It did. Underneath, surprisingly, the entire bottom section of the globe was fitted with a wooden compartment, with a small keyhole in the middle.

She stared at it. The brass key! She tip-toed over to the sofa and pulled the key out of her handbag. She glanced over at Tom, but he was still asleep. Excited, she went back to the globe, lifted the hurricane lamp and inserted the key into the lock. It clicked, and a small panel opened. Inside, lay what looked like a notebook. She lifted it out and went over to the Governor's desk. Standing the hurricane lamp on it, she sat down and opened the book.

On the first page, the name *Clement Pearson* was written in ink, in the top right hand corner. The writing was small and neat. She flicked through pages and pages of entries, all recorded in date sequence, and in the same neat handwriting.

Clement's journal!

She went back to the first page and began reading. Once she got going, she was so engrossed she just kept turning the pages. Occasionally the text was so painful, she stopped to rub her eyes with fatigue. Her emotions ranged from disbelief, to sadness, to shame... until she finally came to the last entry.

<u>*Monday 3 August*</u>

I lied under oath today. I told those British officials exactly what they wanted to hear because I knew they were not ready for the truth. Am I fooling myself as well as everyone else? Am I afraid to tell the truth? No, I am ashamed to tell the truth. The British are proud of their great democracy. They lecture everyone about human rights and good governance. Would they have believed me if I had told them that those two Haitian sloops were deliberately lured onto the reef, and their occupants allowed to drown? It is so wicked I can hardly believe it myself.

What can we do? Those people won't stop coming. There are eight million of them, and only 50,000 of us. Every time we send them home, they come back again. Don't they understand we are in a fight for our own survival? They will destroy us, and our way of life. We are so worn down by the flow of migrants that we are losing our compassion. We are fighting for our homeland, and to keep our communities as they are.

What happened to that first sloop was supposed to send a message to others not to try the perilous journey. That's what he said – just once. But it was so easy, he did it a second time. Now, I know he must be stopped, or more and more people will die.

Already that evil has led to a new evil. When I walked out of the hearing today I knew I could not stand by and watch those children suffer any more. I am going to confront the Governor. He must stop all this. He is the only one who can. After that, I know what I have to do. I simply cannot bear the burden of this guilt any longer.

Dear God, please take care of my darling wife when I am gone, and forgive my own wretched soul.

Jess closed the journal. Clement's words cut through her like a knife. Dear God! Could something like that really happen? Could people deliberately scupper boats and let the occupants drown because they can't cope with a never ending flow of migrants?

She shivered as the wind wailed around the house, moaning and sighing like a wounded animal.

She re-read Clement's final entry. *That evil has led to a new evil… I knew I could not stand by and watch those children suffer any more.* What did he mean by that, she wondered? She thought of voodoo and human sacrifice. No, that can't be happening, she told herself.

She looked over at Tom, who was now wide awake and watching her.

He yawned. "You've been reading that for ages."

"It's Clement Pearson's journal. I found it hidden in the world globe over there. There's a secret compartment in the bottom. The little brass key opened it up."

"Really?" He jumped up and went over to have a look. "Ingenious," he said, as he peered inside. "Who would have thought of looking there?" He turned back to her. "So what's in the journal? Bad news by the look of you."

"Here. Take a look for yourself." She got up. "You only need to read the last entry."

He sat down, adjusted the hurricane lamp and started to read. When he'd finished he looked up and frowned. "This'll cause a stink."

Tom was the master of understatement, she thought.

"What I don't understand is why the Governor would have Clement's journal? And why would he hide it in his study in his Residence?" he asked.

"Hm. Sally said the two of them had a row in the Governor's office after Clement gave evidence to the Inquiry. That was on August 3, the same day as Clement wrote his last entry. That's when Clement must have had it out with him."

Tom nodded.

"Perhaps Clement brought this journal to the meeting as evidence," she went on, "and left it with the Governor for safekeeping."

"But that suggests Clement didn't know the Governor was involved in any wrongdoing. Or he wouldn't have given it to him."

"Not necessarily. Clement uses the word *confront* in his last entry, as if he knew, or suspected, the Governor was guilty of something."

Tom got up and started pacing around.

Jess could see his detective's mind sifting through all the information.

"Maybe the Governor was guilty of the same thing as Clement?" he reasoned. "Maybe he was thinking it would just be one sloop. Or maybe he thought the first sloop to go down really was an accident. But when it happened a second time, the Governor realised it was deliberate and confronted whoever the *he* is that Clement refers to – but doesn't dare name – in his journal."

"And that man, who seems to be the instigator of all this, must have persuaded the Governor not to tell the truth, perhaps by promising it would never happen again."

Tom glanced at her. "Or by money changing hands?"

"We'll soon know the answer to that. London are looking into the Governor's bank accounts." She sighed. "Still, whatever the Governor said that afternoon gave Clement the confidence to hand over his journal."

"And, in return, the Governor handed him a duplicate key for the secret compartment in the globe. So Clement knew where it was hidden."

"You know what I think, Tom." Her mind was whirling. "I think they had some kind of pact. The Governor must have convinced Clement he was going to put things right by confessing. That letter to his wife sort of confirms it."

Tom nodded. "It would make sense."

"The Governor probably couldn't live with himself, any more than Clement could." She frowned. "But what's this *new evil* Clement talks about?"

He shrugged and flopped back down in the comfy chair.

She picked up the journal and went back to the globe. "Let's put this safely back in its hiding place for the time being." She locked the secret compartment and slipped the key into her bag. "Have you still got the other key?"

He nodded.

"What's the time?" she asked.

Tom looked at his watch. "4.30. Soon be light."

"Thank goodness." She went back to the sofa and sat down.

"Why does everything always come back to children?" he asked, quietly. "Sally keeps talking about voodoo ceremonies and sacrifices. I saw Alvita give Maggie a child. Then we find that nursery in the attic, and bottles of sedatives to knock kids out. Now Clement talks about 'watching' children suffer in his journal." He glanced over. "Doesn't look good for Maggie, Jess."

"I know, but I refuse to believe Maggie would ever harm a child. And I think she's been murdered because of it."

Suddenly there was a violent gust of wind, followed by the sound of shattering glass.

"The kitchen!" Tom grabbed the hurricane lamp and ran out.

Jess followed.

The back door had blown open. The glass, in the small, top section of the door, lay shattered on the kitchen floor. The wind howled through the doorway, straight off the sea, almost knocking Jess off her feet.

Tom ran over and wrestled the door closed. He turned the key in the lock and threw the top and bottom bolts. Pulling the kitchen table over, he jammed it against the door. "I should have bolted it when I came in."

"What about that window?" She had to shout above the noise of the wind whistling through the window with no glass.

"Can't do anything about that now. We'll have to wait until the wind dies down."

That's when Jess felt water under her feet. She stared at the door. Water was seeping underneath. "It's the sea... coming into the house."

"Right." He took her arm. "We'll sit it out upstairs!"

38

When Jess woke again in an upstairs bedroom, she could feel a dull ache in her back. She moved forward in the armchair and stretched to relieve it. That's when she heard the silence. No wind. No rain. No rattling shutters. She looked over to where Tom had been sleeping. He'd gone.

Hearing a car engine start up, she jumped out of the chair, and went out onto the landing. "Tom?" she called. No reply.

She looked over the bannister. No water on the stairs. She ran down and stopped on the bottom stair. The hall floor was covered in wet sand and sludge. The watermark on the wall suggested about a foot of water had come into the house and receded again, probably with the tide. She squelched barefoot along the hall and into the kitchen, where the back door stood wide open. Leaves and sand had been forced through the door's shattered glass window by the wind, and strewn everywhere. The same mucky residue as in the hall covered the floor, but everything else looked intact.

She stood in the doorway and looked out. Everything looked calm under a blue sky. What a relief! Were they in the eye of the storm? Or had the hurricane passed over? Taking a deep breath of cool, morning air, she stepped outside.

The retreating sea had dumped a pile of seaweed and other rubbish outside the door, and over the courtyard paving stones. Fortunately, Tom and the gardeners had stored the furniture inside the Residence garage. She could see it was still standing. "Tom?" she called again, as she headed for the garden. Two of the squat palm trees were down, their fronds littering the muddy grass, along with leaves, seaweed and driftwood. The sea hadn't retreated far though. She looked at it nervously. Only a thin stretch of beach separated them. One large wave could sweep them both away.

"Over here, Jess!" Tom waved and disappeared round the side of the house again.

When she caught up with him, he was about to start hammering nails into one of the hurricane shutters that hung off a downstairs window. He looked happy to be outside and busy after being cooped up all night.

"If this is the eye of the storm," he said, "we need to get this repaired before it starts up again."

"I thought I heard a car."

"You did, but it was only me checking to see if ours was okay in the garage." He smiled. "The sea came up right over its wheels, but the engine seems fine. I found this box of tools on one of the shelves. Thought I'd start on some repairs."

Jess nodded. Tom was such a reassuring presence. It would have been a nightmare in the house on her own last night. "I need to report Maggie's murder to the police," she said, "and find Sally."

He looked at her. "Not sure if the road to the police station will be passable."

"What time is it?"

He looked at his watch. "9.30."

"How long have you been out here?"

"Fifteen minutes or so." He paused. "It was totally calm when I woke up. Do you think we're in the eye of the storm?"

She looked up at the sky. "Impossible to tell, but I want to go up to the Disaster Management Centre in case the storm starts up again. I'm not spending another night next to that raging sea."

"Maybe the hurricane's passed through?" He sounded unconvinced. "The house has stood up well, so far."

"It's survived hurricanes for decades." She studied his drawn face. "You look like you could do with some caffeine."

"Coffee would be great."

"I'll go and see if the cooker's working. I'll make us some eggs if it is, in case we get nothing else today. We'll have to be really quick though." She left him repairing the hurricane shutter and went back into the kitchen. She flicked on the light switch. Still no electricity. In the hallway she picked up the phone. Dead. She looked down at her mucky feet and went back into the kitchen. She didn't have time to clean the floors. There wouldn't be much point anyway if the sea came back in. When she turned on the tap, sludgy brown water came out. She'd have to use the water stored in the pans.

The Calor gas tank stood in a tall compartment below the hob, next to the oven. Balanced on a thick block of wood on the floor, it was tall enough for the water not to have reached the top valve that connected to the cooker hose. Brushing the damp sand off the hobs, she braced herself and switched one on. It lit immediately. She rushed around making eggs and coffee.

★

Tom put their bags, with a few things packed, in the boot of the car in case they couldn't get back to the Residence later.

"I think we should check on Maggie before we go?" Jess said.

He looked at her.

"I just want to know if she's... she's at peace up there."

"We'll be back in ten minutes, if we can't get along the road."

"*Please*, Tom."

"Okay. I'll go."

Jess waited at the front door with a heavy heart as he ran up the stairs to the attic. This house was so isolated, it felt like they were the only two people left on the island. Had everyone else come through the storm as well as they had? She looked along the drive, remembering her arrival. Only five days ago, yet it seemed an age. How stunning everything had looked that day, compared to the muddy mess now. She remembered walking along the verandah round to the back of the house, where she'd first met Maggie. Tears welled up in her eyes.

Tom came running down the stairs. "She's lying peacefully up there," he said. "In the house she loves."

Jess nodded. "Thanks, Tom."

"Right, come on." He jumped into the driver's seat. "I'll drive slowly. The road will probably be littered with stuff."

Jess sat quietly in the passenger seat as he started up the engine and drove off.

At the Governor's Office, he put his foot on the brakes. "Want me to have a quick look round the building to see if everything's all right?"

"Please."

Leaving the engine running, with the gear in park, he jumped out.

Jess got out too and turned back to look up at the Residence attic windows. There'd never been anything but warmth and humanity in Maggie's eyes. There was no way she could harm children. No way.

Tom shouted over. "No damage on the outside that I can see."

She turned back and nodded.

"The hurricane shutters have protected all the windows," he went on. "Don't know about the state of the roof though."

"At least it's still on," she said, drily.

He smiled as they got back in the car. It was slow going driving towards town. Tom drove carefully over or round debris, sometimes getting out to drag large branches, or the odd piece of corrugated iron roofing, to the side of the road. He looked at her as they heard something scratch the side of the car.

"The paintwork's the least of our worries," she said.

Large pools of water lay undrained on the main road into town. Tom took each one slowly, worried the car wouldn't come out the other side. But he kept going. Outside town, people were repairing torn hurricane shutters and collecting up any debris the wind could hurl at their houses again. "We must be in the eye of the storm," Jess said, flatly. "Or they wouldn't be repairing things so quickly."

"Yep." Tom was concentrating on the road.

"Wonder how much longer we've got," she mused. The sky was hazy, with no dark clouds on the horizon, yet.

As they got to the stretch of road that ran alongside the beach, the sea looked grey, rather than the usual aquamarine. The storm had churned up the seabed, leaving it cloudy and murky. Even in this calm spell, water lapped almost up to the road. Last night at the height of the storm, it would have been flooded and impassable.

Tom drove through the open gates of the police station, and parked next to a solitary police car. "Looks like someone's here, at least."

"What's the time?" she asked.

"10.35."

Inside, the floor was covered in the same mucky residue as in the Residence. Jess was glad she'd put on her trainers as she squelched up to the reception.

A young constable looked up from behind the desk. "Morning, Miss Turner."

Jess was quite sure she hadn't met him before, but everyone seemed to know who she was. "Is the Police Commissioner here?" she asked.

The young man shook his head. "He's out assessing the damage."

She nodded. "Have there been any fatalities or serious injuries?"

He nodded. "One man killed, so far. Some corrugated iron roofing smashed through his car windscreen. And two young boys are missing, possibly drowned. That's all we've heard about so far, but there's a *lot* of structural damage to houses and buildings."

"What about the Haitian settlement?"

"Flattened."

She sighed. "When do you expect the Police Commissioner back? I need to talk to him urgently."

The young man shrugged. "Can *I* help you?"

She hesitated. She didn't really want to tell him about Maggie, but she had no choice. "There's been another murder, at the Residence," she said, calmly, "the housekeeper."

The young man stared at her. "*Maggie?*"

She nodded.

"Wait there! I'll get the sergeant." He almost ran down the slippery corridor.

Jess turned to Tom. "This is going to be a shock for everyone."

"*Tom!*" A deep voice boomed from the corridor.

Tom turned. "Hi Chuck." He looked relieved to see his contact again. "Have you two met?" he asked, looking from Jess to Chuck.

She went up to Chuck and held out her hand. "Jessica Turner."

He shook her hand, firmly. "Pleased to meet you, Miss Turner. Now, what's happened to Maggie?"

Jess glanced over at the young constable who was all ears. "Can we go somewhere private to talk?" Jess didn't want everyone to know the gory details just yet.

"Sure. Follow me." Chuck led them down the corridor and into an office at the back of the building. The floor of the police station was just as mucky as the Residence, but that didn't bother Chuck. It was business as usual – or almost, with no electricity or computers.

Jess explained carefully about Maggie. She didn't give him the gruesome details because she could barely bring herself to say the words. She just said Maggie had been killed in exactly the same way as Mrs Pearson.

Chuck rubbed his dark-ringed eyes and shook his head in astonishment. He looked at Tom, who just nodded. "When did you last see Maggie alive?" Chuck asked.

Jess looked over to the small window in the office. "Maggie cooked lunch for Tom and me yesterday. That's the last time I saw her. Except... well, except I think I saw her at the Haitian settlement yesterday afternoon."

Chuck's eyes narrowed. "You didn't see her again at the Residence?"

"No." They answered in unison.

"Right," Chuck sounded weary. "I'll get my truck and come back to the Residence with you."

Jess turned to Tom. "Would you mind going back to the Residence with Chuck to do the necessary, while I look for Sally."

Tom stared at her. "Where will you start looking?"

"Rebekah's." She turned to Chuck. "Did Charles Regan come back here yesterday afternoon to collect Mrs Canning when she was released?"

"I was here when they left," he nodded.

"Good. Then I'll go to Rebekah's. I'm sure Charles will be with her. I only hope Sally's with them."

Tom frowned. "I don't think it's a good idea for you to go alone, Jess. The road's a mess."

She looked over at Chuck. "Do you know what the road's like north of town?"

He shrugged. "Passable all the way up to North Creek, I believe."

"Then I'll be fine," she said to Tom. "How long do we have before the storm starts again, Chuck?"

"Impossible to say." He grabbed his waterproof jacket.

"Right, well I'll go north to Rebekah's," she went on, "while you both go back to the Residence." She looked at her watch. "Let's meet back here in, say, an hour. Okay?"

Tom shook his head. "I'd better come with you, Jess."

She could see the worry in his eyes. "I appreciate that, Tom. But I'd be really grateful if you'd help Chuck with Maggie."

"But..."

"Please Tom. It's important. You and Chuck know exactly how things should be done. We don't want any mistakes. We have to catch whoever did this."

He stared at her. "Oh all right." He knew he wouldn't win the argument. "But come back here as soon as the wind starts picking up again, Jess. Don't take any risks."

"Of course not," she replied.

Chuck picked up his keys from the desk. "Come on, Tom. We don't have much time."

39

Passable was not the word Jess would have used to describe the road leading to Rebekah's house. She wasn't the first person to drive along it since the storm, because broken branches and other debris had been dragged to the side. But it was slow going as she picked her way carefully along. Their car was the only means of getting around, and the last thing she wanted to do was damage it.

Drawing up at Rebekah's house, she saw one of the metal front gates had been ripped off its hinges, barring the way. The flagpole lay horizontal across the front lawn, with the Union Jack ripped to shreds. The pretty white plantation shutters had all gone too.

She left the car outside the gates and walked through the debris littering the garden to the front door. There was no no-one around, and no cars in the driveway. No sign of that black cat that jumped at her last time either. At the front door, she had a sense of being watched and turned round, but she couldn't see anyone.

She knocked uneasily on the front door and waited. No reply. This time, she banged on it with a clenched fist.

"Rebekah? Charles? Are you there?" she called. "It's me, Jess." Silence. She glanced over her shoulder again, then walked round to the side of the house. She couldn't see inside because all the windows were boarded up with hurricane shutters.

Round the back, two of the dwarf palms bordering the garden were down. Turning to the house, she jumped...

Rebekah was sitting on the verandah in a rocking chair, with her eyes closed and a shawl around her shoulders.

"Didn't you hear me knocking?" Jess shouted over.

No reply.

She walked over and touched Rebekah's shoulder.

Her eyes flashed open, making Jess step back. She was wary of this woman after yesterday.

Rebekah didn't move a muscle, but her dark eyes appraised Jess. "Charles said you'd come."

That unrecognisable voice unsettled Jess.

"He said you've been watching us ever since you got here."

"And what a fine performance *you've* put on!"

Rebekah said nothing, which annoyed Jess. She pulled a rattan chair round and sat down, facing Rebekah. "No need to play games any more." Jess kept her voice low and calm. "I know your real name's Gloria Diaz, and that you're an actress, and that you and Charles have been... close since your twenties."

Rebekah inclined her head, face impassive.

"So why the English accent?"

Rebekah looked at her, as if surprised to be asked that question. "For Dominic, of course. He's the only man who's ever really taken care of me. Or loved me for... me." Her eyes glistened. "Everyone else in my life has left me. My mother, my father." She gazed blankly ahead of her. "Men along the way."

Jess tried hard to be patient. "Not everyone, Rebekah. I know you and Charles have been close for years. He's never left you, or so it seems."

Rebekah's eyes fixed on her again. "I can't escape him."

What did she mean by that? "Where is Charles?" Jess asked.

"Gone to look for his precious brother."

The way Rebekah drawled the word 'precious', suggested she didn't care for Brad. Why not, Jess wondered? "Is Sally with him?" she asked.

"Certainly not."

"But have you seen Sally?" Jess persisted.

"She's not welcome in this house," she said, flatly.

Jess saw the shutters come down. "Why's that, Rebekah? Because Sally had your number?"

Rebekah gave a dismissive laugh. "You don't know what it's like to be brought up in the slums."

It wasn't said in a self-pitying way, but more as a matter of fact. "No," Jess said. "But plenty of people are brought up in poverty around this world. You're not alone in that."

"I wanted to fit in," Rebekah said simply. "I was only 11 when I was sent to live with an American family. I was nothing like them, but I soon understood what they wanted: the cute, little American girl they'd never been able to have. So I became that girl."

Jess sat back in the chair.

"Then I discovered men wanted an attractive woman on their arm. I played that part too. To survive, you understand."

"Dominic too?" Jess asked.

Rebekah sighed. "I hid my past from him at first, but he found out eventually. Of course he was upset, but he wanted to give it a go anyway." She smiled, fondly. "He's an important man and I didn't want to let him down. So I became the wife *I* thought a British judge, and the Chief Justice here, should have."

The more Jess heard, the more she thought Rebekah was unhinged. Was she telling the truth now? She sat forward. "I have to tell you, Rebekah, I saw you kissing Charles in this garden the other day."

"I just told you," Rebekah said, flatly. "I can't escape him."

Jess suddenly felt a breeze rustle her hair. The storm was coming back. She stood up. "Was Charles here during the hurricane?" she asked.

"Don't ask me any questions about Charles."

"Why not, for God's sake? He may be in danger. Don't you *care*?"

Rebekah closed her eyes again. "Charles is a powerful man, Jess. He's taken his gun, so nothing will happen to him. He'll come back for me when he's ready."

Charles has taken his gun. Those words filled Jess with dread, Sally had gone off with him yesterday afternoon. How come he had a gun? Why would he need one? This wasn't America. People weren't permitted to have guns in this Territory. Was Charles expecting trouble in his search for Brad? Or going to cause it?

Brad! Everything kept leading to Brad. Surely his treasure trove lying on the seabed couldn't be the connection with Maggie and Mrs Pearson?

Rebekah hugged herself. "Those bastards murdered my darling Benji." A tear slipped down her cheek. "I l-loved that dog more than anything in this world." She winced. "They s-sacrificed him," she moaned.

Jess was torn between staying with Rebekah, who looked a tragic figure sitting there, and leaving to find Sally before the storm came back. In the end she ran back to the car. She was responsible for Sally.

Her hands shook on the wheel as she headed back into town. She was driving too fast, bumping over the debris, or swerving to avoid it. She was desperately worried about Sally now. Was she too dead somewhere, like Maggie?

At the main roundabout in town, she stopped to let a mud-covered truck coming from the other direction turn right onto Lighthouse Road. The driver's ponytail was instantly recognisable through the open window. *Brad!*

He looked grim as he drove past, without a glance in her direction.

Her foot hesitated on the accelerator, then she turned left and followed Brad up to the Ridge. He seemed in a real hurry. Fortunately, with less vegetation higher up, there was less debris on the road.

As they climbed, she became aware of the light fading, as if night were rolling in. She looked at her watch. Still only midday.

Passing the Haitian settlement, she saw the makeshift shacks · flattened. But the Haitians were already out, picking through the debris. Such resilience, she thought. She'd stop on the way back to speak to them and assess the damage. Right now, she was hoping Brad would lead her to Sally.

Glancing in her driver's mirror, she noticed a motorbike following. Her heart quickened. The sound of a motorbike revving outside the Disaster Management Centre yesterday came back to her. Gunshots had followed. She slowed to let it catch up and pass. But it slowed too. She strained to see who was riding it, but all she could make out was their helmet and jeans.

She looked ahead, then thumped the steering wheel in frustration. She'd lost Brad. Had he pulled into a driveway? There was no sign of him. *Damn!* When she checked the mirror again, the motorbike was still there. Seeing the turning for the DMC approaching, she swung across the road, tyres squealing on the tarmac, into the track and slammed on the brakes. She peered through the rear window. The motorbike sailed past.

She waited to see if it slowed down or doubled back. It didn't. She flopped back in the seat with relief and looked at the building ahead. There was no reason why Brad should have gone in there, but it was worth a look. Anyway, she wanted to chat to the folks inside and find out what was going on. She looked at her watch, still half an hour before she was due back at the police station to meet Tom. Releasing the brakes, she let the car roll forward and bump along the dirt road towards the building.

To her surprise, there were no parked cars outside, although common sense told her it would have been dangerous to leave them there during the hurricane. She parked and got out. A panoramic view of the island greeted her, and she looked out over the devastation. Many of the flimsier houses were down, or had their roofs blown off. The brick houses were mostly still standing. The little vegetation there was on the island had been ripped up and flung everywhere. Fortunately, it didn't look like the sea had risen any higher than the coast road last night. But the dark sky on the horizon looked threatening. The storm was approaching again, like a black cloak.

She was shocked to find the place completely empty. Where was everyone? The lights were on, and she could hear the generator running. A half-eaten plate of rice and chicken lay on the table, so someone must have been there. Annoyed, she went over and sat down at the computer. She desperately wanted to email London and report what was going on. She tried several times to get online. *Page can't be displayed* was the only response. *Damn!*

Casting her eyes around the room, she noticed a white, hooded sou'wester hanging on the coat rack by the door. Just like the one Alvita had on when she came to the Residence yesterday morning looking for Maggie. Had she been in here all night keeping everything going on her own?

"Alvita?" she called out, but there was no reply.

Jess turned back to the computer and started scrolling through some of the documents. She was so engrossed in what she was doing that she didn't hear or feel a presence at first. Then she suddenly whipped round...

Charles Regan stood right behind her.

"Charles," she jumped up and faced him. "You startled me."

He said nothing.

Careful, she thought, he has a gun. "Have you seen Sally?" She tried to appear unfazed. "I'm worried because she didn't come back to the Residence last night. I'm guessing she's with Brad. Have you seen the pair of them?"

His intense blue eyes fixed on hers. "No."

Jess persisted. "She left me a note yesterday afternoon, you see, saying you were giving her a lift to look for him."

He frowned. "I dropped her at Brad's house. She was going to wait for him there." He paused. "She had his keys to get in."

"Oh, I see." She started moving towards the door to get out, but he stood blocking the way. "Can you tell me where Brad's house is?" she asked.

"One street back from the Dive Centre. No point going round there. I've just been. They're not there."

Jess studied Charles. His hunched posture made him look more exhausted than threatening, which made her relax. "I've just been to Rebekah's looking for you," she said, calmly. "She told me about your long-standing relationship."

He looked away. "I love Rebekah, Jess. It's as simple – and as complicated – as that."

Jess nodded. That was clear, but she was still suspicious of Rebekah's reasons for marrying the Chief Justice. "Why didn't you two ever marry, then?"

"Ambition," he said, bitterly. "We were young when we first met, in our twenties. I wanted to be a banker, and Rebekah an actress. I went to New York. She went to Los Angeles." He paused. "We thought our love was strong enough to survive. It wasn't. Rebekah got married to some film producer."

"And you?" Jess asked.

"Well, eventually I married too, but it didn't last... because, well, because my wife wasn't Rebekah." He sighed. "And by the time my divorce came through, Rebekah was on her second marriage, to the Chief Justice."

"I see." His explanation seemed plausible, and his feelings for Rebekah genuine enough. But did Rebekah feel the same way? Or was it more a case of Charles pitching up all the time to spoil Rebekah's relationships? He seemed as obsessive about Rebekah as Brad was about that sunken galleon.

Charles's eyes narrowed. "I can't believe Rebekah told you about our relationship?"

"She didn't. Not at first, anyway. We ran some police checks after Mrs Pearson's murder."

"On *me*?" He sounded cross. "Just who do you think you are? You have no right."

His arrogance riled her. "We have every right. This is a British Overseas Territory, and we're investigating two murders."

"*Two* murders?" He stared at her. "So the Governor *was* murdered?"

"Almost certainly."

He sat down heavily on a chair at the table.

He looked a shattered man, Jess thought, as she sat down opposite. "The thing is, Charles," she went on, "we were denied access to information on you and Brad." She paused. "Why was that?"

He ran his hands through his hair, but said nothing.

"Why, Charles?"

He put his elbows on the table and looked at her. "I guess I can trust you of all people to be discreet, Jess."

She nodded.

"I work for the CIA."

She sat back in the chair.

He shrugged. "I was the obvious choice. My brother lives here, and we have a business together. It would be natural for me to visit regularly and find out what was going on."

That made operational sense to Jess. Charles's cover was the New York bank he worked for. "And what *has* been going on down here?" she asked.

His eyes became guarded. "How much do you know?"

She said nothing.

"All right," he went on. "Do you know about those Haitian sloops being deliberately scuppered on the reef?"

She nodded.

"Then you'll know the Governor did nothing about it."

She could see him considering his words carefully. "Yes. I'd worked that out," she replied.

"How?"

She hesitated, wondering how much she could trust him. "I found a confession letter from him to his wife, Jayne."

Charles raised an eyebrow. "So he was going to do the right thing, finally?"

"Looks like it."

"Not before time," he snapped.

"It cost him his life," she said, simply.

She saw a fleeting look of panic in Charles's eyes that she didn't quite understand. She had to find out what else he knew. "How did *you* find out about the sloops?" she asked.

"The US *is* just across the water. Do you think we'd let this Territory operate *without* knowing everything that goes on here?"

Jess wasn't surprised, but a question hung in her mind that needed an answer. "Did you tell the British Government?"

He hesitated. "It was sensitive, with the Governor... implicated."

She frowned, unable quite to believe what he'd said. "If you'd told them, they'd have stopped this madness."

He shrugged. "For all we knew, they might have sponsored it. No country can cope with thousands and thousands of migrants pitching up on their shores."

"Oh come on!" He couldn't be serious, could he? "Our Government couldn't get away with that. Not with our media and NGOs on their case all the time."

He looked at her, unconvinced. "That's not what brought me down here in a professional capacity, not at first anyway. We were worried about shady financing being laundered through your British tax havens, and its connection to terrorism." He stood up and pushed the chair under the table. "Now I have to go and find Brad."

"And what about Sally?" Jess said, crossly. "All your brother cares about is that bloody sunken galleon. He was so angry with Sally for telling me about it, he wouldn't speak to her. That's why she's been running around in this hurricane looking for him."

Charles started pacing around. "Brad's obsessed with that shipwreck. Not that he told me about it. My colleagues found out."

"He'd have needed a lot of money to find that wreck," she said, pointedly, "and a whole lot more to get the bullion off the seabed."

Charles stopped pacing and stared at her. "I haven't given him any money, if that's what you're suggesting."

"So, who's bankrolling him, then?" Immediately she asked that question, she knew the answer.

"Oh my God! You think Brad's involved in all this, don't you? That's why you're so upset. You think he was being paid off, and using the money for that shipwreck."

"Yes. It's what I'm afraid of," he said, quietly.

There was a pause.

"Tell me honestly, Charles. Do you have any idea who killed Mrs Pearson, or why?"

He shook his head. "I really don't know."

But she could see the fear in his eyes. He was terrified it was his brother. She took a deep breath. "The Governor's housekeeper, Maggie, was murdered last night... in the same way as Mrs Pearson."

"Jesus!" His face crumpled.

Jess could hardly speak the words. "I found her in the attic in the Residence. She was hanging by her bound feet from the beam."

Charles turned ashen, and sank down onto a chair.

"Her throat was cut too."

"I'm so sorry, Jess," he whispered. "Have you told the police?" he asked.

She nodded. "Tom's back at the Residence with them now."

Charles got up slowly, like an old man rising from his chair. "I must go and find Brad." He turned to her. "If you have any idea where he might be, please tell me?"

She nodded. "I followed his truck up here in the hope of finding Sally, but I lost him before I turned in here."

Charles stared at her. "Why didn't you say so before?"

There was a pause. "I think I know where he was going," she added.

"Where? *Please!* My family are everything to me."

"The lighthouse." She jumped as a clap of thunder reverberated overhead. "Quick. We don't have much time."

40

Jess glanced over at Charles's face as he gripped the steering wheel. Did she believe everything he'd just told her? She certainly believed he loved Rebekah, and cared deeply for his brother. But there was something about him that made Jess wary. Intelligence officers always had their own agenda.

Jess glanced over her shoulder for that motorbike. No sign of it.

Charles drove fast towards the lighthouse, talking as they went. "The Islanders are terrified of voodoo, especially with all this talk of pets being sacrificed, and Mrs Pearson's murder."

"So terrified, they daren't talk about it."

"Ah. So you think it's all nonsense too? A means of silencing everyone?"

She thought of the woman in the Provo restaurant who'd tried to warn her. "You can pull the wool over people's eyes for a while, but some brave soul will always step forward."

He went on: "It must have been a terrible shock, finding Maggie like that?"

"It was." Jess rubbed her eyes as if trying to erase the vision of Maggie hanging from the beam. She wouldn't tell Charles about the children's nursery and sedatives in the attic. Not yet anyway. She refused to believe Maggie was harming children. "I don't think we can dismiss voodoo completely," she went on. "I saw what looked like a ceremony on the beach the other evening, just along from the Governor's Residence. An ideal spot. Very isolated."

He glanced over. "Was my brother there?"

"Why would Brad be there?"

There was a pause. "I found a book about voodoo in his house."

"Really?"

"I know Brad can be impressionable. It got him into trouble when he was younger. Drugs. Gangs. That kind of thing. He put that all behind him when he came down here. Seemed happy at last. That's why I put up the money for the dive business."

"I see." Jess's mind turned back to the Governor. She wanted to find out if Charles knew anything more. "Tell me," she said. "Why do you think the Governor allowed that Inquiry to determine that the sinking of *both* of those sloops was accidental?"

"Around two million dollars, we think. We're still tracing the transactions."

"Oh God." Jess sat stunned for a moment before getting her head around the wider issues. "Do you think the officials who carried out the Inquiry were taking... incentives too?"

He shook his head. "No, but they would rely heavily on the testimony of the Governor and his Ministers. And any local witnesses come to that." He paused. "And it's difficult to determine foul play, particularly when the weather's bad, and no other vessels are involved."

"But two million dollars?" she repeated. "Where does that kind of money come from down here?"

"Selling off land to foreign developers to build luxury hotels and condos on Provo. Some outlying islands too. It's *big* money." He pulled a face. "Tourism's where the money is. The islanders want to become an exclusive destination."

"From what I've seen, they already are on Provo."

"Yes, but thousands of migrants turning up uninvited isn't part of their plan."

"No, I suppose not." Jess's heart felt heavy as she sat thinking about the Governor. Why would he do something like that? Did he think he'd get away with it? Did he really believe it would just be those two sloops? That it wouldn't happen again? Her mind went back to the money. "Who controls the sale and revenue of that land?" she asked.

"The Governor and his local Ministers," Charles replied. "We don't think they were involved in the scuppering of sloops, just in the conspiracy of silence." He went on: "We believe one influential local man instigated all this. He's very charismatic. He persuaded everyone the migrants had to be stopped from reaching shore. It wasn't difficult. People are afraid of being overrun, of losing their homes and jobs. Of course once this man had drawn the Governor in, he got bolder and the violence escalated."

Jess didn't need Charles to tell her who that local man was. "You're talking about Roger Pearson, aren't you?"

"Ah, so you know about Roger, then?"

"I'm just putting the pieces of the puzzle together." She hesitated. "I can't believe he'd get his hands dirty though. Not his style."

Charles's grip on the steering wheel tightened.

Jess could feel his tension and understood why. "You think Roger's drawn your brother into his plot too, in return for money to salvage that shipwreck."

Charles pulled up outside the lighthouse fence and pointed to a parked truck. "That's Brad's!" He jumped out, ran over, and opened the passenger door. There was no-one inside. He slammed the door shut again and raced over to the lighthouse. The door opened when he turned the handle. He beckoned to Jess, and disappeared inside.

As Jess went to get out of the car, the wind almost pushed her back inside. It was fierce now. Steeling herself, she ran over to the lighthouse, and went inside. A black, cast iron spiral staircase greeted her. It was a long way up to the observation tower.

"*Brad?*" Charles called out from the foot of the staircase. "You up there?"

No reply.

"*Anyone* up there?" he shouted again.

"Let's go and take a look." Jess started up the stairs. "If Brad's here, Sally will be too." She could hear Charles clumping up behind her. She didn't look round, or say anything else. She needed all her energy to climb up there.

Her leg muscles were burning when she reached the top. She bent over double to get her breath back.

When Charles arrived, panting and puffing, Jess was already looking out at a staggering sight. On the horizon, an angry violet, red and black sky encircled the island, with streaks of lightning flashing all around. Through windows blurred by rain, she saw waves pounding the north-west reef. Nearer shore, the water was calmer, but grey.

On the observation platform, two camp beds were folded up on one side, with a black bin bag next to them. Peering inside the bag, she saw two sleeping bags. "Someone's being staying here." She went over and opened some cupboards. Tins of food, candles, and other provisions were neatly lined up.

Charles's hand shook as he held up a waterproof jacket. "It's Brad's."

She nodded. "This needs no explanation, does it?"

He shook his head. "I can't believe Brad would switch off the lights, and allow sloops to run aground on the reef."

Jess couldn't believe Sally would either. Was her love for Brad that blind? She walked over to a telescope and looked through it. The sight of the hurricane coming was menacing, yet strangely beautiful. She moved the telescope over the reef, back to the cliff and to the rocks below. Tom must have been crazy to try and get down there, she thought. Now, through the scope, she could see a path running along the cliff top, and further along, a small trail that led down to a beach.

A movement caught her eye. Two figures were hurrying along the cliff path, carrying large boxes. She magnified the lens. "There they are!" She swivelled the telescope to the beach below, where a boat was moored to a wall built out into the sea, like a jetty. The boat was much bigger than Brad's usual dive boats. "They're going down to the beach."

"Where?" Charles elbowed her out of the way and looked through the telescope.

"They're on that cliff path. There's a trail leading off it, down to the beach." Jess stared out the window. "Is that Brad's boat moored along the sea wall? Looks sea-going, with a cabin and everything."

Charles swivelled the telescope from Sally and Brad, to the boat. "*For Chrissakes!* They'll be killed out there." He turned, and started running down the stairs.

"*Wait!*"

"I'm going after them!" he shouted back.

Jess followed.

He was well ahead of her as they ran round and round the spiral staircase. She was getting dizzy going down at such speed.

He reached the door first, flung it open and ran outside.

The sound of two rapid gunshots rang out. Jess froze. She pressed her back against the wall, shuffled along to the door, and peered round to see outside.

Charles lay motionless on the ground.

Roger Pearson stood over him, gun in hand. He looked up at Jess, and raised his arm...

"*Drop the gun!*" a familiar voice barked.

Dexter! The Police Commissioner stood a few yards behind Roger, pointing a gun at his back. Jess held her breath.

"Throw the gun on the floor, Roger!" Dexter shouted. "I'll shoot you if I have to."

Jess could see the sneer on Roger's face, as he turned to face the Police Commissioner. "You don't have the guts, Dexter!"

"It's over, Roger." Dexter's voice was clear, but calm. "No-one here supports you any more. We're all ashamed of you. And even more ashamed of ourselves for not standing up to you before."

"Huh! *You* won't shoot me, Dexter. You're as gutless as that Governor."

Dexter continued in his calm voice. "I know you drove that truck into his car. You wanted him dead because he was about to have you arrested. But you drove away too quickly."

Roger's arm slackened and he lowered his gun.

"Who do you think pulled him out of that burning car alive?" the Police Commissioner went on.

"*You?*"

"After you'd driven off." Dexter paused. "He'd already confessed to me earlier that day, you see."

"You're lying!"

Dexter shook his head. "The Governor asked to be allowed to tell his wife and to make arrangements for his family, before handing himself in. I agreed to that. *His* mistake was having the decency to warn *you* what he was about to do. So you killed him. But what he didn't tell you, is that he'd already told me."

"*The fool!*" Roger spat.

Dexter shook his head. "He was a decent man before he listened to you. Like poor Clement, he was racked with guilt afterwards. He'd taken to driving up to the lighthouse every night to make sure the light was on. He couldn't live with any more deaths on his conscience."

"Listen to me, Dexter," Roger shouted to be heard over the wind. "With me in charge of these islands, we could be independent. A great nation for the whole world to come and enjoy. We'll have jobs, wealth, a good living for our people. *Your* family will be rich. Back me now, and you'll be powerful. I promise you that."

Jess held her breath, wondering if Dexter could be persuaded. He was the only one who could stop this now.

"No, Roger," Dexter said, firmly. "I don't want to live in a country with *you* as President. No-one does. People here know you only care about getting power and money for yourself." Still his voice was calm and even. "Now, drop the gun!"

Roger's whole frame tensed. "You're a spineless fool, Dexter," he shouted as he raised his gun.

Dexter fired first. The bullet hit Roger in the middle of his forehead. He spun round with the force of the impact to face Jess before collapsing to the ground. The surprise on his face was matched by the anguish on Dexter's, as he walked over to where Roger lay, picked up the gun, and bent down to look for any sign of life. He shook his head after a moment and stood up.

Jess ran over to Charles, and knelt beside him. When she pressed her fingers to his neck, she felt a faint throb. "He's still alive," she shouted.

"I'll radio for back-up." Dexter started back to his police car.

Jess saw a motorbike lying close by. So, it was Roger who'd been following her. He must have shot at Tom from the cliff yesterday. He would have killed her too, if he'd had the chance.

She shouted back to Dexter: "Sally and Brad are heading down to the beach. There's a boat moored down there. I'm going to stop them. They'll be killed out there." She turned and started running along the gravel path towards the cliff.

"Jess!" Dexter shouted. "It's too dangerous..."

But Jess carried on running. The wind and sea-spray were blowing her backwards, but she battled on. She could see Sally and Brad nearing the jetty. "*Sally!*" she shouted. But the wind just carried her words back to land.

The going was wet underfoot on the cliff path, and even more treacherous on the trail down to the beach. She slipped and slid her way along, holding her arms out for balance. Suddenly, her foot twisted and she tumbled down the rest of the track, onto soft sand. She lay on the beach for a few moments, dazed, then she sat up. Sally and Brad were just stepping onto the boat. Ignoring her sore ankle, she pulled herself up. "*Sally!*" she shouted again, as she part ran, part hobbled along the beach.

This time they heard her, and turned to look.

Sally waved.

The punch from Brad came from nowhere, sending Sally reeling back onto the deck.

Jess gasped with shock. She ran along the jetty wall and clambered onto the boat, where Sally was struggling with Brad.

Jess tried to pull him off, but he lashed out, winding her.

Suddenly the door of the cabin opened. Carrie stepped out, gun in hand. "*Stop!*" she shouted.

Jess froze. "Carrie?" she whispered in disbelief.

Carrie smiled. "Get in the cabin! Both of you!"

Sally looked from Carrie to Brad. "What's going on?"

Brad responded by pushing her and Jess roughly through the cabin door.

"Sit on the floor!" Carrie barked, as if shouting at her school kids. "Hands on heads!"

When they were on the floor, Sally moved her hand to her cheek and looked at Brad in bewilderment. But she had the sense to stay quiet.

Carrie smiled at him. "Are you going to tell her, or shall I?"

Sally looked from Brad to Carrie. "How long have you been carrying on with *her?*" she asked.

Brad smiled at Carrie. "For ever!"

While Carrie and Brad were tormenting Sally, Jess was desperately looking around. They appeared to be on a sea-going cruiser. There were two berths, the sitting area where they were, and a tiny kitchen. She looked along the surfaces for any knives. None. It seemed their only escape would be back out the door Brad had pushed them through. She studied the door. It seemed to fold into four segments that would open up the entire rear of the boat if needed.

When she looked back, Carrie was watching her intently, as if reading her thoughts.

Jess nodded at Carrie, as if acknowledging she had fooled them all with her different guises. She'd been the quiet and respectful dinner guest, the hard-working and conscientious teacher, the thoughtful and kind friend, and the beautiful, alluring woman. How easily she manipulated people, particularly men. First her colleague David, and then Brad. Or had it been the other way around?

Carrie's eyes gleamed as if she'd heard Jess's thoughts. Then she turned to Sally. "You don't think Brad could *love* someone like you, do you? You're too self-obsessed." She laughed. "You were useful though, working in the Governor's Office."

Sally glared at Brad, and he took a step back.

Meanwhile, Jess was thinking hard. Dexter knew she'd come down here after Brad and Sally. Surely he'd come looking for her with his officers once Charles was safely in the ambulance? She had to play for time.

"So," she said in a calm voice, "you've both been working for Roger Pearson."

They looked at each other.

"We know everything," Jess said. "You switched off the lighthouse light, to make those two sloops run aground on the reef. And Roger paid you to do it."

Sally gasped and stared at Brad, as if seeing him for the first time. "Tell me you didn't."

"Don't look so shocked." Carrie smiled. "We're just doing what wreckers have always done. Where do you think we got the idea from?"

Jess nodded. "I understand why you did it, Brad. To fund your sunken galleon project, and to become a famous diver." She shook her head. "Pity you'll now be known for all the wrong reasons, as a murderer."

He flinched.

"You do realise Roger has just shot your brother, don't you?"

"Don't listen to her, Brad," Carrie said. "She's lying."

"I'm not." Jess shook her head. "Charles was so worried about you, Brad. He went all over the island searching for you. We came up to the lighthouse together, to find you and Sally."

Brad stared at her, then snapped: "Trust him to go and fuck things up. He just won't stop interfering."

Despite his words, Jess could see Brad was rattled. He wasn't the cool, calculating person that Carrie was. "So you and Carrie decided to drown all those poor people on the reef. Murder them."

"Murder them?" Carrie shook her head. "We *saved* them from their own wretched lives."

"By *drowning* them out to sea?"

Carrie stared at her in surprise. "The sea is *magnificent*. Drowning is nothing to be afraid of." She had a far-away look in her eye. "I love the sea. I feel at home in it. Always have."

"You're crazy," Sally said, quietly.

Jess flashed her a warning look. They had to keep talking until help came. Besides, she wanted to know the truth. "Charles told me you had a book about voodoo in your house, Brad. I suppose the two of you killed those missing pets, and started the rumours that they'd been sacrificed?"

Carrie smiled. "It was Roger's idea. He wanted to terrify everyone, to keep them quiet. Brad and I were only too happy to oblige... for a fee of course. And don't sneer at voodoo. It's powerful."

"You'd know all about that from your time in West Africa."

"Of course." Carrie looked at Jess. "You know, I wasn't sure whether you were going to die by drowning, or pleading for your life on the sacrificial altar, or like Mrs Pearson and your meddling housekeeper. We'd have got Maggie's miserable daughter too, if she'd been at the Residence at the time."

Jess stared at her in surprise. "Daughter?"

"Alvita!" Carrie laughed. "Don't tell me you didn't know they were mother and daughter, *and* Haitian!" Carrie laughed again. "And I thought you were smart, Jess."

Jess hadn't guessed, but it somehow made sense. "So *you* murdered Maggie and Mrs Pearson?"

Carrie nodded. "Brad and me."

Sally gasped.

Brad looked away.

All the while they were talking, Jess was still looking round for some means of escape. They wouldn't stand a chance once they'd set sail. Suddenly her eyes lighted on a small rag doll lying on the floor in the corner of the cabin. Carrie must have had children on this boat.

"Oh my God," she whispered, as the realisation sunk in. "You've been saving the Haitian children from those sloops, haven't you?" Her voice shook as she asked: "Why? To sacrifice them?"

Carrie laughed out loud. "I haven't *sacrificed* them." She was enjoying Jess's confusion. "I told you, I've saved them. I've given them new families in America."

Jess frowned, bewildered.

"Do I have to spell it out for you?" Carrie sighed while clearly relishing the opportunity to explain. "I set up a kindergarten in Miami to work closely with mine here. Both registered charities," she said, proudly. "There's a lot of fund-raising going on in the US for our kindergartens. We have visits in both directions by parents and their children too. Lots of exchanges that everyone is well used to." She laughed and patted one of the cabin's wood veneer panels. "Only now, I also take some children to America, who never come back."

"In this boat?" Jess asked.

Brad interrupted. "It's an offshore cruiser."

Jess didn't care what it was called. "What about passports for the children?" she asked.

Carrie smiled. "Easy to obtain with money to pay the right people."

Jess knew that was true. "But America is tough on immigration. They'd never let those Haitian children in."

"No, not through airports they wouldn't," Carrie said. "But the Florida coastline is full of marinas. And it's not so far away. We smuggle them in by sea. Our contacts in America take them, and find them new families."

"You mean they *sell* them!"

Carrie smiled, benignly. "I don't know why you're so shocked, Jess. You must know adoption laws vary from state to state in the US. Some are more relaxed than others. People even advertise children on the internet. Put them up for adoption. Very lucrative."

"You still sell them."

Carrie shrugged. "Put it like that, if you want to. But I haven't hurt those children. Quite the opposite, I've given them new lives. Better lives than they would have had here, or in Haiti."

"But what about their real mothers and fathers?" Jess was incredulous now.

Carrie swept her arms wide. "Drowned out on the reef, most of them. If they made it to shore, we took them back out there."

"*You're a monster!*" Sally couldn't help herself now.

Carrie's smile faded. "It's time to take you out to the graveyard of souls."

Jess frowned.

"That's what the islanders call the area around the north-west reef where so many ships have been wrecked...

the graveyard of souls," Carrie explained. "Very apt, don't you think? Now it's your turn to join all those sunken-eyed skeletons in the deep."

Jess wasn't sure if she were staring at pure madness, or pure evil. Either way, Carrie was beyond reach.

"Cast off, Brad," Carrie ordered.

He hesitated, and looked from Carrie to Sally.

"Don't do it, Brad," Sally pleaded. "Carrie will get the blame for this, not you. You're not the monster she is."

"Brad!" Carrie's eyes narrowed. "I said cast off."

Brad's shoulders slumped, and he went outside.

From where Jess sat on the floor, she couldn't see out the window. But she felt the boat tip as Brad jumped onto the jetty to cast off. She had to stop him, if they stood any chance of surviving. She went to get up. But Carrie leant forward and put the gun to her head. "You can die here and now, if you want to."

Jess could see Carrie meant it. The boat rocked as Brad jumped back on board. Her heart sank when she heard him start up the engine, and the boat pulled away from the jetty. She was powerless to do anything.

"That's better." Carrie sat down on a bench seat, and relaxed back. "Can't bear hurricanes and being cooped up too long on shore."

They were heading for the reef. Jess felt sure of that. "What are you going to do, now? Throw us over the side and let us drown too?"

Carrie nodded.

Jess suppressed a ripple of fear. "Then what? You won't survive the hurricane out here."

"We don't intend to," Carrie said. "After we've buried you two at sea, we'll shelter in North Creek for the rest of the storm."

Jess knew North Creek was an inlet, with only a small opening to allow vessels in and out. It was a natural shelter for boats during hurricanes, and the entrance was just along from the lighthouse.

"Then we'll carry on our lives as normal," Carrie went on. "These islands are our home now. We belong here. I feel I've always belonged here."

The boat started pitching around as they hit choppier waters. Jess knew it wouldn't take long to get to the reef. She kept her eyes on Carrie's face when she said: "It was supposed to be just one sloop, to send a message to the Haitians not to come. But you couldn't resist a second time. And you're not going to stop now, are you?"

"No." Carrie shook her head. "Not if they keep coming. Roger can't have them all here, you see. It's impossible. Just too many of them." She paused. "Anyway, I have families in America waiting for children now. And my job is to make sure they get there safely." She looked at Jess. "You understand that, don't you?"

All Jess understood was that Carrie's logic was warped and dangerous. Carrie's fanatical belief in herself and in what she was doing was unshakeable. But could Jess persuade her to doubt Brad? She had to try.

"You know you can't trust Brad, don't you?" Jess said. "I saw him, the other night, on the beach having sex with Sally."

Carrie's face clouded.

"They were really going for it," Jess went on, "I saw it all. *Heard* it all. Pure, hot sex, and he loved every minute of it."

"Brad!" Carrie shouted. "Will you come in here."

Brad put his head through the door.

"Jess says she saw you having sex with Sally on the beach the other night."

His eyes were hooded. "She's lying, Carrie."

"No she's *not*," Sally piped up. "You said you loved me. *Really* loved me. Couldn't live without me."

Brad shook his head. "Don't listen to her, Carrie."

Jess could see in Carrie's eyes that she knew Brad was lying. "Charles told me Brad was unreliable, and impressionable," Jess went on. "You know you can't trust him, Carrie."

"Ignore her!" Brad glowered at Jess as the boat lurched, and he stumbled sideways. "I've got to get back to the wheel. The wind's getting stronger." He went back out, and came rushing straight back in.

"The police patrol boat's coming."

Carrie jumped up, and looked out the window.

Jess still couldn't see anything from the floor of the boat, but she kept on talking. It was time to tell them they'd get nothing more from their paymaster.

"Roger Pearson is dead too. Dexter shot him, after Roger shot your brother."

Brad looked startled.

"It's over." Jess kept talking. "You'll never get that bullion from your sunken wreck, Brad. You'll never have the fame and fortune you crave. And you'll never take any more children to America, Carrie. It's over," she repeated.

"Brad?" Sally pleaded. "Give it up... *please*."

Brad's eyes lingered on Sally's face.

"Please Brad," Sally begged. "I-I don't want you to die."

Brad looked out the window to the police patrol boat, and then at Sally again. Jess could see he knew it was all over for him. He touched Sally's hand briefly.

Carrie's movement was swift. She raised the gun and shot Brad in the chest, right in the heart.

He slumped to the floor dead.

"Brad!" Sally moaned, as she rolled over to where he'd fallen.

Carrie kicked her hard. "Get up. Both of you." She forced Jess and Sally to their feet and pushed them through the door.

Jess could see the patrol boat pulling up alongside now. Tom and Chuck stood on the deck, guns pointing at Carrie. "Drop the gun!" Chuck shouted.

Carrie smiled at him. "I won't harm the two women, if you let me go," she shouted back over the wind.

But Chuck was in no mood to bargain. "Drop the gun, Carrie! And kick it away from you!"

Carrie hesitated.

The two men tensed, ready to fire.

Then Carrie turned, and threw the gun overboard.

Tom and Chuck visibly relaxed and lowered their weapons.

In the moments it took for them to clamber from one boat to the other, Carrie edged to the side.

Jess could see she was going to jump.

Carrie smiled at Jess, and suddenly grabbed her wrist. "You're coming with me," she said, and they lurched over the side together.

The cold water was a shock. Water rushed into Jess's mouth and lungs as she went under the waves. She resurfaced seconds later, coughing and spluttering, with Carrie's hand still tightly clamped around her wrist. "Don't be frightened," Carrie spoke, softly, as if coaxing a child. "The sea's wonderful."

Jess struggled to free her wrist, but Carrie's grasp was like a band of iron. She kicked out desperately, but Carrie was too strong for her.

"Don't fight me." Carrie smiled again.

The choppy waves splashed over Jess's face and head.

She'd swallowed so much water; she was getting dizzy. She couldn't free herself from Carrie, or hold her breath. In desperation, she trod water, frantic to stay afloat, as Carrie began to pull her under. She looked up at the boat. *Tom!*

She could see his face above, his hand outstretched...

As she reached her free hand up to him, he grabbed it tightly.

"Hang on, Jess," he shouted. "Hang on."

Gunshots rang out from above.

Slowly, Carrie's grip loosened. Jess watched as she drifted away from her, her hair fanned out in the waves, her blood turning the water red around them. Deeper and deeper she sank, until Jess could no longer see her.

She felt herself being pulled upwards. Tom was dragging her to safety. She clung onto the side of the boat, clambered over and collapsed onto the deck, gasping for breath.

"Jess!" Tom knelt down beside her.

She lay looking up at him, but all she could see was Carrie's smiling face drawing her down into the deep. She started shivering, uncontrollably.

Tom pulled her into a sitting position and put his arms around her.

"I'm all right," she choked. "I'm all right.

41

Two days later

Jess stood on the beach, outside the Governor's Residence, looking at the sparkling turquoise sea. The sky was deep blue, the tide back to normal, and the sand as white and fine as ever. It was as if the hurricane had never happened. She glanced at Alvita, who stood silently beside her, then turned to look up at the attic. She felt she would for ever see Maggie's face at that window. "Your mother was a wonderful woman," she said.

Alvita turned too. "Maggie loved this house. I-I'll always feel close to her here, despite everything."

Jess nodded. If only she'd had some idea of what was going on, she might have been able to stop the violence. And save Maggie.

"Don't blame yourself, Jess," Alvita said, as if reading her thoughts. "My mother really liked you."

"And I really liked her."

Alvita's dark eyes still looked sad, but she seemed to have a calmness about her today, as if she'd come to terms with her mother's death. She's a strong woman, Jess thought, just like Maggie. She'd already been in the office for hours, getting things running again after the hurricane. Work was her therapy. Jess could understand that.

"They are good people here, Jess, so don't think badly of them. Living in a small, isolated community is never easy. No-one likes to draw attention to themselves, or speak out against powerful leaders. Life would be made impossible."

Jess knew that from her travels around the world. "You know, Alvita, if you hadn't left the DMC and found the Police Commissioner when you did, he would never have come up to the lighthouse, and I wouldn't be standing here now."

"If only Dexter had found the courage to act sooner." Alvita sighed. "He didn't know what Roger was up to at the beginning. Nor did the Governor. They both believed that first sloop was an accident. So did I."

"I suppose the second sinking set off alarm bells."

Alvita nodded. "People started whispering, and that's when Maggie..." Her voice broke. "And that's when Maggie and I knew." She waited, then continued firmly. "Roger was a very persuasive man. He charmed people into thinking it was the only way to deal with the migrant problem. And those few people he couldn't charm, he paid off."

"Including the Governor."

"Yes, even my Uncle Clement went along with it. But he was a good man and couldn't live with himself." She swallowed. "My aunt would have known the truth. She and Uncle Clement were very close. That's why she was murdered. Maggie too. Roger knew they were both brave enough to stand up to him and speak out. And he used their murders to send a message to others."

Jess remembered Carrie's smiling face as she tried to pull her under, and shivered. "At least it's finally over."

"Is it though?" Alvita hesitated. "It's not the first time sloops from Haiti have been scuppered on these shores."

Jess stared at her.

Alvita nodded. "I was a baby when my mother waded to shore, with me in her arms, 31 years ago. Maggie believed she'd arrived in America, to join my father." Alvita pulled an old photograph from her bag. "This is my real father, Pierre. Maggie only gave me this last month. I guess she must have had a premonition about her own death."

Jess looked at the photo. She could see Maggie in that young woman, standing proudly beside her husband. "What makes you think Maggie had a premonition?"

Alvita poked the sand with her toe. "She practised voodoo as a young woman in Haiti. She had the gift." Alvita smiled. "Don't look so shocked, Jess. Voodoo is harmless, even though the rituals might look a bit scary. In July and August every year, Maggie would hold ceremonies on this stretch of beach when the Governor was away."

So that's what Jess had seen the other night on the beach. Maggie must have been the robed figure, whom Alvita embraced. "What about all this sacrificing animals?"

Alvita smiled. "They usually sacrifice birds, like chickens, or sometimes goats or sheep. But it's not about the morbid death of an animal, it's about offering life-giving energy to the gods. They generally eat the meat afterwards, so it's not wasted." She looked at Jess. "In other cultures, people slaughter animals at home or in their villages, rather than in the slaughter houses or butchers you have in your country. It's a similar thing."

"So Roger put Brad and Carrie up to stealing those pets, and blaming their disappearance on voodoo. Their owners won't ever get them back though. They're gone."

"I tried to stop Maggie holding her ceremonies," Alvita went on, "for fear of what the locals would do if they caught her. Personally, I've never taken voodoo seriously. I suppose because my adopted father was a pastor at the

Baptist church, and my adopted mother a confirmed Christian too." She sighed. "I didn't find out until I was 21 that they weren't my real parents."

"Really?"

"That's when they told me I was Haitian, and that Maggie was my birth mother. They hadn't told me before – or anyone else come to that – because they knew my life would be difficult if people knew I was Haitian."

Jess was shocked. "I'm so sorry, Alvita."

She shook her head. "Don't be. I saw a lot of Maggie when I was young. She was our cook and housekeeper, and in a way looked after me. I always felt like I had two mothers, so it all made sense when I eventually found out the truth."

Jess frowned. "You were saying this happened before?"

Alvita nodded. "People talk about it as if it's just island folklore. They don't want to believe it, but it was as real back then as it is now. I suppose that's where Roger got the idea from. The sloops were scuppered on the reef, with peopled drowned and children taken in exactly the same way. Maggie told me she managed to swim ashore, with me on a plank of wood. She was attacked on the beach, and I was snatched. But my adopted father was out that night trying to stop what was happening. He saved us both. He gave Maggie a domestic job, and adopted me as his own daughter to give me the best life he could." She looked at Jess.

Jess could imagine what a good man he was. "So when you and Maggie found out it was happening again, you tried to save the children?"

"We realised what Carrie was doing. She kept them in her kindergarten until she could take them overseas to sell. Whenever she was away, I'd go in, rescue a child and take it to Maggie. She'd hide the child upstairs in the attic until she could take it to the Haitian settlement. The Haitians trusted my mother, you see, and would only accept the children from her."

"And they were safe in the settlement?"

"Yes. But of course Carrie found out what we were doing. But she never dared come to the Residence when the Governor was around."

Jess shook her head in disbelief at what had gone on. "At least Charles is recovering well in the clinic," she said. "He was lucky to survive. He's cut up about his brother though. Feels he should have known what Brad and Carrie were up to."

"And Rebekah?" Alvita asked. "What will she do now?"

"We'll have to see what happens when the Chief Justice gets back. He's on his way now." She paused. "At the moment Rebekah spends most of her time up at the clinic, looking after Charles. She says she plans to leave the island for good with him when he's well enough to travel."

They fell silent for a while, watching the waves lap onto the shore. "This is such a beautiful place," Jess said.

"Then stay!" Alvita said suddenly. "Help us heal our community and get our lives back on track."

Jess was taken aback by the new warmth she saw in Alvita's eyes. London had implored her to stay too, but she had to leave. "I'm really touched you want me to stay, but I have to go home." She paused. "Sally will help you work with the London team." She looked at her watch. "They should be arriving in a couple of hours now the airport's open again. They'll need all the help you can give them, Alvita."

"Won't you change your mind, Jess?"

Jess shook her head. "I can't."

Alvita nodded. "I'd better get back to work, then," she said, briskly.

Jess knew Alvita's return to business mode was her way of hiding her disappointment. "I'll see you there later," Jess said, as she watched her go. At least they understood each other. She guessed she would always be friends with Maggie's daughter.

Now, she turned and started walking along the beach, away from the house. She needed some time alone to prepare herself for what she had to do next. The sun was fierce on her back as she got further away from the Residence. Suddenly, in the distance, she saw the ponies from her first swim, playing in the surf. As she watched them nuzzling and splashing each other, the horror of the last few days seemed to melt away.

She found some rocks to sit on, and pulled out her mobile. She tapped the code for her voicemail. There was a message she needed to listen to again.

Jess... it's Simon. Look, I know I've been a bloody fool. It's just that... well, I thought I could deal with this on my own. It turns out I can't. I was just coming home for medical tests, you see, but those tests... well, those tests have confirmed the worst. It's cancer, I'm afraid... prostate cancer. I'm going into St Thomas's for an operation in the morning. I feel terrible telling you like this, in a voicemail, but I haven't been able to get hold of you. I know about the hurricane. The Office have told me you're safe. I'm sorry I wasn't there for you, Jess. Really sorry. It was ridiculous of me to say I was going to LA for work. I should have told you the truth and that I'd booked a ticket for you to come home to the UK with me. I was going to tell you everything at the dinner I'd planned but, as you say, life has a way of being unpredictable and you dropped your bombshell about the Turks and Caicos. You looked so happy to get the job, I didn't want to spoil it for you. I hope you can forgive me, Jess, and come home... Sorry.

She held her face up to the sun, and closed her eyes. She couldn't believe Simon had kept something like that from her. What was he thinking? Telling her he was going to LA for work when he was going back to London for tests for prostate cancer, for God's sake. She was cross, and sad, and worried all at the same time. She'd never have come to the Turks and Caicos if she'd known. She slipped her phone back in her pocket and stared at the silvery sea, shimmering under the hot sun. Its quiet lapping onto the shore soothed her frazzled mind.

Now, when she closed her eyes again, she could see Tom's face, and his hand outstretched as he grabbed her before she disappeared under the waves. She could feel Tom's arms around her, bringing her back to life.

★

As she left the Residence, Jess closed the front door behind her, and locked it. She was glad Alvita still loved the place and felt close to Maggie there, but she would never forget the horror of that night. She'd spent the hurricane's second onslaught at the DMC with Tom, working on monitoring and assessing the damage, drawing up reports and a recovery strategy for when it was all over. After that she'd booked rooms in a local hotel for them both. Her excuse was that she didn't want to get in the way of forensics in the Residence, and that it had to be cleaned up. But the truth was she didn't want to spend another night in there after what happened to Maggie.

Now, she was on her way to collect Tom from the police station, where he was saying goodbye to Chuck and the guys, and take him to the airport for his flight home. Approaching the building, she saw him standing outside on the steps. He was bang on time, and with his suitcase packed and ready beside him. As solid as a rock, that was Tom. Always there. What you see is what you get with him.

He waved as she pulled up, threw his case onto the back seat, and jumped in the passenger seat beside her. "The guys are getting ready for the UK police team arriving this afternoon," he said. "Some forensics officers are coming over from the Cayman Islands later." He glanced at her. "Best to get outside expertise in these circumstances."

Jess smiled. "Absolutely. That way there can be no cover up." She paused. "What's the mood like in there... since their boss has been suspended pending investigation."

"Everyone's sad about old Dexter. They all respect him." He hesitated. "They don't think he should take the blame for everything. He didn't take any bribes. Once he found out the Governor had been paid off, he didn't know where to turn to for help. He just tried to keep a lid on things. Anyway, they think he deserves some credit for despatching Roger Pearson." He nodded. "It might have been a whole different story if he hadn't acted when he did."

"Don't I know it!"

He smiled at her. "No-one's sorry Roger's gone. Dexter's a local hero on that score."

Yes, Jess thought. Big Shot had shown his true colours the very first time she saw him in the Provo airport terminal. Such a huge ego, and such arrogant disregard for anyone else. A true narcissist. The island was going to be better off without him, that's for sure. But she was sorry about Dexter. She was fond of him. He was a decent man at heart. In many ways, she understood his dilemma when he found out the Governor was implicated.

"Don't worry, Tom," she said. "Dexter will get a fair hearing. But he couldn't just walk back into his Police Commissioner job after everything that's happened. He should have told me and London everything while he had the chance, before Mrs Pearson and Maggie were murdered. Still, the action he eventually took will be properly taken into account during the investigations. I'll make sure of that."

"Glad to hear it, Jess. Anyway, Chuck's happy. He's been promoted to Inspector to meet the overseas police and facilitate all their investigations." He glanced over. "Did you have anything to do with that?"

"I may have suggested he was the best man on the island for the job."

Tom chuckled. "He asked me to thank you." He reached up to pull down the sun visor and shield his eyes from the blinding sun. "I've invited him to come over to Australia with the guys from Miami when this is all over. It would be good to see him again, and find out how all this works out. I'm going to miss this place." He glanced over. "And you, Jess."

She felt her stomach flutter, but she kept her eyes on the road. "I'm going to miss you too," she replied, as she pressed down on the accelerator. "Now, let's get you to the airport."

"So I'm going, then?" he asked, quietly.

Jess felt his eyes on her. She didn't reply.

"I see." He sounded both surprised and hurt. "You're not coming to Australia, are you?"

She shook her head.

"Not even for a visit?" he went on. "You could see all your old friends again, and relax. Have time to think about what you want to do next."

"I know what I'm going to do next, Tom," she said, simply. "I'm going back to London tomorrow morning, once I've briefed the Director tonight."

"London?" Tom stared at her. "Tomorrow?"

She knew she owed him an explanation. She couldn't put it off. As they drove alongside the main beach out of town, she steered the car into a layby and switched off the engine. Pulling her mobile out of her bag, she scrolled to Simon's voicemail, and handed it to him. "I want you to listen to a voice message I got this morning... from Simon."

At the mention of Simon's name his face became impassive. He took the phone and said: "You sure you want me to hear it?"

"Yes."

He shrugged, pressed play and put the mobile to his ear.

Jess watched his face as he listened to Simon's message, but he didn't move a muscle.

Finally, when the message had ended, he looked at her and nodded. They sat in silence for a while looking at the beauty of the beach and sea. There was nothing to say. Everything was clear. He understood.

Feeling a sadness beginning to well up inside her, Jess started up the car and continued on to the airport. They sat without speaking for the rest of the journey, comfortable as always in each other's company.

At the airport, Jess parked the car and helped Tom check in, and go through security into the departure lounge as she would any other visitor. It was only when she walked with him to the departure gate that her stomach started turning. In just a few minutes he would be gone. She had to say something, tell him...

He turned and looked at her.

At that moment, she could see in his eyes what he must be seeing in hers.

"Thank you, Tom. I..."

He put his finger to her lips to stop her, and kissed her gently. Without another word, he walked through the gate and was gone.

She watched him cross the tarmac and get onto the plane. She stood with her eyes fixed on the door until all the passengers were on board. Just as the co-pilot was about to pull up the steps, Tom suddenly reappeared at the door. He smiled at her, and gave his usual salute.

She laughed and blew him a kiss.

He made a gesture of catching it in the air, before waving and ducking back inside the plane.

As she watched his plane take off into the brilliant blue sky, Jess didn't feel quite so sad any more. They'd been here before. Somehow she knew they'd see each other again.

Also by the same author

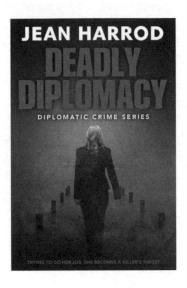

"*Deadly Diplomacy gripped me from page one and made me want to carry on reading until all was revealed ... the insider knowledge for the storyline means that a genuine insight into the world of international diplomacy suffuses the whole book ... highly recommended.*"

(www.crimesquad.com)

"*Brilliant tour de force ... gripping from start to finish.*"

Alastair Goodlad, former Minister of State for Foreign Affairs.

"*A cracking good read. Fast-paced with fascinating characters, and written with all the authority of a seasoned diplomat.*"

Helen Liddell, former British High Commissioner to Australia.